The Last Fernandez

Sandra Perez Gluschankoff

Publisher's Note:

This is a work of fiction. All names, characters, places, and events are the work of the author's imagination.

Any resemblance to real persons, places, or events is coincidental.

Cover art by:

Brenda McCoy - www.ladybbooks.com

Solstice Publishing - www.solsticepublishing.com

The Last Fernandez

By Sandra Perez Gluschankoff

Ernest Hemmingway once wrote that *"Writing, at its best, is a lonely life."*

Thankfully my life as a writer is far from lonely. My journey through the Last Fernandez, my first novel, has been one filled with the constant support of my loved ones who are at either arm's length or oceans away. I am profoundly thankful for your relentless encouragement.

I also want to thank my two wonderful writing sisters and talented authors Brenda Mckoy and Christine Fry, who believed in this Spanish lilted story from the first page.

And special thanks to the wonderful team at Solstice Publishing for giving The Last Fernandez the chance to keep telling its story.

She remembered crazy Don Tomas. Always talking to the empty space, drawing with his hands the shapes of things only he could see. And she wondered—if he, just like her, had discovered a secret portal within him where past and future unraveled the secrets of his today.

Prologue

The year of 1391 was a major turning point in the history of the Jewish people in Spain. It marked the beginning of the Spanish Inquisition. During the fourteenth and fifteenth centuries, Jewish quarters were destroyed, and synagogues were burned in collective *Autos de Fe*, acts of faith, while people prayed inside.

The Spanish Catholic King Fernando and Queen Isabel gave Tomas de Torquemada, a Dominican Monk eager to erase his Jewish past, the task of running the Inquisition. He declared the Spanish Inquisition a process of *Sangre Limpia* or Pure White Christian Blood.

Jews were forced to convert to Catholicism or die. A large number of these *Conversos* kept their Jewish faith alive in the privacy of their homes, while in the eyes of the outside world they led a true catholic life. These Jews were called *Marranos*, a derogatory name alluding to swine.

The year of 1492, the year of the Discovery of America, saw the expulsion of all Jews from Spain. It is believed that many of the Jews held in Spanish prisons escaped aboard those ships on the way to a New World.

This was their opportunity for a new life.

Part I

Chapter One
Exile

Port of Cadiz – Spain, 1492

He could hardly breathe. The rough linen sack in which he hid made him itch all over, but he dared not move. He heard the pounding rain splattering on the cobblestone road and on the surface of the wooden wagon that he rode in. This was it for him. He was to leave Spain forever. He was only ten years old. How could he face a whole New World on his own? The memory of the family he'd lost robbed him of the little air he had in the confinement of his makeshift hideout. He tried easing his breathing by summoning pleasant memories, yet he could not. His mother Sarah, his father Lev, his brothers Yehuda and Yoshua, dead. Gone.

The wagon came to a stop. Without looking out, he could picture in his mind the activity around him. He could visualize the relentless rain falling mercilessly throughout the black night. He could see the dark waters slapping the hull of the large caravel, as the din of rain, wind, and men worked together and against each other preparing the vessel for its departure. Even through his fear, Salomon Fernandez could see himself painting the scene all around him. Putting brush to canvas, infusing them with colors, bringing them to life. That was his gift.

The footsteps approaching him were to be his last contact with all that he held dear. He had begged to stay and he was denied every time. He had screamed out loud, "I don't want to be alone! I am scared." But he would never be alone. His mother had promised to watch over him. She had promised him that one day they would be together again. She had looked into his eyes and sworn to gather their family back in the House of Gardens.

"Perhaps not in this life," she had said. "Perhaps not in this time."

He felt a hand on him and he came shivering forward, shedding the rough sack from his scrawny form. His huge brown eyes moved towards her; Maria. He watched as her hair went up in a short-lived whirlwind before being controlled by the weight of the pounding rain. For a moment he smiled. It was a funny sight and amid the devastation of his life, he was still a young boy.

His senses reacted to every move and every sound. He saw a man working on the ship's platform stand erect at the sight of the wagon. Even through the pouring rain, the cue between Maria and the sailor was evident. They stared at each other for a brief moment. Maybe it was the floating illusion the rain gave, maybe it was the powerful wind moving things involuntarily or the natural swaying of the ship. But the sailor appeared to nod, and with that he vanished momentarily.

Salomon wanted answers to his uncertain future. He stared at Maria, his eyes burning her with anguish. How could she do this to him?

The sailor from the ship materialized right next to them. Maria did not startle or acknowledge him. This was what they all expected. There was no doubt it was their plan. Maria and this man had met before and they had worked in this same fashion several times. Salomon knew it. It was what his family did. It was what had killed them.

The man lifted Salomon out of the wagon. He felt the weight of his body landing on the ground unsteadily, but he still had enough strength to run to Maria and hold onto her tightly. She pulled him away from her and held him at arm's length. She knelt in front of him. It was her way of talking to him when she meant to be clearly heard and understood.

Salomon shivered with cold and undeniable fear. His ragged clothes, which clearly had seen better days, made him look even smaller and frailer than he was. His scrawny figure shuddered with the sobs he fought so hard to keep under tight rein. Then again, he was only a boy.

He saw Maria swallow hard. Rivulets, some of which may have been tears, ran down her face. He knew this could not be easy for her even if she had done this sort of transaction dozens of times. Simple, easy. Out of the wagon and into the ship. No words, no tears. This time around, it was not just a nameless fugitive. This time it was personal. It was him. Salomon.

Although consumed with grief, her voice surprised him when it reverberated. Steady, commanding.

"Listen to me Salomon. You are a man now. The only Fernandez left." Salomon gulped and tried to hold back his tears. Maria slackened her hold on his skinny shoulders. He looked down knowing his battle was lost.

The bells of the ship announced its departure. Salomon's body stiffened. The man pulled him from Maria's grasp. "Time is running out."

Maria glanced from the man to Salomon. Her eyes were desperate, pleading for just a few more moments. The bells chimed once more. Their deafening sound invaded their unavoidable farewell. She quickly searched under her robe and retrieved a pendant the size of a gold coin.

Amid the darkness of the night, the rubies and diamonds surrounding the Hebrew letter, *Fey*, engraved in the center of the pendant enclosed by a golden Star of David, shone at the touch of the flogging downpour. It was his mother's pendant, the one she had worn close to her heart.

The man stared at it. Closing his eyes as if in mourning, he let go of Salomon's arm and stepped back, giving Maria and Salomon the luxury of privacy, if only for a few more seconds, for what was to be their final moments together.

Maria hung the pendant around Salomon's neck. His hand touched it instantly, tracing every bit of the engraved work on it. His voice came out weakly. He understood his unknown fate had been decided beforehand, yet he insisted once more. One last try. "Let me stay with you. I could be your son."

Maria shook Salomon, making him bite his lower lip. A thin line of blood came down his chin which was washed away by the rain. "I could never…" She shook her head, shoving away her emotions from the raw reality at hand. "You will never be somebody else's son." She took hold of the pendant and lifted it in front of Salomon's face. With a firm voice, Maria emphasized her next words. "Salomon Fernandez, you are the son of Lev David Fernandez and Sarah Fortuna Fernandez. You are a brother to Yehuda and baby Yoshua. Do not let their lives and their names ever be forgotten. Never allow their sacrifice to vanish from your memory. Your name, their lives, and their deaths shall be your burden as well as your legacy."

Salomon winced and struggled from Maria's grasp. She held him tighter, waking him into a manhood that he was unprepared to face for one so young. "Never forget what happened. Always remember who you are."

Finally, Maria drew Salomon to her in a powerful embrace. The man snatched him away from her. With a swift move he bundled Salomon back in the linen sack, lifting him like a sailor's duffel bag and running to the ship.

Salomon's last view of what his life had been was through the gritty weave of the sack. A dark cloud, he thought. A bad dream.

Hanging dearly to his mother's pendant he closed his eyes tightly and prayed for her promise to come true.

They will be together again.

Someday.

Chapter Two
Angelina

Pueblo Brugo - Argentina - 1966

Angelina stretched out in her bed and could swear her legs finally reached the edge of the mattress. How could they not? Today was the most important day of her life—she was finally turning six.

For many children in Pueblo Brugo, age probably did not make much of a difference. But many children were not Angelina.

She had a plan and it started with attending school, which automatically rendered her with the status of a big girl, and together with that status came the promise her mother made her, piano lessons at the local church.

Truth be told, Angelina already knew her way around the piano keys, but that was a secret between her and her imaginary friend.

Her mysterious friend sneaked into Angelina's life on a hot summer evening a year or so ago while she struggled through her nightly prayers. Tired of repeating the Our Father for the tenth time, a punishment imposed by her mother for… she couldn't remember why… Angelina welcomed the sudden intrusion of the invisible stranger with alacrity. She inched slightly to her left leaving enough space for the newcomer to kneel next to her. She squinted hard at the friend, and still could not depict her. Angelina was certain her companion was a she.

"My name is Angelina, what's yours?" Angelina felt the stranger shift. The response flowed into Angelina's ears with the sound of a melody composed of raindrops over a tin roof. Angelina counted the beats and sang out loud, "S-A-R-A-H. Sarah." Angelina emphasized the last syllable as if the last *a* were accented. Sarah? Is that your name? Sarah?"

The answer, another raindrop, a confirmation, reverberated through Angelina's room.

In the subsequent days, Sarah proved to be the best friend Angelina had in her short life. The local girls she usually met at the park were too concerned about their hair or their shoes, and did not share Angelina's thirst for adventure. Indeed, every time she walked into the playground area, they would gather by the swings and purposely turn their backs on her.

But since Sarah none of it mattered anymore. This invisible new presence in Angelina's life had more substance than all the hometown girls together. Sarah was full of stories. She was capable of anticipating Angelina's wishes, and above all she shared Angelina's passion for music. Melodies became their common language.

It was their eagerness to play music that drove them to escape the house from under Angelina's mother's nose and reach the church's grand piano unnoticed. Although a difficult task, it did not pose as much of a challenge as she thought it would. It was all a matter of planning, Sarah had explained, and Angelina knew the right time of the day to do it. In Pueblo Brugo naptime was religiously kept as one more sacrament. So at two thirty in the afternoon, when the town lay down to sleep, Angelina would slip into the small music room. She had a faint notion of being naughty, but was not quite sure if playing music without the proper authorization of Mother Superior was considered a sin. All the same, she made a point to always have her Rosary in hand, ready to say a *Padre Nuestro* before starting her piano lessons with Sarah.

One grey afternoon, the week before her birthday, while walking quietly into the convent, Sarah spoke of the important role music would play in her life. "There will be a day when you won't be able to talk to me anymore the way you do now, but you will always find me in the keys of the piano. You will always find me in the melodies we will create together."

The thought of losing Sarah made Angelina's stomach hurt a little. But she knew better than to speak of her worries about her imaginary friend to anybody, especially her mother.

On several occasions, Marta, her mother, caught Angelina having open conversations with what seemed to be the empty air. She was a stringent Catholic and dreaded that her daughter had fallen victim of some demonic possession.

"Who are you talking to, Angelina?" Marta frowned.

Caught, Angelina's eyes sprang wide open. She knew lying was positively a sin, so she went straight out with it. "Sarah, *Mami*. My new best friend."

Marta looked around the cluttered kitchen and swung her gaze back on Angelina. "Do not make up stories, Angelina." She wagged her index finger at Angelina. "God punishes little girls for making up stories."

Angelina shrunk slightly. "But she's here, *Mami*, I swear to God. She is here standing by my side."

Blinded with rage, Marta crossed the floor, and before Angelina could say a word, she slapped her hard. "Enough! Never use the name of the Almighty in vain, and never," she loomed over Angelina like a steel, storm cloud, "never speak of this again. Do you hear me?" Marta's chest heaved, her body trembled. "To your room, on your knees, and pray. Pray hard to be rid of your sins."

Marta watched Angelina scurry to her room. She then turned her palms up and stared at them. She had done the right thing. Angelina needed to be disciplined in the same way her grandmother had disciplined her. There was no other choice. The flesh was weak—her mother had been an example of it, and an imaginative mind was an open playground for Satan. Marta righted her kitchen apron and mouthed a prayer as she walked to the sink.

Fear... Marta had been raised over a foundation of fear. And so she was the kind of person who feared her soul drifting away from the right path if not under the submissive control of strict religion. She thrived with the borderline sadomasochistic relationship of sin and punishment that she established with God. Her unwavering faith and her immediacy to impart discipline to her boisterous daughter were rewarded with God's unconditional protection from evil.

For that reason, it became customary for Marta to drag Angelina to church, Monday, Wednesday, and Friday, and have Padre Aparicio sprinkle holy water over her as divine confirmation that the child was still under the Lord's wing and not within Satan's grasp. Deep in her heart, Marta knew that Angelina's behavior was not a matter of good and evil, but that of a little girl whose free-spirited ways could not be dampened with holy water.

Marta's other obsession was to make a lady out of Angelina. Her daughter was the town's tomboy. Angelina's knees were constantly skinned and raw from climbing on trees, and her long brown wavy hair was in constant disarray from fighting imaginary monsters. If someone would have depicted Angelina's personality, her unruly mass of curls would have been a good place to start. Just like its owner, her wild locks would break free out of carefully groomed pigtails, before Marta finished tying the last of the ribbons.

Still, Marta persisted in raising an obedient, religious daughter, and was fiercely determined to achieve it. For this reason, the house seemed like a permanent burning shrine filled with every possible image of saints and all the different representations the Virgin Mary ever had.

In Angelina's playful mind, the effigies of saints and Mary were no other than houseguests, and more often than not, Marta found Angelina entertaining the many statues around the dinner table. Sometimes it was a lavish tea party served on Marta's great-grandmother's Italian tea set, the one saved for special occasions. Other times, she would gather all of Marta's burning candles at the center of the table. Positioning the statues right next to the candles, Angelina would throw a big birthday bash, song and all, for her inanimate honorees, concluding with the blowing of every candle at once.

Angelina was a trial Marta never thought she'd have to face, nor one that she felt prepared for.

Chapter Three
Marta

Feelings of regret for the way she had raged at her daughter chased Marta to the foot of the shrine in her bedroom. Perhaps if Grandmother was still alive, she would know how to handle Angelina better. She missed the old woman terribly, and she missed her mother too, even though she could not remember her face. Everyone she had loved had left her. Angelina was all she had in this world that she could claim as hers, and she lived in constant fear of losing her too.

Marta grew up in a little stucco house, with tiny windows and a blue door, a few blocks away from the house in which she lived now with her husband and daughter.

Before she learned to say the word *papa,* her father left for the big city never to come back. Soon after, her mother, who was too young and felt too lonely, was swept off her feet by a handsome fisherman who came to look for work and women at the docks of Pueblo Brugo.

For many days Marta waited in despair at the bottom step of the house's front porch for her mother's return. As the days passed her anxiety increased and her hopes waned. With a heavy heart she understood that like her father, her mother would never again set foot in the little stucco house with the blue door.

Her mother's body was found in a field outside of town. Her death became the biggest event a forgotten town like Pueblo Brugo ever had. Life in that part of the world was dull and plain boring. Given the exciting turn of events, the model citizens of the dusty settlement by the river, proud of their model behavior and model attendance at Sunday mass, like dormant coiled snakes grasped this tragic opportunity to slither from their everyday boredom. And with venomous tongues they conceived the most obscene versions of the last dreadful moments of the doomed young mother.

As much as her grandmother tried to protect Marta from the relentless gossiping tongues, Marta heard it all. From dismemberment, to missing body parts eaten by wild animals, to rape by Satan as a result of fornicating with a stranger out of wedlock.

The death of her mother had left Marta under the care of her stern grandmother, and of course the Church. She was not a bright student and dropped out of school halfway through the sixth grade. Spending all her subsequent afternoons helping the sisters at the convent with cleaning, cooking and sewing was a natural transition for Marta.

Looking back at her childhood, Marta got a glimpse of the way Grandmother finely orchestrated her life, carefully placing her onto a path where she would not pose a threat to the old woman's ailing heart. No, she couldn't blame her. The old woman did everything possible to prevent Marta from following her dead mother's footsteps.

Falling under Grandmother's care was a blessing sent from heaven intended to shape her into the dutiful wife and mother she was to become. Unfortunately, the old lady never got to see the fruits of her labor. She died quietly a few months after Marta started dating Ramiro.

Marta never considered Grandmother's age. Perhaps that was the reason her death caught her by surprise. She had a strong constitution and Marta often wondered if the immeasurable liters of *mate*—the Gaucho's legendary concoction—the old woman ingested throughout the day gave her the immune system of a tough bull. She thought Grandmother invincible. She never complained and kept up with a rigorous work schedule, one that Marta saw fit to implement to withstand the constant ups and downs of the economy.

The sewing work they performed for the locals was not enough to support them throughout the whole year any longer. Marta started paying close attention to the chitchat of housewives at the local market when going out for groceries. Medicinal herbs such as chamomile, lemon balm, or valerian, which the women swore by for their magical soothing effects on their men's nerves, were in high demand but scarce in inventory. With a rocky economy responsible for the unemployment of many of the local men, stress and anxiety were at their peak, leading to drunkenness and plenty of wife beatings. Certain to have found the answer to their money problems, Marta laid out before Grandmother the profitability of growing an herb garden. Although she hadn't finished her formal education, Marta was business savvy and foresaw great financial potential for her intended small investment.

Slowly but surely the herbs grew. Grandmother and granddaughter established a small business which allowed them to do more than to cover their basic expenses. Moreover, with the extra income, Grandmother started amassing a wad of bills under her mattress in a way of a savings account.

It was with talks of expanding to a second plot of land that Marta parted from Grandmother the night before her death. She hadn't noticed anything out of the ordinary, at least not until she went to bed.

On any other night, as soon as her head sunk into her pillow, she would drift immediately into a deep sleep. Sometimes she believed that her lack of dreaming was due to the extra effort it required to be in a dream. That was not to be the case that night. She was fully conscious of falling asleep right away as she always did, but a whisper in her ear, and a soft touch on her cheek, startled her. The familiarity of the whisper and the softness of the touch were disturbing. She had felt them before, many, many years ago. Maybe two decades past. It was the one feeling she would never forget. It was the touch of her mother.

Her mother used to come back home late at night from her routinely fervent search for love. Reeking of sex, cigarettes, and cheap cologne, she would curl up next to Marta, and while caressing the little girl's face, she whispered empty promises as though she could undo the actions of that night.

Marta had been a young child when her mother ceased to curl up next to her, and although she fantasized about being held by her mother the feeling had never been as vivid as tonight. Why now?

After some serious praying and silent tears for what had never been, sleep won out. Marta fell into the bitter stupor that was the result of a restless night of soul ache.

The next morning the quietness in the air woke her. She got out of bed with the same effects one suffers after a long night of heavy drinking. Forcing her limbs into action she walked to the kitchen where her grandmother's radio should have been chatting away the town's gossip, accompanied by her loud assent or disapproval of the news. The radio was off and its faithful early morning co-host, who held her Alpaca and calabash gourd *mate* instead of a microphone, was not standing at her usual spot.

At once Marta knew something was amiss. She went out to the small herb patch. Maybe Grandma had decided to do some early clippings that morning, instead of drinking *mate* and listening to the news. But no, the garden looked undisturbed and stalking fear crept up her spine.

She knew before she set foot into her grandmother's room that the form lying on the narrow bed was not her beloved grandmother anymore. Her body was rigid and blueish-white. Grandmother bore a relaxed expression on her face. For a woman who constantly pursed her lips, as though in disapproval, in death her mouth almost had the touch of a smile.

She did not need confirmation. It was Marta's mother who had come the night before. She had felt cheated, dejected. The two women, the one that gave her life and the one that kept her alive, had conspired against her and decided to leave her alone.

Her initial reaction was one of anger. Throwing herself on the floor, she punched the rough concrete slab over and over again until the stickiness of her knuckles, soaked with blood, brought her back to the life who was not there anymore. A surge of blurring tears brought understanding for what the naivety of youth never allowed her to see until then.

Grandmother had lived with a festering emptiness in her heart from the moment Marta's mother was murdered. Too late Marta realized why no amount of good behavior or love for the old lady, was enough to fill up the void the soul suffers when a child is gone forever. She was a mother now and could understand the eternal emptiness losing a child could cause, leaving an open yet hidden wound that never healed.

Marta could see now that Grandmother had chosen the right moment to depart. Ramiro had come into Marta's life and the serious young man had already asked Grandmother for Marta's hand in marriage. Grandmother's job on earth was done. She had raised a pious granddaughter that would surely become a dutiful wife and mother. It was time for the old lady to reunite with her daughter—wherever she might be.

Before Grandmother's grave was fully covered with dirt, the landlord rented the house to a family who had just moved into town. Forced to leave the only home she ever knew and the life she had built to herself, the sisters at the convent took Marta in.

Grief and desolation drew Marta closer to her fiancé. He became her protector, a constant presence in her life, rousing unsettling feelings in her, sinful cravings, which had lain dormant under the stern supervision of the old lady.

Disgusted with herself, after nights of lusting for Ramiro, and scared to fall under the same trap of desire her mother had, Marta begged the sisters, amid seas of tears, to let her enter the order as a novice. Time and time again her request was flatly denied with the simple explanation that her grandmother would have never wanted her to grow old without feeling the life of a child of her own flesh.

Even in death, the old lady had the power to impose her will on Marta, and as always, Marta obeyed.

With the Lord's help, she knew she could do the same for her free-spirited daughter, Angelina. Fiercely attached to her beliefs, Marta drew a plan of her own which included excessive praying and daily visits to the church, aimed to finally set her daughter straight.

She prayed for that too.

Chapter Four
River Tales

As Marta finished tying off a big bow in the back of Angelina's white pinafore dress, she turned her daughter around to face her. With the innate tenderness of motherhood, she tucked a few stray locks behind Angelina's ears. "Now, go to the kitchen and don't move until we're ready to leave."

Angelina frowned, drawing her big brown eyes together almost to the bridge of her nose. "What if he arrives before we get there?"

"We will be at the docks on time." Marta smiled.

"But I promised I'd be there waiting for him. If I'm not, he might leave again. The girls at the park told me that's what happened to your papa. They said he left you because he couldn't find you."

Marta felt slapped by the cruelty of the blunt statement. She was not ready to face these kinds of questions from her daughter, not so soon. The painful reminder of his abandonment always brought her down to a state of uncontrollable shivering even though she could not remember her father's face, a face she never met. The mention of her absent father stripped her down to her bones and she used the only weapon she had to protect herself. "Angelina, go to your room."

"But why, Mamá? I didn't do anything wrong."

With trembling hands, Marta yanked Angelina's ear and dragged her to her room. Angelina's eyes filled with tears, but she knew better than to give in to them. Marta pushed Angelina down to her knees.

Angelina looked down submissively and pressed her palms together in prayer. Surely her mother intended for her to pray again even if she hadn't ordered it yet.

Marta, already regretting her actions, stood behind her little girl. She reached out almost touching Angelina's head with her unsteady hand. More than anything she wanted to tell her daughter she was sorry, that it wasn't her fault if the gossiping snake-tongues of the town enjoyed hurting her. She felt responsible for handing down such an ill-fated legacy to her daughter.

She knew the story better than anybody else did. The sisters at the convent as well as her grandmother never missed an opportunity to remind her of the bad blood running through her veins. It was for her benefit, they insisted, so she wouldn't follow in their footsteps. She was the fruit of a philanderer and a whore. Their legacy was a rough and unavoidable truth, one she had grown used to since early in her life that switched her back into the facade of the stern woman she pretended to be.

Behind a mask of righteousness, Marta felt weak and unprotected, and she hated that feeling. In a way she envied her daughter's confidence. She often wondered if Angelina would be able to keep up that attitude while Marta worked so hard to break her. She quickly retrieved her hand before the tips of her fingers reached Angelina's head, turned on her heels and left the room.

As Marta's footsteps faded down the hallway, Angelina snapped her eyes open and gazed directly towards her window. She felt Sarah's presence on the other side, a fact confirmed with her melodious laughter enticing Angelina to break all rules.

Angelina did not think twice. She slipped out her window and, alongside Sarah, she ran all the way to the harbor.

By the time they reached the docks, Angelina's knees were peeled, the bow on her dress was undone, her hair was flying in all directions. And her white dress wasn't white anymore.

With her heart thumping and careless of the freshly torn piece of cloth at the hem of her dress, Angelina climbed up the rusted wrought iron fence that led to the pier and sat at the top. She set her eyes on the horizon, and waited anxiously for the first sight of her father's vessel.

Ramiro, her father, was finally coming back home after a three-week long absence, one of his longest fishing trips ever. She couldn't remember the last time he was gone for such a long period of time, and in Angelina's young life span three weeks meant an eternity.

Before his departure, he had promised that upon his return he would take her on short fishing trips. Angelina didn't enjoy the fishing that much, but the idea of sailing in the open waters away from Pueblo Brugo was thrilling enough to rob her of her sleep.

While her father was away, she ran to the riverbank every day to stare at the steel colored waters. She learned to tell the imminent changes in the weather by the depth of color of the water or the flow of the streams. Being able to dispel the secret messages the water carried made her love the river even more. She was drawn to it by its strength and the illusion of infinity the river lent. She could feel a pull, a call from the other side. She knew that someone or something was waiting for her in a faraway land. She was not sure what was beyond the water. She did not know if there was anything at all outside the limits of her Pueblo Brugo, because she had never been past the dusty roads that led to the river.

"Have you ever been on the other side, Sarah?" Angelina gazed to her right, her legs swinging down the iron fence.

"Yes, I have." Sarah embraced Angelina with a melody.

"How is it?" Angelina squinted hard at the far distance as if she could reach the other side of the world.

"One day you will see it all. I promise." The voice vanished with the roar of the strong current.

The weather had been stormy for the past few days, and a vast accumulation of water hyacinths populated the immediate shore. They frightened her to no end. She closed her eyes tightly in an effort to erase their image from her mind.

She wouldn't be scared of those water logs if it weren't for Don Tomas. He was the town's crazy; an old fisherman who travelled the world, or so he said. He once told her that the presence of water hyacinths was a bad omen.

Her mother had strictly forbidden her to talk to Don Tomas, but there was something about him that drew her to him. Maybe it was the sadness in his eyes, or the fact that he was constantly on his knees, praying and thumping his chest on the spot where a heavy silver crucifix lay close to his heart. But most definitely, she thought it was because he always talked to somebody who was not there, to an invisible friend, just like she did with Sarah.

Even if she had considered obeying her mother, it was almost impossible to avoid meeting him on a daily basis. On her secret expeditions with Sarah to the church, Angelina had to walk across the town's main square. Actually, that was not entirely true. There was a shorter way to the church, but taking the alternate route would have meant missing Don Tomas, and she just didn't see the point. As for her mother, she would never have to find out.

Don Tomas was full of wonderful tales that filled the void of her father's stories while he was away on his fishing voyages. The old man's recollection went back all the way to the time when he was the captain of the

Augusta, "a sweet tender girl," he often said with a toothless melancholic grin along his thin, dry lips.

There was a particular story that haunted her for many nights, leaving her sleepless and waking her up in sweating nightmares as soon as she would fall asleep again.

This particular story was about the time Don Tomas and his five-man crew survived a fierce storm, or so they thought. The waters of the Parana River pushed the small vessel angrily through a whirlwind of rapids that entrapped the hapless boat.

"There was nothing left to do other than pray to Saint Peter." His words had flowed like a mournful whisper, his eyes remained shut, and his right hand, which Angelina noticed was horribly maimed, touched the heavy, silver crucifix centered on his sunburnt chest.

Don Tomas' eyes sprang wide, adding the drama that a story of such caliber needed. Angelina held her breath and shook slightly. She knew something bad was about to come.

"The storm suddenly stopped as if Saint Peter had sheltered us under his protective hands," the old man recounted, fixing his stare on Angelina. She was too scared to look away, and also too scared to look straight at him. There was no escape from the story and she knew the worst was not over yet. Confirming her fears, the old fisherman delivered the blow she dreaded.

"My men fell on their knees and in silent prayer they thanked our savior, *bendito sea*." His voice filled with emotion. "For a moment I gave in and closed my eyes too, not so much as in prayer, because I didn't believe back then, but just out of plain exhaustion. Then, the screams came. I opened my eyes and all I could see were dismembered bodies being attacked by vicious beasts climbing up on the water hyacinths, those cursed *camalotes*, surrounding my beautiful Augusta. River monsters, such as snakes and piranhas, jumped on deck. We fought them with our bare hands," reminisced Don Tomas looking down at his mutilated limb, "but the Devil was on their side and he was laughing at me. I was being punished by Saint Peter for not believing."

The old man lowered his head, and when he looked up again, sad and defeated, he cupped his mutilated hand with the good one. "I lost them all."

It took Angelina a moment to recover from the dreadful story. "Is that who you're always talking to, Don Tomas? Your sailors, are they here with you?"

Don Tomas grinned and looked down at her. "Yes, *preciosa*. Just like you and your friend next to you. I have my sailors all around me."

Angelina's jaw dropped. "Can you see her too?"

Don Tomas leaned closer to her. "Of course, but let's keep it a secret between us."

A few raindrops brought Angelina back to the present and she thought about the dangers her father could face out in the open water. That was Don Tomas' story, she reassured herself. Her father would come back safe and they would share tons of adventures together. Her mother was right, she should not talk to that crazy old man again. Angelina looked at the *camalotes* once more and stuck her tongue out at them.

The horn of an approaching boat resounded throughout the docks. Angelina squinted. There it was. A dark dot in the distance. "That's him, Sarah. My *papi* is home. Do you have a *papi* like me? Is he a captain too?"

The answer came with the sound of hoofbeats. Angelina wrinkled her nose while thinking, *oh, so your* papi *is not a captain, he has horses, right?* Angelina knew that was right because she could feel Sarah's smile around her.

The dot she had seen only moments before was gradually shaping into a boat. Excitedly, she waved her arms. "*Papi, Papi.*" She stepped down the fence and ran to the pier, stumbling in between rocks and some slimy garbage, to the very spot where the ship would dock. A small crowd was slowly gathering, and amongst them, Marta, as anxious as Angelina, stood waiting for the impending arrival.

Angelina elbowed her way into the packed crowd to reach the closest spot to the edge of the water, but every time she advanced two steps forward she was pushed three steps back.

A firm grasp on her shoulder made her impossible fight stop. She needn't turn to know it was the hand of her mother. Marta surprised her by clearing a path all the way to the quay as if she was parting the waters of the Red Sea. She gave Angelina a gentle shove on her back. "Go ahead, *mi amor.*"

She reached for her mother's hand and looked to the other side, feeling Sarah's presence near her. They all walked together. Angelina ran her free hand through her hair just enough to notice she was a complete mess. She looked up at her mother with some apprehension. "Sorry about the dress, *Mami.* I just—"

Marta kissed the top of her head and rearranged Angelina's hair as best as she could. "Don't worry about it, my love."

The approaching fishing boat was a worn, warped, and ragged old piece of wood. But, judging by Ramiro Fernandez's proud and stoic posture when standing at the bow of the Gloria, one would assume he was the captain of one of those big caravels Queen Isabel gave to Columbus back in the old days.

Chapter Five
Ramiro

Ramiro was a young man of thirty, fairly young to be the captain of any boat new or old. His soft brown eyes, surrounded by fine lines, mirrored each one of his emotions. The gentle contrast of youth and radiant olive skin that appeared immune to the constant beating of the sun made women sigh after him, even though they knew he was taken.

Sighing women or imprudent offers never sidetracked Ramiro. His gaze stayed forever focused forward, not on the crowd anxiously awaiting the arrival of the ship, but on the finish line.

He did not consider his job to be done and did not rest until the last bit of cargo was unloaded off the boat, until he saw every one of his men safe in the arms of their beloved families.

Every one of Ramiro's trips represented a challenge. Growing up in an eastern province by the river and trailing after his father, the way his father did after his own, Ramiro never fathomed that manning a ship required more than good fishing skills or a good nose to find a large school of fish. The task was one of a politician.

His crewmembers admired Ramiro's temperament. He was a great captain, and they all looked up to him with respect. The greatest respect from his men came from the fact that Ramiro did not impose his authority by standing above the crew imparting orders. Instead he earned his place as captain by working harder than anyone else.

Ramiro had the highest regard for each member of his crew. He knew their personal stories, the number of children or women they had, and most importantly, he knew their weaknesses.

Aboard the Gloria, Ramiro became a mediator. Brawls erupted often amongst the crew during long trips, and their outcome could determine the fate of the fishing expedition. His motto was, happy crew meant good production and greater dividends for his men. Unhappy crew… they were all screwed.

This particular trip had been a success. Crew, weather, and fish worked in harmony as though conscious of the approaching rainy season that would keep them away from each other, at least for a couple of months. During those months of inactivity, some of his men tended to move to other areas in search of seasonal jobs. Others would venture out to close-by *pueblos* finding shelter between a pair of tender breasts, guaranteed to keep them warm and safe from trouble until work resumed. But mostly, they stayed in town, working small jobs around the docks, taking care of their families, and certainly taking care of their women. The local midwives knew to be prepared to welcome the massive arrival of babies the rainy season would deliver.

Ramiro wanted more babies, a large family. At least that had been his and Marta's plan before they married. Throughout their days of courtship he would steal innocent kisses from the painfully shy Marta while talking about their future in between nervous giggles meant to mask their strong carnal desire. He was experienced on how to sweet talk a girl, to get what he wanted, and Marta looked like an easy target. But he would never trick her in that way. He loved her. Moreover, his restraint was connected with a secret. What would she think of him when she saw him for what he was…

***

He lost his virginity at the age of fourteen. A good family friend, who earned the title of uncle by mere affection, was self-appointed to take Ramiro for his first visit to a brothel.

This uncle, a dandy and know-it-all, instructed Ramiro to take matters in his own hands, literally, before the scheduled rendezvous with a legendary prostitute responsible for initiating most of Ramiro's friends. The uncle made it clear to Ramiro he wanted his money's worth, and if Ramiro were to cum as soon as the whore would lay a hand on him, it would be a waste of money for the uncle and easy business for the whore. No, under his uncle's orders, Ramiro had to keep it up for as long as he could and make the whore work for it.

With that in mind, Ramiro found a quiet spot behind a shed at the docks and set out to work on it. On any given day, his penis would just stand up on its own. In fact, he was having problems keeping it down most of the time. But on that day, it would not rise for anything. He fondled it, and rubbed it, and summoned to his mind all the dirty stories he had heard the fishermen bragging about at the local cafe. Yet nothing happened. His penis remained limp as rubber. He must have groaned out in frustration, and before he could stuff his inert organ back into his pants, Antonita, a girl a few years his senior, materialized in front of him.

It was a humorous sight, he remembered now. He had both his hands choking his unresponsive member and his pants around his ankles. At Antonita's unexpected emergence, his hands spread out like a Chinese fan over his crotch. He was sweating profusely out of irritation, humiliation, and heat. With a hand covering his shame, he quickly reached down for his pants, lost his balance, and went down like a sack of potatoes, exposing more than he ever wanted in front of a girl. By then, it was not only his shaft that was hurt, but his pride.

Antonita laughed until her sides hurt. Still struggling with his pants and shaky hands, Ramiro huddled against a wall, curled up into a ball, and hid his face between his knees. Silently, Antonita sat next to Ramiro by the wall. Her presence intimidated him and he closed his eyes trying to forget the embarrassing moment she witnessed.

She didn't seem fazed by a boy with his pants down and reached out for Ramiro's hand. She slowly unclasped his arms from his knees and looked down at the offending appendage. Her hands ventured down in between Ramiro's legs. "I've never done it with a Jew."

Ramiro pushed her hand away and got up abruptly not caring about exposure anymore. He was red in the face, more out of anger than of shame. "I am not a Jew."

At school, the *padre* had made it very clear that Jews were the murderers responsible for killing Christ. Ramiro was not that. He was not a murderer.

Up to the day of his first time with Antonita, he pushed the possibility of being a Jew aside, although the doubt hovered over his mind ever since he could remember. He learned to be careful of his privacy. To avoid side-glances and cruel remarks from other boys he was cautious not to take a piss when others were around in the school's urinals. Yet, he felt there was something different about him and his father. They never went to church, they had no religious images in their home, and there was the matter of their misshapen penises. When he asked his father about being a Jew, he replied, "We eat pork, Jews don't."

Not satisfied with the answer, Ramiro braved a second question. "But, what about..." He looked down at his crotch.

The answer came in the form of a slap across his face followed by five short words. "You were born that way." Ramiro knew better than to press the matter any further, he sensed he would not get a satisfactory answer from his father.

Antonita had noticed Ramiro's member shrivel after she called him a Jew. She was determined not to let Ramiro's snipped penis or his anger get in the way of adding another virgin to her list. She went down on her knees, crawled like a cat in heat towards Ramiro, lifted her head with a wicked smile in her eyes, and worked Ramiro until he was hard as a rod.

Ramiro's fears and misgivings left him and he surrendered to a sea of lust and flesh. He never made it to the whorehouse. Instead, he stayed back at the shed discovering the intricate channels to Antonita's ecstasy.

***

Standing at the bow of his boat he narrowed his focus on the distant shore. They still had some time before reaching the port, the crew was readying to dock and disembark, all seemed to be in place, so he allowed his mind to wander a bit more.

He reflected on the two women that had made a mark in his life. Two polar opposites, yet both as significant. He thought back upon the time when Marta came into his life and the way he was taken aback by her simplicity. The women he had held in his arms during his short life were not by any means sophisticated. Rowdy women ready to lie on their backs to sate his needs.

He was unaccustomed to the presence of a woman who blushed when meeting him, and shuddered when his warm breath touched her delicate neck. Marta puzzled him from the start and made him hot with wanting her. It had been a long time since he had touched his wife. His body ached yearning for the feel of hers. Thoughts of Marta made him feel like a virgin all over again.

Chapter Six
Deadly Secrets

Marta opened Ramiro's eyes to a new meaning of a woman, a new gender yet to be discovered. Maybe his mother had been that way. He would never know. His mother died in childbirth. His own.

His father never spoke of her. Guilt, perhaps. Truth be told, his father never spoke of anything at all. As far as Ramiro could remember, he only shared one intimate moment with his old man.

A tale as old as time. A brief moment within minutes of death. The spirit, leaving the restraints of the physical body, yearning to be accepted and loved.

He had been merely eighteen the last time he walked into his father's room. It was just the two of them, but not for long. The priest would soon arrive to give his old man the last rites.

He had never before looked directly into his father's eyes, and it pained him to see the effort this dying stranger—whom he called father—made to meet Ramiro's gaze. Their eyes settled upon each other, the mirror of one another. No words were spoken, it was too late for that. Ramiro's father reached for his son's hand and grabbed it with the force of a man desperate to live. Ramiro felt a hard object on his palm. He attempted to pull his hand away from his father's iron grip, but the old man would not let go. Ramiro's eyes never left his father's face. While the last signs of life flowed out of the dying man's body, the word, *remember*, formed on his lips. He closed his mouth, then his eyes, and before Ramiro could ask any questions, his father exhaled his last breath.

Ramiro sat stunned for what seemed like ages. The priest came and left, and so did a few neighbors and fellow fishermen. People talked to him and patted him on his back. He found himself nodding at their words of sympathy, not really registering what they said. Only one thing was very clear and immediate, and his hand was still wrapped around it. What had his father meant by his last word?

Hours later, he was still sitting by his father's bed. The body had been removed. Somebody had mentioned the sacristy, but he wasn't sure. The silver glare of the night entered the room through an open window. He suddenly felt tired. His right arm ached. Only then he noticed that his fist was tightly clenched about the object his father passed over to him in a secret first and last handshake.

He uncurled his fingers to find that his palm was sticky with sweat and blood. The object had dug into his flesh. He held it up against the intrusive moonlight. It was a piece of jewelry, a pendant. It hung on a chain. Gemstones surrounding a star with six points sparkled with the touch of the night's gleam.

"Remember," he whispered. Ramiro clamped his fist around the pendant and left the room, closing the door behind him.

As he plunged out into the dusty road he nearly ran into an old woman. Her eyes fixed anxiously on his face and then dropped down to the pendant he held in his bloodied fist. She slowly reached out for his hand and he stretched out his fingers to reveal once more the shining star.

"I found you," she had said with the heavy Spanish accent of the old world, "at last," her voice filled with emotion. "You are not alone, nor am I."

Ramiro, stunned, stared at her for a long time while she identified herself as Fortuna Fernandez, and talked about Spain, and a ship, and a myriad of other things Ramiro could not begin to grasp. His head was crowded with a cacophony of questions, and the only voice he could hear was that of his father whispering his last word, *remember.*

"Remember," he said to himself. He stuffed the pendant in his pants front pocket and left the blabbering old woman behind. He needed to distance himself from a past where there were no footprints of his existence and move toward a future where he could find himself.

Six months later he stumbled upon the first tangible traces of his path in life. It happened on a hot summer night at the local fair, where the whole town gathered to chatter, when he came across the local midwife that had so laboriously worked to bring him into this world. The woman was an open book of town gossip, she loved to talk and tell the stories about everybody's birth. After several glasses of red wine, the midwife's tongue loosened a bit more than usual and she answered some of Ramiro's questions.

Her tale went back all the way before Ramiro's birth. His mother and father had moved to Pueblo Brugo right after their wedding. Nobody knew them back then, but Clara—Ramiro's mother—was a sweet girl that slowly won the heart of everyone in town. After more than a dozen miscarriages, the midwife had advised the couple to abstain from having children. Still, a few months later the young couple found hope with the blessing of yet another pregnancy.

Ramiro's birth had been a difficult one. He came six weeks early, and it took twenty-three long painful hours for his tiny body to come out of his mother's battered womb. He emerged from the birth canal red in the face from the effort of grasping life, and screaming for air.

His long body was wrinkly, and his egg-shaped head made him look like a little specimen not associated with the human species. Amid the baby's incessant wailing, the midwife assured the overjoyed mother that he would look somewhat normal in a few days' time. The young mother did not seem to care. She looked at her baby with that special amazement only mothers have when looking at their children at the time of their birth.

Forgetting about her exhaustion, Clara stretched out her arms to hold her tiny baby. She cradled him to her bosom and by pure animal instinct the newborn found his way to the engorged breast laying invitingly only inches from his face. Ramiro clamped his hungry lips around her nipple making her jolt with the newfound painful experience of breastfeeding.

A blanket of bliss fell over the room at the miraculous picture-perfect sight of Madonna with child. Ramiro's father walked in and knelt at the side of the bed. Tears rolling down his haggard face, and the foul stench of alcohol emanating from his every pore, were the traceable scars from his own labor pains.

Speechless, the young couple locked eyes, clasped hands and shared a smile of pure joy and relief. No one noticed the crimson puddle forming under the mother's body. Her hand slowly lost strength, hung limp from her husband's grasp. Her smile lingered on. But her eyes glazed over, wandering, leaving, dying.

Ramiro, forgotten for hours lying on his dead mother, fell asleep after suckling laboriously on a dry breast. His father, thinking that both mother and baby were gone, did not let anybody move them until the wee hours of the morning, when the baby, smeared in his mother's blood, woke up with a sudden wail.

Ramiro screamed for hours, starving for a breast to suckle. A nearby neighbor, alerted by the crying, walked into the death-scented room and snatched Ramiro from his mother's cold body. His father never heard him. He never saw him. Maybe, he never loved him.

Before Ramiro bid the midwife goodbye, she added one last detail to her story. A week or so after his birth, his father had taken him away from the *pueblo*. Both father and son were gone for almost six months before they returned to Pueblo Brugo to stay. As much as he pressed her for answers about a possible family away from the *pueblo*, the midwife did not have them.

"You were motherless and we took you in like one of our own, even though we never knew your people. Your father never spoke of them, but it was all the same to us."

He could now make sense of the steely scent of blood embedded in his nostrils that woke him up in a dreaded recurring nightmare. A nightmare in which he lost grip of the very edge of his beloved boat Gloria. His cherished ship was the only solid platform in his life. It served as his anchor, a place where he stood out from the rest of the townspeople. It was aboard his boat where he felt complete, where he felt contained as if he were embraced by his mother. The Gloria gave him that special touch he yearned for while growing up, and was never granted. He never had it, except when he was aboard the Gloria. Why was that torturing nightmare coming to haunt him, making him feel so terribly alone?

The nightmare was about the utter sense of being left alone and lost in the middle of the waters. In his dream he fought the force of the waters, and with every desperate attempt to reach the Gloria, he succumbed to the raging river. The river's victory drained him of his age and experience and turned him into a defenseless baby.

Night after night Ramiro woke up drenched in sweat. It was as if he had just come out of a battle against an opponent he couldn't beat. More often than not he would cry himself back to sleep. It was that feeling of hollowness that left him worn out and devastatingly empty. Longing for his vessel to embrace him tenderly, rocking him to sleep like only a mother could. Cradling him with love was what he fathomed his mother would have done if only…

"What was your *mami* like, *Papi*?" Angelina had asked him one evening as he was tucking her in bed.

The question had caught him unaware and he was forced to lie to his daughter. "She was the best *mami* in the world, and she looked very much like you," he said, knowing that those were the words his little girl yearned to hear.

But his only memory of his mother was the smell of blood left on him forever. His only memory of his mother was that he killed her.

Chapter Seven
To Love and To Hold

The wedding celebration was a humble one. Both orphans, Marta and Ramiro lacked a cheering crowd of relatives to help them with the wedding preparations. They settled for a small ceremony in the church, followed by a meal of red wine and empanadas the sisters at the convent made in honor of the celebration. It was simple and memorable.

Marta and Ramiro were highly regarded in Pueblo Brugo and their marriage had brought in a considerable number of well-wishers to the wedding. Even Padre Aparicio brought out his guitar and sang a few *sambas*, which encouraged rhythmic clapping and some daring dance moves from the attendees.

They were a handsome couple, both young and very much in love. Marta had worked on her gown for months. She had designed it herself. A dress of pure white satin buttoned up all the way to her throat, complete with a princess-like ball gown skirt. The gown swayed smoothly around her ankles when she walked. Her long, black lustrous hair was pinned up with pearly clips. For Ramiro it had been a lot easier. He fell in the hands of the local tailor, accustomed to dressing all grooms in the same fashion. A plain navy blue double-breasted suit, a crisp heavily starched white shirt, a blue and red tie, and shiny black shoes.

Showered by a downpour of rice, good wishes, and some imprudent winks, Marta and Ramiro were sent home long before the party ended. Marta insisted in helping the sisters clean up, her last attempt to delay the unavoidable forthcoming events about to develop in their marriage bed.

The short drive to Ramiro's house had been deathly silent, except for the grinding protests his old beat up blue Citroen made every time Ramiro changed gears, and for the jangle of traditional tin cans tied to the rear bumper of the car of any newlywed couple.

Ramiro parked his car right outside the house. He glanced at Marta, but her eyes were downcast, glued to her shoes. She looked nervous. It was evident in the way she bit her upper lip every time he looked at her. Ramiro had felt jittery himself knowing that he would have to pace his moves, mollify his anticipation of finally being with the woman he loved.

Anxiety turned against him and he was out of the car opening her door before he could actually realize he had done so. With mechanical movements and avoiding eye contact, Ramiro swept her up into his arms and walked towards their love nest. After pushing the front door open with his elbow and stepping over the threshold of the small home, their eyes finally met.

Here he was. Standing in the middle of the kitchen, holding his bride in his arms, feeling pretty stupid, not knowing how to proceed forward. Luckily, Marta broke the awkwardness of the moment with her shaky little voice.

"If you put me down..." He looked at her as if he was waking from a dream. "The bathroom, I have to..."

"Of course... it's the last door." His gaze remained upon her, still holding her tightly. She raised her eyebrows questioningly and finally he put her down. "You know, the one to the right."

At that moment, he realized that it was Marta's first time in the house. They had never been alone there or anywhere else. She was a girl with a good reputation and he swore to honor it until the end. They always met at her house, before the death of her grandmother, and after that at the park. They would always be surrounded by people—never alone. This day was a first for many things. It was their first time alone, her first time in his house, the first time for Marta, his first with his wife, and a virgin.

Since his father's death a few years before, Ramiro had lived alone and the only women who ever crossed that door were not the marrying kind. But, Marta was. He even made the necessary arrangements to acquire and transport a new mattress from the big city, Entre Rios, since the little cooperative in their town did not carry such luxuries. Ramiro thought it would be a fresh start for both of them.

He also planned a short trip to Entre Rios, a honeymoon, for the following weekend. With his savings, he planned to take her to the movies and a nice restaurant. Marta had never been to the city and he swore to give her everything she never had. He loved her so.

Ramiro waited in the kitchen for what seemed like an eternity. A few minutes later, he decided to go check on her. Before knocking on the bathroom door, he hesitated. She was a lady and needed her time, but he was anxious, and she was his wife.

With macho determination, he knocked. "Marta!" No answer. He knocked again, this time a little harder, and got nothing in response, except for a faint sob.

The door was unlocked and he slowly opened it. He found Marta sitting on the floor, on a cloud of white satin, crying silently. His macho attitude came undone and his heart broke at the sight of her. He sat next to her and reached for her hands. She didn't resist, but would not look at him. He brought her hands to his lips and brushed them with feathery kisses.

"You don't have to be scared of me. Marta, I love you."

She drew her hands away and lifted her tear streaked face. She cleared her throat and squared her shoulders. Without a word, she stood up and reached down for his hand. He slowly got up on his feet, followed her out of the bathroom and across to the door leading to the bedroom.

The sisters had taken care of their marriage chambers, as well as stocking up the fridge with sufficient food to last a couple of days.

The double sized bed, which belonged to Ramiro's parents, was covered with a white bedspread embroidered with tiny red roses. Above the bed a heavy hand-carved wooden crucifix was pinned to the wall. Jesus' eyes were staring down intently at the site where the carnal act would take place. Next to the only draped window in the room there was a small shrine, with the effigy of the blessed virgin surrounded by burning candles. This last detail completed the marriage alcove, overwriting its former reputation of the fornication room.

Ramiro let go of Marta's hand and stood in front of her motionless. He had already resolved to let her be until she was ready to give herself to him. He meant to spend the rest of his life with her. He needed somebody in his life to finally love him deeply without reservations. If time was what she needed to get used to his skin, then time she would have.

Marta took a step back and Ramiro reached for her hand and kissed it again. His next words came out of his heart and they even surprised him. "Thank you for marrying me." With that he turned on his heels and began to leave.

The rustle of satin on floorboards followed him. Marta grabbed his hand before he reached the door. He stopped dead in his tracks and his heart suddenly throbbed. Marta slipped her hands around his waist and rested her head on his back. She inhaled his scent and exhaled softly. He could feel her heartbeat pounding like a set of African drums. He did not move. It was for her to make the call. She relaxed her hold on him and walked around until they were standing face to face. She loosened her long, black, shiny mane from the pins constraining it, and dropped their pearly heads on the floor one by one.

Ramiro felt his chest tighten, his hands ached to touch her, but he controlled his urges. It was her time to initiate things between them.

She reached for his tie and freed him of it. Then, she unbuttoned his jacket, careful not to wrinkle it, and slid it off his shoulders, hanging it neatly on the doorknob. Ramiro swallowed hard while a thin line of perspiration formed above his upper lip. His eyes never left her face as she slowly unbuttoned his shirt and slipped her hands across his chest. This time he couldn't contain the groan rising in his throat. He clenched his fist as she stepped closer to kiss him. She played with his lips, torturing him with desire. Ramiro, the gentleman, did not raise a finger... at least not yet.

Next, she went down on her knees and untied the laces of his shoes and removed them one by one. She then proceeded to remove his socks.

Her hands went to his belt and pulling the strap back she unbuckled it. Ramiro felt the waist of his pants loosen. He heard the gritting of the zipper as she pulled it down. The unbearable pressure of his mounting penis hardened when she slid her fingers beneath the waistband of his briefs, releasing him of the last piece of clothing that once dressed him as a groom.

He didn't dare to move. She stood once more facing him, and then looked down at how much he wanted her. She laid a finger on his stiff organ. Her minute touch was enough to make him groan again. Enjoying his response, she ventured another finger, and another, until her whole hand was wrapped around it.

Ramiro thought his heart would explode if he couldn't have her and soon. Still sensible to her feelings, he didn't move.

Marta slid her soft fingers up and down, tilted her head, and closing her eyes she bit her lower lip. Was that an invitation?

Ramiro raised his hand to her face. His fingers brushed her moist lips and she instantly tightened her grip on his penis making him jolt in pain. With her eyes closed, she loosened her fist but did not let go. Ramiro's hand slid to the small of her back and pushed her to him. Until that moment he hadn't noticed how badly he was shaking.

When she didn't resist, he bent his head to kiss her. She answered with a hungry, lip-biting kiss. His repressed desire unleashed. He thrust his tongue into her mouth. Both of his hands were on her now, but everywhere he touched there was slippery satin, and all he wanted, all he needed was flesh. His mouth, hungry for hers, left her lips for a brief moment, long enough to breathe sufficient air to survive. Her fingers dug into his well-built muscular shoulders, asking... no, begging for him to take her. That was the moment when he lost himself to her.

He grabbed the neck of her gown and with one swift motion he ripped the front open. He took a step back to admire her small, but perfectly round breasts.

His mouth went to them. Marta's breath became a mixture of gasps and moans, the sole response he needed to proceed. He pushed her against the bedroom wall and lifted the ballooned skirt. Finding it a nuisance, he pulled it down and the whole dress fell around her ankles in shreds.

Too aroused to care, Marta stepped out of the puddle of fabric and into Ramiro's arms wearing nothing but her skin.

He looked at her as though it was his first time with a naked woman. She was beautiful, fragile, and soft. His desire for her ever increasing, he gripped her hair. With his mouth never leaving her mouth, neck, or breasts, he laid her on the floor pinning her under his weight.

It was too late to back down and they both knew it. Marta's legs shook uncontrollably while Ramiro rose over her and spread her thighs with his knee.

Blind with wanting and hard as a rock, he plunged into her soft core with a single, powerful thrust. Marta's eyes went wide, she held her breath for a short moment, and whimpered in pain.

His hands went to her hips keeping her steady as she cringed under him. He waited until he saw her initial pain had eased, until she welcomed every one of his strong demanding thrusts, touching him, kissing him, moaning in pleasure.

Ramiro could read her responses. At the peak of her ecstasy, he boosted his intensity until they climaxed together.

Bathed in sweat, they lay on the floor, wordless. Once he came to his senses and his breathing returned to normal, he reached over to Marta. He meant to apologize for acting like a caged animal. He wanted to cradle her in his arms. But, she surprised him.

She threw her arms around him and brought him down to her bosom. She rocked him and caressed his hair. She pressed her lips to the top of his ear and hummed.

He felt small. He felt loved. He cried.

A short while later, the two of them managed to make their way to the bed. They cuddled under the warm covers, and spent most of the night exploring each other and making love with the hungry novelty of new lovers, tasting each other and trying everything possible on every inch of their skin. Their lovemaking surprised Ramiro in a way he never imagined. He made love to Marta not only with the thirst of their first time, but also with the underlying knowledge of being their last.

Late into the night, Ramiro woke from a deep sleep. Marta's side of the bed was empty. He rose up on one elbow and surveyed the room. He found Marta kneeling at the foot of the shrine where the virgin stood. She was sobbing silently. He started to go to her, but her words froze him.

"Please forgive me for being like her. Forgive me for being a whore like my mother. Father, burn me with the flames of hell for being a whore to a Jew."

That moment, when he witnessed the agony of her inheritance and the torture his marked body brought to her, he resolved never to touch her again. It was a hard decision, and it was going to be even harder to carry it out. The touch of her skin on his was still fresh and he felt like taking her again, disregarding her torment. The thought of never having her in that way was torturous, but the mere notion of losing her pierced his guts. The idea of living without having to prove himself worthy of anything, and still be loved, was enough for Ramiro to settle for a life without her flesh.

All he wanted from their union was for her to love him unconditionally. He knew he could always get his sexual desires satisfied elsewhere. He had never experienced love before that night. The pure sensation of another soul mingling with his made him feel dizzy, close to fainting. She made love to him and loved him, sacrificing herself in the process, even though she had recognized the shameful appearance of the shorn head of his penis.

No, he wouldn't dare ask for more.

Ramiro was resolute in his decision. Although they never discussed it between themselves, Marta welcomed the silent decree. He secretly blamed the outcome of that night on the miniature church the sisters had mounted in their room, with Jesus on one side and Mary on the other. He was surprised at the fact that he got hard amid the prude witnesses.

Every time they looked back at that passionate night, they fervently believed they were granted the miracle they had prayed for before meeting, and before laying with each other.

It was on that fateful night that Marta and Ramiro were rewarded with the seed of their love, the biggest joy they ever knew to exist. God acknowledged their unselfish sacrifices and in return He blessed them with Angelina.

Chapter Eight
Pueblo Brugo

After the methodical unloading of the Gloria, although filthy, smelling like rotten fish, and dead tired, Ramiro didn't pause until he delivered his men safely to the many outstretched arms waiting anxiously for them.

He was the last one to leave the ship. Working side by side with his men, he too was exhausted beyond words. Yet, the thought of coming home to the loves of his life kept him running on pure adrenaline.

It had been a long trip and it promised to last a bit longer if he hadn't pushed his crew to their limits to make it back on land in time for Angelina's birthday. His men did not mind. In fact, the closeness Ramiro had developed with them made those special allowances possible.

Captains from other ships had criticized Ramiro's leadership methods, and because of them they had to work harder to meet the expectations of their crew throughout the season.

When the fishing season was set to start, the Gloria was the most sought-after vessel to work on. Men wanted to be part of Ramiro's journeys. They wanted to work for him simply because it meant they would get to work with him. Ramiro shared his life with them, so the men naturally knew about Angelina's sixth birthday. With that in mind, they drove themselves harder to arrive in Pueblo Brugo in time for the celebration. And they did.

However, there was much more to June the twenty-ninth than Angelina's birthday for the people of Pueblo Brugo. June the twenty-ninth was Saint Peter's Day. For a fishing community, it was one of the most important days of the year, second to Christmas. Saint Peter was the patron of fishermen. The statue of Saint Peter, held in the arms of the *padre*, shone as a beacon for the returning sailors. The saint's golden halo represented a point of reference that the crewmembers associated with home.

It had been the first time Angelina's birthday, and the arrival of a successful fishing expedition, coincided. An expedition where her father was the captain, and reckoning the revenues this trip would bring the townspeople, Ramiro would be idolized as a fisherman, surpassed only by Saint Peter himself. Of course, the relentless gossip generated by the men from other boats who had not been as successful as the Gloria, alluded to the matching dates not as a mere twist of fate, but as an intentional display of power on Ramiro's behalf.

Ramiro saw that coming and quickly dismissed the rumors as pure idiocy. He was too tired and way too anxious to come home to the warmth of his family, and couldn't care less about the cold statue of a saint.

Ramiro was not a practicing Catholic, his father had not been, and he had his doubts he was baptized. Nevertheless, he held a deep respect for the religion if only for Marta's sake.

For a man used to the infinite breadth of nature, religion posed too many barriers. He was a spiritual being and held the most intricate conversations with God especially when the waters were calm and the crew was mostly asleep. There was something about the rare combination that was brought together by the depths of the night and the soothing rush of water that transported him somewhere he'd never been before, but someplace where he suspected he had existed somewhere in time.

Talking to God in his heart felt as real to Ramiro as having ten fingers and ten toes. Talking and praying to a statue made by the local plasterer, a good man with whom Ramiro had done some handyman work during the off season, felt as real as talking to one of Angelina's dolls during one of her lavish tea parties at the kitchen table.

It was with that in mind that Ramiro blindsided the aging Padre Aparicio by lurching forward, almost tripping the chubby priest and his holy doll, when the *padre* attempted to hand him the saint. It was a high honor, Ramiro knew, to lead the procession, but his heart was not in it.

In a sweeping move he picked Angelina up with one arm and held Marta tightly to his side with the other, making the whole incident look like a mere oversight.

Angelina hung tightly to Ramiro's neck. He nuzzled her. "So tell me, what's new? Have you been playing in the park with the other girls?"

Angelina eyed her mother who was distractedly walking beside Ramiro and took the opportunity to whisper in her father's ear, "I have a new best friend, *Papi*."

Ramiro turned to Angelina. "Oh, and who is she?"

Angelina cupped her hands around his ear. "Sarah, but no one can see her. Don Tomas says I must keep her a secret."

Ramiro raised his eyebrows. "She's one of those, eh?"

Angelina nodded.

"Don't worry, your secret's safe with me." He winked at her.

She exhaled with obvious relief and winked back with her own version of a full owl-like blink.

He gazed around him and was met with smiles and friendly nods. The citizens of Pueblo Brugo were the kindest Ramiro had come across throughout his life, even if they were not too forgiving of those who did not follow the ways of the church.

The *pueblo* was a town of about five hundred living souls. At any given time two or three were always ready to depart. Fewer than ten handpicked transients increased the population during the peak of fishing season, and a couple dozen stray dogs, which had become everybody's at one time or another.

It was a *pueblito* by big city standards. The streets were not paved. The church stood tall and proud in the middle of the town, serving as a point of reference for vagrant drunks. To the left of it, a decent size cooperative served as a general store as well as Pueblo Brugo's Town Hall whenever there was a need to assemble the town to discuss matters of the community.

The park lay naturally to the right of the church. It was a perfect square of bright green grass lined with yellow daffodils, which contrasted brutally with the dusty brown face of the rest of the village.

Most of the homes, plain stucco-covered boxes, were built at a decent walking distance from the town's square. This layout made everyone always available for events held at the park. The spot the whole town headed to at the culmination of Saint Peter's procession.

Food took center stage in all of the *pueblo's* gatherings and this one was no different. The sisters fried their legendary beef and potato empanadas. Marta made her grandmother's famous flan bathed in liquid caramel, served with her trademark delicious homemade vanilla-scented whipped cream. However, everybody knew that no get-together was complete until the traditional *locro*, a stew consisting of beans, chopped pork, corn, and spices, was served.

For this particular occasion, a group of ten fishermen's wives succeeded in borrowing the local rotisserie shop's kitchen. The owner, Don Nino, a grubby, old Italian man, always quick to strike a good bargain for himself, allowed them the use of the kitchen in exchange for a deep cleaning of his cockroach infested shop. The rotisserie's kitchen was the biggest in town second to the convent's, which never rested from the constant baking and cooking the sisters did. Out of options, the women shrugged their reservations away and accepted the dirty bargain.

Like many times before, the women of Pueblo Brugo proved their ability to enjoy a good time. In between lukewarm *mates*, sweet rolls, and loads of heavy gossip, mostly about brow-rising sightings of Padre Aparicio around the shabby shacks by the docks, the high spirited ladies barely noticed the grime in Don Nino's shop.

The party at the park concluded with a huge birthday cake for Angelina. The candles were lit. Angelina held her breath, silently wished her three birthday wishes, and exhaled with full force blowing all the candles at once. Her first wish was obviously about school. Marta and Ramiro did not have to guess that one. Her second wish was about her friend. She itched to see her face, to know who she was. Her friend had promised her that they would meet one day. That Angelina would go to her and all her questions would be answered. And lastly, the third wish was about her and Ramiro. She couldn't wait to go out on the many adventures the two of them had planned on their many walks along the docks. Angelina was ready to encounter pirates and river monsters. And if she was lucky enough, she would even come across the lost tribe of river mermaids the old ladies of the town talked about so much during their incessant rounds of *mate*.

The story of the river mermaids had become part of the town's folklore. Many years ago, more years than Angelina could count with all her fingers and toes, fifteen young girls vanished from the *pueblo*. Every living soul in Pueblo Brugo, including dogs and drunks, looked for the girls for thirty days and thirty nights. To their dismay the girls were never found.

Some months later, as a group of fishermen were getting ready to depart, they found fifteen dresses and fifteen pairs of shoes neatly folded at the edge of the riverbank. They matched the dresses and shoes the girls wore on the day of their disappearance. A note was attached to them. It was from the River King. The short missive read that the girls had become part of his kingdom, his mermaids, and they were never to return.

The story haunted Angelina, and days before her birthday, she finally came around to asking her mother about it. They were in the kitchen, Angelina casually poking her little fingers in a soft mass of dough Marta was shaping into a golden loaf for dinner. The moment was perfect.

After hearing the question Marta held her hands over the dough as in blessing. Angelina knew when not to push an issue with her mother, stood flat on her feet and waited.

"My mother, your grandmother, is a River Mermaid." The hands came down on the dough along with Marta's answer.

Angelina's eyes opened beyond their usual big size. "So Nana... she's not dead?"

Marta's next statement was pronounced with vehemence. It was her truth, the one she had lived by since she was a little girl. It did not matter what others had said about her mother. There was a truth between Marta and the fantasy she believed her mother to be, and now it was to be passed on to Angelina. "Nana is a beautiful River Mermaid."

Angelina's excitement was hard to contain. She stepped up on her tippy toes, and her gaze burned in her mother's eyes looking for a flick of deceit in what she had heard. But Marta did not waver. She was telling her truth.

"Can we see her?"

"Nobody can see her."

"Not even you?"

"It's a secret."

Angelina's feet were flat on the floor once again. She stared at her floury hands and chanced her next question. "Is her name Sarah, *Mami*?"

Marta shook her head.

That made Angelina very sad. She desperately wanted Sarah to be her nana or somebody real, and then her mother would believe her. She looked down at the tip of her worn shoes. This time her voice shook with emotion. "Why did your mamá leave you? Why didn't she take you with her?"

Marta wiped her flour-coated hands on her apron and took a deep breath in. She then knelt on the floor, lifted Angelina's chin softly and looked at her daughter's beautiful face. Angelina's lips trembled and her eyes filled with fear.

Marta would die before hurting her daughter. She gathered Angelina into the safety of her arms. She felt so fragile in her hold, so small, so innocent.

"I will never leave you," Marta pronounced. Another truth she would live by.

Angelina's shoulders relaxed. Her eyes smiled once again. In an instant, with the resilience children have to overcome their fears, she was back on her tippy toes poking the mass of dough and chattering away about River Mermaids.

Chapter Nine
The Visitor

The party dissipated quickly. The women were anxious to take their men to the two Bs—bath and bed.

Angelina, Marta, and Ramiro walked hand-in-hand down the dusty roads towards their house. The sun was setting and even if unseasonably warm for winter, the evening had a bite of chill to it.

Angelina was suffering the effects of too much sugar and was gradually running out of steam. Ramiro saw the little girl yawning and swaying with deep exhaustion, and so, he picked her up. She cuddled her head in the hollow of his collarbone as though she was still a baby and in a matter of seconds she was asleep. A pang of pain took hold of Ramiro when he noticed Angelina's legs dangling along the length of his torso and past his hips. She was growing fast and she was to be his one and only child. He felt content about coming home, about his family and the way things had worked out for them. Still, he wished things were different.

He knew ahead of time how his day would develop once in Pueblo Brugo. After putting Angelina to bed, he would share some of the stories about his most recent voyage with Marta and she would tell him what happened at home and in town during his absence. Then, he would kiss Marta goodnight, and he would quietly slip out of the house and into Antonita's arms which were still as welcoming to him as their first afternoon at the docks.

When they turned the corner onto their street, they saw a luxurious black sedan parked a few meters from their house. Angelina felt Ramiro's body tense. She turned her head to the side, murmured something unintelligible and lolled back into a deep sleep.

The last time Ramiro saw such a car in Pueblo Brugo was the day his father died. He had removed that event from his mind and did not expect to be confronted by that memory again as long as he lived. Yet, the car was there and it was only a matter of time until he had to deny his past once more.

They kept their steady pace until they were a few feet from their front door. Ramiro laid a protective hand on Marta's shoulder and steered her into the house closing the door behind them.

Ramiro placed Angelina on her bed. Careful to not wake her, he changed her into pajamas, covered her with a blanket, kissed her softly on the top of her head and left the room.

Marta was in the kitchen making coffee for the two of them. Ramiro walked in, hugged his wife affectionately and kissed her on the cheek.

"I missed you." His voice was filled with longing.

Her body trembled at his touch. Although he swore not to lie with her again he never lost hope. He knew she wanted him as much as he wanted her. Perhaps one day.

The knock on the door didn't surprise Ramiro—he expected it from the moment he spotted the car on the street. What he didn't anticipate was for Angelina to answer the call.

Before he could warn her against it, she was already greeting a refined older woman. "You're here. Sarah said you would be coming today."

The old woman was taken aback. "Oh, she did? Sarah, is she…"

Angelina lowered her voice. "She's my friend. She plays the piano."

Ramiro stood behind Angelina and placed both hands on her shoulders. His eyes, stone cold, glinted with recognition. The lady fixed her bottomless dark eyes on Angelina. There was a glimmer of emotion in them.

"Does it ever move with the wind?" Angelina asked. "Your hair, does it move with the wind?

The woman smiled and knelt next to her. "Blow hard as you did with your candles and see for yourself."

Angelina blew against the woman's hair with all her strength. The hair moved a little, but kept its coiffed form. Angelina touched her wild ringlets and looked back at Marta who stood frozen over by the kitchen's entrance as though she was an ornament on the doorframe.

"See, *Mami*, that's how I want my hair so you don't have to pull it with the ribbons." Angelina massaged her scalp. "It hurts."

Marta shook slightly with what seemed the beginning of a chuckle, but it was cut short by the stranger's quick response.

"Your hair looks just like mine when I was your age. If I counted the years correctly, you are six today." The woman touched Angelina's hair with transparent tenderness. Her voice was clear and tinged with the Spanish lilt of the Old World.

By then, Marta was already standing by Ramiro's side wondering why a stranger would have knowledge of their lives. Ramiro stood guard behind Angelina, his constraint wearing thin and his apprehension increasing. It was a matter of time before this stranger would open the Pandora's Box which concealed his family's many mysteries. He suspected she held the key to his father's last word before his death. Yes, he had wanted answers and had sought them, but that was before Marta, that was before he found the love of a family.

Angelina smiled with delight. Her eyes stared directly into the stranger's that were the twins of her own. "You talk funny."

Amused by the little girl's bluntness, the old woman chuckled, letting some of the tension on her shoulders relax. "I do, don't I?"

Angelina turned to look at Marta, who stood stiff holding Ramiro's hand. An idea formed in the little girl's head. She turned back to the woman and whispered, "Are you a River Mermaid? Are you my nana?"

The old woman straightened up slowly, wincing slightly with the weight of the years lying heavily on her lower back. She stared at Ramiro, who had gone completely pale. The tension in the room rang with a deafening buzz. Every move and every sound was enhanced. The creak of the old wood plank floors, every breath that was carefully inhaled, even the slight graze of clothes against skin.

Ramiro stepped forward, his hand up in warning.

He didn't faze her and she stood her ground. She would not leave before saying what she came here to say. She was not young anymore. Her time to claim what was rightfully hers would soon run out.

***

She had tried once before when Ramiro's father died. She had stood outside of this very same house waiting for an opportunity to speak to him. She had bought an extra ticket for him to go back to Spain with her in the same luxurious cruise liner in which she had arrived in Buenos Aires. She made sure to get Ramiro a spacious suite as a preview of what his life would be as a Fernandez of Cordoba.

She could hardly wait to take that lonely young man under her wing. She was aware of his rugged upbringing, to say the least, and had booked the best tutors in Spain to enlighten him in the arts of surviving the Spanish aristocracy.

Ramiro had to be told. It was her job to unravel before his sad, dark eyes the unspoken truth of the Fernandez family.

She remembered him walking out of the house, his aimless steps on the dusty road, his hand gripping something so tightly that a thin trail of blood ran down his wrist. When his fist relaxed, she caught a glimmer of the sparkling precious stones, caught a glimpse of the object.

He was in possession of the pendant, Sara's pendant, or like Angelina called her Sarah, her rightful name. After all those years searching for the lost thread of the Fernandez's in South America, the proof was in front of her in the form of the one thing that had belonged only to Sara Fernandez. Perhaps it had been the parting gift she had bestowed to her only surviving son, Salomon, before he fled the devastating hand of the Inquisition.

There was no doubt. Ramiro was her blood.

Fortuna hadn't had any children. She was a barren woman, or so her ex-husband said, when to her relief, he petitioned a *get*, the religious annulment of their marriage before the rabbi.

She was convinced that her childless marriage was the result of the repulsion she suffered at being pinned down every night underneath her foul breathed husband. It was an arranged marriage—of course, she never loved him or even liked him.

Fortuna Fernandez was a woman of the Cordoban hierarchy. The Fernandez's belonged to a long lineage of prominent bankers. Many members of the Spanish aristocracy had singled them out as eternal turncoats. According to the social climate in the country the Fernandez's had been openly Jews one day and Catholics the next. The truth of what they really were lay in the depths of their fifteenth century palace in the heart of the *Judería* in Cordoba, where the Fernandez's of Spain had never wavered from their Jewish faith.

Centuries of continuous survival, at times cropped, had taught the Fernandez's of Cordoba to swathe their tongues with gold, a language that spoke more eloquently than words. Hence, the influence of the Fernandez family reached the highest political spheres.

Fortuna had always had an eye for politics even from the back of the sewing room, the one place her mother saw fit for her only daughter. She never dared voice her well-analyzed opinions about the state of Jewish affairs in the Spanish society in front of her chastising mother. She saved her arguments for her late-night chats with the man she admired the most, her father, when serving him his customary after-dinner shot of Arrack.

Once married, she paved the way for her useless husband to occupy a high position in the Ministry of Finances. No one cared that he could not articulate more than two consecutive meaningful sentences. All they cared about was the work that the Jews of Cordoba, the few remaining, were doing to sustain the Spanish financial institutions.

Things haven't changed much in the past four centuries. Fortuna had the situation dissected to the last detail. While her husband acted as her pawn in the political orb, she made sure her family's wealth kept a hindrance-free path for some of the most eligible Jewish leaders of Spain. These appointed agents, who underwent the severity of her approval before she would allow them to act on her behalf, would discreetly slip their peseta-laden-paws into the ever-wobbly Spanish government, seeing to the welfare of the Jewish community.

All her power and arrogance did nothing to help her during her second visit to Pueblo Brugo. Fortuna, a woman who had withstood Franco's hatred, not only for Jews, but also for her personally, was suddenly reduced to a mumbling, incoherent old lady, standing in a shabby shack facing three humble individuals.

She stepped forward, and like all those many years before, she lightly placed her hand on Ramiro's.

He didn't resist her touch. He didn't have to. His eyes were as empty as on the evening of his father's death, when the pendant shone amid the veil of his blood.

Angelina was her only hope. She had nothing to lose.

With her free hand, Fortuna reached under her elaborate silk blouse and produced a thick gold chain that ended in a heavy pendant, a reproduction of the original.

Ramiro knew without looking up that the old woman's pendant was a replica of the one his father handed to him on his deathbed.

He decided right there and then that the dark chapter of his life, where mysteries were its only inhabitants, ended the day his father exhaled his last breath. He didn't want to know. He didn't want his daughter to know. Even if this woman might hold the answers to his unknown origins, he was not interested in them. Ramiro had no past. His life was made out of the present, supported by the love of his wife and daughter, a love he never thought possible. A life he would not jeopardize for the sake of a faith his wife despised.

"Get out," he blurted in a warning whisper.

Marta quickly pulled Angelina from between Ramiro and Fortuna and ran with her to the kitchen, closing the door behind them.

Fortuna stood unmoving. Her hand grasped the pendant as though her life depended on it.

"Get out," he said again. His voice was cold. He made sure to slap Fortuna with his rejection.

She wavered for a quick second. The hand placed on Ramiro's went instinctively to the pendant, protecting it, protecting herself.

He opened the door and looked out, directing the old woman to the orange slice of the dying sunset.

She didn't move. She waited. Ramiro would never put a hand on her and she knew it.

She was buying time, so her voice would not crack with the words she had rehearsed all those many years ago.

"We are the sons and daughters of Rabbi Leon David Fernandez and Sarah Fortuna Fernandez. Our name doesn't belong to us but to the future generations. You are my future as that beautiful little girl is yours." Her voice betrayed her and was trapped in a sudden sob.

"Get out," was all he could mumble.

"You can't escape the pull of your blood. You are a Fernandez, as was your father and his father before him."

He lost his self-control. A roar of anger rose within him. "Get out."

Fortuna grew pale and held onto the door, as strong as she could amid his towering fury.

Her chauffeur, who was standing dutifully by the car, noticed the old lady's vulnerability and dashed to her aid. Fully conscious, she surrendered to his care. Her eyes drowned in a flow of tears.

Her possible weakness of heart or advanced age did nothing to soften Ramiro's fierce determination to extract this woman from his life like a cancerous tumor. Whoever she thought she was to him was part of her history and not his.

The chauffeur peeled Fortuna's fingers from her hold on the door and walked her carefully to the back seat of the sleek black sedan.

Before the chauffeur had finished helping her into the car, the door of the Fernandez family of Pueblo Brugo had closed on Fortuna Fernandez forever.

Chapter Ten
The Sins of our Fathers

Many strange things happened in those next twelve hours following the visit of the woman with the stiff hair and the heavy accent. Angelina always knew her sixth birthday would mark the day her life would change forever. However, the chain of events unleashed soon after were beyond her wildest imagination.

For starters, that night she slipped into her bed with the naughty knowledge she had skipped her nightly prayers.

Her parents, always so peaceful, argued heatedly, and not even Sarah's soothing melodic presence was able to muffle the angry screaming of her mother. Her mother kept yelling out the word *infidel*, and other words like swine, and Jesus killer. And her hysterical insults were suddenly stopped by what sounded like a slap of skin on skin.

Immediately after, a dreadful silence took over the house. Angelina tiptoed out of her room and peeked into her parents' room. She found them both on their knees in front of the Holy Mother, hugging each other, rocking back and forth with grieving moans.

Her father's shirt was torn at the front. His bare chest showed a fresh raked trail.

Angelina went back to her bed and covered herself up all the way to her head, feeling scared for the first time in the short six years of her life.

When she opened her eyes she thought she had only slept for a few minutes, but was surprised by daylight. The house was silent. She jumped out of her bed, and went into the kitchen as she did every morning. Her mother was not there, and neither was her usual breakfast of *café con leche* and toast smeared with *dulce de leche* on the table.

She walked from one room to the next finding the house empty, and in a disturbing state of complete tidiness. She felt the presence of her mysterious friend, but decided to ignore her. Angelina did not feel like playing. At least not until she knew that everything was all right.

The front door opened. To Angelina's relief her parents walked in. Her mother's face looked swollen on one side. They both looked as if they hadn't slept.

For a moment they stopped and looked at Angelina in a way they had never looked at her before. She knew something important was about to happen. The inexplicable fright that had crept into her the night before made its way back into her stomach. On any other day, Angelina would have started an endless chain of questions, aimed to tire out her parents and find out what the matter was. Today was not the case. She was scared of asking questions to answers she would rather not hear.

Ramiro took the first step forward. He opened his mouth determined to say something, but nothing came out. She looked into his eyes and could see her fear in his. He broke down crying. He reached for her, pulled her to his chest, and hugged her as if by doing so he could make her part of his own living flesh.

Marta, on the other hand, was cold. She spoke the first words. "Angelina, go to your room and get dressed."

Angelina turned on her heels, and for the first time since she came into the world, she did not defy her mother.

Marta followed her. She opened Angelina's closet and one by one she took out all her clothes. She folded them neatly and stuffed them into the small suitcase stored under Angelina's bed.

Angelina had hidden that suitcase under her bed, thinking it had escaped Marta's notice, before Ramiro left for his last fishing trip. Some of her most valuable treasures were in there ready to depart with her on her long-planned trips across the water with Ramiro. Her favorite doll, a slingshot made of bone and a thick rubber band, and a picture of Marta and Ramiro on their wedding day.

Angelina watched her mother's calm demeanor with absolute terror.

Ramiro materialized at the door. Angelina felt this was her only chance to ask questions, and though choked with fear, she did so.

"*Papi*, are we going on the water trip?"

Ramiro shook his head no. Marta kept folding Angelina's clothes. She looked at the contents in the suitcase and ventured a second question. "Why aren't you packing?"

Marta was done folding the last of Angelina's socks and sat on the narrow bed. Angelina walked to Marta and kneaded her fingers into hers in the way she had done so many times before when she wanted something out of her mother. "*Mami*, where are we going?"

Marta found her voice and propped Angelina next to her. When she spoke to Angelina, she did it enunciating every single word, trying to make sense of the news she was about to break to her little girl. "You are going away to school, Angelina."

"But school is not until your birthday." Angelina walked to a calendar pinned up on a wall and set her finger on a date marked with a shiny pink X. She turned around, beaming at them with the gap-toothed smile of a child.

"You are going to a different school, one close to Buenos Aires. Padre Aparicio says it is the best place for you."

Angelina ran to Ramiro and held on tight to his legs. "*Papi*, I don't want to go away. I promise I'll be good. I promise I won't talk to Sarah. I promise I'll say all my prayers. I promise I won't play with *Mami's* candles. I promise I won't climb trees anymore. I promise—I promise—I pro-mm-mise."

By then, Angelina was crying and all her promises had hammered Ramiro's heart to pieces. He thought he was going to die, for the pain he felt was unbearable.

Ramiro picked her up and, unable to restrain his agony, he cried. Three hard knocks on the door silenced Ramiro's sobbing. He turned pale and held onto Angelina tighter. Marta, cool and detached, picked up the suitcase and walked to the door.

A nun stood there, rigid and sour faced. Marta acknowledged her with a quick nod, and went out to the small car waiting at the curb with its engine running, anxious to finish with the unpleasant business at hand as soon as possible.

She placed the suitcase carefully in the trunk. Then, with the same coldness that she had conducted her previous moves, she walked back into the house and attempted to peel Angelina from Ramiro's grasp. The little girl's legs and arms locked around Ramiro's body. He didn't help Marta extricate Angelina from him. When Marta finally pulled her from him, every part of his body, which was no longer in contact with his daughter, died.

Marta carried a kicking and screaming Angelina to the waiting car. She shoved her in the back seat and ran back to the house.

She never saw Angelina's attempts to throw herself out of the car. Nor did she see the way the good sister slapped her until Angelina finally lost the will to fight.

***

Night crept into the Fernandez house. The place seemed darker than ever. Smaller. Suffocating.

Ramiro stood by Angelina's bedroom door. He would never see her again. The *padre* had forbidden it and he had agreed. The curse of his family had to reach an end and Angelina had been the ultimate sacrifice.

Maybe it was a test, he thought. Abraham, the biblical patriarch, had to endure the same test to prove himself faithful to God. He was driven to the point of almost sacrificing the life of his son Isaac to earn God's trust. Maybe, this was a challenge, and after proving himself worthy of Jesus' love, the Lord would return Angelina back to him.

It was his fault. Marta had been right, he was an unbeliever. For years he had tried to deny his heritage. His body bore the mark of the covenant Abraham had entered into with God when he was chosen as the father of the Jewish people. Just like Isaac, Abraham's son, and any other Jewish man, Ramiro was circumcised.

The undeniable truth of his personal history took him back to the last gift, or maybe the last curse his father slapped him with before his death. A pendant in the shape of the symbol that distinguished the Jews from the rest of the world. It was a shield that had protected King David from his enemies, a shield that had ultimately exposed Ramiro's buried identity and had cost him his most precious jewel, Angelina.

Remember, his father's last word scourged him. He knew now what the old man had meant. It was better to accept than to renounce. It was better to remember than to forget. But he was a victim of silence and secrets, and he did what he thought best for him and for his family. He ignored the brand on his manhood. He turned away from the Star of David—the inheritance his father had entrusted to him. And then in a final act of denial, he shut away Fortuna Fernandez, the only person with all the answers he craved for all his life.

It was too late now and he was desperate. In the enclosure of Padre Aparicio's office he had fallen to his knees and sworn to find his way to the Lord and the way back to his daughter.

Nothing mattered anymore, not his vows, his past, or his present. Surrounded by the deafening silence of a life without Angelina, he stood paralyzed. Not feeling. Barely breathing.

Marta was busy tidying up the house and closing all the windows. She lit up candles in every room. The undisturbed golden glow flowing through the house made Angelina's absence more evident. Marta went into their bedroom and shed all of her clothes. She hung the accursed pendant around her neck and stared at her nakedness in the mirror. She fixed her eyes on the jewel that shone in between her bare breasts.

Wearing just the pendant, she went out to find Ramiro, who still stood in Angelina's room. Marta reached for his hand and guided him back to their bed. She closed the door and stripped him of his clothes. She touched him with the same fear and hunger she had touched him on their first and only night together.

He rose to her touch because the man living in his body was not him anymore. Any human traces he ever had, had left him when Angelina was taken from him. He was an animal.

She took him to bed and savaged him. She bit him, scratched him, made him want her to the point of pain. She took pleasure at the thought of committing her biggest sin and consequently being rewarded with the final punishment.

A candle sparked sending a spit of fire to one of the window's drapes, delivering the sentence she had waited for so patiently for almost seven years.

In the midst of their mutual physical assault, Marta felt that vague yet familiar touch on her cheek. She recognized the reassuring whisper of her mother's empty promises flowing through her like a lullaby. Her mother had finally come for her.

Marta lost track of time and space. She stopped feeling. She dissolved with each and every one of the blows her body gave and received.

The blazing fire danced around them like an ancient sacrifice. Even if taken away by madness, they were fully aware of their actions. They willingly paid the ultimate price in exchange for a life free of their torment and the loss of Angelina.

They stared at the room burning around them while they did the best to kill each other before the fire got to them.

They succumbed in a final embrace to either redemption or damnation. They would never know.

Part II

Chapter Eleven
The Trapa

Hinojo – Argentina - 1966

Time stopped for Angelina Fernandez, on a mild winter morning, the day after she turned six years old. The developments following that day became part of the haze she sank into, a silent and lonely place which had conveniently become her safe haven.

Keeping true to her word, she fulfilled all the promises she made to her father during those dreadful last minutes they spent together. She never played with candles again, she never climbed a single tree, she prayed obediently, and she never spoke a single word again, not even to Sarah.

Despite Angelina's desire to be alone, Sarah was always around her. She had made a promise when Angelina was so desperately trying to hold on to Ramiro.

"*Don't cry little one,*" Sarah had said with the protective assurance of a lullaby, "*for I will lead you back home where you belong.*"

During her first days at the convent, the sisters were bent on making Angelina talk. They tried different threats, briberies, and forms of punishment, finally giving up when they couldn't find any signs of life behind the girl's impenetrable dark gaze.

The small convent was on the outskirts of the Buenos Aires Province. There were about twenty girls of different ages who shared the everyday simple life the Trappist sisters offered.

The routine in the small *Trapa,* a Cistercian convent, had not changed much since its opening in 1958. It still followed the principles of its founder, Bernard of Clairvaux, an eleventh century French abbot who was later declared a saint. At the age of twenty-two Bernard, a lover of literature and the Holy Scriptures, found refuge in the Cistercian Order after his mother's death. Three years later he was sent out to the Aube department to found his own abbey. He named it Claire Vallée, later developing into Clairvaux.

Bernard, who came from the highest nobility of Burgundy, lived an austere life and considered the riches of the world meaningless. He regarded the world as a place of temporary banishment and trial, and men nothing but strangers and pilgrims. As for heretics, he preferred to subdue them. *Not by force of arms, but by force of argument,* an opinion he conferred in one of his many speeches. However, if a heretic refused to see the error of his ways, Bernard of Clairvaux would, without compunction, put the intellectual fight aside opting for the decisive blade of a sword instead.

The Trappist order lived by the Cistercian philosophy. The sisters at the convent led a life of austerity, devotion for the Virgin Mary, and, to Angelina's advantage, silence.

Angelina's rebellious and adventurous demeanor diminished to a dull shadow of her former self. She stopped counting the days to anybody's birthdays, she walked by the convent's grand piano as though it was nothing but a piece of useless furniture, and blocked out the ever-loving presence of Sarah.

The decision to stop talking was not conscious at first. True to her inquisitive nature, Angelina was accustomed to finding logical explanations for the things she saw, smelled, touched, or felt. The new feeling she experienced from the moment she was torn from her father's grasp was unsettling and completely foreign to her. It was akin to the physical pain she felt after the cruel punishment by the sister during the long car ride, but not exactly it.

This new sensation had also left a bad taste, like that of the bile stuck to the back of her throat, that had not left her after throwing up three times during the car ride. She knew that what she felt was not physical pain. This was a new kind of pain, one that had robbed her of her speech, her laughter, and that mischief that made her who she was.

Even if she could put into words what she felt it was of no use, because her interest in relating to others was lost. The world, as she once knew it, disappeared. Any traces of who she was, or what she had ever envisioned becoming, had vanished with it.

The tight grip keeping her throat closed didn't dampen her hopes of seeing her parents walk through the doors of the convent, putting an end to this bizarre situation. So, she waited.

She lost track of time, and without the river to consult with, she couldn't predict the weather anymore. Yet, she did notice the changing of seasons. The weather got colder and the nights longer, leaving her with the unpleasant company of the most frightening, recurring gory nightmare.

The ordeal started the very first night she slept at the convent. The car ride had been excruciatingly long, arriving at the small convent in the wee hours of the morning. As much as she refused to close her eyes and give in to her new reality, exhaustion won out. After several hours of continuous crying and many more attempts to jump out of the car's window, followed by another severe beating administered by the ever-ready fleshy open palm of Lucia—the accompanying sister—Angelina was exhausted.

Carrying her little suitcase, Angelina followed Sister Lucia through a seemingly never-ending dark corridor. The hallway was aligned with several heavy wooden closed doors that did nothing to block the funny snorts seeping from under them. Hours before, she would have done everything in her power to work out the mechanics of such sounds. Not anymore. All she wanted was to crawl inside her suitcase, as if it was a womb capable of protecting her from a place she refused to belong to.

Strong disinfectant breathed through the bare walls of the *Trapa*, assaulting Angelina's sense of smell. She abhorred the scent instantly, for it was the same stinking smell of the sister that ripped her from her home. She hated her.

After some walking, they reached a small, mostly bare room at the end of the hall. The room consisted of one narrow cot against a wall, a dwarfed wooden nightstand topped with a clay ewer, and a small statue of the Holy Mother placed next to an armoire on the opposite side.

Sister Lucia walked in and turned on the light, which was no more than a hanging bulb dangling from the tip of a blue wire. She then opened the armoire and retrieved what looked like a nightgown.

Angelina stood by the door and watched as Sister Lucia went about disrobing and getting into something very similar for bed. This was followed up by prayers at the foot of the Virgin's statue. Angelina had the faint notion of the nun telling her something about a cot, or a room, but her words got lost when she turned the light off, got into bed, and joined the loud snores of the other residents of the convent.

Her night became a nightmare, literally. After Sister Lucia sank into a deep stupor, Angelina waited. She could have rested on the floor using her suitcase as a pillow, but she refused to lie down and make her stay at the convent official. Thus, she stood still, staring into the darkness, with her hand firmly wrapped around the handle of her suitcase, waiting for the morning to arrive, and hopefully her parents with it.

She didn't notice when she slid into a sleep state, the images and sounds of that night taking on a familiar feel like the life she had lived before. It started with a beautiful melody that overtook the snores and farts that came from the sleeping form of Sister Lucia.

The melody was one she played repeatedly under Sarah's guidance back at the church in Pueblo Brugo. At the familiar sound, Angelina had the vague memory of easing her grip on the suitcase and walking through the convent's dark hallway in search of the origin of the music, or perhaps finding her way back to Pueblo Brugo.

With every step she took towards the music, the convent hallway turned into a dark labyrinth of winding, narrow passages.

Unable to see anything, and free of the weight of her suitcase, Angelina spread her arms wide in order to get her bearings. On one side she felt the roughness of a stone wall. It was not a new feeling for Angelina.

With her fingertips she had traced that very same wall every day, when sneaking into the church back in Pueblo Brugo, while rushing through the empty hallways on her way to the grand piano. Her other hand stroked flower petals. She smiled. Those petals belonged to the carefully manicured garden the sisters of her hometown kept at the convent.

Her heart skipped a beat with anticipation. Could it be that the music pulling her through this dark labyrinth would lead her home? With that thought, Angelina gave herself over completely to the sensorial experience that embraced her. She stopped fighting the black space and opened her senses to the sound of rushing water, to the riverbank where her father most surely would be waiting for her, ready to take her on the adventure they had planned for months.

As her pace quickened towards the direction of the water, the music grew faint. She stopped for a moment tuning back to the music, until the melody drew her in another direction.

Her feet, which until then had stepped on a hard, rocky surface, sank on a bed of tender grass. Beyond the power of the melody, Angelina was lured in by the pungent fragrances of fruit trees, herbs, and flowers. She recognized the heady scent of aromatic plants her mother grew in their own little garden on the side yard of their house.

With both hands, she reached into what felt like a patch of thick shrubbery and picked a handful. She crushed rough herbs in between her fingers and inhaled deeply. Rosemary, yes! That was it. There was no doubt in her mind that she had stepped into her mother's garden.

A wave of emotion overwhelmed her for she had finally come home.

Angelina's exhaustion from the earlier lengthy, torturous journey, finally overcame the strength in her legs. She slumped down on the cushioning tender grass and felt the caress of a warm spring sun tuck her in for a nap. Her aching heart felt at peace and she drifted into a sweet slumber.

A sudden moment of stillness and silence interrupted the perfectly choreographed sense of security. The music played a deafening silent beat. The rosemary leaves in her hand turned into spiky thorns stabbing her tender flesh, and the soothing rush of the water turned into an agitated rising menace.

The dark space surrounding her filled with a mantle of grey fog pierced with screams of terror. She jumped to her feet and searched along the dense fog for a way out. She was lost in the darkness. But, she was not alone. She could hear the presence of others, hear their desperate pleas, smell their acrid fear.

The stormy water was closing in, chasing her, ready to swallow her. Angelina ran blindly, with no direction, until she was finally cornered against a hard surface, by cries, and a moonless night.

She awoke, startled from her nightmare. Her screams echoed down the hollow hallway of the silent convent.

She found she was still leaning on the same door frame she had stood by a few hours before. Her muscles felt stiff and achy. Her feet were swollen from standing for so many hours and her hand was numb from clenching onto the handle of her suitcase so tightly.

She tried opening her closed fist. Her fingers were rigid, barely moving. With her free hand she pried them open one by one. Something fell on the floor when she finally stretched out her hand.

Angelina knelt down and picked up a sprig of rosemary.

Chapter Twelve
Lucia

Sister Lucia stirred under her bed sheets, opened one eye and saw Angelina standing. Not for a minute had she dared to put her suitcase down, she was ready to go back home.

Sister Lucia was a woman of few words, which fit perfectly with the Cistercian order, yet she was a person of action. Her first encounter with this little girl had been more than unpleasant. Removing a child from her family was a nasty job. She knew the child was innocent. How could she be blamed for the sins of her father?

Of all the sisters in the convent, she was usually the one chosen for such duties. Lucia was known for her immunity to sentimentalism, and was not shy in exercising her right hand when a beating had to be administered in order to tame her subject.

Sister Lucia felt too old for this job already. She was well into her forties, and although strong and filled with energy, she was over with disciplining girls who hadn't the slightest desire to become Cistercian nuns. She would rather work in her rose garden and deal with weeds she knew she could pull out for good.

As a common rule, the girls that came to the convent were strays. Some were sent to them to conceal a pregnancy, others to prevent one. But mostly, girls stayed with them for a short period of time until their wealthy families found a good match for them and married them off, making their new husbands responsible for the behavior of their wanton daughters.

She still had a hard time understanding the way of things in this part of the world. Sister Lucia was born into a devoted Catholic family in Torino, Italy. Her parents, stern and reserved, did not say much and their voice was rarely heard except when they mouthed their daily prayers and during the routine nightly moans, which had religiously delivered a new baby every eleven months.

From the moment she could articulate her first words, Lucia declared her intentions of becoming a nun. Used to scarce talk and an ample spiritual life, the Cistercian order was a perfect match for her.

She was in her early twenties when World War II erupted in Europe. Many of the nuns at the small convent she entered left to join the resistance and be trained as combat nurses. They claimed that as women of God they were needed more than any other skilled nurse. After all, the healing of the body was not possible without the healing of the soul.

Sister Lucia tried to follow their motto, but became queasy at the sight of bloody stumps and spilling guts. She left her deserted convent and joined a makeshift orphanage, in an abandoned mansion that had once belonged to a rich Jewish family.

After a couple of years, when shortage of food and basic goods made the survival of the children at the orphanage impossible, she gathered up her few belongings and sailed across the ocean to South America in search of a new convent, away from the horrors of war.

***

She glanced at the mass of curls crowning the bent head of Angelina. Almost twenty-four hours had passed since they had left Pueblo Brugo, and the stubborn little girl in her room, stoic as a Greek statue, would not budge. How could she still stand by the same door she had left her at all those hours before?

The sight of the rigid girl by the doorframe did not trouble her at all. She knew the child would eventually tire and lie down. What haunted her was the depth of sadness that had settled in the girl's warm brown eyes. She had seen those eyes decades before in the children that the war had stolen from her hands.

Lucia waved away the disturbing memories she left behind in Italy and looked forward to her every day, predictable, stable routine—prayers followed by a simple breakfast, school followed by prayers, needlework, some more praying, dinner, more praying, and finally bed.

On her first day Angelina went through all the right moves. She knelt and clasped her hands together when she had to, sat when instructed, and held a needle between her small fingers when told to. However, she did not utter a single word, stitch a stitch, or touch her food.

Sister Lucia kept a close watch on her even though she avoided eye contact with the little girl. She was certain her behavior would change in time and that she would eat when she would feel hunger. For the rest, she knew too well about the resilience that came associated with childhood. Angelina would not be an exception.

On her second night at the convent the sisters allocated a cot for Angelina in a room with five other girls. The girls were part of a group attending a three-month long spiritual retreat.

The girls were from the Buenos Aires high society, and were four to five years Angelina's senior. Their stay at the convent was one of the many steps these girls were required to go through while completing their well-rounded education. Throughout their formative years they would become an authority in religious matters, world culture, the arts, and the latest French fashion.

The moment they saw Angelina walking in their room, they regarded her with a wary eye. The girl seemed out of focus and out of place. She just stood silently by her cot holding a beat-up suitcase to her chest with her eyes pinned on the door. And her dress! How could anybody dare to walk out in public in that?

Angelina was immune to the mocking faces and cruel comments darting her way. Eventually the laughs and jokes subsided, and one by one the girls fell asleep forgetting about the new addition to their room as though she were a piece of furniture.

When the convent drifted into the sounds of the night, Angelina walked out of the assigned room straight to Sister Lucia's door. She leaned on the doorframe and gave into the melody that once more filled up the hollowness in her heart, transporting her to a place she had never been, but where she believed she belonged.

By the end of the first week Angelina's behavior had not changed. Sister Lucia tired before the little girl did, and moved the cot inside her bedroom. She forced the girl to lie on it, which she obediently did, clutching the suitcase that had become an extension of her right hand.

Before she realized it, Sister Lucia bent each one of the rules she set up the moment she left Italy. Sick with war and death, she had sworn to herself never to let a child warm her heart to the point of pain again.

**

The very morning before she removed Angelina from her home, Padre Julio, the Cistercian monk who ran the order, called Lucia into his office. The case she was assigned to was one she had never heard of before. *Dubious fate*, were the exact words of Padre Julio. Sister Lucia knew better than to suggest a handful of alternatives for the family to stay together instead of breaking it apart.

In her vast experience as a nun, dubious fate, as the *padre* suggested, could be easily remedied with mandatory attendance at church on weekdays as well as weekends, catechism classes for the parents and the child, peregrinations, or even to be sent as missionaries to a remote village in Central America where they could follow the Lord's work. Lucia had a hard time understanding the reasons behind the single-minded decision the priest in Pueblo Brugo made. But nobody had consulted with her, nor would her word have any leverage in this matter anyway.

Apparently, Marta, the child's mother, demanded their daughter to be taken immediately from their house. She suspected her husband of having some sort of association with the Devil. The mother saw permanent exile to a convent as the only chance to save their daughter's soul.

The *padre* at Pueblo Brugo considered it to be the best solution. Removing the matter out of his parish represented fewer headaches and longer naps. Thus, without hesitation he contacted the *Trapa*. Padre Julio told Sister Lucia that throughout the proceedings, the father of the child had remained silent, that the father's face had been drained of color, and his eyes remained pinned to the crucifix pinned on the office's wall as though waiting for a miracle.

The miracle from heaven Ramiro Fernandez prayed for that morning in the priest's office never came. The only answer he got was Lucia.

***

Unlike all the other girls who used the convent as a diversion, the little girl was not a temporary case, she was there to stay. Lucia considered the seriousness of the case and the brown eyes drifting sadly about her room, and took a personal interest in the child's education. As far as she knew, it was only the beginning.

Lucia was an expert in administering tough impersonal discipline, but with Angelina that was not necessary. Although the little one had put up a good fight when she was taken from her house, once they arrived at the convent she adjusted to the rules. The only big problem Lucia could spot, without going too deep, was the unmanageable mass of chestnut curls framing Angelina's face. Discipline was not needed to tame that boisterous mane, only a pair of sharp scissors.

What was she to do with this little girl? Lucia felt that her chastising methods were not the way to get to this child. In fact, she was not sure as to how to get to the core of the little girl whatsoever. As far as she could see all that was left of Angelina was her shell. The girl looked vacant, almost transparent, as though she could vanish into thin air in front of her very eyes.

Chapter Thirteen
The Wait is Over

Again, she had followed the music and slipped out of the *Trapa* and into a strange, new place. The length of the wall she had thought belonged to the church in Pueblo Brugo, stretched out beyond the limits of Angelina's imagination. A tiny city could fit inside the grounds encircled by the perfectly aligned stone enclosure.

This time around, the melody did not guide her into the grassy grounds. Instead, she wandered outside the walls, tracing with her fingers the softness of the many flowers that cascaded from the solid stones, and inhaling the exotic scents that turned her imagination into a rainbow of vivid colors. The familiar melody kept playing in the backdrop. She could feel her fingers tingling with the urge to sit at a piano and play this music she knew so well.

Her last venture across the stone walls and into the garden had been a traumatic experience. It wasn't because of the raging water washing away the beautiful harmony of nature, or because of the horrific screams of pain and desperation coming from the heart of the blinding fog. Her uneasiness came from the subliminal knowledge that once she crossed the darkness and stepped into the light, she would cease to exist as Angelina.

She could envision her hands at the piano keys. Hands that did not feel like her own. Every note reverberating, filling up the emptiness that came over her the moment she was torn from Pueblo Brugo. Here in this strange place, filled with music and fragrant colors, she did not feel like a child. There was something about her awareness of what was to come that told her that her childhood years were long gone.

She recalled the last moment in her father's arms, and knew that nothing would ever be the same. She would never again revel in Don Tomas's stories, in the depth of the river, or in imaginary adventures. Since her arrival at the convent she didn't care if she was six or sixty. Time and space did not matter anymore for they belonged to an existence that was interrupted. Her life at the *Trapa* had become a meaningless period determined by the sum of days without the pangs of living—a conscious, comatose state.

Angelina's eyelids fluttered, the faint hint of dawn was reflected into the dark pools of her eyes. She was still suspended in that lethargic state experienced by most when awakened. For a few seconds, she was Angelina of Pueblo Brugo. Her eyes were not seeing and her nose did not perceive any particular smells. During this short period of timelessness, Angelina was in her old room ready to welcome her mother's soft footsteps in the outside patio and her father's constant humming while preparing his early morning *mate*.

With the blink of an eye the moment was gone.

Sister Lucia was already up and dressed for early morning matins. Angelina stared at her with empty eyes.

"Don't just lay there. Get up!" Angelina jumped off her cot on command, grabbed her suitcase and waited for Sister Lucia by the door.

Lucia shook her head with some annoyance. "You slept in your clothes again!"

Angelina looked down. Her hands tightened on her suitcase.

Sister Lucia softened her tone.

"Come over here. You have to wash before we go."

Angelina walked to the basin by the closet. She freed one of her hands, washed her face and brushed her teeth.

Sister Lucia stood by her studying Angelina from head to toe. "Your clothes are wrinkled. I'm sure you have a fresh dress in there. Let me see." Sister Lucia tried to take hold of the suitcase, but Angelina backed against the wall and refused to let her near it. At the sight of Lucia's determination, she threw the suitcase on the floor and slumped over it as though her life depended on it.

The church bells rang and the girl was not moving from the suitcase. Lucia sighed, summoning patience she didn't have. There would be time later to deal with Angelina's wardrobe and the contents in that battered, old suitcase.

"Get up. We cannot be late for prayers." Angelina leapt to her feet, lifted the suitcase, and followed Sister Lucia out of the convent and into the church.

Nothing changed much for the next few months. Angelina did as instructed, never putting up a fight except when it came to the wretched suitcase. Sister Lucia decided to leave that issue alone for the time being. It was as if that beat up leather bag, which was peeling rapidly, had become a part of Angelina's anatomy, an extension of her limbs. She counted each of her victories as a blessing, especially when she succeeded in changing the girl into clean clothes everyday after giving her a challenging bath, suitcase and all.

Angelina adapted to the rhythm of the *Trapa* with indifferent resignation and became Sister Lucia's shadow. In a way she developed a certain closeness to this tough woman. After assessing her current situation, Angelina made the conscious decision of sticking to the sister. For starters, she knew where Angelina lived. She had met both her parents. Sister Lucia was the closest thing to a link to

Pueblo Brugo, the only one with the power to take her back home.

The signs of the upcoming spring loomed over the convent grounds. The colors turned brighter, the nights warmer, still long enough to give Angelina plenty of time to explore the outlandish world beyond the confinement of the *Trapa*.

Her journeys around the outskirts of stone wall were hardly a product of her imagination. The dried leaves and flowers she brought back with her and accumulated under the covers of her cot were solid evidence that her visits to that place with music and flowery scent were a far cry from a recurrent dream. As with everything in her life, Angelina needed to try and test her theory. A figment of her old self resurfaced, her curiosity was piqued.

During daylight hours, while trotting behind Sister Lucia, she managed to explore the surroundings of the convent and found no signs of the many plants she had collected during her nightly expeditions.

In a way she started feeling happy when her nocturnal adventures to the unknown became recurrent. Soon enough, she discovered that the water that had threatened to swallow her during her first dream was not a river. The music finally led her to the core of the rushing sound. It was a fountain. Shutting her eyes, tighter than they had been before, Angelina pictured a tall marble fountain towering above her. The centerpiece rose with the shape of an angel over a pool of crystalline water. She stepped into the fountain, the water fresh and clean reached her knees. She jumped back as something ticklish swam past her ankles. She giggled.

Angelina reached down into the cool water until her hands found the source of the silky caress. It was an undulating body with dancing wings, elegant and graceful as a ballerina. Without counting them she knew that there were six of the same. They were fish, but not like any other she had seen in the river. These fish swam in distant waters, perhaps the ocean.

She racked her brain trying to remember their name. Had she seen them in a book? No, not a book, in a fountain, this fountain. She could swear she had seen the exotic creatures proudly expanding their orange and royal blue oversized pectorals in a majestic dance, synchronizing their movements with the cascading water. The melody seeped deeper through her senses and the name of the fishes played in her mind. They were *flying gurnards*, and she was certain that once upon a time they had been hers.

At times, the after-dark journeys along the stone wall and into the garden turned dreadful when filled with the horrific screaming muffled by the impenetrable fog. But those moments didn't deter her from giving into them. It was a strange yet familiar feeling, for the more she frequented that place, the more she developed a remembrance of events past and of the certainty that she had once been a part of them.

Without once transcending the darkness, without seeing what lay across the stone wall, she developed a vivid recollection of every path in the garden and the position of every flower. She knew of the existence of a special patch—an orange rose garden, which filled her with joy. When they were hit with the first rays of dawn, those roses speckled with gold, and reeled her back to moments of laughter and love.

Although Angelina had been assured that the *Trapa* was her new home, a conversation she overheard from some of the girls at the convent filled her with renewed hope of going home. The girls were counting down the days to the end of winter break, which was to come in six days and marked the end to their tortuous stay at the *Trapa*. Angelina had no doubts hers was about to be over as well.

That's where the matter of the suitcase made sense. At least it made sense to her. Angelina was young, but not stupid. She was well aware that everybody, even the most devoted nuns, regarded her as strange for carrying her suitcase with her at all times. Nobody had bothered to ask her why, though she would have not answered anyway. She had an explanation for it and it was short and simple. She couldn't wait to leave the convent. The moment her parents were to cross the heavy wooden door of the convent to fetch her, she would dart out of its grim interior without glancing back. Not having the suitcase with her would mean wasting time to look for it when she could be out of the door and back into her life. Simple.

She waited patiently. Although her arms were in constant pain due to the weight and the odd shape of the suitcase, she didn't mind. She waited.

Angelina grew accustomed to waiting. At the convent she was patiently waiting to leave, while in her dreams she was waiting for the right time to open her eyes to the light. Her life was on hold.

One by one the girls left. Angelina noticed how the number of people at the dining table decreased gradually, until one night she realized she was the only girl amongst seven old nuns.

That night she refused to go to Sister Lucia's room. Instead she perched herself by the main door with her suitcase clutched tightly against her middle and waited. The sisters walked by not minding her. So did Sister Lucia. Angelina did not sleep or wander through the cobblestone road towards the mysterious palace. She ignored the music regardless of how taunting it was. She kept her eyes on the door. She waited.

When the sun rose the next morning, Angelina opened the heavy wooden door of the *Trapa* and stepped outside. She stood on tippy-toes and squinted, so her sight could reach as far as possible along the dusty road that led to the main route. No one was coming. But, she knew it was still too early, so she waited.

The day grew damp and grey. Heavy steel clouds covered the sky and thunder broke, unleashing the most powerful rainstorm. Still, Angelina waited. By nightfall Sister Lucia walked out of the convent with an umbrella and stood facing Angelina. She found the little girl looking out in the distance. She was soaked, blue and shivering.

"You can't stay out here anymore, you'll catch a deathly cold." Angelina kept her gaze on the road as though Sister Lucia was not there.

Sister Lucia let out a deep sigh. She knelt so that she was eye to eye with Angelina. "They are not coming. Not tonight, not tomorrow. Never." Angelina didn't move but her eyes met Sister Lucia's, and the nun delivered the final blow. "Your parents are dead."

Angelina's suitcase fell on the damp ground with a heavy thud. The copious rain washed the hapless bag to a ruin, and Angelina's strength dissolved with it. Sister Lucia was quick to catch the little girl before her knees gave way. She picked her up and walked back to the convent. Angelina's body racked with sobs, and made Sister Lucia ache with each one of the spasms that hit her chest.

In silence, Sister Lucia carried Angelina to her room. She put her down, undressed her and got her into some of her own warm clothes. Dressing her like dressing a Raggedy-Ann Doll, the girl was weak and unresponsive. She picked her up again and laid the little girl beside her, holding her to her bosom as if her embrace could undo all the wrong that had been done to her.

Drowned in tears and confusion, Angelina drifted to a somnolent state, engulfed in Sister Lucia's solid arms and disinfectant odor. In her sleep she felt the sturdiness of Lucia's arms become hard as stone. It only took Angelina a brief moment to realize that she was no longer at the *Trapa*, but was leaning on the stone wall. The fog that usually surrounded it had dissipated giving way to light.

Angelina opened her eyes wide and found herself at the main entrance of a palace.

Chapter Fourteen
A Childhood Cut Short

Lucia rose early the next morning and slipped out of bed quietly, careful to not disturb Angelina. She was well aware of the little girl's sleeplessness throughout the night. But unlike any other day, she allowed her to stay in. Angelina needed to come to terms once and for all with her new life, and if Lucia's judge of character had not been impaled by her emotional actions the previous night, the girl needed to be alone.

What had come over her the night before? She rubbed her numb arms back to life thinking about the chain of developments that had evolved under the pouring rain— and what had preceded them. Telling Angelina about the death of her parents was long overdue. It was plainly obvious that none of the other nuns at the convent were going to step up to the unpleasant chore of relaying the tragic news to the child.

***

As soon as the news of the devastating fire reached the *Trapa*, the nuns held an emergency meeting. From the moment Angelina entered the convent, they were all aware of the permanent status of the girl.

As obliged, as the nuns were to be of service for a greater purpose, their tolerance for minors never extended further than the period of a short season. The prospect of twelve consecutive years of daily dealings with a youngster was well beyond what any of them had signed up for when taking their oath. Anybody in their right mind would have reached the same decision. Even in silence, the girl exhibited a stubborn streak that threatened to explode, a reason sufficient enough for six old nuns to take a step back and let Lucia, the one who brought Angelina to the convent, deal with her. Yes, of course they would all help raise the child in the Lord's way. Nevertheless, the unanimous vote went to Lucia to become the unofficial guardian, since the Church was the one holding official guardianship of the new orphan.

The voting was done under the elaborated premise of Lucia's qualifications for the task at hand. She had grown up in a big family and had dealt with countless orphans during the war.

Regardless of her previous experiences with children, Lucia knew better than to get emotionally attached to any of them. She had heard about the resilience of children many times over. People were always quick to judge as to the way children managed loss. In fact, when she first joined the group of nuns at the orphanage back in Italy, she was instructed not to do more than feed them and bathe them. "The less you communicate with the children the better," the older nun in charge had advised her with a stern eye.

Lucia dismissed the warning and poured her heart and soul into those young casualties of war. She not only groomed the children to a bright sparkle, but also managed to brighten their tiny hollow faces with temporary smiles. Smiles she later understood were only a natural reflex of the brain, but meaningless in spirit. She would often wake up next to a rigid, cold body nestled in her arms, one that just hours before had filled her with the hope of life.

Grief was worse than the Devil, because there weren't prayers powerful enough to banish it. Instead, grief acted as the Angel of Death itself. Lucia had wondered many times, while she stared at the statues of angels depicted as chubby children, how anybody with their heart in the right place could find anything angelic about the death of a child.

The damage to her heart was done and she had learned the lesson the hard way. Lucia hid her emotions behind a rough façade and did her best to keep the children alive. In the meantime she watched their little souls struggle with the alternative of living the rest of their lives based on a foundation of sorrow.

***

Watching Angelina the night before standing under the pouring rain, clutching her silly bag to her body, finally broke the lock Lucia had set all those years ago in her heart.

The child's situation was not the result of hostile gunfire. It was a result of adults' ignorance and stupidity. Lucia was a religious woman, to say the least, but she was opposed to fanatics.

The brief exchange that she had had with Marta Fernandez was enough for Lucia to recognize the young woman as a fanatic. The urgency and cold calculating way in which the young mother had ejected her daughter out of her life, as though Satan was in the house ready to jump the girl, had struck Lucia as insane. Maybe Satan was in that house after all, and had already crawled under Marta's skin. The signs were all there. Lucia remembered the hollow darkness in Marta's eyes. The young mother looked lifeless, as if she had already committed to walk down the burning hell that consumed her and her husband hours later.

Luckily, Lucia had been sent to them to keep the girl from harm. Lucia shrugged, and a ghost of a smile lit the creases around her eyes, while she came to the understanding that the Lord had used her to do his dirty work in order to save a life.

***

After receiving the news of her parents' death, Angelina spent the night consumed by a burning fever, which did not budge with the administration of cold compresses or the baby aspirins Lucia struggled to press into the girl's mouth. The fever was unmitigated despair and it would not be placated with all the medicine in the world.

The matter of Angelina's fate, the decision to keep on living or not, was still at bay. Lucia did all she could to reaffirm the girl of her unconditional presence. She held her tight to her ample bosom through the night, taking in Angelina's rattling sobs. Sobs that had woken Lucia's buried feelings, shocking her heart back to the land of the living.

When walking out of the room that morning, Lucia looked back at the still form of Angelina under the covers, and said a silent prayer in hopes for the girl to make the right decision. Whatever it might be, either continuing her journey to adulthood or ending it in order to join her parents in heaven, Lucia was ready to face the challenge. Angelina's life had been spared for a reason, and Lucia had to remind herself as she always did when struggling with earthly emotion, that God had a plan.

Around noontime, Lucia went up to the kitchen and prepared a small plate of food to take back to Angelina. Her pace was somewhat sluggish, she was in no haste. If anything, she was fearful to find out what had happened during the child's morning deliberations.

More likely than not, Angelina was to be found in the same state Lucia left her earlier that day, and she refused to witness the slow downfall of an unwanted life.

What Lucia encountered when she opened the door to her room was way beyond what she had feared.

Angelina was not in the bed or on the cot. A trail of shorn, dark locks led to where she was. Dressed in one of Lucia's habits, which hung loosely around her tiny frame, the little girl knelt solemnly at the foot of the shrine of the Virgin, clasping a Rosary in her hand, mouthing prayer after prayer.

The sight of little Angelina was more than Lucia could have prayed for that morning under the comforting shade of her favorite cedar tree. From the moment she left the room, Lucia had relinquished her daily obligations at the convent, and walked straight out into the open space, free of walls and doors, to have a heart to heart conversation with God. She spent the morning on her knees begging for the life of the child, and before she came to realize it, she had begged for a child.

She had never yearned for a child of her own before, but the prospect of losing another one filled her with the urge to have one she could call hers. A child she could see grow, a child she would give her life for.

The awe of the miracle overwhelmed Lucia. She left the plate of food on the floor by the door without a sound, and closed the door behind her holding on to the handle. She fell on her knees as soon as the door was shut, and with her hands pressed in prayer, she gave thanks.

Angelina had reached a decision and the *Trapa* was her new home. She didn't mind Sister Lucia's disinfectant smell any longer. In fact she noticed she started smelling like it herself and found it somewhat comforting. Maybe Lucia would want to keep her if she found out they shared something in common, even if it was only a scent.

The night before had confirmed Angelina's fears. As much as she tried to convince herself all those many months that it was natural for her parents to disappear from her life so suddenly, she knew there was something amiss. She thought her self-imposed muteness was an effective way to impede her from asking about their whereabouts. She dreaded knowing the truth, but the truth always made itself known. She really didn't have any other options. The convent was all she had for now. However she did have another place to go...

***

A magnetic attraction reeled her back to the entrance of that stone compound. The entrance to the palace stood open invitingly. Angelina felt she had to walk through the gargantuan gates, for she belonged in that place and in that time.

But before taking her first step, she took in the enormity of the place where the familiar melody had led her to. Her eyes did not betray her. What she had perceived beyond the thick fog, what the black dreams had revealed in the previous months, was indeed an Elysian landscape. A slice of paradise divided by pathways made of fine mosaics which in turn lined rectangular gardens that stretched symmetrically before a striking marble angel fountain. Angelina smiled at the memory of rushing water. The water was as crystalline as she had pictured it, and although she could not see that far ahead, she sensed the elegant fish dancing about, a beautiful picture complemented by a surrounding patch of orange Valencia roses.

The walls encircling the property were a work of fine masonry which harbored an array of flowers set to disguise the solid stones for a waterfall of bright colors.

Standing at the edge of the grand arch that marked the entrance to the palace, she felt the pull from the other side. It was Sister Lucia's voice calling her name. But, the Angelina of Pueblo Brugo had vanished along with her hopes of ever reclaiming her old life. With her sight set forth, Angelina decided that Sister Lucia would have to wait. There was someone summoning her here, someone she had once known. Perhaps someone she had once been.

The distant flickering light of the candles drew her in. Angelina peeked around while she stretched out her neck and stood on her tiptoes. The place looked empty. As

Sister Lucia's voice faded away, Angelina became certain that the moment she would set foot inside, the palace would gain life. And that the moment she would play the music that so intoxicated the air she would finally become herself.

There was nothing to lose now and no place to go other than forward.

Angelina took her first step through the threshold and suddenly the music stopped. One foot followed the other, and soon enough, her footsteps echoed on the limestone floors all the way through the grand salon that made the impressive foyer of the palace. The layout of the construction indoors was very much like the garden surrounding the building. The entrance hall did not consist of just one room, but several rooms of quadrangular shape all connected through passages ending in a central courtyard. Each room depicted a different area of the outside grounds, giving the palace a flavor of an indoor heaven. Columns, archways, fountains with running water, reflecting pools, foliage, and painted tiles largely used as paneling for the walls, were amongst the chief decorating details of this magnificent stronghold.

Angelina walked slowly through each one of the chambers touching the tiled walls as though getting reacquainted with her surroundings. Her wandering stopped at a particular room, where a lustrous wooden harpsichord was the central object. A handsome hand carved bench of tulip poplar, the same wood used for the construction of the harpsichord, was set at the front of the instrument waiting for somebody to sit on it and strike the first key.

Footsteps came towards her. She watched as her hand, a fine feminine hand with long slender fingers and round nails, hovered over the keys. Her index finger sank on a key, and a note reverberated throughout the halls of the palace. The twin of that hand joined it and the familiar music came to life in the hands of the woman she had become, in the hands of …

"Sarah." A deep male voice mingled with the intensity of the music. His strong hands took hold of hers, and the tender lips of this olive-skinned man, with the deepest blue eyes, kissed the soft neck of the woman he called Sarah.

He whispered something in her ear that made her smile. His lips moved to hers and she answered his demands with an urgent kiss.

Angelina, no longer in Sarah's skin or her own, felt removed, suspended, weightless, a mere spectator of events to unfold.

She heard a message flowing around her, embracing her with the warmth of sweet melody. It was a whisper, the voice of the relentless presence in her life, Sarah's voice. Following the directives of the melody and with the eyes of an outsider, she narrowed her attention on the room she was in.

Unlike the other rooms in the palace, this particular one was quite austere in appearance. None of the wooden tables decorated with blue, green, and yellow mosaic were present in this chamber. This room was also not connected with any of the other ones nor did it end in the flowery courtyard that made the cornerstone of the palace. This room had only two things—a harpsichord and the portrait of a woman.

I promised you will see me one day...

The woman in the portrait stood out after the words swirled around the room. She was young, maybe in her late twenties, slender, with beautiful olive skin, light brown eyes, and rich long brown hair, which cascaded in a mass of soft curls.

The portrait depicted the face of the woman who was the heart and soul of this palace. The artist who had painted it had captured with his brush the immortality of her image. This was an image that was intended to express more than beauty. The accent of her high cheekbones, her round upturned chin, and an intense honey colored gaze that shone out of her almond shaped eyes, incited curiosity if not passion to anyone who laid eyes upon her exotic features.

This woman was more than a face, and her story was hidden in the determination of her soft, yet commanding stare. A stare her successor—Angelina— would inherit almost five centuries later. A descendent that would not only resemble her almost identically, but one who would finish what she had started.

Had she foreseen it? Had this young woman, with skin as soft as rose petals and hair the color of ripe dates, planned her future upon her death, as well as the future of the generations to come? Had she transcended time and space in search of the one heir who would carry out her legacy?

The only remaining member of the Fernandez lineage had been lured into unveiling the secrets of the family, blending into a world as foreign to her as it had been to Sarah Fernandez at the turn of the fifteenth century.

Hovering between two worlds Angelina Fernandez understood that the moment she entered the palace, she ceased to exist as the six-year-old orphan and became Sarah Fortuna Fernandez in the flesh.

Chapter Fifteen
Sara

Sara Di Laurenti looked down at her needlepoint lying upon her lap and wondered once again, why? While she envisioned herself cantering on a forbidden horse, the one her father refused to give her as a present for her seventeenth birthday, she absentmindedly toyed with the needle held in between her forefinger and thumb until it finally poked her. With some fascination, she watched as a single drop of blood made a slow descent from her index finger to the fine white linen she was working on. The red dot quickly spread out in the center of the white cloth, and Sara could not help but think of the repercussions a single act of violence could have when it unfolds in the heart of a city.

Sara laid her needlework aside, and walked towards the large windowpane. The window took up an entire wall of the room. It was intended to be the greatest source of light for the sole purpose of sewing and embroidering. Textiles were the core of her family business.

Massimo, her father, was a wealthy textile merchant who imported the finest yarns from the Orient, India, and Italy. Once the yarns arrived in Cordoba, Camila, her mother, was in charge of designing the patterns in which the fabrics were to be woven. Camila's fabrics were sought after by most monarchs across Europe. She designed each sheet of cloth uniquely, never repeating a pattern or detail. Her work was famous for their elaborate designs, embroidered in gold and silver thread, encrusted with pearls, and even sewn with precious stones. Camila was an authority in fashion design and had an eye for beauty and class, being herself the most beautiful woman Sara had ever seen in her life.

Although Camila was a statement of finesse and elegance, women across Cordoba paid close attention to what Queen Isabel the Catholic wore as the reigning fashion of the times.

Queen Isabel had a comely appearance. Her hair was strawberry blonde, her complexion fair, and her eyes shifted between blue and green according to the weather. In the eyes of the men in court she was a rare beauty, one that exuded vitality, youth, and determination. Isabel was the first woman to rule in the ancient kingdoms of Castile and Leon. She stood proudly while she was crowned Queen in front of a crowd filled with the cynical nobility, before her husband, Prince Fernando, had time to arrive from Zaragoza, preventing him from being crowned as King Consort.

Isabel's magnetism came more from her charismatic persona than from her physical attributes. She had a long history of decisive actions which backed up her strength of character. After the death of her father, King Juan II of Castile, Isabel—only three years of age—was exiled together with her mother and siblings. That left her half-brother Enrique IV at liberty to sit comfortably on the throne without the nagging companionship of some drooling toddlers with a future threatening eye on his comfy chair.

Enrique IV had allowed the nobles to ascend to power unrestrained. He was not only the weakest king Castile had come to know in the feudal years, but was also rumored to exercise the same feeble behavior in bed. His first childless marriage to Blanche II of Navarre had left the bride as virginal as the Madonna herself. After thirteen years of failed attempts, of poking and prodding with a limp, useless member, Blanche was sent packing home with a divorce granted by the Pope. She was formally accused of having cursed her husband's penis to hang like the leaves of a weeping willow, and worst of all she left court horny as a rabbit. Soon after, Enrique married his second wife Juana of Portugal, and a daughter, her namesake, was born six years later. Enrique, who doubted his paternity of young Juana, decided to summon Isabel and her brother Alfonso back to Madrid to keep a closer watch on them, and possibly name one of them his successor. The nobility demanded Alfonso to be named Enrique's heir, upon the dubious origins of Princess Juana and the raucous behavior the queen displayed in every bedchamber across the kingdom except the king's.

Enrique agreed to the demands of the nobles, but Alfonso died shortly after, leaving Isabel next in line to the throne. Isabel stole this opportunity to defy her half-brother, and against his will, she married her second cousin Fernando of Aragon in 1469. After Enrique's death, Isabel had herself crowned Queen of Castile, even before the dead king was settled comfortably in his coffin. By then, her niece Juana was her biggest adversary to the crown. Two years later, her warrior husband, Fernando, had no trouble defeating Juana, leaving Isabel as the sole and rightful heir.

The bond between Isabel and Fernando became stronger after the death of his father in 1479. They formed the strongest alliance Spaniards had seen until the point they united the two kingdoms of Castile and Aragon. After receiving the troublesome reports about the existence of Crypto Judaism amongst *Conversos*, Isabel and Fernando drew up their strategy for the unity of Spain based on ethnic cleansing. The monarchs convinced the reluctant Pope Sixtus IV to authorize the creation of the notorious Spanish Inquisition, where a political tribunal, disguised as a religious one, would examine the genuineness of recent converts from Judaism to Christianity. In reality, the tribunal was dedicated to ultimately eradicating Judaism from Spain altogether.

Sara admired the queen's attributes and wished to become as strong and influential as the queen herself. Because of their stable financial status, her family—the Di Laurentis—were deeply involved in the business of the court, having financed the king's army on more than one occasion.

Even if Isabel was the symbol of power in Spain, it was Sara's mother who turned heads when attending formal functions. Camila's origins were a mystery to Sara. She was undoubtedly of Spaniard ancestry. No lilts in her speech or foreign practices ever betrayed her true Spanish roots. Sara could easily tell the difference between a native and an immigrant, because her father was one, and she could identify at a distance who the true Spaniard was and who was the imposter.

That was as far as Sara had ever gotten when it came to finding out about her mother's past. One thing she knew for sure, there was something about Sara's name that made her mother's voice tremble at times. She had also noticed her mother's eyes glistening when she watched Sara doing certain things like combing her hair, or simply smiling. On more than one occasion, Sara wondered if she was her grandmother's namesake, and the idea of being kept in the dark made her want to shake her mother violently with the sole purpose of making her speak.

Many times she had asked her mother about her childhood, her family, and her beginnings, getting always the same response in turn. "My life started the day I met your father." That answer was not satisfying by any means for somebody like Sara, who was the kind of person who could not leave any stone unturned until she discovered the truth.

To her dismay, her father had a very similar line to the one her mother used over and over again. "I never knew life could be so thrilling until I met your mother." An obviously rehearsed line they had agreed on long before they decided to start a family.

There was something amiss, though. Sara was fully aware that Massimo's family had severed ties with him since his marriage to Camila. But none of that ever came between them, and Sara admired the strength of their relationship. When together, which happened infrequently as a result of both of their occupations, they always seemed to be alone in a room, regardless of the crowd that might surround them. Camila was a woman accustomed to being admired not only by men but also by women. When in Massimo's arms, her eyes never wavered from his. The words flowing between them were barely audible as though they could read each other's thoughts.

Camila's dominance in the fashion world earned her the title of Queen Isabel's chief wardrobe advisor. "Style, elegance, class, go beyond exterior looks, Sara," her mother always stressed on her tirelessly. "They could strike alliances as swiftly as a marriage bed."

Isabel was fully conscious of the power a beautiful woman could have in a world dominated by men, and her need for Camila's expertise became a must if she intended to expand her kingdom throughout Europe.

Sara's father, Massimo Di Laurenti, spent many months away from Cordoba due to the nature of his business. He was originally from Verona, and was often referred to as a dark-skinned stallion by most women who laid eyes on him. He worked in the exceptionally profitable textile business that had made his family richer than monarchy. He could sit comfortably at home and enjoy life in their lavish estate. But Massimo had the spirit of an explorer, and the mere thought of sitting at home contemplating his lush garden from an oversized window, made him claustrophobic.

Sara had inherited her father's dark complexion along with his inability to sit still. From her mother she had some of her beauty, except for those rare green eyes her older sister Paola inherited. Sara's eyes were amber in coloring and shaped like almonds, set above high cheekbones. She was a rare beauty and she knew it, but she did not want to be known only as such.

Sara was fully aware there was more to life than riches, parties, and good looks. Well, that wasn't entirely true. She loved her life, it was fun and privileged and she enjoyed being beautiful. She was not the type who liked being fussed over by serving maids working laboriously to make her look good. She had seen her own sister going through that painful treatment since waking in the mornings, while she merely escaped with brushing her hair and freshening up her face.

Unlike Sara, her older sister Paola was a long nosed, green eyed, pudgy young woman who was content with what life handed to her. Camila had arranged her marriage three years before to a wealthy spice merchant from Portugal, and she had resided there with him since, having already birthed two babies, soon to be three.

Sara sighed and eyed the piece of stained linen left half-finished on her couch which corroborated the superficiality of her every day. Life in Casa Di Laurenti was not one she was proud of living. She aspired to be memorable, not for her looks but for her courage, like Queen Isabel.

The queen had suffered some major scrutinizing ever since she had revived the Inquisition. Sara understood Isabel's reasons and in fact was a fierce supporter of the edict. The only way Spain could become the most powerful kingdom in Europe was to become a solid unity.

With the Moors and the Jews exercising freely their heretic practices, the kingdom would always have to watch its back, in the event infidels would decide to sell out to foreign kingdoms, taking with them their wealth and impoverishing their homeland. As long as they would not embrace the Catholic Church as their Alma Mater, showing full commitment to the true faith as well as to their queen, they could not be trusted.

The queen was benevolent in that regard. She had offered the heretics the chance to convert to the Catholic faith or leave. There were many families she knew whose ancestors had been Jewish, but in 1391, when the Inquisition was first declared, Jews saw the logic to it and fully assimilated to the country that welcomed them.

Since then, these families thrived in Spain attaining the most influential positions in government, the world of finances, and the Church. Wasn't that proof enough that embracing Jesus and his holy virgin mother was the answer to prosperity?

She related her political vision to her mother and found that her mother was not agreeable to her point. "Nobody wins when blood is shed, Sara. Eventually, blood speaks, if not in a torture chamber, it spreads its truth throughout time." Camila's statement was somewhat of a shock to Sara. Her mother was one of the few the queen had allowed into her inner circle. They spent countless hours in the queen's chamber and she thought her mother was a close friend of Isabel. She never imagined that even with her closeness to the queen, Camila held Isabel's decisions in suspect.

Sara and her mother never spoke of the Inquisition again, and Camila went about her business with the queen as usual. The warning tone in her mother's voice when answering her questions was not one to be ignored. As much as she admired the queen, Sara was not immune to the devastating effects the tribunals of the Inquisition had in many families she held dear to her heart.

The week before, it had been the father of her best friend Ana the officers of the Inquisition dragged out of his home, while the family entertained guests. Last she heard he was still imprisoned in the dank, murky underground cells of the Alcazar charged with practicing the Jewish faith in secret.

Rumors of torture were gushing through the streets of Cordoba. It was difficult for her to reconcile acts of violence and bloodshed with her beloved queen. If there was any truth to them, Sara was sure they were not performed under the queen's orders. A woman with Isabel's religious convictions would never resort to torture as an approach to conversion. Jews and Moors converted to Catholicism out of love for their queen and their country, and that was all there was to it.

Sara glanced at her unfinished work. She decided she did not share her mother's passion for design and detail, or her father's interest in bargaining for the finest threads around the world. She was seventeen years old and thirsty for knowledge and adventure. But that might remain as a squandered dream, because according to the last conversation she had with her parents before their year-long departure, her time to marry was upon her.

Her mother had her sights set on a couple of eligible bachelors in Portugal. Portugal again. Sara could not understand her mother's fascination with that wretched country, when her family was so influential in Spain, and she could be a most desirable match even for the son of a queen.

No, she would not be forced into an unwanted marriage. She would be the one to decide who she was going to give herself to, just as her mother and the queen had.

Setting thoughts of marriage aside, Sara concentrated on the void she had in her life. She needed a purpose. Aside for her love for riding, reading and writing were her other passions. She also had an ability to master languages that was surprising to her tutors and made her father call her an intellectual.

There was the work with the children at the orphanage, but that had come to her as easy as anything else had in her life. Yet, that work in itself was not enough to make her a memorable woman. She feared sinking into a marriage, impregnated every year like her sister, and ultimately have nothing to show for on her deathbed other than a belly criss-crossed with stretch marks, and a load of jewels on her fingers.

With two long strides, she reached her unfinished embroidery. She hastily threw it in the flaming hearth as though getting rid of an unwanted life before it suggested itself as a possibility.

Before the swatch of linen was completely consumed by the fire, Sara was out of the sewing room, and taking two steps at a time she ran up to her chambers. She desperately needed to go out riding, feel the wind on her face, renew her lungs with fresh air. When she reached her room, she realized that she could not do so in her present confining garments, and that her favorite riding attire had been removed from her chest before her mother's departure. Camila had ordered Sara to wear more feminine clothes while riding during their absence. "It is time you start behaving like a lady befitting of your station, Sara, you're not a child anymore," Camila had said firmly as she gathered each tunic and trouser in her arms and took them out of Sara's room.

"But, Mother, I promise to ride within our property line, no one would ever see me," Sara had pleaded with her best rendition of innocence.

Camila smiled at her daughter. "You have your father's blood, my dear daughter. You do not respect boundaries, Sara. You cross each and every one of them until you reach your destination."

Sara remembered how angry she had felt at her mother's distrust. But, in all honesty, Camila was right— she was short sighted when it came to limits.

It had only been a week since her parents' departure and Sara was already going back on everything she had promised her parents before they left, especially when it came to her riding habits. She had never ridden horses like a proper lady, nor was she going to do it in uncomfortable dresses any longer.

She walked into her mother's chamber and eyed the few chests scattered around the room. She sighed deeply, and began riffling through them. To her dismay all she could find were Camila's old gowns. She threw herself on the floor and felt like kicking and screaming like a sulky child, until she caught a glimpse of a small chest hidden under Camila's bed.

To Sara's surprise the chest was not locked, as if waiting to be discovered, and her riding clothes were atop the pile of treasures stashed in the wooden crate. "Thank you, Mother. I love you."

Under her riding garments, Sara found a stack of old letters tied with ribbon with her father's handwriting on them. Massimo was a romantic and he wrote letters to Camila when away and even when he was home in Onuba. She set the pile of letters back in its place and covered it with loose swatches of fabric, when her hand struck something hard, a sharp frame of some sort. Sara pushed the fabrics aside to reveal the offending frame containing the miniature of a young woman. She lifted the miniature and stared at it in shock. She turned it around and found the name *Sarah*, written in perfect block letters. Sara turned the miniature around again, and looked into the eyes of a woman that looked so much like her. Eyes, the twin of her own, that whispered, "*You have found me.*"

Sara's heartbeat raced as the miniature slipped from her hands. The room closed in on her and she had the feeling of being smothered by thick smoke. She needed air, space. She had the sudden need to break free from her golden cage, to run away. Questions about this woman,

Sarah, assailed her. Their likeness was too strong to deny the blood ties between them. Her mother had left the chest unlocked, hidden in plain sight fully aware that Sara would find it. As the air in the room grew thicker, Sara found herself gasping for air. Black spots danced before her eyes, she could not think straight. Riding the chestnut Andalusian would help her clear up her perplexing state of mind. Perhaps later, she would sit in front of the harpsichord, that odd new instrument her father had acquired in Italy, and play around with some of its keys once again. She could swear she was creating music.

Chapter Sixteen
Falling

Children learn by example. No matter how prosperous or poor the living conditions a child grows up in, they tend to emulate their elders. Camila often wondered why her girls had not inherited all of her attributes instead of alternating with some of Massimo's, when she was the one parent who was always around. At least she was, most of the time.

Due to Massimo's excessive travelling, Paola and Sara spent limited time with their father while growing up. But, when Massimo was home, he knew exactly how to make up for lost time with his three adoring women. With Camila, it was in the privacy of their bedroom and the extravagant public affairs they enjoyed attending. With the girls, it was outdoors.

When Massimo had decided to make Spain his home, he didn't hesitate as to where to settle. A cultured man himself, he had full knowledge of the role Cordoba had played in the past eight centuries in the spheres of business and letters, a consequence of its affluent and highly intellectual Jewish and Moorish population. The mixture of both, plus a vast concentration of nobles around the Alcazar, were the perfect combination for a man like Massimo. He was a lover of society, money, culture, and opportunity. To him there was no other choice but Cordoba. Once this extraordinary Italian man had laid his eyes on what he wanted nothing could steer him away from his goal.

So was the case when he singled out Camila, as she stood amongst a herd of Andalusian foals. He was currently surveying the village of Onuba in the Valley of Guadalquivir, seven and a half common leagues east of Cordoba. He wanted a secluded, sizable expansion of land where he could enjoy breeding horses, riding, and hunting, yet be close enough to the main city to keep his name buzzing around in the right circles.

While weighing in on his options, he stood at a shady spot on the road that wound down from the famous Carpio, the castle on the hill built by Garci Méndez de Sotomayor in 1325.

Enjoying a respite from the sun, he settled his eyes on Camila gracefully moving around the playful foals, enticing them to follow her as she zigzagged along the green path. Massimo was struck by her dark hair free falling down the length of her back, and by that thin, almost transparent muslin tunic that did nothing to conceal the definition of her curves and the perfect roundness of her breasts. For a moment, he wished he was one of the foals in the herd, or better yet, the stallion.

Massimo shook his head and could not help but laugh out loud at the sight of the foals following their mistress devotedly. In that instant, he knew he was watching the most beautiful woman he had seen in all the thousands of miles he had traveled. He had to have her.

In a day's time, Massimo bought a large estate in Onuba with a sizable lake defining its rich boundaries. Two weeks later, he bought the foals he saw beside the road. And that same night, he made love to Camila over and over again, in their marriage bed.

Camila went through a series of heart wrenching miscarriages before she finally got pregnant with Paola. Anxious to deliver a healthy baby for her beloved husband, she relinquished the daily activities that had made up her life up until then.

Her horses were long forgotten, her long walks with Massimo along the lake were suspended, parties in or out of the house were on hold, and their sex life became non-existent. For the sake of their unborn baby and their marriage, Massimo and Camila found a new common ground where they could enjoy each other, without being naked in bed.

It was then that out of boredom, Camila began playing around with some of the fabrics Massimo brought back from his trips, and before his very eyes, she designed the most luxurious embroidered patterns on them. What had started as a pastime, swiftly evolved into a solid business partnership that once again reaffirmed their union as soulmates.

Camila's hidden talents evolved rapidly in the world of fashion and design. After the birth of their daughter Paola, her time was limited and the temporary halt of activities set during her pregnancy became almost permanent, except for her intimacy with Massimo. Having made a name for herself in the highest spheres of Cordoba as a fashion goddess, her days had to be cleverly planned. Consequently, the baby was always with her no matter where she went, accompanied by a wet-nurse, a nursemaid, and a servant, except when Paola was out riding with Massimo.

During Paola's first year of life, Massimo avoided travelling as much as he could. His absences never exceeded a week at a time. He couldn't bear being away from home.

Before meeting Camila, he had never opened his heart to anybody. His mother had attempted in vain to match Massimo with a handful of eligible young women from several of Verona's noble families, but he elegantly declined his mother's efforts with the excuse that his constant voyages were needed to ensure the family's fortune.

His excuse wasn't entirely true. The family was already wealthy and his travelling was not necessary at all times, since he had a network of agents in every city he sourced for product. The truth was that he was terrified of committing to only one woman. The notion of encasing his life in a marriage, becoming a prisoner under his own roof, was an act of sheer insanity to him. He was not ready to settle down, not yet.

He often laughed at how much life had fooled him. He had not only settled under one roof and with one woman, but he was also crazy with lust and love for her and filled with tenderness for his daughter. Massimo took the role of parent seriously. He was a good father to Paola, and constantly came up with new ideas to include the baby in his own activities.

One day he walked into the nursery as the baby was finishing nursing. Tapping a foot on the wood floors, Massimo waited patiently under the stern scrutiny of the baby's nurse. As soon as he was able to snatch the baby from the obliging hands of that dutiful woman, he held Paola to his chest and swung a piece of sturdy linen around him. With ample dexterity, Massimo bundled Paola to his chest like a bag of grain. The baby kicked his middle with excitement and giggled with joy. At the baby's sign of approval Massimo walked out of the nursery, out of the house, to where his horse groom waited with his mount.

The baby's entourage followed after him, crying in horror, fearing injury to the baby's back, possible decapitation, and permanent bowel dysfunction. Deaf to the staff's protestations, Massimo swung up on his horse's back and waved charmingly at the ladies. Keeping an eye on his baby's fascinated expression, he slowly took off on the first of many rides together.

The same routine was repeated years later, this time around with less agitation on behalf of the nursery staff. Some token of resistance notwithstanding, Sara was about the same age as Paola when introduced to the world of horses. By then, the Di Laurenti servants grew accustomed to their master's oddities and found most of their undertakings somewhat charming.

As soon as the girls were able to mount their own ponies, Massimo officially declared them his new riding companions. Gradually, he added new activities such as jumping, hunting, and the girls' all-time favorite, splashing mud at the bank of the lake until their clothes were no more than brown crusty shells.

So full of love for his daughters and wife, Massimo often wondered why was he the recipient of so much luck. He hadn't done anything beyond extraordinary in his life to deserve such joy. These moments of unguarded reflection brought him down to his knees. Not in prayer, because Massimo was a man who doubted the power of religious submission, but with weakness. He feared life could be teasing him and happiness could be taken from him without a moment's notice.

The Di Laurentis' eccentricities went further than Massimo becoming his daughters' playmate. He transgressed into grounds a man should never venture: the girls' riding attire.

Sara was a young girl of four when she faced her father with the most logical question a child could ask a parent when learning from him.

"When do I get to ride like you?" She looked up at her father from her pony, with those impossibly beautiful honeyed eyes, while struggling with her skirts and petticoats.

Massimo looked around him, and her pony, and replied in a bit of confusion, "Well you are, my love. You have a horse, I have a horse."

Sara frowned in frustration. "I know we have horses, Papa, but I want to ride like you. I don't like this silly skirt. I want to wear what you wear." She turned around and nodded at Paola seeking her sister's consent on the matter. Paola was a few steps behind them and nodded back. By then she had become accustomed to Sara being the one in charge.

Massimo halted his horse and the girls gathered around him. He frowned at the elaborate dresses they were wearing and after a short moment he laughed heartily. "Your mama will love this."

By the time they were back at the house, Massimo had a plan. The girls were to ride astride within the confinements of their lands. As for the attire, he talked Camila into recreating the type of loose fitting trousers he'd seen Turks wear. Camila embellished them with as many types of embroidery she deemed necessary to make the Di Laurenti riding trousers look as feminine as possible, and with that matter settled neither woman in the Di Laurenti household ever rode sidesaddle and in dresses again.

Sara still remembered that day and a smile stretched across her lips as she donned her riding clothes. By now Sara's riding attire had evolved dramatically, discarding all the unnecessary niceties her mother had used in the past to beautify it. What had emerged was an outfit that was meant to be functional to withstand mud, dirt, and working around horses. Her trousers were loose and baggy, her tunic was long, and she wore a scarf on her head, concealing her long hair under it. From afar, she looked like a Turkish warrior.

Everything in her life had always been so easy, given to her without asking, she never had to fight for what she wanted. Fighting, she could not grasp the concept of the word. Here she was now, a girl no more, filled with monstrous energy, yet unable to find a goal, or even fight for one.

The face of the woman, Sarah, in the miniature was still in her mind. She needed to ease her troubling thoughts to be able to come up with a plan. Riding her new Andalusian would do.

In reality, this chestnut beauty was not hers, but promised to some man on his way back from Italy. Even though the colt was foaled at her father's stable, and she had been there when he made the first tottering steps on his long legs, she was forbidden to bond with it.

The chestnut was stubborn and spirited, a combination that made his training difficult by even the most experienced trainers. Its feral nature was stronger than any strict workout administered to tame him. The horse was gentler towards Sara than to anybody else who dared approach him. With her father's approval and only in his presence, she had trained the chestnut colt for the past three months. Despite the closeness she had developed with the colt, the chestnut beauty was still skittish of her and somewhat unpredictable.

Her father had forbidden her to ride the chestnut Andalusian during his absence, but he was not there to stop her. She couldn't think of anything else but the stallion's energy to reach the point of exertion she needed, to feel something else beyond frustration. Moreover, she wanted to surprise her father upon his return with a fully trained rebel. There was no doubt that the horse could do with some more discipline than what the head groom had administered thus far.

When she approached the stables, the groom had already saddled a sedate grey mare for her. Sara strode by the mare with complete disregard and turned to the groom with authority. "Saddle the chestnut."

The groom, a young man of fifteen, stood still for a short moment. Overcoming the shyness his mistress triggered in him, he finally croaked a firm, "No."

She was fully aware that the groom was following her father's orders. With both parents away, she was ready to test her authority over the servants.

With dramatic mastery, her eyes grew bigger than their usual size at his impertinence. All the fury and frustration she carried throughout the day came out in a furious scold, the worst that any servant had ever received at Casa Di Laurenti.

"You are nothing but a groom. You must obey me, unless you prefer the life of a beggar than living under the protection of my father."

The groom stood stunned and so did Sara. She couldn't even believe her own words. She took a step forward and he stepped back at once.

"I apologize. I didn't mean any of it. I don't know what came over me. Please, I will ride him only to the line of trees. You are a good man and I will commend your faithfulness to my father." She followed up her apology with a slight smile, a gentle batting of the eyes, and a tilt of the head. After a moment's hesitation, the groom gave in and the chestnut was saddled.

The ride started choppy and strenuous. The horse was determined to assert his authority over hers. He bucked and reared a few times. They struggled for dominance for a couple of hours, before they came to the understanding of who was playing the role of horse and who was the rider. Ready for a break, Sara dismounted the horse by the lake, and let him wander around a copse nearby while he chewed on some tender shrubs and quenched his thirst.

She looked over what she called her horse with pride. There were many horses in her father's stables that she could have except for this one, especially now that the Andalusian was promised to some acquaintance of her father's agent in Padua. The new owner should have arrived in Onuba two weeks ago to ride away with the horse. But they had received word that he had been delayed because of some storm, sickness, or some other kind of trouble that kept the royal-privileged caballero, or was he a physician... Whatever he was, she didn't care at all. He was to take her horse, reason enough to dislike the idea of him with or without a royal appointment.

Since the birth of the chestnut Andalusian, the grooms in the stable behaved warily around this particular foal. Unlike most of the horses of his breed, he was not grey, but of a deep chestnut color with white socks. The popular belief was that horses with markings could signify ill temper, bad luck, or good luck. The grooms could not make up their minds, but without a doubt, they treated this magnificent beauty with feared respect.

Sara fell in love with the colt as soon as she laid eyes on him. He was not easily approachable but she was up for the challenge. She yearned for a horse that belonged solely to her, a faithful companion. It took her several weeks to secretly name him. He was big, strong, and arrogant. A true warrior. Over and over again, she returned to the same name, El Cid.

Sara, a lover of literature, was well acquainted with the poem, *El Cantar De Mio Cid*. It was the story of a true warrior that inhabited the Iberian Peninsula more than four centuries before. His real name was Ramiro Diaz de Vivar, but to the eyes of the people, he was a hero, a true champion, and they named him *El Cid Campeador*, The Lord Champion.

Her hot-tempered horse was the picture of a champion and a fighter. Although cliché, she reluctantly gave in, and Cid was finally named.

Cid looked content nibbling around the copse, his vitality regained after the much-needed rest, and was eyeing Sara inquisitively as to their next adventure. She took the naughty insinuation with humor, and stroking the bridge of his nose, she asked him if they should surprise the cook back at the house with some fresh game. As though he understood the perspective of their mischievous adventure, he replied with a sound neigh.

Against her father's warnings, Sara ventured out of the perimeter of their property and into the dense woods. She had left the stables armed with a small knife, which she always carried in the event of an emergency, securely tucked beneath the waistband of her trousers. Stashed in her saddlebag, she had a bag of fresh figs, and a canteen with diluted wine. As routinely done at Casa Di Laurenti, a stable groom insisted on accompanying her and, as predicted, she was successful in waving him off. She was to be away for only a couple of hours and everybody assumed she would never cross the limits of the property wearing such scandalous garments.

In reality, this was not the first time Sara had crossed over the property line. She knew the area like the palm of her hands and was well aware of the dangers. Throughout the years, when she had gone out riding with her father, they had encountered only a few red deer, the occasional Egyptian mongoose, small rodents, and plenty of vultures. Her hunting skills were pretty decent when armed with bow and arrow, assuming the animal she aimed for was either half asleep or on the verge of death. Nevertheless, she felt compelled to try her luck in the open space, with just a small knife and plenty of female arrogance.

After half an hour of riding without any animal sightings and with some ominous grey clouds looming over them, she decided to call her adventure off. It was fall, and even if mild, the weather was known to turn from pleasant to stormy in a heartbeat. The prospect of being drenched by a sudden storm, out of careless stupidity, was not an appealing prospect.

Although still haunted by the image of the miniature she had found in her mother's chamber, her frustration slowly ebbed. While outdoors, her reality did not look as gloomy as it did in the company of her sewing kit. "Maybe I should be a farmer," she whispered in Cid's ear.

Cid shook his head as if he understood her and thought it a terrible idea. "You're right," she replied in agreement. The mere image of working the fields from dusk till dawn raised a hysterical laugh in her chest that echoed throughout the desolate wilderness.

A booming thunder mingled with her laughter and in no time, as she had predicted, she was soaked to the bone. Lightning ripped the sky, scaring Cid out of his wits. He reared up on his hind legs in alarm, and lurched forward, catching Sara completely off guard as she was thrown from the saddle.

Sara's head hit the ground with a loud thud. Through a haze, she noticed one of her feet was still tangled in the stirrups. With a surprising clarity of mind and innate means of survival, she struggled to free her foot from the saddle. But, Cid's wild speed and erratic cantering around trees and overgrown roots, made all her efforts impossible. She strained to keep her head above the ground, for she was sure she would smash her skull on the next density of trees and rocks. She felt her clothes rip and her skin tear. Her body was soaked with rain, she was lathered with mud and warm blood.

She fought to what she thought to be her last breath until her body stopped dragging along the jagged trail. Was she dead? Why weren't they moving anymore? Though brutally injured, her senses were still sharp, and she could discern the faint hoof beats of a distant horse. She could not tell if the horse was approaching or moving away.

The searing pain cutting through her body confirmed that she was very much alive. She tried moving. A bestial groan frightened her. She tried moving again and the same sound followed her failed attempt. The immeasurable pain made her wish she was dead. A pang of fear gripped her aching chest. If she couldn't move it wouldn't be long before vultures would feast on her body.

She tried opening her eyes, but her eyelids were already swollen shut. Through narrow slits, she could identify something moving towards her. Instinctively, she screamed to scare off what might approach her. If she was to be devoured, she wanted to be completely unconscious. Not a chance, at least not yet. Pain kept her miserably awake and alert of her surroundings. But, there was nothing she could do other than wait for death to claim her. Her body did not respond to her commands. Her limbs felt disengaged from her body, she could not move and run from the imminent danger upon her.

The approaching shape was not an animal, but a man. He knelt next to her and placed his hand on her forehead.

"Mother of God!" he exclaimed.

She writhed under his gentle touch and mouthed something through a slobber of saliva and blood.

"Hush now, you are safe with me." Her breathing became more agitated and short at times. Through the constricted opening of her eyelids, she could partially see a few of his facial features. His eyes were gentle and blue.

He placed his palms firmly on her hips, causing her to whimper in agony. "I know it hurts, but I must do it now. Please forgive me, my lady."

He pulled both her legs downward with all his might, and with a crunching sound that ripped through the thunderous storm, he readjusted her dislocated hips.

Her last breath before fainting was sufficient to make her vomit. *The rain will wash it away*, she hoped before giving into the pure bliss of deadened darkness.

Chapter Seventeen
The Physician

The prospect of sailing back to Spain was not one that Leon Fernandez had contemplated with enthusiasm. True, he had never gotten seasick during any of his previous trips, but it was the stench of others that did get sick he could not withstand.

It was to be a busy crossing for him, especially since his natural healing instincts would send him straight to the aid of the unfortunate travelers who would heave up their insides unmercifully. He could have waited for spring when the stormy season was over, and travel on calmer waters, but as he had expected, the moment he graduated from the School of Medicine at the University of Padua, he got an official sealed letter from his family's protector, the Marquis of Alazar in Cordoba, requesting his services as the family's new physician.

***

The appointment was one more of the many natural successions of events his life had been predestined for by simply bearing the name Fernandez. His father and his father before him had been the marquis's father's physician, a position that had been held by the Fernandez males for the past century.

Ever since he could remember, Leon had practiced the arts of healing. When he was a little boy, he would sneak out of his grandfather's surgery with scalpel, needle, and thread, in search of fatally wounded rodents who were missing body parts or were torn beyond recognition. His fascination was not so much with the inner work of their inert bodies, which he was already familiar with, but with the many ways those injuries could be mended leaving behind the slightest of scars.

During his medical education in Padua, he demonstrated his fine surgical capabilities. In doing so, he earned his professors' trust and respect. Leon became the one physician his peers called upon to serve members of the Italian nobility who got injured in brawls and were too vain to display the earned marks.

Through this practice, he added a decent amount of riches to the Fernandez family coffers, significantly increasing the fortune his family had accrued throughout decades. His services were valued and well rewarded, because along with his magical surgical touch, his oath of secrecy was priceless. Most of the cases he attended were the results of passionate encounters, sometimes ending in grueling duels, which happened in the wrong chamber and with the wrong partner.

He expected this voyage to Spain to be one of permanency even though there was no family to go back to. His father had died the year before, his mother perished to putrid fever when he was ten years old, and his only sister was happily married and living in Venice. Still, Spain was home to him.

The appointment by the marquis was one of the two reasons he was destined to return to Spain. The other one was a promise.

When he parted from his father four years before, he knew that to be their last time together. He remembered hugging him for the last time, memorizing the lines on his face, his robust build, the timbre of his voice as he spoke his last words of advice. When Leon learned of his death he wished he could turn back time for one last word, for one last blessing.

Leon feared for his father's life the moment he departed Spain. A fear born out of the carelessness in which his father conducted his personal affairs, the matters of the *Anusim*, the unwilling ones.

The Fernandez family was a family of *Conversos*. It was widely known that the nature of the conversions which occurred at the beginning of the century was a pretense intended to maintain the status quo of the Spanish hierarchy. After all, most of its constituents were wealthy Jews desperately needed to keep the economy of the kingdom in balance. Spain could not afford to lose them.

The Fernandez family vowed to wear the newly adopted religion like a cloak just to endure public life. But like any other accessory, such as jewels or a pair of gloves, they shed the imposed identity once in the privacy of their homes.

It was around that time that the late Marquis of Alazar and Doctor Fernandez—Leon's great-grandfather—developed a friendship. The two men were known to sit for hours over games of *Tables Reales* and a bottle of Arak and share their most intimate secrets. Leon's great-grandfather knew of the rakish nature of the marquis, of his addiction to gambling and women. Dangerous habits that drove his family to ruins. At the verge of an apoplexy, the marquis sought the help of his friend Dr. Fernandez. The doctor, a shrewd man, foresaw this moment and made the marquis an offer he could not refuse. The deal was plain and simple. The Alazars needed the financial solvency of the massive fortune of the Fernandez's, and the Fernandez's needed the protection of a good Catholic family close to the Church and with heavy influence in the Spanish court that could help them conceal their double life. The huffing and puffing marquis, a finished man, agreed on the spot. His debts were higher than ever and he had more mistresses than he could bed, or support. The only way he could justify his existence was by being the way he was, a useless noble. Still he was a man of honor. The only man the good doctor would trust with the fate of his family.

The alliance was struck over another one of their games and after a full bottle of their favorite drink. Besides being doctor and patient, noble and intellectual, Jew and Catholic, the marquis and the doctor were friends.

As generations passed, nothing changed. The Alazars kept producing marquises and the Fernandez's, doctors. Most importantly the original vows to protect each other were never broken. It was now Leon's turn to take the reins of the alliance formed a century ago.

Leon's journey to becoming the next Fernandez started with his first degree of *licenciado* from the University of Salamanca. But the man he was destined to become required further education in Padua.

Besides becoming a doctor, Leon was bound to be secretly instructed at the Yeshiva of Padua, the famous center for Talmudic studies, under the care of rabbi and doctor Judah Messer Leon. Rabbi Leon was responsible for mastering a combination of traditional study of the Jewish texts with lectures on the non-Jewish program of the secular curriculum. It provided leaders of *Marrano* communities across Christendom the right tools to approach their highly compromised double lives.

The solid foundation the Fernandez's established through generations in the Cordoban hierarchy, made other *Converso* families look up to them as leaders of a community that existed only by candlelight.

Leon's great-grandfather took the title to heart, considering himself the contemporary Moses responsible to deliver his people to religious freedom. The truth was, there was no freedom or a way to achieve it, yet there were feasible channels to outlive the tight reins of the Inquisition. Thus a secret society was born in the hidden tunnels below the Fernandez estate where practices of the Jewish faith were solemnly observed. Rituals for births, deaths, marriages, and *bar mitzvahs* were all performed. Jewish life in the heart of the Fernandez home was untouched by the bloodthirsty fanatics of the Inquisition.

***

The retching sound of another hapless victim of the rough Mediterranean Sea took Leon out of his thoughts. Unfortunately, there was nothing he could do for the sickly passenger other than mixing some diluted wine with a few drops of opium and let him sleep it off. Leon considered the option for a while. It would have been wonderful to diminish the putrid pools of vomit on deck, except that such a course of action meant for him to monitor each and every one whom he put under the magic spell of opium. It was his duty as a physician.

Duty. Responsibility. Was that to be his predicament?

He looked at the man still retching over the rail, almost falling overboard with each powerful heave, and sighed irritably while he reached him in three quick strides. Why was he doing it? He could have said no to his father and put an end to everything his family had stood for for the past century, before his earthly existence had ever been conceived. He wished he could simplify his life and allow the Catholic faith to saturate his flesh, in a way that he would wholeheartedly mean what his tongue had been trained to say.

He yearned to forget everything he had ever experienced as a *Marrano*. The sense of completion when gathered in the confinements of the Fernandez underground tunnels with other *Marrano* families. The awakening of a dormant community brought to life when the Torah scrolls were exposed under the golden glow of burning torches. His mother's hands embracing the light of the *Shabbat* candles bringing a magical sense of uniqueness to their family which helped preserve within him his identity. His father's touch over his head in blessing reassuring Leon he was not a lie as he feared every time he was spoken to under his real name Lev and not Leon.

Lev. He could hear the voice of his mother. He could see her eyes as blue as his, calling him her Lev, *her heart.*

And what about the bloodsucking Alazars? Was he to trust them? Their demands had increased significantly throughout the last decade. The initial alliance made on grounds of honor, friendship, and necessity, shifted abruptly to one of ruthless extortion. Keen to be on the crown's good side, hungry for additional fiefs necessary to replace the ones the Alazars lost shamelessly, the parasitical new marquis had taken on financing King Fernando's latest delusional campaign—the re-conquest of the Kingdom of Granada, which had been in the hands of the Muslim Moors since their invasion of Spain in the eighth century.

The marquis had wined and dined the king at the Fernandez's expense. Worst of all, he pledged to the king a fortune without previously conferring with Leon's father. Leon was aware of the ugly confrontation his father and the marquis had over the subject. The relationship between the two families showed obvious marks of irreparable damage. Then, the worst happened.

An all too familiar pain assailed him again leaving him short of breath. His father had died because of the marquis's intentional neglect to shield him from the murderous interrogation of a young officer of the Inquisition. He had gotten a letter from the marquis a year before informing him of the sudden death of his father. He also advised Leon not to set foot on Spanish territory until further notice. From his colleagues at the Yeshiva, he got the gruesome details of his father's last days. He was arrested and charged with performing the Jewish ritual of *Brit Milah*, a circumcision, to the newborn son of Manuel Pedrosa, a renowned architect responsible for the building of several churches across Spain. A kitchen maid from the Pedrosa household followed the murmurs of the ancient Hebrew chants all the way to the baby's nursery and secretly witnessed in a state of shocked horror, what she later described as the sodomizing of the baby in a satanic ritual.

The Pedrosas vanished from Cordoba overnight. His father was not so lucky. The questioning was said to be gruesome. It took the marquis three long days to get a full acquittal for his father. Too late. His flesh rotted from the wounds inflicted and he died feverishly, mouthing, "*Shmah Yisrael Adonai Eloheinu, Adonai Ehad,*" the centerpiece of the Jewish prayers.

To his last breath Leon's father was true to his beliefs. The word *ehad*, one, kept on resonating painfully in Leon's head. His father took his last breath dying for his *one* truth.

Leon burned inside to finish with it all. The memories. His absence. His impending appointment as the new rabbi.

But he wouldn't. He didn't believe in conversions. His heart would ultimately follow its way home. To his family. To his faith. *Shmah Yisrael*, he silently prayed as a shudder crept up his spine.

Damn it! The sickly man threw up on his shoes and looked up at Leon. The poor man was exhausted like a deer after rutting season. Leon laughed at the visual.

He had gone hunting with his father many times near the Guadalquivir River in the outskirts of Cordoba, where the woods thicken, and had observed the herds of deer, literally out of breath after mating season. The happy memories helped Leon keep his composure together summoning the excellent bedside manners that he had learned as his grandfather's assistant. He put the sick man out of his misery, diluting a few drops of opium in the man's flask, and forced him to drink it in a couple of gulps, to ensure it stayed down.

After his patient fell asleep like a drunken sailor on deck, Leon surveyed his ruined shoes. How would he meet Signore Di Laurenti smelling like rotten cheese? It would have to do.

Chances were that Di Laurenti was no longer in Cordoba this late in the month. As far as he knew, the man was due in India for business right around this time. Weeks of stern procrastination over the most important decision he would ever make in his life had delayed his arrival in Spain. That could mean that the horse his tailor in Padua had told him about, the one Massimo Di Laurenti was anxious to give away to a fine horseman, was most likely in the hands of another.

Leon had laughed, enjoying the tailor's accounts about the demonic traits of the Andalusian. He was not superstitious, and Signore Di Laurenti seemed anxious to get rid of that four-legged demon before his younger daughter broke her neck riding it. When Leon heard about the Andalusian, he knew he had to have it. He was a skilled rider, and if he was to go back to Cordoba, he was going to do so with the most handsome mount his gold could buy.

Between suit fittings and the purchasing of the finest custom-made shoes, Leon had reached a decision. He was to fulfill his promise to his father, yet he would never marry, nor sire children. The deliberate imposition he suffered as a *Converso* through his life would end with him. He would be the last Fernandez.

Another interesting thought crossed his mind, gradually turning the myth of a man, one who became the divine inspiration centuries after his death, into something more tangible.

It was said that Jesus died at the age of thirty-three a childless bachelor. For a Jewish rabbi, the way he was referred to countless times in the books of Luke and

Matthew, Jesus should have married and conceived children in order to comply with the first precept of the Torah—be fruitful and multiply. Still, there was no evidence of his fulfillment of said precept.

If he was truly the son of God, wouldn't he have to set the example for the rest of humanity and obey each one of his Creator's rules blindly?

The notion of Jesus as an ordinary Jew pressured to keep his traditions alive, made more sense to Leon now than ever before.

Jesus, like any man with a sense of duty for his community, became a leader merely because he was chosen to do so. He had a voice, he represented the oppressed, he fought for justice. He was the chosen one, not his unborn child, not the child after him. He endured all the pain and suffering his opposition caused not only to his family, but also to his followers. What if he didn't want his seed to endure the cruel scrutiny he had endured from the moment of his birth?

Leon was resolute in his decision to terminate the Fernandez lineage with him. His judgment was final. Apparently there was no sin in it since the man once known as Jesus ultimately became God.

Leon closed his eyes. He was exhausted, and judging by the size of the waves that battered the ship, the storm was far from over. The air was getting colder, and although his skin rippled with goose bumps, he would rather stay on deck inhaling the last of his freedom before officially assuming both of his new titles.

He crossed his arms over his wide chest to shield himself from the relentless wind and ocean spray. His hands touched the fine wool of his suit. His Italian tailor insisted on getting the finest fabrics which could only be found at the Di Laurenti mill in Padua.

Leon was familiar with the name and with the man. He had met Signore Di Laurenti briefly in Padua at the

Yeshiva. Massimo was a regular visitor since he had business with some of the rabbis who managed a network of the finest silk houses across Italy.

When Massimo learned who the interested party for his horse was, he sought Leon at the Yeshiva and extended an invitation for him to stay at their estate in Onuba upon his arrival and until he was completely settled in Cordoba.

Leon accepted Massimo's offer eagerly. He vehemently refused to live on the marquis's grounds, neither would he go back to the place where he failed to accompany his father to the end. He envisioned himself as the master of his own manor, a small token for not being the master of his own life.

The painful groans of another passenger fallen prey to the rough seas reminded him that once more, duty called.

Chapter Eighteen
Landfall Over Heels

A deep line of brown above the steely colored ocean popped up in the distance bringing some relief to the passengers who thought death by seasickness was upon them. Leon was always amazed at the way those suffering from strenuous retching revived when sighting land on the horizon.

Besides showing signs of dehydration and in some more severe cases early signs of wasting sickness, the process of compulsive vomiting could be painful due to the constant contraction of the stomach muscles. Leon had some success in helping patients relax and mentally visualize firm land. Nevertheless, the actual sight of the Port of Malaga, even if from afar, revived the most wretched of them into a state of euphoria. The good news for the survivors was that after a good sleep and a good meal, life would resume as usual.

Leon had made previous arrangements to travel by carriage from Malaga to Cordoba, find lodgings in the city for a couple of days, and subsequently ride to the Di Laurentis' estate once recuperated from the anticipated arduous work on board. His mood during the sea voyage had plummeted dramatically. He could not endure another minute in the company of anybody who demanded medical services or advice from him.

The grateful passengers, now in a state of hyperactivity, had gone as far as offering him valuable jewels or their most precious daughters in marriage to show their admiration and gratefulness for his help.

By landfall, Leon succeeded in shrugging everybody off, escaping through a narrow alley where he spotted a lanky youth with a lame horse. Perfect.

The negotiations with the overly attached owner of such freak of nature were unbelievably difficult. Leon offered the young man a fair price to start off the transaction. The boy shook his head and held on tight to his animal.

After tears, recommendations on the horse's likes and dislikes, the exorbitant sum Leon offered the sentimental owner overtook his feelings and finally he let the mare go.

Leon surveyed his investment with a critical eye. It surely was a bad cross between donkey and horse, of a dirty grey color, hair spotted sparingly, large floppy ears, eyes as tired as a bloodhound's, and the fattest rump Leon had ever seen.

He really didn't care overmuch about the looks of the horse at that point as long as he could enjoy some peace and tranquility on the way to his destination.

The acquisition of his own transportation, if that was the proper way to refer to the mare which ignored every single one of his commands, helped him make a quick change of plans. After arranging for the transport of his travelling chests to the Di Laurentis, he made a final decision. He would not go to Cordoba. Astride his new mare Leon was on his way to the Di Laurenti manor in Onuba.

The ride was somewhat interesting. To his surprise the plump creature proved to be sweet tempered and fairly fast.

After Leon allowed the horse to sniff him in order to familiarize itself with its new master, he mounted her slowly and jabbed the heel of his riding boot close to the mare's fat rear. But instead of a fast pace trot, the only thing he got in return was a reproachful look that spelled out, "Treat me like a lady or I won't move." True to her ladylike nature, Señorita—the mare's name—was to be treated as such. Leon whispered into her ear sweet words in Italian sure to weaken a woman's heart and caressed her neck. The trick worked, and with a soft gait they were on their way.

The terrain of the road was in fairly good condition. The route from Malaga to Onuba was about forty-four common leagues. With luck and good weather he would make it by next morning.

So far luck was with him. Señorita was a great companion and did not demand anything from him besides the occasional rest, flirting, and sweet snacks. The weather was a different issue altogether. The sky soon covered with heavy clouds. The storm which had followed him since Rome brewed with dark menace. Flocks of birds flew their way to refuge at the unavoidable break of thunder and lightning. Personally, he did not mind getting wet. He just hoped that Señorita would not fret with the rain.

The storm did not hit until late that night. Leon found lodgings at a lice infested inn, where after not finding a half decent spot to lay his head on, he ultimately decided to accompany his beautiful Señorita—as he thought of his hideous mare this far in the trip—in the stables. The mare snuggled next to him providing him with nurturing warmth. For the first time since leaving Padua, Leon slept. Before dozing off he understood the poor lad's resistance to depart from Señorita. He would never give her up.

After a quick breakfast of cheese, goat milk, and bread, Señorita and its proud rider were back on the road. Even though they left the inn under partly cloudy skies, it didn't take more than an hour for the first cold drops to darken Señorita's already spotted pelt.

Leon looked further into the horizon. It was going to rain and hard. He stopped at the side of the road and gently patted the mare. "What do you think, my sweet princess, should we ride any further or look for shelter?"

As though considering the question, Señorita tilted her big head to one side then the other, farted soundly—making Leon's eyes water—and slowly picked up a rhythmic trot. She had reached a decision, they were going to reach the Di Laurentis as first planned.

As they neared the dense marshes surrounding the perimeter of the swollen Guadalquivir River, which had now turned into lakes due to the massive flooding from the intense rain, Señorita grew impatient. At that point in the journey, Leon trusted his mare blindly and proceeded with caution.

They were nearing the woods which harbored small animals as well as the occasional wild boar. Leon carried his surgical case with him that contained the most exquisite collection of handmade scalpels. Each one was made to fit his right grip. The handles were smooth, letting the muscles in his hand and arm relax, applying the right pressure when making an incision. It was doubtful whether he could fight a wild animal with any of them unless they were under the effects of a sedative.

Instinctively he reached for his breast pocket. He felt the familiar contour of his *navaja*, a folding knife his father had given him as a special present at the age of thirteen for his *bar mitzvah*—the day he became a man in the Jewish tradition.

His father was a skilled swordsman and had trained Leon to be fierce. The *navaja* required an array of skills far from the elegant dance and athleticism of swordplay. A victorious *navaja* fight involved cool calculation. The small knife was one for finality and quick action. A precise wound to the lower abdomen was to be fatal. Jabbing a *navaja* into human flesh called for an intimate death. It was a haunting experience that involved the closeness of the bodies, the reek of fear from both opponents, the warm feeling of the last breath from the departed.

The small knife gave him some comfort, even though reaching for a wild boar's abdomen could be almost impossible, the slashing of the carotid artery seemed more feasible. He shook his head wanting to rid his mind of morbid thoughts. Thunder and lightning were sure to keep anything, with the minimal instinct of self-preservation, under safe shelter.

Señorita acted skittish. She fought Leon on the trail he chose to take and took a turn at a fork in the road. A faint scream broke through a thunderous boom followed by a crack of lightning that parted the sky in two. It could have been the howl of a stray wolf. Maybe a vulture. Señorita picked up her pace in the direction of the sound that by then he recognized as human.

Leon saw the crushing of tree branches in the distance. A magnificent horse was wildly scurrying through the slim spaces in between the heavily populated forest. The rending screams of a woman were clearly audible. Another ray of lightning illuminated the dark woods. That's when he saw her. Plainly hanging on for dear life by her foot. The right stirrup held her prisoner in the saddle. He could see her struggling to free herself from the leather strap, but the frantic flee of her scared horse made every one of her attempts fail.

Leon intensified his push on Señorita. The woman could succumb to a blow to the head if he didn't get to her on time. The forest was thick with overgrown branches. Scattered boulders emerged on the uneven terrain, making it a dangerous place to ride, least of all a place to be dragged on at full speed.

"Lift your head from the ground!" Leon yelled, desperate to prevent her from decapitation. His riding grew desperate. Her screaming became spaced indicating to Leon her slipping in and out of consciousness. Then it stopped altogether. The horse disappeared in the forest as if the Devil had opened the gates of hell and swallowed the possessed beast.

Leon was able to halt Señorita a hairsbreadth from stomping on the limp, yet awake mangled body lying in a pool of blood. He jumped off Señorita before she could settle entirely, and anxiously examined the horrific prospect of a person struggling to breathe. At least she was breathing. Or was it a young boy? Hard to tell.

The facial features were disfigured with deep cuts, bruises, and blood smeared with dirt. The clothing was reminiscent of the Turkish attire he had seen on some merchants in the streets of Padua. The figure was slim, but the curved lines of hips were visible through the damp muslin. Then, the obvious jumped at him, a detail he purposely averted his sight from when assessing the immediate danger of his new patient. Under her blood soaked tunic, the mound of her round breasts was hard to ignore.

Leon quickly took his coat off and covered her to keep her warm. The issue of her nudity did not faze him. He had seen his share of naked women professionally and privately. She moaned in pain. The initial weight of the coat over her broken body was seemingly unbearable. That was the least of his concerns.

By the looks of her, if she survived the next forty-eight hours she would have to get accustomed to pain. Her battered state would not withstand her body temperature to drop any further. His priority was to keep her warm.

The young woman tried opening her swollen eyes to identify her companion. Leon bowed his head briefly at her, closed his eyes and gently explored the damage to her body with his fingertips. The deepest of the cuts would require stitches. He counted three broken ribs and a broken fibula. Luckily the bones on face, neck, and head were intact, but the odd angle in which her body lay indicated dislocated hips.

By the way her breaths were coming in short desperate gasps it was obvious that her pain was intensifying. The hips were probably the first area he should attend to in order to lessen her agony. He hoped she would sink into unconsciousness to make her transporting easier.

She squirmed in pain, but looked alert, and could hear him most likely. He murmured some gallant reassuring words and pulled her hips back into place with a decisive yank. Her bones popped and crunched. She screamed the last of her strength, piercing his eardrums, giving Señorita a jolt.

After her painful outburst, she vomited, and slipped into a state of unconsciousness. Good. He could do without a screaming patient while he tried to improvise, with whatever rudimentary resources he had, to attend to the most dangerous injuries. He was highly concerned about the ribs. Under the pouring rain, his vision faltered and he could not fully assess the extent of the breakage. The wrong move could send one of the crushed sharp bones plunging into her lungs or heart. Life and death. He had chosen this path. "Bear it," he muttered to himself.

As he stripped off her tunic, he was sure to find an undergarment of sturdy structure he could use to bandage tightly around her ribs. He was wrong. Whoever this lady was, she did not bother with such accessories. She wore a wide silk strap instead, tightly secured from her nape, coming down to her chest in a criss-cross fashion, keeping her breasts firmly in place. All right. He would work with both the tunic and the strap. He carefully lifted her arms to fasten the fabrics around her torso. He felt sorry for the young woman. The sight of her fragile body was pitiful. Once more he lifted his heavy coat from her to survey his next move. The fibula would have to be strapped for now.

Later, in a dry place and with proper tools he would splint the broken bone, extend it, and adjust it. Leon removed his shirt, his only remaining piece of linen strong enough to secure a makeshift bandage. The leg was slowly becoming morbidly blue and horribly swollen. Hopefully, the break was a clean one and there would be no need for an incision where he would have to insert a fir branch into the cavity of the bone marrow. The procedure was extreme and the threat of infection was high. In most cases, doctors resorted to amputation against risking patients' lives to such dangerous measures. He hoped he wouldn't have to go that far.

Satisfied with the temporary dressings, the subject of transportation was next in his mind. He reached into his saddlebags and retrieved some of the shirts he had stashed in there. He would have to hold her as immobile as possible on their way to Casa Di Laurenti. The slightest jolt could signify her death if a broken rib would inadvertently pierce her heart. He lifted the young lady, careful not to move her too much. His hands became soaked with blood and sticky as soon as they made contact with her skin. Her back was skinned, as he had expected, due to the violent dragging she suffered on the rough terrain. He pressed his lips on her battered forehead, closed his eyes, and cried out looking up to the darkening skies, "*Shmah Israel Adonai Eloheinu, Adonai echad*. Please, help me mend this broken body back to health. Please, give her strength to survive the ordeal ahead of her." With the utmost care, Leon strapped his patient to his chest with the few shirts at hand.

With the prayer still fresh in his mind, and the shallow breathing of the ailing young woman flowing around him, he mounted Señorita. His clever mare took the cue and they rode away slowly.

****

Sara felt the odd, yet liberating sensation of being sucked into a vortex. It was an endless fall, except she was not scared. Her body bore no weight or pain. It was good and she welcomed it. She didn't mind falling endlessly. Suddenly a voice suspended her in mid-air. Was it the voice of a little girl?

Like an angel, arms spread wide, Sara turned. Yes, it was a little girl. She was standing at the end of a dark passage. A faint light shining over the child allowed Sara to see the girl's wild curls framing her innocent face.

"Come play with me," the girl called out as she disappeared into the retreating light.

Chapter Nineteen
Maria

"Where could this blasted brat be?" Maria paced up and down the top balcony of the Di Laurentis' manor from where she had the view of the whole valley. Of all the glorious days they were accustomed to enjoy in Onuba, today was the exception. The torrential rain came down in thundering sheets obscuring the otherwise clear view. When home, Camila and Massimo enjoyed the privacy of their balcony, from where they could see everything and not be seen. When the nights were warm they loved sleeping under the stars. It was a little piece of heaven that always brought them back to the cornerstone of their love affair.

They had left on a trip together the week before on what was to be their longest absence since the birth of their daughters. Up until then, Camila never felt safe leaving Sara behind in the house to venture away with Massimo. Especially since the child with the most common sense of the two, Paola, was married and living happily in Portugal. They had planned this trip for a long time. Massimo wanted to take his wife to the Orient. He had his mind set on acquiring some of the most legendary silk houses in China, responsible for crafting a number of highly original silk tapestries, exclusive to the artistry of the Ming Dynasty. It was a milestone he wanted to achieve with Camila by his side.

The voyage was to be an adventure, the Silk Road, as merchants called it, would take them through Africa,

India, and ultimately China. Under the starry nights of Onuba, they had dreamed of living their own *One Thousand and One Nights*. It was one of Massimo's favorite private entertainments with Camila, where she impersonated the sensual Scheherazade, and he the tyrant King Shahryar. Massimo had confided in Maria some of the details he had been working on for the year long trip and she had helped him with some of his ideas. The planning of such journey had taken Massimo over a decade, which gave him sufficient time to build two small palaces for their stay, one in the Sultanate of Adal in Africa, and the other in Jaisalmer India, a secret gift to his queen.

Since the birth of the girls, Massimo had to exercise a skill he was not aware he possessed—patience. He developed said trait earnestly but lost it all together when the girls became old enough to be left at the manor under the care of the little army of trusted servants working for them.

Even though Maria was not Camila's blood relative, their bond was tight as that of sisters. Maria had entered a convent in Toledo at the ripe age of four after the death of her mother. It was there she met Camila.

Ten years her senior, Camila was said to be the daughter of one of the artists who secretly crafted paintings in the convent, hidden beneath the veil of a common nun, and signing her masterpieces under a male nom de plume. The rumor was never confirmed nor did she ever ask about its truth.

Two years after Maria's arrival, Camila disappeared from the convent, stunning the little orphan with the sudden abandonment. Word amongst the other girls and some of the naughtiest of the nuns, was that Camila was of noble birth and her grandfather finally claimed her as his own. Maria never asked about that story either.

A heavy bag of coins was deposited on Mother Ignacia's wooden desk—the prioress at the convent—a year after Camila's sudden departure. The convent's new benefactor, Massimo Di Laurenti, demanded two conditions before allowing the prioress to assess how much the precious bag was worth. First, he wanted to keep his donation anonymous, and second, he requested the release of the orphan Maria into his care.

From that day on, Maria grew up as a Di Laurenti. She became fiercely protective of her new family, and before reaching the age of twelve, she displayed a marvelous ability for leadership and multitasking. The task of running the estate became her passion. Nobody moved a finger within the Di Laurenti grounds without her scrutinizing the consequences of such a move beforehand. Even Massimo and Camila went to her for advice when matters of the manor were concerned.

She kept a detailed account of the household provisions and valuables, and had a team of trusted domestics kept on a tight leash, who assigned the different duties to the various servants. Maria made a perfect administrator because everything she did, she did out of love. The Di Laurentis were all the family she ever knew. If necessary at any point in time, Maria would give her life's blood for them.

Amongst the three reigning adults of the house, they had discussed long and hard about what the next year would bring, especially concerning Sara. Maria was of the opinion that Sara should be married before Massimo and Camila's departure. Even though Paola's marriage had been an arranged union, the couple fell in love from the moment they met. It was meant to be, and all three, Massimo, Camila, and Maria, sighed in relief when they witnessed the jolts of excitement Paola experienced on every occasion her beloved called on her. But Sara was no Paola, and the chances of her falling in love at first sight with an appointed suitor were a remote possibility.

At one point they had even entertained the idea of sending Sara and Maria to stay with Paola in Portugal. As expected, Sara put up a most articulate argument stating that she was a grown woman with a life of her own. She declared her parents free to roam the world as they pleased while she was free to explore hers without having to be added to her sister's nursery like a foster child. Maria for once stayed out of the argument. She could not leave the manor behind for a whole year. If absent, she feared the collapse of the painstaking enterprise started a decade before when she officially took on the running of Casa Di Laurenti. And, there was also the matter of Señor Jaime Moreno.

The final decision was to leave Sara and Maria in Onuba. Sara, always deep in her studies, was to dedicate herself to the new musical instrument Massimo had brought back to Spain after his latest visit to Italy, as well as expand her knowledge in languages.

There was another reason that kept Sara from leaving—her very first project. Most afternoons she got into the habit of riding to the bottom of El Carpio, a gathering point for beggars. Once there, after handing out coin sparsely, she rounded up the children and took care of their basic welfare, such as clothing and food, and made sure to find shelter at the local convent for the ones who didn't follow Sara home like a row of ducklings.

The sight of stray children wandering around the Di Laurenti grounds became normal. Assessing the situation, Massimo put a halt to it by donating a large sum to the local orphanage in order to accommodate the ever-growing orphan population. Sara still visited the children and asked her father to ship a second harpsichord to the orphanage so that she could enlighten the youngsters with the hidden language of music.

***

Another look at the steely skies increased Maria's worry. If Sara had gone out to El Carpio to lead stray children to the orphanage, she should have been back hours ago. The last Maria had seen of the girl that day, was in the morning when entering the sewing room. Maria had noticed she had that look on her face—a deep crease above the bridge of her nose, while she chewed her upper lip—and it was no good. Sara was up to something, Maria felt it in her guts as if she had borne the girl herself. "Well, not a girl anymore," she murmured while closing and opening her fists trying hard to ease the tension mounting in her body. At seventeen she should have already been married and with child. But, no, in the Di Laurenti world, Sara was still a girl.

As the day progressed without sightings of Sara, the stable lad finally confessed under fear of death, in between bawling and self-administered head butting on the dusty ground, about Sara's departure atop the chestnut demon.

Maria was confident of Sara's ability to handle a horse. "But that thing is not a horse," she had yelled out to the five men that made up the search party. Fear gripped her chest as she imagined the most horrible scenarios of her dear child lying lifeless by the side of the river. It was her fault. She had seen Sara's face that morning and did nothing to stop what she suspected to be trouble brewing.

Since leaving the convent at the age of six, over two decades before, Maria did not see the need to pray much. She saw her prayers answered when Camila and Massimo took her in. Was her faith being tested with Sara's disappearance? Or was she being punished because of her carnal knowledge of Jaime Moreno?

He had proposed marriage time and time again while entangled in her meaty thighs, to which she always answered with a soft flutter of lips upon his and a quick dismissal. She loved him dearly and yearned for his warm embrace every night. Still, she was not ready to give herself entirely to him. She had watched her mother die of a broken heart and that had been enough of a lesson for Maria not to commit to a lifelong relationship.

"Sara, *mi niña*, where are you?" In her muddled state of mind she was ready to swear to right her ways and consider Jaime's proposal. But who should she pray to? Jesus? Mary? God? Maria pleaded to all three during her improvised prayers, while keeping an anxious eye on the valley below.

She heard dragging hoof beats slogging through the mud and water before she could catch a glimpse of any shapes. Then, an ugly excuse for a horse broke through the curtain of rain and made its straining approach to the manor. A shirtless savage, with dark shoulder length hair stuck to his face, and a bundle strapped to him, was the commander of the ridiculous ride.

He dismounted the horse carefully and went down on his knees as in prayer. The man undid the layers of rags that held the bundle tight around him, revealing what seemed to be a person. With the body lying in his arms, he walked up to the entrance of the manor. Maria ran down the steps to the entryway of the house, shouting orders to the few men remaining on the property. "There's a stranger outside. He looks dangerous. Seize him."

Leon at once found himself surrounded by a circle of armed men. One by one the men put down their swords when they noticed who the stranger was holding.

"The Lady Sara," one of them whispered in a strangled voice. The men stood paralyzed at the sight of the youngest Di Laurenti.

Leon did not have time to deal with shocked men or the orders of their mistress. "I must tend to her or she dies. Let me by."

They cleared his path and the door to the house opened before any of them reached it. Maria held her breath for a moment when she laid eyes on Sara. No time for sorrow now, she had a task at hand that required her immediate attention.

"Follow me," she instructed Leon. With the back of her hand, she swept clean the long wooden dining table of candelabra and gold embossed runners.

Leon positioned Sara softly upon the smooth surface and started undressing her gently. The rain had soaked his improvised dressings and had helped keep them from sticking to her wounds. "Good," he said deep in concentration. She couldn't afford to lose any more skin.

Maria put a restraining hand on his, which Leon jerked away angrily. "Do you want her to die? I know what I'm doing." He removed one of the bandages. Maria gasped. Their eyes met and she nodded.

"Boiled water, clean dressings, comfrey, St. John's Wort, blankets," Maria ordered.

"Marigold," Leon added.

Supplies flowed in from what seemed a hundred helping hands. Leon was silently grateful for this small women's initiative. Maria stepped back and watched the stranger work with professional knowledge. By the looks of his ugly mount and his ragged state, he could easily be a barber surgeon doing his rounds in the valley, and perhaps her prayers had put him in Sara's path.

The nervous shifting of feet behind her and the soft murmurs of the men pulled her out of her thoughts. She suddenly noticed that Sara was openly exposed from head to toe to everybody in the room. Maria turned around and saw a row of stunned men white with fear at the painful sight of Sara. "Out!" she screamed. The men scuttled out of the house like arrows.

A ghost of a move came from Sara's mangled form accompanied by a cry of pain. Leon scowled at Maria and laid a reassuring hand on Sara's forehead. "Bear with me, I beg you."

He got a whimper in response.

He turned to Maria. "My saddlebag... there's a bottle of opium. I cannot allow her to suffer any more." Maria turned to leave but was stopped by the stranger's voice. "My horse," he added, "there are some dark figs in the saddlebag for her. She must be tired and cold." Maria assented with a quick nod and went out into the wet darkness.

After administering a few drops of opium into his patient's mouth, Leon kept his touch on the girl's forehead as if he could wipe away her pain. Her face, now clean, showed some of its original features. She had been a beautiful woman. *Had been and will be*, he would see that through. "I will fix you, I promise," he said softly to her sleeping form.

Hours later when Leon was done with his medical ministrations, he carefully moved Sara to a wooden pallet he requested from the woman Maria. Two men were called in and moved the pallet to Massimo's study which occupied the right wing on the manor's ground floor. Leon examined the layout of the study. A large room furnished with the latest trend in Italian architecture, a reminiscence of furniture and fine arts from ancient Rome. He moved a carved armchair next to the pallet and checked Sara's pulse for the hundredth time. Weak, but steady. He put his hand to her neck, abdomen, and feet. She was still cold. He covered her with a blanket he found stacked neatly at the foot of the pallet. It was going to be a long night, he was certain of it. He had done everything medically possible to help this young lady, all there was to do now was wait.

Even in a state of unconsciousness the choice of healing was entirely hers. Fevers would be fought in the following days. Wounds would eventually heal. Yet, the decision would be solely hers. He had seen patients too weak and too sick to survive, but they had a purpose in life that kept them from stepping through death's threshold. He hoped that this young woman had unfinished business in this life and would not succumb to the specter of death. *Fight*! he urged her in his mind. *Fight*!

A sudden wave of tiredness washed over him. He was cold, hungry, and wet. He had forgotten about his disheveled state until he met the inquisitive eyes of Maria, who was standing on the other side of the pallet, arms folded across her chest silently demanding an explanation. He looked like a criminal bent on mayhem. He regained some of his composure and although half naked he cleared his voice and bowed cordially in front of the horrified lady.

"Doctor Leon Fernandez. Pleased to make your acquaintance."

Chapter Twenty
The Pact

A blanket of smothering darkness surrounded Sara. It prevented her from following the light that was encircling the little girl she spotted at the end of the pathway.

The weightlessness she felt in her arms, that made them feel like angel wings, was replaced by the tightness of a shroud. Still, she felt no pain. *This must be death*, she thought. So much for the afterlife. Maybe she was to face a trial. An amusing idea. *Let's see, what do I have to repent for? Stubbornness? For sure. Vanity? Well... But if I am dead, last rites would have been given to me and I was surely absolved. Everybody is... no, not dead then*, she concluded.

The fog surrounding her was slowly dissipating, clearing the now visible path ahead of her. An open invitation. Temptation. Sara considered these possibilities before making herself free of any corporal restraints.

Wherever she was it was against her nature to sit still waiting for something to happen. She looked over her shoulder where thick darkness was accumulating. Not an appealing prospect. She looked the other way and spotted a golden glow beating rhythmically like a heartbeat. Was she at the crossroads of life and death?

Music. The chords of a finely tuned harpsichord interrupted her inner debate. She knew the melody. It was the one she had been composing on her new instrument. She followed the trail of music coming from the direction of the pulsating light.

Sara stopped feeling fearful for the first time since drifting into this unknown dimension. The light was shining invitingly in front of her. She slid her fingers through it and saw them disappear. She retrieved her hand and counted all five fingers making sure a demon had not devoured them on the other side. Her next move was more daring. She immersed half of her body into the light which now felt comfortably warm. Still whole, she took a step back.

The music kept playing, but there was a chord that was always struck wrong. It bothered her considerably. She had poured her soul out when composing this beautiful melody and somebody on the other side of the light was trying their best to destroy her masterpiece. Sara crossed over to the light.

The place she entered was bare of any of the architectural features she was accustomed to. The walls were plain, so was the floor.

The music kept playing. Following the intermittent glow, Sara found her way to the origin of the chords. A strange version of a harpsichord sat at the far corner of the room. With her little hands on the keys, the girl from the pathway sat with her eyes closed in abandonment as the resonance of the musical notes harmoniously blended together, until the impossible note she hit over and over again made her open her eyes.

"Angelina." Sara called her with certainty, but there was still a questioning tone in her voice.

Angelina did not startle at her presence. Instead she frowned. "I can't get this part right," she sulked in frustration. Angelina closed her eyes again playing the melody from the start. Sara slid on the bench next to the girl and placed her hands on hers. Both hands moved at unison along the keys. This time, the result was flawless. The girl smiled, pleased. "I already made my decision," Angelina announced. "Because of you I will stay."

Sara attempted to retrieve her hands from the keys but the girl held on to her tight. "You are what is left of me. If you leave me I will never exist."

Sara looked into Angelina's face and saw a younger version of herself staring back at her. The little girl nodded knowingly. Sara was aware of having been in this room many times in her dreams. What made her hesitate were not the choices ahead of her, but the dreams—events—that succeeded this one. Could she put this little one through what her life was about to become?

Sara cupped the youngster's face in her hands. "You have knowledge of what is about to happen as do I. We might not be aware of it when the fog surrounds us again, but we won't be surprised."

Angelina stared back at Sara with her huge brown eyes and nodded.

"We might not be able to change the outcome of events, but we will fight." A pang of fear gripped Sara's chest, yet the smiling girl before her gave her the courage she needed to go on.

"Do you understand what will happen if we follow the light?" Sara asked.

"We will cross it together," the little girl said with a maturity beyond her years. "Now, play with me."

Sara's hands caressed Angelina's, and the beautiful melody they played brightened the pulsating glow of life.

Chapter Twenty-One
Rebirth

The fever lasted seven days and seven nights. Although slowly healing, Sara's wounds infected easily due to her weakness. Added to that, the pain cause by her many injuries worked against her recovery. She floated in and out of consciousness, and Leon's efforts to pour some nourishing broth down her throat were met with choking and vomiting.

The dreadful fever was on its seventh consecutive day, leaving behind a ghastly picture of blistered skin too close to the bones. Leon pried Sara's eyelids open one by one. Her eyes were yellowing. He proceeded to check for her pulse with the tips of his finger around her collarbone, armpits, and groin. He knew the discouraging diagnosis before he rearranged the covers neatly back around Sara. Her body was slowly dying.

Leon shook his head, overcome with concern. He feared for her recovery for the first time since his arrival at the manor. Maria, who had stationed herself on the other side of the pallet, stood up alarmed and reached for Sara's hand.

"I don't know how much longer she'll be able to last without any food... or water." His words trailed off while he contemplated Maria steadily. "She is dying," he blurted out.

Maria sat back down. Then got back up. Her throat was dry, and she was scared of opening her mouth because nothing but a deep wail would come bursting forth. She had to get busy. Take action. That was all she was good at. Maria inhaled until her lungs had enough air to keep her through her next moves.

Maria's hands worked busily around Sara's hair and encircled her gaunt face with her beautiful, lustrous mane. Next, she opened a bottle of lavender oil and began to massage Sara's hands, her bare shoulders, and her sunken stomach.

Sara had been a fussy baby, and at day's end everybody in the Di Laurenti household was exhausted after the grueling job of tending to a screaming baby. On one occasion when all attempts to calm the howling little creature, who tussled violently under the many layers of silk covers, failed, Maria took the baby from Camila's arms and intoned a lullaby she had embedded in her mind.

She could count with the fingers of one hand the partial memories she had from her mother, but the lullaby stayed with her always bringing her comfort. The lullaby worked its magic, slumbering the baby into a peaceful rest. A silence gratefully welcomed by every inhabitant in Casa Di Laurenti.

The knot gripping Maria's voice would not allow her to sing to Sara the way she did so many years ago, so instead she hummed.

The tune Maria hummed brought words to Leon's lips as soon as he heard it.

"*Durme durme, mi alma donzella Durme durme,sin ansia y dolor.*

Que tu 'sclavo que tanto desea ver tu suenyo con grande amor.

Hay dos anyos que sufre mi alma por ti joya, mi linda dama."

Had he not heard this lullaby countless times before falling asleep while his mother tucked him and his sister in bed?

When singing only to him the words shifted from *donzella* to *itzico de madre. Sleep, sleep my beautiful son.* Her sweet chant would appease him before falling into a tender dream sealed by the last words of the lullaby, *con her hermosura de Shma Yisrael*, with the beauty of God.

Why would a maid at the Di Laurenti household sing a Ladino lullaby sung by most of the *Marrano* mothers across the Iberian Peninsula?

The sense of peace the lullaby brought to Maria unnerved him. He could not allow himself to sit back and let his young patient fall any deeper. He didn't want her to feel comfort. He wanted her to feel pain and scream from it. It was the only way for him to know she was still fighting.

"Stop!" he yelled. Maria froze. Her oily hands suspended in the air imploring for answers. He lifted Sara off the pallet and ran out of the room with her. She was weightless, yet the feel of her body ached in Leon's arms. He had never lost a patient before. His professors at the University of Padua as well as in the Yeshiva taught him about God's will. "Pray, Leon, always. Pray for the Almighty to be with you every step of the way. And when the sick and the suffering leave this world welcome it as His will, not your failure."

He couldn't reconcile the will of a God with the loss of a seventeen-year-old life. No, he would not. It was not God's will. It was his own failure. Leon had to show God the face of the young woman he was about to deprive of life. He would not pray. He would demand.

With Sara in his arms, he strode through the house, and propelled by fury he went out into the starry night. The air was cool, a yellow moon hung suspended in the dark sky. A silent witness to his furious rant.

Leon knelt on the ground and peeled off all the garments that covered Sara. Her body was fevered and he felt her skin burning his fingers. "Is this what you brought me back for? Is this why you drove me to her path?" he screamed to the empty space. "To witness death? To see life slipping out of my hands unjustly? Tell me! Tell me! Tell me what to do! Tell me how to fix her!" Leon's voice turned hoarse from screaming.

He held Sara to his chest protectively and raised one fist up in the air. "I will fight you for this one like I've never fought before. Do you hear me? You will not have her."

Leon remained holding Sara to his body, on the spot where he dared defy God, all through the night under a glimmering sky. He did not know if God was watching. He did not know if there was a God. But if there was one, he wanted him to know that he was watching him too.

Maria stood in the foyer watching, she did not have the nerve to intrude on Leon. She had not talked much to him save for the basic necessities to care for Sara, still if any of her prayers had been heard when Sara was missing, Leon Fernandez was what she got in return. She didn't know him, nonetheless she trusted him. Maria's legs buckled under her while she kept watch from a distance waiting for the fate of a woman and a man to be decided.

Sara felt cold all of a sudden. She also felt pain, lots of it. Her eyelids fluttered in an attempt to open them. They felt so heavy. Perhaps she didn't have to open them fully. Through slits she surveyed her whereabouts. That damned horse! How long had it been since he ran spooked as if possessed? The rain must be over because she was only cold, not wet. How long had she been lying here? she wondered again. She turned her head away from a solid form that kept her confined. Was she lying outside of her home at dawn? Odd. Awfully odd. Her eyes travelled down her body. There were some dressings covering parts of her arms and legs, and she was… naked. She was naked! Her head suddenly swiveled to the trunk supporting her. No, no, not a trunk. The limbs enfolding her were warm, she could detect the beat of a heart. It was the torso of a man that held her naked in his arms. If her arms did not hurt so much she would have pushed him away from her. She was experiencing the same problem with her legs. She could not run away from him. The man was dressed. Thank the heavens for that. *There is still a possibility that part of my dignity will remain intact,* she pondered. Except that if he wanted to have his way with her all he needed was a little outlet to let his, his … Oh no! Her eyes flew open.

His hold of her was firm yet gentle. She looked at his face. His eyes were blue, deep blue. He was not looking at her. He was intent on a spot in the sky as though waiting for something. His roman nose gave him an air of rough determination, as well as the thick dark hair that fell on his burly shoulders.

How could anybody from her household let this happen? Maybe they were all dead. It had to be. He killed them all. He killed Maria. Her heart sank at the dreadful conclusion. She was at the mercy of this beast. She was all on her own.

Whatever had happened there was nothing she could physically do at that moment to fight him. Her mouth felt dry, pasty. Her throat ached. She was thirsty. She needed water, now!

"Water," Sara mumbled. Her captor did not stir at her request. "Water, I want water," she croaked with as much strength as she could gather. How could she make herself heard? The man's attention was miles away from her. She considered several options, which included all sorts of physical maneuvering she was not able to perform. That infuriated her further, added to the fact of lying naked in the arms of a savage who may have killed everybody in the Di Laurentis' lands.

There must be something she could do. She tested her fingers. One by one she lifted them and then closed them into fists. She could feel her knuckles standing up.

Strong enough, she concluded as she mentally measured the proximity of her right hand to the groin of this murderer.

On several occasions when Sara had helped in the kitchen preparing meals for the orphans waiting at the foot of the El Carpio, her sexual curiosity was quenched by bawdy talks amongst some of the kitchen maids. Their stories were hilarious and caused Sara to blush at times.

Elmede, a heavyset Livonian maid, with a rough accent but the sweetest of smiles, recounted the time when she made her flirty husband pay for his infidelity. He had knelt filled with regret and tears as she crushed his balls in one hand while holding a butcher knife with the other, until he swore never to lie with another woman again. After vulgar comments and loads of banter, they had all agreed that Elmede's rough method also served as an excellent defense move in the event of rape.

Sara had stored that piece of information, and now was the time to put it to use. Careful to not wake him from the apparent stupor he was in, she inched her right hand between the man's upper thighs. Her eyes followed the slow advance of her fingers until she reached the designated bulge. She had never seen, and least of all touched, a man's private part, but right now it was not the time to be shy about it. After all, her long exposure to horses taught her to view a penis objectively as a merely reproductive organ.

You will regret the moment you stuck yours in me— the words burned in her silent mouth. Her hatred for him was inflamed at the thought of being ravished by the murderer of her household. She inhaled, gathering whatever strength was at her disposal, and grasped his bulge with all her might.

Leon jerked and held onto Sara tighter. The blue of his eyes pierced deeply into her vengeful stare. "Bitch!" he yelled. "Let go."

Sara smiled for the first time in eight days. "As soon as you take your filthy hands off me, you rutting bastard. And fetch me water while you are at it, I'm thirsty," she replied with an unwavering whisper.

Leon reached for her clutching grasp, kissed her hand and laughed out loud. He got up on his feet, held her tight to his chest, and screamed louder than ever. "She wants water. Water. She wants water."

Maria took off running from the spot she kept vigil the whole night to where Leon was twirling round and round, holding Sara as if she were a precious offering. Her muscles were stiff and sore and she fell once on her way, but scrambled to her feet not minding her scraped palms. Maria embraced them both, and broke down crying. Sara could not be more confused. Didn't anybody notice she was naked? What about the dressings and bruises?

"Bring water, fresh water," Leon asked Maria. Maria made her way to a nearby well and brought back a bucket of cool, crystalline water.

Leon sat back down and pressed a clay mug to Sara's cracked lips, feeding her short sips of water which she swallowed desperately. Her aching hands took hold of the mug when Leon pulled it away from her. "You'll get sick if you drink it all at once," he explained.

Unusual knowledge for a rapist and murderer… She then glanced at Maria who was kneeling next to them allowing this man to touch her. Nothing made sense. It was time to get a detailed account as to why she lay naked and horribly battered in the arms of a man who smiled at her stupidly while Maria cried.

"You better have a good explanation for not being dead," she mumbled as she struggled to keep her eyes open.

Maria opened and closed her mouth like a gaping fish, unable to voice any coherent words. Instead she chose to laugh heartily for the first time in a week.

Chapter Twenty-Two
The Missing Rib

Sara's waking moments became more frequent as days went by. The fever had receded significantly, still not entirely, due largely to the forceful feeding at the hands of the hefty Elmede.

The decision to have Elmede care for Sara took place in the kitchen when Maria walked in one morning bathed in soup from head to toe. Elmede clicked her tongue between her tiny front teeth and announced without being asked, "I take care of the girl."

Maria's attempts to tend to Sara were answered with indifference at times, foul language for the most part, and the occasional thrown object by the ailing patient. Still, Maria insisted on popping into the room at least five times a day at her own risk.

Leon stood in the hallway outside of the room when he saw Maria barely escaping the latest of Sara's attacks. As soon as the door closed a porcelain ewer hit it, crashing into pieces before falling on the floor. Leon raised his eyebrows. "She shouldn't have anything within her reach, we agreed on that."

Maria shrugged. "Jasmines are her favorite. I want to see her happy. I am to blame for what happened to her."

Leon held his hand up putting a stop to Maria's endless guilt. "Your little lady in there manipulated the young groom with her charms in order to ride that demon horse. Do you know that the poor lad preferred decapitation instead of admitting to you what went on at the stables?"

Maria gasped. "Is he... was he?"

"No, of course not," Leon replied sharply. "He is whole and taking care of my Señorita. A good lad he is." Leon was seething with anger. He pointed at Sara's closed door accusingly. "Your young lady is the only one responsible for what happened to her and I will inform her of that shortly." Leon put a hand on the doorknob and Maria pulled him back.

"What?!" His temper rose.

"There's a second ewer with jasmines on her nightstand," Maria replied sheepishly. Leon pushed the door open and closed it behind him with a firm thud.

Sara's complexion had improved in the seven days since she mumbled her first words to Leon. Her cheeks were regaining some color and her eyes had lost the yellowish cast, an indication of the proper function of her internal organs. She was painfully thin, a fact Leon was not overly concerned about because Elmede, the maid in charge of her daily feeding, was tougher than Sara, and that was a mere understatement.

"It is obvious you are regaining some of your strength." Leon smiled warily. The collection of broken artifacts at his feet was a testament of her improving aim and strength, a result of his ministrations.

Sara was plumped up on a sea of plush feather pillows which seemed to swallow her fragile frame. Her eyes had opened instantly at the sound of the door. The sight of Leon annoyed her. She hated him. She hated his blue burning stare, his strong build, and his perfectly polished bedside manners. She had forbidden him from examining her, a matter he had dismissed completely, and he went about his business like the infuriating professional he was.

Her tibia fracture was healing beautifully and no further signs of infection had manifested in the past forty-eight hours. "The fever should ebb shortly," Leon informed her. Sara replied by glancing intently at the wall in front of her.

Since she became conscious, Leon had not been able to examine her back. The skin had been raw the last time he conducted a full checkup and he feared the possibility of permanent ugly scars, should she not let him attend to the nastiest of abscesses.

He moved towards the bed and proceeded to lift the covers off Sara. Aware of wearing nothing but a few dressings over her wounds, she held onto the sheets and pulled them all the way up to her chin. The open wounds on her back were still oozing, she felt the heat emanating from them. They were surely painful and she could not bear any further pain. She would not let him touch her.

"I am a physician, my lady. I have the duty to examine you." Before she could muster a cruel response he added quickly, "Furthermore, I am pretty acquainted with the human body and I am definitely," he remarked matter-of-factly with a hint of a grin, "not unfamiliar with yours."

Leon's last words and his intended mockery made Sara see red. Her hands which had clutched the sheets so fiercely to cover her nudity, now moved swiftly to the nightstand, and took possession of the last of the water-filled porcelain ewers with floating jasmines Maria left only minutes before. Leon had foreseen her intentions, and seized the opportunity to jump on the bed on all fours and restrain her, when she turned on her side.

Sara struggled, with the ewer in hand, to lie back down. His firm grasp on her shoulders made it impossible and he was hurting her. "Let go of me, you beast," she yelled at the top of her lungs.

"I will if you allow me to examine your back." He kept his tone under tight rein.

"You will never lay another hand on me while I live." Sara struggled against him, reluctant to let the ewer fall on the floor. Her strength gave out under the strength of the physician.

Leon pinned her flat on the mattress. He felt the rolling tremble of tears rise up her chest. He had gone too far and he was sorry. But she was impossible. Even from her sickbed, the house leapt at her demands. Still, it was neither appropriate nor his job to put her in her place. His frustration increased at the notion of being barred from doing what he knew best. It might be too late to cure the wounds her back suffered during the long haul across the rocky forest. His hands slacked on her shoulders, yet she didn't move.

"It hurts. You hurt me." She stifled a sob. "I want Doctor Zaragoza. I want you gone."

Leon got off the bed and stood back. "Doctor Zaragoza, he is, he is not..." Leon sighed. "He died last week."

The porcelain ewer shattered as it fell to the floor. Sara closed her eyes and let her hands lay limp.

She was right. He was a beast, but somebody had to tell her about Zaragoza. The old man had been the Di Laurenti's chief physician since before Paola and Sara were born. He was old then, and his time had run out days after Sara's accident. Leon did not know what else to do or say. He slowly retreated to the door. "I will ride to the city tomorrow at first light to find you a suitable physician. You need not worry about me hurting you anymore. I will be leaving your residence shortly."

He got a shaky hiss in response which he acknowledged as a sign of relief from his patient. "I apologize for any harm I may have caused you, Lady Di Laurenti." With those last words he opened the door not realizing the conversation was only starting.

"You will be going to the city in search of another man to see me fully exposed? Don't you think I went through enough humiliation with you?"

Leon, stunned, turned to look at Sara. "I have no personal interest in you, Lady Di Laurenti, other than that of a physician. I am certain that any other respectable physician will share my same interests."

Sara struggled to lift herself up on one elbow. She had to look at that conceited Dr. Fernandez in the eye. Who did he think he was?

The covers slid off her torso revealing what Leon had feared the most. The scrapes on her back from shoulder blade to shoulder blade, oozed sticky yellow pus from their angry red tracks. The rest of the skin on her back showed signs of healthy regeneration. But it would not be long before the healthy tissue would be compromised by the spreading sepsis.

His reply to her taunting died on his lips, replaced by deep medical concern. Leon could not imagine the unbearable pain she was under. He had never sustained an injury more serious than scrapes and bruises resulting from mischief as a child. What Sara bore on her back had to feel like being stabbed with thousands of blades.

He closed the door softly and walked back to the bed. This time he faced her. "I will take my leave tomorrow morning as I said before, but for now I must take care of your wounds—that is—if you allow me to do so."

She could not look at him for fear of breaking down. She would not give him the pleasure of seeing her reduced even further. On the other hand it was time for her to drop the act. She was well aware of the monster tormenting the flesh on her back, and the pain was such that it did not allow her to breathe other than in short gasps.

She finally relaxed on the mattress, her arms spread wide. There he had it. The whole of her ravaged back to work on. Leon took this as a sign of surrender.

A burning hearth was at the far end of the room where a cauldron held boiling water. Leon scooped out three cupfuls of water and poured them into a smaller pot, in which he dropped some garlic cloves, marigold, and witch hazel. He immersed a number of clean dressings in the pot and walked back to Sara's bedside.   In complete silence he reached for his surgical box and chose a tiny scalpel. The sight of the sharp blade made Sara cringe and bunch the corners of the bed covers in her hands. "I will give you opium," Leon said.

"No," was her reply.

Leon nodded in compliance and went about his business. The first steaming piece of cloth on Sara's skin made her wail. Leon's hands were firm. His jaw tensed at her pain, but he stayed focused on the matter at hand trying to justify the excruciating agony he would put her through in the name of saving her life. First he had to soften the inflamed scar tissue with the warm solution to be able to cut into the affected area and drain out the pus. There was a strong possibility of finding rotten flesh that would have to be cut out. He would only be able to tell once the infected area was fully open to his viewing. He hated to do this to a patient that refused to be asleep. He pressed a second dressing on Sara's back and got the same response as the first time.

Her hands were digging into the mattress and she had stuffed the corner of a pillow in her mouth. Her face was damp with sweat and tears, yet she shook her head when Leon uncorked the bottle of opium.

During the long procedure, Leon stopped a few times when Sara vomited or fought to catch her breath. Every time he wiped her face with fresh water and allowed her enough time to gather strength to go on. At one point she reached for his hand and dug her nails into his palm until he bled.

By the time Leon was done cleaning up her wounds, they were both exhausted. The place where Sara's face lay on the bed was damp and smeared with mucus. Leon's shirt was drenched with sweat and his face contorted in pain. Unfortunately, he'd had to cut out a small portion of her flesh. He was hopeful that a part of it would regenerate. If there was to be a scar, it would be an indentation under her right shoulder blade which could be shadowed by the bone.

Face down on the bed, Sara gave out to exhaustion and fell asleep. He heard her steady breathing. A sign of the pain subsiding. Only then did Leon slump down on the floor inches away from Sara and close his eyes.

"Damn, damn woman," he cursed under his breath. "With a hell of a courage." He smiled to himself before dozing off.

The house was dead asleep when Leon opened his eyes. He felt the effects of the stressful evening in every one of his muscles, topped off with a sore neck from leaning sideways on the side of the bed. It had grown colder overnight and his first thought was of Sara lying covered from her waist down. The last thing she needed— or for that matter, he needed—was to catch a chill. He forgot to light candles before falling asleep. Not even the fearless Elmede had enough guts to walk into Sara's room after hearing the loud screams mixed with foul words in Spanish, Italian, and French, coming from the lady as well as the doctor. As a result, the room was left in complete darkness.

Leon got to his feet. Amid shadows he felt for the shape of Sara on the bed. Instead, his hands encountered bunched bed sheets, covers, and pillows, but no Sara. His senses, only just awakening, noticed the door to the room ajar and a distant melody flowing through the opening.

She could not have gone too far, not with her weakened state, and a splint strapped to her leg. Once more he found himself amazed at the oddity of this woman. How could she slip out of the room without him noticing it? He did not blame her. She had been held prisoner to painful doctoring from the moment she fell off her horse. He too would have liked to be left alone away from prodding hands. To find solace.

Leon decided against taking a candle with him, and moved silently through the manor. His eyes grew accustomed to the darkness as he was drawn by the melody coming from the far end of the house.

***

Sara had managed to slip into a thin silk shift and had made her way to the music room half leaning against walls and half dragging her body down the stairs.

She had seriously considered giving up on her way down to the music room, where her instrument was left untouched since the morning of her accident. Despite her bodily pain, there was an inexplicable urge inside of her that could only be tamed by the keys of the harpsichord.

When she awoke in her room shivering from cold, she had found her fingers entwined with those of Dr. Fernandez. He had fallen asleep at the side of her bed that night. She was well aware that all the other nights he slept outside of her bedroom on the floor by the door—rushing to her side every time he heard her moaning in pain.

During Maria's attempts to comfort Sara, she had related to her the events leading up to Dr. Leon Fernandez becoming her physician.

"The man saved your life and you should be grateful," Maria said before dodging one of two ewers she brought that morning to brighten up Sara's spirits.

Sara was furious at herself. She had become the victim of her negligence, and a *caballero* with scalpel in hand came to her rescue. She was done being rescued and she was done being spoiled.

He had seemed unaffected by her pain until that evening. Her insane decision not to take any opium to numb the butchery she went through had a motive. She intended to make him feel what she felt. Not her physical pain—no, that was a curse she did not wish upon her worst enemy. She wanted him to see through her anger for what she had done to herself and to those around her. She felt helpless, exposed. It was not her outer nakedness that upset her. It was the loss of self-control when at the mercy of others.

All she wanted was for him to drop the act and show a sign of empathy. Everything about this man was perfectly structured, measured. Even when she insulted him he never seemed to lose his temper, and she wanted someone to yell at her, to stop protecting her.

The morning of her accident she came to the conclusion of what her life was made up of—a fantasy world crafted by her parents, designed to shield her from the world. Sara was sick of living a lie, she was done living a meaningless life. That same morning, before she was reduced to a scrap of useless broken bones and a mass of bruises, she vowed to find the truth behind all the unanswered questions she had compiled throughout the years. The first place would be with her name... Sara.

Then, the unthinkable happened and she stared death in the face. Was she being warned from unveiling something that should be kept hidden? Or was her strength being challenged to see how hard she was willing to fight to escape the pedestal her parents had placed her on?

All those thoughts chased her during each one of her wakeful hours since the accident. When pain roused her not one hour ago, she pushed them aside. At that moment the only thing that mattered to her was her music. When she sat at the harpsichord she felt every note resonating inside the wooden chamber. With each plucking of the strings, she watched a new chapter of her life unfold. When she closed her eyes the vision of that unruly little girl came back to her again.

Things seemed so clear in that bare room. Next to Angelina her life was worth living. The girl showed her a purpose. Angelina's life depended on Sara's. After the brief encounter with the girl, she understood that without her, the future would fade into a blinding light.

***

Leon stood outside the music room. The flickering of a single candle danced atop the harpsichord. He allowed the sweet melody Sara played to calm his racing heart. There, shadowed by the light of the candle, she was beautiful. Damn woman. She got his heart and he was lost to her forever.

Sara rested her fingers on the keys and stared at the candle flame, unblinking.

"Stay," she said to the light, to the empty silence, to Leon.

He walked into the room and lifted her in his arms. "As long as you want me to," he replied as she rested her head in the hollow of his collarbone.

Chapter Twenty-Three
It All Starts from the Beginning

Leon kept his distance from Sara during the following days. He tended to her wounds, which were improving daily, and made sure she got some sun and fresh air to encourage her appetite.

What went on between them in the music room, Leon convinced himself, had been the result of the bewitching melody Sara played. Its magic led to that single private moment they shared away from their worldly burdens. A world without obligations, without resentment, only populated with the language of golden candlelight and music. It had been an accidental lapse, it would never happen again. He was determined to stick to his original plan of remaining unattached to a woman, and that included Sara Di Laurenti. Soon, he would be departing the Di Laurentis to report to the Marquis of Alazar and establish himself in Cordoba.

Regardless of his resolve, he found it difficult to be close to her without wanting to be more in her life than her provisional physician. Reason enough to leave as soon as he could.

Sara made nightly visits to the music room after that first night Leon found her playing the harpsichord. He cursed himself for it, but he could not stop from hiding like a fugitive behind a stone column every night. He watched her in awe, stealing any piece of her he could from every melody she composed.

She probably knew of his silent companionship. They never talked about it or about anything else. She answered his questions regarding her welfare with monosyllables and he acknowledged them with nods. Their relationship reverted to one of physician and patient, underlined by restrained feelings buried under a fragile veneer.

The day before Leon was to depart from the Di Laurentis he removed Sara's splint. Although the bone had healed completely it would take several months for her to regain the full strength of her leg. Elmede and Maria were present in the room, while Leon showed all three of them the different exercises Sara would have to do on a daily basis in order to recover the use of the leg and avoid a permanent limp.

With the help of Elmede and Maria, Sara stood up for the first time in almost two months. She leaned heavily on both of them, nervous to stand on her own. She had to take a step. The first of many that would free her from the restraining chains of her privileged life. She squeezed Elmede's hand, and then turned to her. She loved that rough woman. She had always been kind to Sara especially during her convalescence.

"Thank you, Elmede," Sara said with a warm smile, "I will do this on my own. You shall return to your friends in the kitchen. I have no doubt they could not go another day without your amusing stories."

Elmede hesitated, but Sara responded with an encouraging smile. "I will walk to the kitchen to visit you." Teary eyed, Elmede bowed quickly, a comical gesture for such a large woman, and left the room.

Maria still held Sara tightly. "You can let go now, Maria. It's time." Leon nodded and Maria took a step back.

Sara placed the whole weight of her body on her left leg and slowly balanced onto both. She was sure to fall flat on her face. The two persons that were waiting expectantly for her to take her first step, as if she were a baby, had witnessed more embarrassing things from her than a tumble and a fall. So if falling flat on her face was the next thing they would have to witness, so be it.

Her first step was shaky. The right leg, immobilized for the past two months, felt weightless and hard to control. She could hear both Maria and Leon holding their breath as her second step almost sent her flying against a solid oak armoire. Sara stabilized herself holding onto the heavy brass handles protruding from the armoire's doors and proceeded toward her third step which was more stable and less wobbly.

Sara stood victoriously in front of her small audience and addressed Leon formally. "I was informed that you would be leaving us today."

Leon's demeanor and tone was no less formal than hers, although his eyes never left hers. "As soon as my luggage is loaded, Lady Di Laurenti."

Sara's leg throbbed. She wished she could sit down and rub the spot where her ankle met her foot. She would endure a few more minutes, and then, after he took his leave, she would be able to relax. "Very well, Doctor Fernandez, I gave orders at the stables to have Cid saddled for your departure." Sara nodded towards Maria. "Mistress Maria will pay you for your services rendered in the past two months."

Leon smiled feebly. He gave her a short bow and caught her in his sapphire blue stare. "Your kind hospitality was more than I could ever ask for. It is my duty as a physician to see you well. Your full recovery is all the payment I request for my humble services to you."

She couldn't peel her eyes from his. He must leave immediately. Another day under the same roof would surely bring disastrous consequences which they would both regret for years to come. "Thank you, Doctor Fernandez." She nodded candidly. "I will never forget what you've done for me. You will always be welcome as a guest of honor in our home."

Keeping his eyes on Sara's, Leon walked to her, took hold of her hand and brushed it with a soft kiss. "Until we meet again, Sara Di Laurenti."

Sara remained speechless as he bowed cordially to Maria and left the room.

"You can sit now." Maria scowled at Sara helping her to the closest chair.

Maria watched as Sara limped laboriously to the chair sitting down hard with exhaustion. "Are you done acting like Cleopatra?" Maria bent at Sara's feet and gently massaged the afflicted leg.

Sara retrieved the leg and stood up amid the discomfort. "I will not be reprimanded like a child, Maria."

Maria stood eye to eye with Sara. She was back to her wits now that Sara looked stronger and on her way to a full recovery. "Then stop acting like one," she snapped sharply. "I went mad with worry when the men found that wretched horse all alone, and the forest scattered with bloody pieces of your clothes. We thought you were dead, Sara. Dead! You were blessed to have been rescued by an honorable gentleman who cared for your life more than his own. Some other man would have..." Maria waved her hand trying to dismiss the horrific possibility.

"What?" Sara asked in anger. "Raped me? Left me for dead?" A line of sweat was forming on Sara's upper lip bearing the toll her ailing body was taking with a heated row. The argument was long overdue. Kept on hold from the moment Sara woke from her injuries. Neither woman could wait another moment to spew out what they had held back for the past two months.

"You know what? It would have been the first real thing that would have happened in my life. My first real problem." Her leg could not support her any longer, and finally she flopped down on the chair.

Maria looked at her in disbelief. "The fall damaged your head more than your leg, Sara. You are devoid of sanity."

Sara chose to laugh at that. "You might be right at that, my dear Maria. At times I'm convinced my sanity was lost the day I fell. I hit my head horribly hard... a good thing I finally got to see things for what they are."

Maria's eyes were at the verge of popping out.

"This," Sara opened her arms wide trying to enclose the whole compound within the empty space between her arms. "All of this, Maria, is a lie. I'm a lie. My name. Sara. It belonged to somebody else. I saw her face. She lived and I hold her name. Was she my grandmother? My mother's mother? Tell me about her. Tell me about the woman who bears the name of the first matriarch of the Jewish people."

Maria's face showed an array of emotions and none of them were joy. "I don't know." Maria pressed her hands on her face. "I don't know what ideas got into your head, Sara. I could get Doctor Fernandez before he leaves," Maria said while walking to the door hurriedly.

"Don't!" Sara got up abruptly, mindless of her condition. She lost her footing and fell beside the chair.

Maria started but did not move. Why did they have to call the girl Sara? Even if nobody had spoken about the matter out loud, the veil covering that name was thin. How many Saras existed in Christendom?

Sara stayed on the floor. "I don't need a doctor. I need you. I need the truth. You were there. Or at least that was the fairytale told to me. You knew my mother before she married my father. You know who she is."

Maria walked over to Sara and sat down beside her on the floor. She took both of her hands in hers. "Nobody ever knew who Camila's mother was, my dear child. Only Camila did. She never spoke of it. Leave it be, Sara. Please."

Sara withdrew her hands from Maria's grasp and bunched up her fists on her sides. "I cannot," she said. The conversation was over.

During the next few weeks, Sara limited her activities to short walks in the gardens, meals taken regularly during daylight, and the privacy of the music room until the wee hours of the night. She did not speak a word to Maria or anybody else. Maria did not have to be a seer to predict Sara's plan. She was strengthening her body to leave the Di Laurenti sheltered grounds in search of answers.

On the day of her departure Sara woke up before sunrise. To her astonishment, she found her riding clothes neatly folded next to a basin with fresh water. Sometimes Sara wondered if her own mother knew her as well as Maria did. Sara freshened up her face, put up her hair in a tight bun, and slipped off her shift in front of the mirror. Her ribs still showed through her skin, even though she had gained some of the weight back. There were some yellowish bruises determined to stay a while longer as a warning of the danger she could encounter riding on her own. "I will be careful," she promised as she stepped away from her reflection.

Sara reached for her tunic after fastening the ingenious, functional undergarment her mother had created to hold her breasts steady while riding. She meant to ride hard for several days until reaching the old convent, for that reason any garment that would constrict her movement was completely out of the question. As Sara slipped into her tunic, a short note fell on the floor. *Ask Mother Ignacia*, it read, written in Maria's round handwriting.

"Thank you," Sara whispered, and without further delay she made her way to the stables.

The sight of Maria standing by Cid saddled and ready to depart startled her. "Doctor Fernandez refused to take him, even though they became good friends during his stay. But he knew Cid was yours," Maria said flatly.

Sara stood in front of Maria, speechless.

Leon had worked Cid hard every day at dawn. Sara had watched him from her bedroom window, and she had admired his power to conquer Cid's wild nature.

Sara hurried to Cid, as if by doing so, she could erase the memory of Leon. She looked into the horse's eyes and stroked his forehead. "You'll be a good boy, now. None of that skittish business this time. It's just you and me on this journey." The horse responded by gently nuzzling his wet nose on her shoulder.

"There are enough provisions in your saddlebag for three days. Since you will not allow a groom to escort you, I sent word to the Medinas and the Garcias to watch out for you when you cross their lands. A rider from each one of their territories will be on the lookout for your arrival and will escort you until you reach their dwellings. You will stay as their guest as long as you need to. Once you are off the Garcias' lands, it will take you no more than a day's ride to reach the convent."

Sara took in all the information without protest. She felt guilty for putting Maria through such heartache. Before she could say a word, Maria stepped forward and held her in a tight embrace. Sara welcomed Maria's arms like the little child she once was.

"I know you have to do this, *mi niña*," Maria whispered in her ear. Maria took hold of Sara's shoulders and kept her at arm's length. "Please, be safe and come back to me."

The ride across the neighboring lands was smooth and somewhat liberating after being confined to her bed for most of the past three months. She was thankful for Cid's sensibility. It was as if the horse was aware of the danger he had put her through due to his wild behavior. He had become an extension of her body, reading her intentions before she could command him fully. His awareness of her made the journey all the more easier than she had envisioned. Even though recovered from her major wounds, she was far from healed and the strength in her legs was not sufficient to withstand the length of the trip.

***

Two weeks had passed since her departure from Onuba. She had planned it silently during her daily pacing around the perimeters of Casa Di Laurenti while considering all the odds against her.

There was no indication that Mother Ignacia or anybody that knew of her mother's precedence would be alive or even willing to disclose the story to a young woman claiming to be Camila's daughter.

Her heart raced as she came upon the stone convent. The building had been one of the many palaces erected upon the reconquest of Toledo in the year of one thousand and eighty-five by King Alfonso VI—the Brave, as he was commonly called by the people of Castile, and Leon. Right after his death in the early part of the twelfth century, the castle became a convent where his mistress Ximena Moniz was said to have spent the last days of her life.

Cid slowed his pace into a gentle trot, finally settling into a walk when they approached the convent walls and heavy iron gate. Sara dismounted by the convent's stables, where a young groom of no more than thirteen almost danced with excitement at the prospect of caring for Cid. He confessed to Sara that he had never ridden anything more than the nuns' donkeys, and he dreamed of becoming a warrior worthy of a beauty like Cid. Warning him of Cid's hot temper, Sara left the stables only when the young groom promised not to attempt anything but feeding and brushing him.

Maria's influence along Sara's travels transcended the arrangements for safe passage through the neighboring lands. A good humored, small framed nun welcomed her as if she had been expected.

Sara barely mouthed a cordial, "Good afternoon, Sister. I am Sara Di Laurenti," and she was swept through the building, almost dragged, into a large bedroom where a large tub with warm water was awaiting her. The tempting aroma of a steaming bowl of goat stew on top of a small table by the only window in the room made her stomach growl with hunger. An invitingly soft bed turned up from corner to middle, with the whitest sheets, completed the welcome reception.

The smiling nun, who mutely guided Sara to the room, closed the door behind her and left as soon as Sara stepped in. She felt filthy, ravenous, and saddle sore. She opted for the bath, the meal, and the bed in that order. The day was dying down, and she would have to play by the convent's rules if she were to obtain any information at all. Clean, with a full stomach, Sara fell asleep as soon as her head sank into the feather pillows.

A soft knock on the door startled her. For a moment she forgot where she was. It was the first time in her life she found herself away from home and without the company of a tutor, an escort, her parents, or Maria. Even though she had secretly doubted her power to endure a trip of such strenuous nature as the one she had embarked on, the thrill of adventure had surpassed any physical barriers or fears.

There was a second knock on the door, this time a little louder. Sara jumped out of bed and quickly reached for her shift which was still in her travelling bag.

The door to the room opened while she was still getting dressed. The oldest woman Sara had ever seen in her life, with folds of wrinkles on every inch on her face, walked into the room with a slow but sure stride. The woman, a nun, had her gnarled hands folded. Her bony fingers were thin as twigs, and thick blue veins protruded from them. Reflexively Sara touched one hand with the other to confirm that her hands were still young and soft.

The nun noticed and smiled. "Don't worry my child, old age is not contagious. I am Mother Ignacia and I believe you have questions."

Chapter Twenty-Four
The Untold Story

Sara felt foolish and at a disadvantage. Mother Ignacia stood stoically in front of her, while she, the one who initiated this odd encounter, was consciously off guard, speechless, and had nothing on more than a thin shift to cover her embarrassment. Sara cleared her throat a couple of times before responding to the unnervingly serene nun. "Mother, I apologize for—" Sara gestured at her half-covered body.

"Nonsense, my child," Mother Ignacia dismissed the issue with humor, "at one point or another in our lives we were all in possession of some of your noticeable attributes. Although I may ask, do you own any ladylike clothes?"

Sara immediately thought about her riding garments and the impression it might have caused on the small-framed nun who welcomed her. "Yes, yes, certainly. Of course I do."

The answer pleased Mother Ignacia. "Very well, my child. We will have a private breakfast in my study in thirty minutes. I believe we have much to talk about... or it may be not that much. It all depends on you, my child." Mother Ignacia fixed Sara with a sharp gaze and left the room.

On the previous day Sara had felt anxious, but after Mother Ignacia's unexpected appearance she turned into a bundle of nerves. She had ridden for two weeks to get to the convent looking for answers to her past. What was she to do with them if she was to get the truth out of Mother Ignacia? She really didn't know.

The carefully thought out scenario she had staged in her mind had not gotten any further than that precise moment. She inhaled deeply and decided to play it out like a tennis match, a toss and return game she used to play with her father. Another eccentricity afforded by the leniency of her father, an unladylike sport favored since the twelfth century amongst monks in Europe.

She would throw the first ball, and would be ready to catch the first stroke back from Mother Ignacia's bony hand. Not until their first leveled encounter would Sara be in a position to draw up a strategy upon the tenacity of her unknown opponent.

Sara had decided to travel light. All sorts of fanciful wear were left behind in her heavy armoire. Instead she chose a plain woolen peasant dress, which had folded easily amongst her riding outfits and was needless of frills. She quickly washed, pulled the dress over her head, and left her appointed room. She met the gentle nun from the day before standing guard at the door, a fact that did not surprise Sara. She knew she was being watched.

Throughout the length of the corridor leading to Mother Ignacia's study, her footsteps echoed loudly, increasing her anxiety for the meeting. She suddenly realized that she could only hear her boots on the floor and not the nun's. The nun's steps were another one of her noiseless traits. The absurd thought kept her entertained until they reached the heavy wooden double doors to Mother Ignacia's study, from where Sara's companion departed as quietly as she had arrived.

Sara knocked on the door once. It was opened by another nun who motioned for Sara to step into the room, and then left closing the door behind her, leaving her alone with Mother Ignacia.

Mother Ignacia sat by a large windowpane on a couch of sophisticated French workmanship that all but swallowed her frail frame. A matching couch was set next to her separated by a low table where an array of fruit, cheeses, fruit preserves, and fresh rolls were arranged on a large porcelain platter for the promised breakfast. Mother Ignacia waved Sara closer, and poured two cups of the steaming tea that she favored.

Sara stood still by the door, debating silently how to behave around this unapproachable character.

"Please, come sit, my child. It is way past my breakfast time and at my age, hunger makes a person short tempered."

Sara blushed again with embarrassment. There was something about this old nun that intimidated her. She had never blushed before in front of anybody, and today it happened to her twice. "I apologize, Mother, I did not mean to keep you waiting," Sara said while she took her seat opposite the nun.

Mother Ignacia dismissed her apology with a wave of her twisted twig fingers, a gesture she seemed to own, and offered Sara a steaming roll of bread with a dollop of fresh butter topped with a teaspoon of apricot preserve. Sara's mouth watered at the sight of the food and accepted it graciously as a truce. They ate and sipped their tea in silence.

Once they finished their breakfast, as though it had been timed beforehand, the door to the study opened. The nun who welcomed Sara walked in and retrieved the dirty dishes and the almost empty platter. Mother Ignacia refilled the two cups of tea and waited.

Sara cleared her throat, a newly acquired habit when addressing Mother Ignacia. She put her teacup down and placed her palms down on her knees. "I have a few questions for you, Mother. Questions that have been troubling me for the past few months. I do understand if you see it as an imposition... me being here, but I hope you might be able to help me."

Mother Ignacia set her cup down on the table and studied Sara's anxious demeanor for a long time. A smothering mantle of silence hung over the study. Sara's hands tensed into fists, unable to feign calmness.

Mother Ignacia's voice broke out. "Some of you wonder and some of you prefer not to. You could enjoy our hospitality until you are fit to ride back home or..." Mother Ignacia's voice trailed off when she looked into Sara's honey colored eyes.

How many times had she looked into the same eyes in the past? "I do not believe that to be an option for you, young lady."

Mother Ignacia rose from her couch. "Remember your life as it was till this day, my child." The prioress walked to the door and looked back at Sara. Sara saw that as an invitation, and followed the old woman out of the study.

The former palace, now turned convent, was laid out with a series of hidden alcoves and stairwells, which appeared out of nowhere, connected to passageways that led to the different stories of the stone structure.

After climbing up and down what seemed like endless flights of stone stairs even Sara began to feel breathless. Mother Ignacia did not appear to tire. In fact the endless staircases might have been the secret to the old nun's longevity.

Sara counted eight long flights of stairs before they arrived at their destination. By the looks of the building from the outside, and by their steep climb, Sara surmised them to be in the tower. Unlike the other stories they passed on their way up, this one was lined with windows, giving Sara the impression of being outdoors. Sara noticed this particular floor was lacking doors and corridors. The tower was a single chamber separated by only one wall and one door. Sara held her breath. She was afraid to talk and break the spell of whatever was awaiting her in the large room.

Mother Ignacia's talent to read Sara was revealed once more when she turned to her. "We can still go back, my dear Sara. Once you cross that door I doubt you could come back from it."

Sara looked at the closed door and then at Mother Ignacia. "I don't understand, Mother, why would a simple room in a tower change the course of my life? All I want to know is who my grandmother was."

Mother Ignacia dismissed Sara's plain statement and made her way to the closed door. She didn't knock, she opened it. The glow in the room was as bright as in the anteroom even though the walls did not have as many windows.

Unlike the previous chamber the walls in this particular one were painted with scenes of a family in different stages of their life. The paintings told a story of a woman. She looked young and beautiful, very much like Sara but not exactly. The eyes seemed to be the same and so were the massive cascade of soft waves that fell down the young woman's back.

Sara followed the painted story in awe. Whoever had painted the murals was a gifted artist. The vivid colors made by the skillful strokes of the paintbrush evoked an almost metaphysical emotion. Their images drew the viewer into the artist's world as if entering a fairytale book.

The first mural showed the maiden, the main figure in the story, painting a landscape on a panel under the shade of a large tree. The second mural portrayed the same young woman elegantly dressed and adorned with jewels, sitting at what looked like a family dinner. On the table there was a set of candles, a loaf of braided bread, and roasted lamb on a platter. The young maiden had her hands raised above the candles, her eyes closed deeply in prayer. By her side, a handsome man holding a cup filled with wine looked at her with devotion. The next few murals were a reflection of the love story between the young woman and the man, shown with the unspoken language of sensuality the painter had given the colorful figures. The fairytale then progressed into murals that depicted terror and darkness. The dinner scene was repeated, however this time the couple had their eyes open, as if waiting for something ominous to happen. The language between the lovers shifted from carefree passion to uneasiness. Their eyes were not lost in each other like in the previous paintings, but fearful of the world outside of theirs.

The next painting explained it all. A ring of fire encircled the couple. The handsome man was lying on the floor looking up. Where his eyes had once held a tender gaze they were now hollow pools of blood. Sara took a step back wanting to run out of the room. Her legs did not respond. Mother Ignacia stood by the door watching Sara's every move.

"Why are you showing me this? What does any of it have to do with me?"

"The house was burnt to ashes. Before the soldiers left, they cut the girl's tongue and dismembered her husband before her eyes. They locked all the doors and sealed all the exits of their home, so that she would be burnt alive."

Sara felt faint. Mother Ignacia noticed but the girl had insisted on the truth and she would do her job. She had kept the secret buried in the tower for forty years. Mother Ignacia was a lover of life and she believed this secret would shed truth onto whoever asked about it. Nobody had come to claim it before and taking it to her grave would signify the death of a story God had intended Ignacia to tell. When she got word of the youngest of the Di Laurentis heading to the convent, she fell on her knees and thanked the Lord for giving her this opportunity before she died.

Perhaps that was the one reason why he had kept her alive for so long.

***

Throughout the years the convent had served as a temporary hideout for Jewesses running from the murderous hand of the Inquisition. Disguising women as nuns was an easy task especially in this former castle with so many hidden passages and chambers. Most of the women Mother Ignacia harbored were literate in many languages, and in exchange for shelter they had copied large tomes of scientific encyclopedias and works of literature, which in turn helped her build the convent's library. Most of them left when it was safe to seek passage to North Africa or Portugal. Some of them were horribly injured when Mother Ignacia took them in and then died shortly after their arrival.

The case of Sarah Espinoza had been completely different from anything Ignacia had dealt with before. The nuns at the convent got word of the Espinoza castle being burnt to the ground with all their inhabitants locked inside. An *Auto de Fe*, a procedure the Inquisition was known to use when *Conversos* resolutely denied the Lord Jesus Christ as their savior. Ignacia had a deep revulsion for the Inquisition and their methods. In her mind Inquisitors were after only one thing, wealth. She saw them as criminals disguised under holy robes, using the distorted memory of a man who died for the sins of others, as their shield for their hypocrisy.

When the flames died down, Mother Ignacia led a rescue party to the Espinozas' castle. It was her mode of operation. She could not rest until she personally saw to the hopeful possibility of finding a living creature within the domain of the destroyed residence.

The rubble was still steaming when Ignacia arrived. The acrid smell of burnt flesh hung in the air over what once was the envy of Toledo. Total devastation. The lady of the house had been a famous painter, one Mother Ignacia had gotten to know personally. She had used her services on many occasions to create some of the most beautiful murals in the convent's chapel. The nun had a clear picture of what the castle looked like before its destruction, and she was certain to be standing in the middle of what once was the large dining room. She bent down and picked up scraps of glass. The castle had a large room devoted to its artist. Sunlight and moonlight lent inspiration to Sarah Espinoza's art. Mother Ignacia remembered feeling the hand of the Almighty when contemplating the painter's masterpieces. That light was gone, so was her life.

After hours of looking for survivors, Mother Ignacia called off the search. The five nuns who made up the rescue party climbed back into the cart in which they arrived. They waited for Mother Ignacia to take the reins of the donkey that would pull them back to the safety of their convent.

Mother Ignacia was always the last one to board the cart after surveying another criminal casualty of the Inquisition. She had a ritual of her own in which she took extra care to leave certain things neatly arranged in a way that the souls of the departed felt respected even after being unjustly massacred. She also said a prayer which begged God to put an end to the killing of innocent people in the name of religion.

Just as she began gathering together loose pieces of porcelain that would have made the most beautiful platter, the sound of a faint moan froze her. Her hands stayed on the hot gravel. She held her breath, so that the sounds of her own breathing would not block the possibility of a miracle.

The moan came again. It was nearby. Ignacia crawled over the hot stones certain that what she had heard was human. Her hands dug under a mountain of steaming rocks and iron. The moan was growing fainter, but she could still feel the existence of a heartbeat. "Please God," she repeated over and over again. The rest of the nuns saw Mother Ignacia struggling against the weight of the burning stones and ran to help her. Lifting one slab at a time, they finally reached Sarah Espinoza's half-burned body.

***

The memory of that day rattled Mother Ignacia. It always did. Except now she could pass it on hopefully to the right bearer. "It was a miracle, but she survived. She was meant to live because she had a life inside of her. Four months later, we were blessed with the arrival of a baby, Camila, your mother."

Sara leaned on the closest wall. Ignacia could not refrain from revealing the whole story. "It took years for Sarah to become somewhat functional. She loved this part of the convent and I believe it was the light seeping through the windows that made her want to paint again. She couldn't speak—of course, her tongue had been severed the night of the burning. Her paintings became her speech and told the story on the walls of this tower as a testament of what horrors have been done to them all."

Sara's eyes were closed, she could not look at the paintings anymore or at the woman in them. The same woman from the miniature. There was no doubt she belonged to her.

"Sarah was a wonderful mother to Camila, but she had to let her go. That was when I tracked down your great-grandfather, Doctor Espinoza, a convert who lived by the rules of the Church. Camila married soon after that to who I believed was the perfect match for her, considering."

"Considering what?" Sara snapped leaving all politeness aside. The blunt disclosure of her past had been raw without the need for pleasantries.

"Considering she was not marrying a Catholic." Mother Ignacia shrugged casually. "I owed that to Sarah for what my people did to her. I owed her that much."

Sara felt like she was being swallowed by a beast, chewed up, and spat out, all in the span of a brief moment. "You are lying," was all she was able to blurt out coherently. She was crying but it didn't matter. The simple question about the name she bore would change her world as she knew it forever, unless the nun was not telling the truth. "You are lying," she yelled this time.

"Why would I lie to you, my child?" the nun said regaining her composure. "You are the reason why God kept us both alive."

"Both?" Sara asked choked with panic.

The nun nodded and walked to the farthest end of the room where an alcove was hidden behind heavy blue velvet drapes. Mother Ignacia pushed the drapes aside. Sarah Espinoza was alert, sitting straight up on her cot. She had been listening to the conversation and her honey colored eyes, the only portion of her face spared from the fire, shone with expectation.

Sara stood behind Mother Ignacia taking in the disfigured features of the woman who had once looked so much like her. She couldn't deny it any longer. Mother Ignacia was right. She had reached the point of no return.

When her grandmother took her in her arms, Sara swore to fight with every drop of her blood whoever dared to make her renounce her rightful name.

Chapter Twenty-Five
Sarah

Sara Di Laurenti spent the following ten days with her grandmother in the tower. At night she would snuggle up tightly next to the old woman, listening to their mingling heartbeats that soon gave birth to a melody playing inside of Sara's head. On the tenth day, with the help of Mother Ignacia, Sara took her grandmother down to a room where a dusty harpsichord waited for somebody to lay their fingers upon its keys.

Apparently, a generous donor had sent it to the convent. None of the nuns had yet developed the right skills to play such an unusual instrument. There was no need to reveal the identity of the donor—Mother Ignacia knew it came from Massimo like the donation of luxury articles, such as soap, clothes, and shoes she could not afford for the orphan girls and the stream of fugitives she hid at the convent.

A quick glance at the wooden music box confirmed this to be an exact replica of the one her father had exclusively commissioned for her in Italy.

Sarah Espinoza devoted the days after meeting her granddaughter to relating the story of her people, the Jewish people, in the only way possible to her. With trembling hands the old woman compiled a booklet illustrating the life of Abraham, the son of a polytheist, who after a pact with God became the father of the People of Israel. The treachery Joseph suffered at the hands of his brothers, and yet he did not turn his back on them when they needed him. The massive exodus from Egypt with Moses—a man raised as a prince of Egypt—as their leader. The danger Queen Esther chose to go through, while impersonating a pagan maiden, to save the life of Jews in Persia.

Sara admired her grandmother and loved her for not surrendering her beliefs despite what had been done to her and to the man she loved. For the first time, Sara felt a sense of belonging. The stories in the illustrated booklet and the disfigured face of her grandmother, who lost her tongue while praying in Hebrew, defying with unmitigated audacity the soldiers of the Inquisition, were the most vivid confirmations she had ever had of who she was. Sarah Espinoza's drawings reflected the true essence of her namesake, better than any full-length mirror found in Casa Di Laurenti.

Young Sara was filled with the moral obligation to follow in the footsteps of so many before her. She also had an undying duty, born out of love and blood, to the courageous woman staring back at her doe-eyed awaiting for her to press down the first keys of the harpsichord.

Sara closed her eyes and let her mind memorize the breathing of her grandmother. The language of her heart, the strokes of her brush on the pages of the booklet. Sarah Espinoza inspired a melody in her granddaughter's soul, and she played it. Music granted the old woman a portal to transcend the physical boundaries imposed by horrors of the past. Sara's music would allow her speechless grandmother to become an undying voice.

Later that evening, Sarah Espinoza climbed up the infinite flights of stairs leading to her safe haven feeling light as a feather.

Her heart was content for finally being able to achieve what she once thought to be impossible.

***

197 • The Last Fernandez

She had chosen not to burden her daughter with the weight of her own fight. The poor child had enough to cope with growing up with a mute, half-burnt mother, who moaned in pain like a dying animal for most of the day. It had been Sarah Espinoza's decision to seek out Camila's sole surviving relative.

Mother Ignacia, the woman who throughout the years had become her best friend, acted as her tool in the outside world and took care of Sarah's wishes. The wounded mother yearned for her daughter's happiness. She wished she could erase Camila's memories of the monster that tried to raise her with love, but could never tell her how much love she had for her.

Sarah was resolved to let Camila go. But her child was as stubborn as the man who gave her life, and would not leave unless Sarah died. The morning Camila was collected from the convent by her reluctant grandfather, she was informed of the sudden death of her long-suffering mother on the previous night.

Camila was forbidden from climbing up to the tower room to kiss her mother one last time. She was ushered out of the convent with the strict warning to never come back. Sarah could hear Camila fighting Ignacia for the chance to spend one last moment with her mother, but Ignacia was impervious to the heat of tears.

Ignacia kept Sarah informed of Camila's life up until she married Massimo. Only then, when Sarah was assured of her daughter's safety and happiness, did she gather strength and start painting her story on the murals of the walls of the tower room.

***

The child she saw in front of her now was different from Camila. Her granddaughter had come to her out of necessity. She had the choice to back down and leave when

Ignacia slapped her with the shock of her past. However, she stayed.

It had become a tradition during the past nine nights before bed—Sara would comb the sparse, frizzy snowy hair on her grandmother's scarred scalp, while telling her stories about Camila.

The old woman rejoiced with the knowledge of her daughter's exciting life.

On the tenth night, the eager granddaughter was suddenly interrupted by the old Sarah. She grabbed Sara's hands with all her strength and looked at her with determination. Sara spelled out the urgent request in her grandmother's eyes and responded with a firm, "I promise."

The next morning, Sarah Espinoza rested serenely on her cot and for once in forty years did not feel pain, anger, or shame. She exhaled her last silent words of love into her granddaughter's sleeping ear and departed in peace.

Sara Di Laurenti was awarded the opportunity her mother was denied. She arranged her grandmother's hair one last time, kissed her scorched face twice, one for her mother and one for her, and took away the booklet that had become the cornerstone of her new beginning.

From that day on her name was no longer Sara. Her name was to be Sarah, pronounced with a heavy accent on the last consonant. The *H* in her name symbolized the protection of God and her Jewish lineage, and she would wear both with pride as her shield.

After a tearful goodbye from Mother Ignacia, Sara mounted Cid and was ready to leave. But where? She knew there were others like her long before she discovered her roots. She could not go back to her old life and pretend the last two weeks were no more than a mishap soon to be forgotten. Sara was a woman of action and she had promised her grandmother the night before her passing that she would become a warrior for the People of Israel.

Mother Ignacia gave Sara the name of an inn outside of Cordoba where a woman with the name of Florica could help her, should she choose to join the secret life of the *Marranos*.

Sara had already dispatched a letter to Casa Di Laurenti informing Maria of her impending arrival in Onuba. The net of guardsmen from the neighboring lands were probably already lined up waiting to escort Sara back to her lands. However, this time she would decline their help and hospitality. She had the need to be completely alone. She would fare for herself during the long journey home. Without succulent meals and feather beds waiting for her every step of the way, she calculated that her traveling time could be shortened by half.

Before mounting on Cid, Sara looked back at the tower where she had spent the last ten days with her grandmother. Going back to a sheltered life in Casa Di Laurenti did not feel right. There were plentiful provisions in her saddlebags, and if she were to ration them properly, she could make them last until her meeting with the woman Florica.

Sara wrote a quick note for Maria explaining briefly her change of plans without disclosing them fully, and handed it to the stable boy who cared for Cid while she spent her time at the convent. "Please, make sure it goes out today."

The boy could hardly contain his excitement of being of service to the owner of such a magnificent mount. He jumped on his mule and headed for Onuba shortly after Sara rode away.

Sara made it to Cordoba in less than a week, thoroughly ravenous and filthy. Her riding outfit was covered with dried mud from sleeping in the damp caves she found along the road. Her hair was tied up under a thick scarf, and still her scalp itched badly. Sara was fearful of letting her hair loose. She was sure to find all sorts of crawling living things having a feast on her head. She yearned for a warm bath and a fine comb.

The inn Mother Ignacia told her about was on the outskirts of Cordoba. It was a greasy, rundown tavern which suited Sara's present appearance as though it had been planned. The stench of the inn was overpowering. The odor of stale wine, unwashed bodies, and urine made her eyes water. No hot baths in here, she thought with disappointment.

Sara stood at the threshold taking in the scene. Inside, a drunken crowd sat along wooden tables that were set at both ends of the tavern. A couple of serving maids walked around, filling up empty mugs and offering a full view of their mostly exposed breasts. Her eyes surveyed the room until she located, at the far end corner, the only woman sitting in the dimly lit establishment.

The woman, a Gypsy, stared at her intently. As Sara started her way to the Gypsy, a drunken patron groped her from behind, intent on sliding his grimy hands down Sara's Turkish trousers. The foul breath coming from his rotten teeth made her gag. She felt his touch on her bare skin and reached for the small knife she always carried strapped to her hip.

Sara managed to turn around and put her hands down on the man's half-erect penis. While she grabbed him firmly with one hand, she shoved the point of the knife at the base of his testicles with the other. The pressure of the knife on the man's balls was enough for him to feel the prick of the sharp blade. The man's eyes popped open, as round as two pigeon eggs. He eased his grasp on Sara but did not dare move.

"If you don't take your filthy hands off me I will cut your balls off and feed them to you one by one," Sara said with a calmness she did not possess, while enunciating every word clearly. The man let both of his arms drop to his side and staggered back until he was at a safe distance from her. He then sprinted out of the tavern howling while grabbing his crotch.

Sara held her knife out, spinning around, in the event anybody else attempted to attack her. The drunken patrons did not notice her, and went about their business, which was drinking, as if nothing had occurred.

The Gypsy woman came up to her. She squinted hard at Sara. "And what do we have here? A harlot?" The Gypsy tilted her head, and grabbed Sara's chin with her grimy hands. She inspected Sara's face as if she were about to buy her. "No… I don't think so."

Sara jerked her head back, but was clearly taken aback by the woman's gruffness, a fact that made the Gypsy laugh with her mouth wide open, displaying her missing front teeth. "What makes you think I'm not a harlot?" Sara countered defensively.

"Your teeth are too white, and you have all of them," the Gypsy replied, shoving Sara's shoulder in jest. "You look dirty as a mule, but your clothes are those of a wealthy maiden. What is a lady doing here alone?" the Gypsy demanded this time without any traces of humor.

"I'm looking for Florica." Sara's eyes fell upon the plate of cheese and bread laid on the Gypsy's table. She could not stand another minute without food or water.

The Gypsy scrutinized Sara, taking her time. She knew the girl was famished, still she made her wait. Sara tried hard to control her breathing and think about pretty things, things that did not involve her empty stomach.

The Gypsy tugged on Sara's shoulder and gestured for her to sit. "Eat," she ordered.

Sara did not have to be told twice. She dug into the plate of food, dismissing all manners taught by her awfully expensive tutors.

The Gypsy filled Sara's mug twice, while topping off her own. "Where did you hear about Florica?"

Cleaning the last scraps of cheese from the plate with her dirty fingers, Sara mused over the right way to answer. Her mind was working more sharply after the food and drink, and she did not trust or like this woman. Furthermore, as tired as she was she would not allow the Gypsy to bully her. Sara dropped a silver coin on the wooden slab and made to leave.

The woman looked at the coin which was enough to pay for ten of the meals she had offered Sara. The girl was rich and Florica had a price. "How much will you pay?" the Gypsy asked.

"I've already paid you more than your food and cheap wine are worth. And by the looks of this place, I presume I covered for most of these drunkards who do not have a *real* to their names." Sara had planned her response while chewing the last bits of food. She would not engage the Gypsy in chat. She was dead with exhaustion and mind games were not her favorite at that stage of her travels. The Gypsy would bend for money, she had no doubts about that.

Before Sara reached the door, the Gypsy's attitude changed from arrogant to amiable. "I can help you, for a price, and yes I am Florica."

Sara choked down the urge to laugh. "That's exactly what Mother Ignacia told me you would say. She also said you could guide me to the House of Gardens."

Florica looked at her sharply. Sara could not tell if it was the mention of Mother Ignacia's name, or of the House of Gardens, but the Gypsy reached for her hands and looked at her with respect for the first time since she had set foot in the shabby tavern. "I will take you at sundown. You fooled me. You don't look like the others. Your clothes…" Florica waved her hand in Sara's direction. Her tone was apologetic.

Sara looked down at the grime covering her. "You don't happen to have a tub large enough for a bath, do you?" Florica looked at Sara in disbelief. Sara shrugged. "It didn't hurt to ask."

Florica led Sara to a bench in a dark corner of the room. She sat down, and within minutes sleep claimed her. As promised, at sundown, Florica nudged Sara gently, rousing her from a fitful sleep. "It's time," she said.

They rode into Cordoba when the sun had completely gone down. It was the time of the night when women like Sara did not wander around a city unguarded. At least she was with Florica, a woman who didn't seem fazed by late hours out in the open. She also relied on Cid's speed to run to safety should they encounter danger.

The narrow road they had been following for over an hour ended abruptly. A palace that was more like a fortress rose up before them. Florica reared her mule to a halt. "We are here," she said in a hushed tone. She dismounted and so did Sara.

Amid the darkness, Sara could see a grand entrance in the shape of an arch, which opened up into a vast garden that looked endless. Florica led her to a low pool, where they let both their weary mounts drink of the cool, clear water. Then, they made their way to the big house, which stood elegantly like a sculpture, with alabaster terraces lushly cultivated with trees and flowering plants, and surrounded by a collage of nature.

Sara's insides were in turmoil. She did not know what to expect once she entered the palace, and in the company of strangers. She was dirty and smelled like goat. Fear and vanity were warring inside her. From the moment she left her home in Onuba, Sara had endeavored to validate her right to inhabit this world. Her grandmother gave her more reasons than she ever imagined could exist. Sarah Espinoza had presented her with a tough choice, and Sara took it without hesitation.

The arduous ride from Toledo to Cordoba had served her as a period of mourning. She mourned the death of her grandmother, but mostly she mourned her own death. The decision Sara made while at the convent was no different from the decision many *Conversos* were forced to make. In both instances, the conversions were made out of basic survival instinct. *Conversos* would rather live than perpetuate a faith that would eventually lead them to death. Sara found that she would rather die than perpetuate a lie. Although assertive about her decision, she did not feel ready to claim her new status out loud. She needed more time.

She hesitated on the threshold until Florica, stunned, pushed her forward. "Do not back out now, *mujer*!"

Stricken with panic, Sara looked back at Florica.

"Go on." Florica pushed Sara forward again. "Tell the rabbi, Florica brought you here." Then, the Gypsy took off running, leaving Sara alone before the imposing entrance.

The never-ending vegetation did not allow for visual boundaries between house and gardens. The continuous greenery lent the sensation of entering the Garden of Eden.

Sara's echoing footsteps on the limestone floor announced her arrival. A young maidservant met Sara and curtsied respectfully. Conscious of her ragged appearance, Sara was not certain the curtsy was directed to her. She looked about her, confirming there were no other more adequate persons in the room being addressed with such respectful greeting.

Sara did not know what to say or do. She opted for the Gypsy's advice. "Florica brought me here," she parroted Florica's words.

The maid nodded acknowledging the information provided, and motioned for Sara to follow her through a long hallway and into a study. She curtsied again before closing the door, leaving Sara alone.

The study was covered from wall to wall with books of all sorts. She recognized a few philosophy tomes in Italian, French, and Arabic, some of which were part of her library in Onuba. It had been some time since she read anything in French. It was not the right time to take up on reading, but she could not find what else to do with herself while waiting for the rabbi, probably an old man who had retired to his chamber and was already snoring in bed.

She pulled a heavy book out of the shelf and made herself comfortable on a deep leather chaise lounge. She propped the book on her lap, and tried to read it despite the weight of her eyelids. Suddenly, she realized why she hadn't read in French for a while—the romantic language put her to sleep.

From her somnolent state, Sara felt she was being watched. Her suspicions were confirmed with the opening of one eye. Yes, she was being watched. By a man. A man she knew.

"Lady Di Laurenti?"

Sara stood up proudly smoothing down the front of her hopelessly crumpled garments. This was to be her first formal introduction in this new stage of her life.

In her fantasies, she pictured herself wearing a breathtaking gown made out of her father's best silks, embossed with her mother's finest embroideries. She had envisioned her long, wavy hair cascading free down the length of her back, with a touch of seed pearls randomly braided in between her soft curls glinting like stars. The stench coming from her armpits defused her fantasy bringing her back to her current state, and back into the home of a man who did not require a formal introduction. He knew her better that she wished him to, yet she still had a surprise for him.

"No, Rabbi," she sneered at the word rabbi, "I am no longer Lady Di Laurenti. From now on I only respond to the name of Sarah," pronouncing the name carefully, so that the last consonant was lilted with the Hebrew accent, "my Jewish name."

Leon Fernandez, the man in the room, looked up addressing God directly as though they were the best of friends. "God, you are the King of Jesters."

Chapter Twenty-Six
The Jewess

At the sight of Sara standing in his study Leon would not have been more astonished if someone had told him he had grown a second head. The months that had passed since his departure from Onuba had worked to Sara's advantage. Although grimy, raggedy, and with dark circles under her eyes, she looked healthy and more lovely than ever. Her skin was tanned, and her eyes shone like two polished ambers.

He had fled Casa Di Laurenti like a coward, thinking it would free him of her. Yet, the memory of her haunted him. His mind was held hostage by the image of her delicate fingers on the harpsichord, of her hot temper, her beautiful body, and of the way she let him share her most private moments every night when playing her music. It had to end. She had been an accident in his path. He found her, healed her, and moved on to other patients the way physicians do. But she was back, standing in front of him, claiming a name and a heritage that was meant for trouble.

Leon gathered his thoughts before addressing Sara. She hadn't moved from her spot other than to scratch her head twice, and her back once. First things first, Leon decided.

"You are in need of a bath," he said leaving no room for objections.

She didn't flinch—moreover she threw the offense back at him. "I don't need a physician or a rabbi to diagnose my urgent need to wash, Doctor-Rabbi Fernandez," she replied sardonically. "Yes, I would very much appreciate a bath if a room of that sort could be found in this monstrous palace."

Leon bit his tongue to restrain himself. They could spend hours bantering back and forth, shooting daggers at their most sensitive spots. This and the emotions it invoked was something he wanted to avoid.

"Yes, there are baths in this monstrous palace, Lady Di Laurenti, to which I will be delighted to guide you."

Sara stood rooted to the spot, and made no attempts to follow Leon as he reached the door. He turned around and raised one of his thick, dark eyebrows.

"I expect a maid to show me to the baths, perhaps your wife, but not you," Sara demanded.

"I apologize for the inconvenience, Lady Di Laurenti, nonetheless, I must make it clear to you—here, in my dwellings, there are no servants or wives, only free working men and women who have retired for the evening. You could either follow me or join the beasts in the stables for the night. Although, I suspect, even they would be offended by your odor."

The last cynical remark escaped his mouth before he could stop it. In view of her limited choices Sara tilted her head sideways mulling over the only option which did not mean getting back on her horse, as much as she felt like leaving.

She followed Leon through an impressive maze of hallways lined with pots of lush foliage. Sara walked a step behind Leon, free to admire her surroundings. This place was the closest she would come across on earth to what scholars depicted in their writings as Paradise.

Sara wondered silently why an honorable man like Leon, who claimed to not have a wife with whom to share this piece of heaven, would want to live alone in a palace that ought to be bursting with music, laughter, and plenty of children running around.

The baths he led her to were the traditional baths found in Arab palaces. The room was rectangular, and although lighted by flickering bronze lanterns, Sara could still admire the greenery and the tiled walls surrounding the chamber. She inhaled the heady scent of the perfumed waters that floated in the air, and felt magically transported to the many stories she had read in her father's library about the life of harem girls.

Her eyes grew accustomed to the dimness of the room as she entered the main chamber where three pools, one warm, one hot, and one cold were arranged in a pyramid like setting. The place exuded sensuality, and she wondered with a surprising pang of jealousy, if Leon had guided many women to the baths, or perhaps a special one.

Sara noticed a large tub placed at a corner of the room by a hearth. A copper cauldron with steaming water hung over the fire, and a couple of cakes of soap sat next to a pile of fine linen, neatly stacked sheets. Obviously the girl who admitted her into the palace, had anticipated Sara's bath—how could she not? —and rushed to make the proper preparations at the sight of her disheveled state. Sara smiled at the subtle gesture. She would never dare pollute the clean water of the thermal pools with her grime. She walked to the hearth, lifted the cauldron with the hook that was intended for that purpose. Then, she poured the water into the tub, which had been previously half filled.

She noticed that Leon stopped just inside the bath's antechamber. According to the stories she had read, the antechamber was the strategic place where Moorish kings usually surveyed their flock of naked concubines and made their pick for the night, by choosing her with the throw of an apple. She wished for Leon to throw her an apple. Not to spend the night with him, but because not only was she filthy, she was ravenously hungry. But, he made no attempts to throw her anything, either to feed her or ravish her. He stood, brooding, arms folded across his chest. Sara decided to ignore him.

Her skin prickled for the warmth of water and the silky touch of the olive oil soap. She needed to get out of her clothes and her scalp was screaming to be scrubbed. Sara undid the tight headscarf covering her thick mass of hair, finally freeing it from its smothering restraint. She then proceeded to remove her tunic but her arms betrayed her. She had reached the edge of exhaustion brought on by her hasty ride to Cordoba. Her muscles would not obey her, and she got tangled in a knot of hair and clothes in the process of undressing.

If he was to stand there staring at the empty air, she might as well make him useful. "Doctor Fernandez!" came Sara's muffled voice.

Exhausted, she gave up and sat down on the floor, trapped by the mass of fabric of her clothing. She could have actually fallen asleep bundled in her own hair and filth, had it not been for the awful smell coming out of her pores which kept her senses at bay. "Doctor Fernandez!" she cried.

"Yes, Lady Di Laurenti." His clear baritone voice rang only inches from her.

"As you can see, I could use some help." She barely lifted her arms and let them fall like two heavy boulders.

"I see," he replied with the same soft tone he had used to calm her during the worst of her pain after her accident.

"Aren't you going to do anything about it?" She suffered from a different kind of desperation now, one coming from tiredness.

"Sara…" This time his tone was doing more to unnerve her than to calm her.

"Sarah," she snapped back before he could articulate what he intended to say. Her interruption was answered with a prolonged silence, in which she opted for lying flat on the floor, waiting to be lectured by the scholar.

"I do not know what brought you to my home, but you will be on your way to Onuba as soon as you are fit to ride. I will make sure of it myself."

Sara scrambled back into her tunic, she went over to the tub and sank into it clothes and all. She reached for the soap, submerged her head under water, and began to lather her hair with the oils released from the soap. Her fingers fumbled, the soap slipped from her hands and skidded across the marble floors. She glanced at it with longing. Resigned to be humiliated once more in the presence of Leon Fernandez, she chose to close her eyes hoping he would tire and leave.

She was mistaken again when it came to Leon Fernandez. He picked up the soap from the floor, walked to the tub, pulled her head back towards him, and finished lathering her hair. His fingers dug deep into her scalp massaging it, releasing the knots of tension she had held since her departure from Toledo. Sara kept her eyes closed. She did not want to see his blue-eyed gaze on her. His hands moved down to her tunic. Although wet and sticky he managed to rid her of it by simply ripping the garment at the seams. Her Turkish pants were next, leaving her barely covered in her makeshift bodice.

"Might as well rip that one off, too." She shrugged. "I've lost my dignity to you once before."

He did as she ordered, and discarded the wet cloth on top of the pile of wet, shredded clothes beside the tub. Leon knelt and clasped his forearm under her ribcage. He held her straight up, and with his other hand scrubbed her back with a soap-lathered sponge. He stopped at the spot below her shoulder blade, where he had been forced to cut out a piece of her flesh to prevent her death. As he had predicted months before, a slight depression of the flesh was noticeable and would stay there as a reminder of her ordeal. Leon dropped the sponge in the water and let his fingers trace the edge of the scar as though counting the invisible stitches.

"It does not hurt anymore," Sara whispered.

Leon released her gently, allowing her to relax on the back of the tub. He sponged down the rest of her body, leaving nothing untouched.

The soothing actions of Leon's touch had a cathartic effect on Sara. His hands held a healing power over her. Their relationship had been a battlefield from the start, where they were both intent to outsmart the other. However, the physical contact of this man on her skin did not trigger a hostile response from her. Every cleansing stroke on her surface slowly melted away her defensive wall ultimately purging her heavy heart.

"Her name was Sarah Espinoza and she waited forty years to die."

A wave of tears came over Sara. She cried until she was unable to shed more tears. Leon picked her up from the tub and wrapped her in a soft linen sheet. He held her close to his chest until her trembling ceased. It was then that she recounted her story and the story of her grandmother. When she was done, she looked up at him and asked, "How could I be called anything other than Sarah?"

"You can't. You won't." His words had the effect of opium on her, that at one time served to sooth her physical pain, and now it did the same with her heart. She rested her head on his shoulder, and gave way to slumber.

Sara woke up in a large bed snuggled under a mountain of soft covers and protected by the safe arms of Leon. It was apparent that he put her to bed, yet he lay dressed by her side on top of the covers, offering the sanctuary of his body. She slowly disentangled from him, careful not to wake him, threw a heavy blanket over her naked body and walked around the immense room.

Unlike the rest of the house, this room was devoid of luxuries. There were several windows dressed with heavy brocade drapes. The big bed was of dark cherry wood, of a sturdy yet plain design. There was a large desk in the corner, matching the bed's craftsmanship, and a chair next to it. The desk was covered with papers and books. His papers, his books, his room, Sara observed after she quickly glanced over some medical writings.

Sara's stomach protested with a loud growl. She felt ravenous. Her stomach yelled at her for a second time, reason enough to wander out of the room in search of food.

There were two doors, facing each other from opposite ends. Which one to take was the question. Her body moved instinctively to the door at the right end of the room. The door opened easily. The flickering of candles lit her way into what it looked like another chamber. It felt wrong to intrude into somebody's secret space, but the glowing light lured her to its depths.

It was an empty chamber, except for a harpsichord taking center stage. Sara forgot about her hunger and even about her surroundings. She walked straight to the harpsichord and traced it with her fingers. Her hunger for music was stronger than her physical need for nourishment. She sat on the beautifully crafted bench and lost all sense of time and space when striking the first key.

Sara felt weightless as she floated towards the light.

***

Angelina sat by Sara as they had on every occasion that they had met. They had long stopped communicating with words, instead they shared their lives with the sound of musical notes. Angelina was no longer a little girl. She appeared to Sara as a tall and slim young woman. Her facial features were much like Sara's except for their eyes—Angelina's bore a darker brown with specs of amber.

Side by side they could be mistaken as twins, except for their vestments.

During their unplanned encounters, Sara had worn everything from fashionable gowns to bare skin, while Angelina never changed out of her nun's habit.

However they were dressed, or to what time in space they belonged to, their relationship was one of twin souls. Unrestrained and worldless.

Sara played the melody of her grandmother to Angelina, and Angelina played it back to her, remembering every note, every detail. Angelina was a sponge ready to absorb all the stories of the only friend she ever had.

Her life at the *Trapa* was still a waiting game and she believed her time would come when music would break her silence into action.

Sara could not yet determine the role her somber companion played in her worldly life. She was compelled to share every intimate detail of her every day with her, even the ones she had trouble allowing herself to admit, like her feelings for Leon.

She played a melody of love and lovers to Angelina. Her prude looking friend blushed at Sara's desires and encouraged her, with a melody of her own, to explore the world of romance and flesh.

They parted as always with their hands blending together on the keys of the harpsichord.

***

The music had woken Leon, and as he had done before, he stayed hidden in the shadows, unseen by Sara. Her melody played tricks with his heart and his body. The sight of Sara half covered by a blanket at the harpsichord was more than he could bear. He knew it was not her intention to drive him mad with desire, at least not consciously. He had awoken to a melody that touched his heart. It felt as if she was calling him to join her in body and soul. Or, it could have also been a dream resulting from his longing for her.

Sara sat staring at nothingness while coming out of her daze. A state he had witnessed when she had played the harpsichord back in the Di Laurentis' music room.

Her hands rested on the keys. That much she could tell. As for what happened when she sat at the harpsichord, she could not tell. She felt cold. The blanket had slid off her shoulders and lay bunched up at her feet. She picked it up and wrapped it around her. She left the harpsichord room and went back to the adjacent chamber where Leon was still resting.

She had a slight recollection of waking up hungry, but she did not feel hunger anymore. Instead, she had a different physical need. She longed for Leon's warmth. She was not shocked at her bold thoughts. Leon Fernandez was a far more delectable prospect than a loaf of fresh bread.

Sara climbed back onto the bed and nestled back into the width of his chest. His arms closed around her in the same way he had done before. However, he was no longer asleep. His breath was warm on her neck.

His lips brushed her ear forming words she longed to hear. "You can be Sarah, but only here, only with me."

Chapter Twenty-Seven
A Man, A Woman, A Broken Oath

They lay in the darkness, not moving, not talking, only listening. There were many sounds that arose from the silence—their breathing, the faint shuffling of their feet against the soft bed sheets, and the thunderous beat of their hearts. As with everything else Sara translated the experiences of her world into melodies. She thought of the heart as the drum behind the symphony of life. It never played solo. Her thoughts were mixed with a new flow of emotions, ones that scared her. Slowly she stopped thinking. Images of what her melody looked like flashed before her eyes, playing a harmonious tune, explaining her feelings...

From the moment of conception, before a baby announced its existence with a funny bump in its mother's belly, its heart beat rhythmically with the one of its keeper. Out of the womb, when free and untamed, the heart played numerous melodies until it met a partner. The proud would swear by their loneliness, they would convince themselves that their heart was meant to beat only for them. Eventually, solitude led to despair, and inevitably to heartache and heartbreak.

Loneliness was not what Sara sought, for she had realized that her heart was already engaged in one of those rhythms meant to beat as one for eternity. She was in love.

She turned to Leon and looked into his eyes. So blue and filled with desire, they mirrored her feelings as if he too could hear the music. He had seared her skin with his touch. He had shaped her heart only to fit his. She could have never understood this feeling before. Before her accident, before him. Her departing from Onuba had taken her to a forked road and she had chosen a path from which she could never return. Her oblivious innocence had come to an end. Sara had become a woman.

Returning her gaze, Leon yearned to take her in his arms, touch her with the same hands that healed her, cleansed her, protected her, and now he ached to own her. He did not wait for an invitation. He cupped Sara's face with his hands and pulled her closer. He brushed his lips with hers and kissed her, tasting her like he dreamed he would. They kissed for a long time. He was surprised the effect her mouth had on his. He had been with more women than he would like to admit, but her kiss made him feel dizzy as though hers was his first kiss. Her initial clumsiness gave him a sense of pride. He was undoubtedly her first. Her first, he suddenly realized. Sara was not an experienced woman when it came to affairs of the bedroom, and they were in his bed. She was naked under the covers, and he was still fully dressed, and about to burst if he didn't have her.

Panic took hold of his rising desire, bringing him back to his senses. He held her at arm's length. She looked at him almost offended.

"I don't trust myself—I cannot Sara, I—"

She threw her head back and laughed. The sight of her soft neck, which he had been kissing only moments before, unnerved him. "I won't make you marry me. I would not do that to you."

Her words struck him hard. She stung his pride by giving him what he wished for the most—a woman in his bed asking for nothing in return. In Italy he had been against love and marriage. Yet he fell in love with Sara, and she was offering him what he thought he wanted, a casual affair, no ties. She was out of her mind if she thought he would let her slip out of his grasp, and share somebody else's bed. Leon's passion turned into anger. He grasped her upper arms and shook her until her teeth rattled. "You won't marry me, huh? You won't marry me?" He managed a low, raspy growl filled with menace.

She pushed him away and made to get out of bed, but he was too quick for her. He pulled her back to him.

"No, I won't," she said with sadness. "Like I said before, I would never do that to you."

She had the ability to blind him with passion, pushing him to the verge of violence. He felt ashamed for his behavior and loosened his grip on her without letting go completely. "Why?" He was calmer, his voice had lost its threatening edge.

Her hands took hold of his and she placed them on a soft spot in between her breasts. "Because of the decisions I have made. Because of the life I intend to live. Because I am thirsty for revenge. Because I love you."

With her last four words, she broke his heart. She disarmed him. He felt naked.

"We can be together, tonight. Tomorrow?" She shrugged.

Sara moved closer to him and unbuttoned the bone buttons of his linen shirt. The shirt slid off his shoulders and she leaned against him. Bare chest on bare chest.

He held her tightly to him, the bristle on his face rustled softly against her neck. "Promise, I'll be your only one."

She laughed silently. He discarded the rest of his clothes and laid her gently down on the bed, kissing every inch of a body he knew too well, but not as a lover. With every kiss he savored a piece of her, claiming her as his. He wanted to own all of her. The proof of his desire throbbed painfully. He sought relief with a strong deep thrust that startled them both. Sara bit her lower lip, gasped and recoiled under the firm weight of his body. He kissed her

219 • The Last Fernandez

face until he felt her muscles relax, and gazed at her with eyes filled with love and desire. "Promise, I'll be your only one."

Sara pulled him close and kissed his demands away. She lifted her hips to meet his and brought him to her. Together they melted in waves of unrestrained passion, claiming each other without the promise of forever.

They spent the next few days locked in the bedchamber, in the way new lovers would. They made love, they tested their limits and went over them.

"How did you come upon this palace?" Sara asked while feeding Leon a piece of roasted lamb leg, part of a succulent meal left at their door.

Leon chewed his meat carefully, washed it down with a cup of wine, and frowned. "I could not tell you the story without marring your morals more than I already have. A lady of the most refined tastes, sitting in my bed, bare as a leaf," Leon kissed her breasts, and then her mouth, "and me, the scholar, taking her like the beast that I am."

Sara rested on her back, propped her legs on his shoulders and pushed her hips towards him. Leon held his breath, she was a temptress and he loved every bit of it.

Before he could move within her, Sara sat back up, stuffed a piece of roasted lamb in her mouth and smiled at him. "My dear Lev, this greatly educated lady read the Ananga-Ranga," she waved her hand as though it was a common read, "the legendary Indian sex manual, in its entirety. In the original language, of course."

Leon looked at her dumbstruck. This outwardly chaste girl had probably more intellectual knowledge about sex than a married woman. During their passionate games, Sara was uninhibited and capable of taking Leon to a point of ecstasy he had never known before. Consumed by her irresistible smile, Leon pushed the food aside and climbed on top of her like a horse in heat. Sara shrieked playfully.

"I will tell you everything, after you instruct me in some of your learning of the Ananga-Ranga."

**

At night, when everybody at the palace retired for the day, they crept into the bath chamber and soaked their exerted bodies in the thermal pool. They talked mostly about their past—their parents, their sisters, their childhoods. Leon told Sara about the marquis and about his promise to his father before leaving for Padua. Sara listened intently and her eyes burned with rage when Leon told her the story of his father's last days.

They both avoided talks about the future, and when it came to the question of the present, the immediacy of their flesh was their only answer. In the privacy of the bedroom, they were Lev and Sarah. Names they could only use under covers.

Leon was able to conquer almost every bit of Sara except for one.

In the middle of the night, as though it were a religious ritual, Sara would leave his side and sit at the harpsichord immersed in a space which did not seem real. He always watched her from afar, afraid of interrupting what he felt was an out of body experience. A moment taken over by her deepest emotions. A place where her soul played stories of passion and love. Afterwards, she would go back to bed and be all his as if nothing had interrupted them.

"Teach me," Leon asked her one morning when sitting at the harpsichord.

Sara looked at him with distrust. "Teach you? You have a wooden monster in your chambers and you don't know how to play it?"

Leon looked down sheepishly.

"You don't really know how to play it?" she said bewildered. "Why do you own one?"

He was caught. Time to confess. "Because of you. I thought that—I thought that if I learned to play the harpsichord I could always keep a part of you. There, I said it!"

He was flushed, and embarrassed. What had this woman turned him into! He was a physician, a businessman, a rabbi, yet he felt like a young boy when he was with her.

She sat on his lap and kissed him gently. First, the upper lip, then, the lower lip. "I will never be with another man. I promise."

Leon was a quick learner, but lacked musicality. She would not dare tell him that even though he needed not to be told. He was not deaf and could distinguish between the splendors she created when she touched the keys, against the choppy, discordant sounds that came out of him.

On the fifth morning together Sara woke up alone in bed. She bolted upright and found Leon staring at her, standing by the bed. She ran her hands through her tangled hair and blinked a couple of times until her sight was in complete focus. "Has anything happened?"

He shook his head in response.

Sara was up on her knees. "What's the matter? Why are you looking at me so?"

"You won't marry me," he said plainly.

Sara slumped back on the bed. "Lev, we talked about this already."

"No, Sarah, you talked about it. I haven't had my say yet."

Sara sat back up. "Speak your piece."

Leon stood as straight as he could. He looked taller than usual, and his body seemed broader than Sara remembered. "'If a man find a damsel that is a virgin, which is not betrothed, and lay hold on her, and lie with her, and they be found; then the man that lay with her shall give unto the damsel's father fifty shekels of silver, and she shall be his wife; because he hath humbled her, he may not put her away all his days.' This is from the book of Deuteronomy," he explained.

He had taken pains to memorize every word of the verse before confronting her. Sara broke into a fit of laughter that had tears streaming out of her eyes, accompanied with some funny snorts that made Leon lose some of his composure.

"I mean it, Sarah, you will be my wife. I pledged an oath to God and my community when I became a rabbi. I cannot break the rules in my own house."

Sara darted out of the bed with the speed of lightning, and struggled to get into a gown Leon had one of the maids sew for her. "You don't have to worry about breaking the rules in your own house, I'm leaving. And keep your miserable fifty shekels. My father has a big enough fortune already."

Before she reached the door, she was pulled back by his large hand. He brought down his face very close to hers. "You are free to leave after you marry me." Every word was firmly said in between gritted teeth as though they were separate sentences. "I mean it."

She hated him at that moment and wanted to hurt him as much as he was hurting her with his total disregard for her wishes. "*If* I marry you, you will never see me again."

"So be it," he snapped back. "Be ready in an hour." He left the room, slamming the door behind him.

***

Two days before, back at Casa Di Laurenti, Maria had been anxiously awaiting the arrival of her lover Jaime Moreno. Besides missing him terribly, he was to bring her news from Cordoba. When the young boy from the convent delivered Sara's note, Maria screamed in rage. What did that wretched girl want from her? Did she want to kill her before she reached old age?

After feeding the lad and letting him rest for a day, Maria sent him to Cordoba with a note for Jaime Moreno. Jaime knew everybody and everybody knew of him. Jaime was involved in an array of businesses, and people seemed to be one of his commodities.

It had never been discussed between them before, but Maria was sure that many of the temporary workers he brought to Casa Di Laurenti were fugitives of the Inquisition. Furthermore, she suspected Massimo of being involved in the operation as well. Nothing about Massimo surprised her anymore.

Before his yearlong departure with Camila, he had had a private conversation with Maria. Their trip could take longer than a year, maybe two, maybe more. He had to leave Spain immediately, but he wanted to do it in a subtle way. She was to follow with Sara a year later when news of their delayed return would hit the upper echelons of Cordoba. Before the trip, Massimo had encountered a young man in Padua whom he trusted to become their protector during his absence. He lured the man with the excuse of a fine horse and temporary board until he found himself settled in Cordoba. The young man, Leon Fernandez, was a medical doctor, and a scholar in philosophy and in other areas that Massimo avoided disclosing.

The old fox's eyes had glinted when he said to Maria, "I believe we won't have to worry about Sara after his arrival at Casa Di Laurenti. Wait and see."

So far Massimo's plan had failed. Yes, both Sara and Leon had feelings for each other as far as she could see during his stay with them. But then he left and Sara had let him go. Now she was gone on a soul-searching journey riding all over Spain on her own. She could end up murdered, if not raped, or she could be taken prisoner by some slave trader and be sold into bondage.

Maria could always rely on Jaime and once more he showed his trustworthiness by coming to her with some important news.

Jaime was a head taller than Maria and proportionally well built. His most captivating assets were his dark hair and dark soulful eyes.

Maria had met Jaime Moreno at Casa Di Laurenti five years before, when Massimo had invited him for a three day feast. Another one of Massimo's plans, Maria remembered while smiling. It was an instant connection. It worked perfectly well for both of them. Jaime travelled frequently for business, and Maria was a busy woman administering to the Di Laurentis. Yet, whenever she needed him he was there for her.

Jaime strode into the house, propelled by his usual vibrant energy, swept Maria into his arms and kissed her thoroughly. Before Maria could mumble a word he said, "She is fine." He smiled with the devil in his eyes. "I would venture to say that she is more than fine."

Maria recovered her breath after the kiss and the good news. "Why are you smiling? What do you know?"

Jaime groped Maria's buttocks roughly and made her squeal. "Because, my love, she's been locked up in a room with Doctor Fernandez for the past three days. And when I say room, I don't mean his surgery." His eyebrows rose up, and he fixed Maria a mischievous stare. "Something we should be doing right now." Jaime lifted Maria like a sack of grain over his shoulder, and marched up the stairs towards the direction of her room, while she laughed.

The news of the impending wedding arrived in Casa Di Laurenti a day after Jaime did. "Thank the heavens," was all Maria could say.

She felt responsible for setting a bad example for Sara because of her relationship with Moreno. Now, her conscience felt cleaner even though she did not regret the way she chose to lead her life. Suddenly, she thought about Massimo and his carefully orchestrated plan to set up his youngest daughter with the doctor. Well, it worked, slightly backwards, still, it worked. But how was she to fulfill the rest of Massimo's plan? With Sara married it might not be at all possible to ship her out of the country unless her husband agreed to go along. And if he did, Massimo's plans could move forward, granted that Sara was not with child at the time of departure.

First things first she decided, waving away all her troubled thoughts. Sara needed a dress, a wedding gown to be more precise. Maria knew exactly where to find one that would fit Sara beautifully. She walked into Camila's chambers and dug into one of the many wooden chests where old clothes were kept.

She found Camila's wedding gown, wrapped in silk. It was of rose-colored silk, with simple lines. She had not been present at Camila's wedding, but the gown looked like it had fit suggestively around the curves of her body. Sara had her mother's build, and she would look exquisite in this dress.

With five chests full of clothes and necessities for a bride, Maria and Jaime left Casa Di Laurenti in a carriage destined for the House of Gardens in Cordoba.

Maria's arrival at the Fernandez Palace could have not been better timed. She was welcomed by an ill-tempered Leon who mumbled words like crazy, unreasonable, and stubborn. Maria knew exactly whom he was talking about. She searched around and found her way, in between floating gardens, to Sara's whereabouts. Her location was relatively easy to find. A dramatic melody lured her to the far end of the second story.

Maria knocked once out of courtesy. Without waiting for a reply, she strode into Leon's room, and into the chamber adjacent to it, where Sara was doing her best to smash the keys of the harpsichord.

"Stop!" Maria yelled.

Sara looked up, noticing Maria for the first time. She jumped off the bench and threw herself in Maria's arms, nearly knocking her down on the floor.

After the exciting welcome, Sara looked at Maria suspiciously. "How did you know I was here, and why are you here?"

"Jaime is the answer to your first question, and your marriage to Doctor Fernandez is the answer to the second." Maria frowned. "Did you not have me called for the wedding?"

"What wedding?" Sara exploded in anger. "I already told him I shall never marry him. No, of course I did not have you called. Why that—sly, bastard pig, and that—that—"

"Man," Maria volunteered. "The man you've been sharing a bed with for a few days now," Maria added waiting for Sara's denial. "That's a yes, then. You must marry him."

"No, I won't. I can't. I won't."

Maria sighed. "So you've found some secrets about your family, I gather."

Sara responded with silence.

"You are a Jewess."

Sara looked at Maria intently. "How long have you known, Maria?"

Maria sat by Sara, and considered that breaking the news of her parents' indefinite departure was not going to be so difficult after all. "Oh, I never actually knew. I believe I always suspected it."

Sara pressed a key on the harpsichord. "Maria, I've seen things I cannot come back from."

Maria pressed a key also. "Then don't, *mi niña*. But you must not take it upon yourself to fight this fight on your own. This is a work of many men and women. I know you as though you were my own flesh, and I know that you would have never given yourself to a man if you were not madly in love with him."

Sara folded her hands on her lap. Maria caressed her hair and Sara leaned on her as she had done countless times when she was a child. "What about you? I can't lose you."

Maria sat up and set Sara straight in front of her. "My chests are down in the carriage waiting to be taken to my new quarters."

Sara hugged Maria, letting go of all the tension she had accumulated since Leon's proposal.

"Your bridegroom is awaiting and anxious," Maria said fighting tears.

"Good," Sara sniffled, "he deserves it."

A few minutes passed and the door to Leon's room opened. Leon and Jaime stood in the hallway, hands clasped behind their backs, expecting their women to come out at any moment. Although Sara had finally abandoned the refuge of the harpsichord room, the warm embrace Leon expected from her never happened. Instead, he stood watching as Sara and Maria marched out.

Leon rushed after Sara. His face masked with anxiety. "Where are you going?" Leon walked fast to catch up with her.

"To find a chamber of my own." Sara quickened her pace, but his strides were long enough to keep up with her.

"Sara, this is ridiculous. I beg you reconsider. As your husband, I will not allow you to leave after the wedding." He was pleading and that made Sara feel slightly guilty, but not so much that she would back down from her original decision.

She stopped walking and turned to him. "As my husband?" she retorted. "Doctor Fernandez, you are not my husband, you don't own me. I will inform you if a wedding will take place, and when. It appears to me that the fact that you deflowered me has you in moral turmoil," she added with a sneer, "and you will not rest until you make a respectable woman out of me. In the meantime while you dwell with your conscience, Doctor Fernandez, Maria and I have plenty to talk about."

Leon was left agape at the top of the stairs, while Sara and Maria chatted all the way down to the bottom of the stairs, as though they were strolling along the central market.

Maria and Sara were shown to adjacent rooms. Both chambers had direct access, through private patios, to one of the many gardens surrounding the house. "This place is paradise, Sara. How did he come to acquire this palace?"

"That is quite a unique story." Sara glinted with mischief.

Maria and Sara relaxed on Sara's bed and put their feet up on a pile of cushions. "It was given to Leon as payment for his services by a Moorish prince."

Maria frowned. Sara continued, "As soon as Leon arrived in Cordoba he called on the Marquis of Alazar to attend to some pending business. The marquis was delayed for the meeting—Leon was told upon his arrival that the marquis was unavailable due to a mishap with a house guest, the Moorish prince to be more precise. You see, apparently the two men were kind of—in the middle of—you know—"

"Sodomites!" exclaimed Maria covering her mouth with her hands.

Sara nodded. "Lovers, yes."

"Sara, *mi niña*, how do you know about these things?" Maria looked more outraged about Sara's knowledge of the various sexual practices of men, than about the story she was relating to her.

Sara looked at Maria matter-of-factly. "I've been educated in seven different languages, all of which I can speak, read, and write. My father's library holds more than classics of literature and philosophy. The books behind the heavy tomes of Plato are highly enlightening, I must say. Especially the ones about the secret life of Alexander the Great."

Maria nodded with some resignation. She gestured for Sara to carry on with the story.

"Leon heard screaming coming from the floor above, and pushed the servant aside, who was determined to not let him through. The whole staff stood crowded at the bottom of the stairwell, looking up towards the marquis's chambers."

"The marquise, his wife, where was she?" Maria asked.

"The wife was in the room, with them." Maria's eyes popped in surprise. Sara nodded, her eyebrows raised almost to her hairline.

"Leon had to bring the door down since it was locked from the inside, and found all three of them on the bed in a much compromising situation. The marquis and his wife were looking up the prince's—" Sara's chest was shaking with suppressed laughter. She composed herself as much as she could and continued the story. "The Moorish prince had something stuck in his—up his—"

Maria shook her head in disbelief. Sara nodded again, slowly, in confirmation.

"With the help of oils and some maneuvering Leon got it out. This prince is known to have three hundred and sixty-five concubines, one for each day of the year," Sara could not control her laughter anymore, "and he, he left Cordoba with a tarnished reputation and a s-so-sore behind." Both women erupted in hysterics.

When their laughter died down, Sara reached for Maria's hand. "I am sorry Maria… for everything I put you through."

Maria sat up and took both of Sara's hands. "You did what was right for you, *mi niña*. I have the obligation to help you, because of the love I bear for you. I could have pretended that there was nothing dark and unknown. But it is not in me. I vowed to protect you, not lie to you."

Sara hugged Maria. "Thank you. As my second mother, you are dearest to my heart."

"Well then," Maria stood up, "as your second mother I command you to marry that pitiable man looking like a tormented sheep, no later than tomorrow sundown."

The wedding took place in the privacy of the harpsichord chamber. If Leon felt he could barely breathe until Sara entered the room, he lost all the remaining air inside of him at the sight of his bride. Sara wore her mother's silk gown and it showed each of the delicate curves Leon knew all too well. Maria had carefully arranged Sara's hair to fall in waves of brown and amber down the length of her back, smooth as the silk of her gown. Leon wore a white shirt, and long white doublet embroidered with sapphire blue and silver silk threads, with matching blue hose. His dark hair was tied up neatly at the nape, and his head was covered with a white *kippah*. Over his shoulders he wore a prayer shawl matching the blue, white and silver of the rest of his attire, turning the blue in Leon's eyes as deep as the Mediterranean Ocean.

Five men and Maria entered the room after Sara. Jaime was one of them, the older man Sara recognized as the groom, and the other three men were as Leon called them, workmen at the palace.

The groom turned out to be a rabbi from Bilbao, who had escaped the hands of the Inquisition and found temporary asylum in the House of Gardens. The other three men were also Jews awaiting safe passage to Portugal.

Jaime and the three men erected four wooden poles mantled by a large *tallit*, the traditional Jewish prayer shawl, making up a canopy. The rabbi called the canopy, *chuppah*, a symbol of the newlyweds' home. The ceremony was conducted under the *chuppah* and in Hebrew.

Sara did not understand the meaning of any of the words, but the chanting choked her with emotion. The one thing she did understand clearly was her name, which was pronounced Sarah, with that special Hebrew lilt on the last consonant. Leon had a plain gold band ready to claim Sara as his, and he slid it onto her right index finger, trembling like a nervous boy. Nearing the end of the ceremony, Sara and Leon pledged eternal love to each other, and repeated a verse from Solomon's Song of Songs, "*Ani ledodi vedodi li.* I am for my beloved and my beloved is for me..."

Before stepping out of the *chuppah*, Jaime handed Leon a chalice made out of glass. Leon wrapped it with a piece of white linen, and stepped on it with all his weight. The cracking glass brought joy to the five men standing in the ceremony who shouted, "*Mazal Tov*," in unison.

Rabbi Lev David Fernandez and Sarah Fortuna Fernandez were officially declared, by the beaming rabbi from Bilbao, husband and wife under the Jewish law.

***

Later that night, while Leon held his wife in his arms and enjoyed her light snoring, he laughed at the way fate had tricked him. Six months before, he swore never to marry and sire children. On his wedding night, Leon could not imagine his life without Sara. While stroking her soft back, counting each one of her vertebrae, Leon mouthed a silent prayer, asking God to bless them with a child.

Chapter Twenty-Eight
Marranos

The morning after the wedding, the Fernandez household woke up to a hearty breakfast, served in a secluded alcove designated for private meetings. Sara, Leon, Jaime, and Maria sat at the table for a formal assembly.

The table was piled high with several early morning delicacies and fruit. Ceramic bowls, filled with an assortment of melons, were served at both ends of the solid cherry wood table. The center of the table, nestled between loaves of wheat bread with dates and walnuts, was crowned with a ceramic platter containing steaming glazed sweet rolls filled with figs, almonds, and honey, which had everybody's mouth watering. A jar of citrus juice and another of fresh cow's milk was also provided for the morning meal.

Sara barely ate, although she did make small talk. Maria could see the signs of Sara's mind working. She had chewed the insides of her mouth more than she had chewed her food, and the bridge of her nose was folded in a deep frown. Leon looked at Maria begging for clues to which Maria responded with the bite of a sweet roll and the rise of her eyebrows.

"What's troubling you this morning, my love?" Leon asked Sara, when he noticed her eyes had not left the watermelons for an over extended period of time.

Sara stared at Leon as though she had just seen him for the first time that morning. She opened her mouth, and then closed it. The same motion was repeated a couple of times. Leon stared back at her, silently waiting for his wife to form words that were apparently still fighting their way out.

Sara squinted at Leon, and then her eyes travelled past Maria and finally rested on Jaime. "It is fair to say, Jaime, you've been hiding fugitives at Casa Di Laurenti."

Jaime looked at Leon, who sat as blank as a piece of new parchment. "You, and my father, I gather as much…" Sara paused and bit her lower lip. "Mother Ignacia, the Gypsy Florica, my dear Lev is the newest addition to the ring, of course—" Sara's full attention was on Maria. "Where do you fit in this scheme, Maria?"

Maria was on her fourth sweet roll. She put it down, and wiped her hand on a linen napkin. "I manage a secret fund and I make sure that bags of coins are available when your father requests them." She smiled faintly. "I never ask questions."

Jaime reached for Maria's hand and brought it to his lips brushing it with a soft quick kiss as a sign of support. Jaime took on where Maria left off. "I arrange safe passage on cargo ships, mostly. Florica is one of the agents in Cordoba, as you may have already guessed," he explained while savoring a piece of melon. "Mother Ignacia harbors women. A woman looks as much as the next one draped under a nun's robe." Jaime laughed enjoying his own humor. Leon joined in with a wide smile.

Sara disregarded the comment with a quick question. She turned to Leon. "What about the children?"

Leon inhaled deeply before answering, as if more air was needed to continue Sara's interrogation. "The ones who survive, the ones we cannot get to in time, end up in brothels. When fortunate, at the bottom of El Carpio, or on the streets as beggars. Some of them succumb to the Church when they cannot withstand the physical abuse of living unprotected."

Sara felt as if the air had been knocked out of her. She stood up abruptly from the table and knocked down her chair in the process.

"The orphanage—" Leon cut in. "The one you started has been a miraculous help. But they often escape and we lose them. It's hard for them to stay in one place…" Leon shook his head. "These children were forced to stand and watch the butchering of their parents or older siblings. The only thing they can bear is the open air, the streets."

"And what about the ones you do get to in time?" Sara's voice sounded slightly choked.

Leon stood behind her, put a hand on her shoulder. "We hide them in good Christian homes, until we find relatives in other parts of Europe. When wanted, we send them off, when not…"

Leon looked down in despair. "This is bigger than all of us, my love. Europe is siding against us, one kingdom at a time. Portugal is not bending to the Inquisition, but it is only a matter of time. However, we are strong. We have been surviving for centuries. We shall live through it, too."

Sara turned around and looked up at Leon. "And you?"

Leon inhaled deeply again. "I, sometimes… after indulging the marquis's monetary demands… I use the name, his name, to be admitted into the dungeons of the Alcazar and persuade the guards to release prisoners. I bring them here," Leon looked down at his hands and closed his fists, "and I try, I do try healing them as much as I can. Sara, when I get them, they are broken. The guards— vile bastards that they are—only release the ones that are upon death's door. Some live and I help them escape." He clenched his jaw. "I have access to some of the names, to lists of names the Tribunal of the Inquisition plans to interrogate. We seek them out and make them disappear before it's too late."

"How?" The air in the room closed tightly around Sara, and she felt a drop of sweat running down her back.

Leon was actively involved in all aspects of the operation and a grip of fear took hold of her when she realized she could lose him. His voice brought her back to the breakfast alcove, and she saw him, strong, determined, disclosing every detail of his dangerous secret activities.

"The friar responsible for creating the official parchments suffered from a serious case of the pox. I was called in to see him. It did not take a physician to diagnose his condition, the signs were obvious. His skin was covered in red sores. He was fevered, heavy discharge." Leon waved his hand as though further explanation was not required. "The man was in need of urgent care. To this day, I think his condition worsened with the fear of facing eternal damnation for his weakness of the flesh. I used his fear to my advantage. My silence for the names." Leon closed his eyes, putting an end to that part of the story.

A sudden smile lighted his face as in bliss. His eyes opened wide, bright with enthusiasm. "On the other hand, I rejoice when I witness the reunion of our community for a holy day, a birth, a wedding, a *bar mitzvah*." His arms spread out wide, in an attempt to show Sara the immensity of those gatherings. "And there in front of my eyes, I see and I hear the little ones chanting along, pronouncing the same words our ancestors uttered centuries ago. That's when I know there's hope. In their young tongues, those words symbolize the promise of the survival of our people. This, what we do, is all very new for you, Sara." He bunched up her hands in his. "We do it for the ones who live and for the ones who died. We do it, my love, because every day could be our last."

Sara lifted a hand to Leon's face and traced it with her fingers. Although she was looking into his eyes, she was not focused on him. Her mind floated toward the streets, to the crude reality of rejected children who failed to find refuge and found death instead.

"The unwanted," she murmured under her breath. A searing pain rose up her chest. She stepped back from Leon and paced around the room. Her mouth went back to the twitching tic, a sure sign of forethought.

She turned to Leon. "I'm confident this palace has a hidden area built to accommodate the secret pleasures of the Moorish Prince, am I right?"

Leon nodded slowly. "An underground pleasure palace to be more precise. I dismantled one of the rooms." He rolled his eyes. "I'm no innocent, my love, but I swear I have never seen so many interesting objects before. The prince appears to be a creative man."

Jaime chuckled at Leon's subtle statement and joined in. "Indeed. It made me blush! Imagine that!" Jaime said with a roaring laugh. His contagious outburst broke through the iron tension that had settled upon the breakfast room, making everybody feel more at ease.

Jaime rose from his chair, cleared his voice and spoke up without pleasantries as was his manner. "You must marry in church, before word gets out of the new Señora Fernandez."

Sara was about to protest but was stopped short by Leon's stern look. "We will have a small ceremony at the marquis's chapel in two days' time."

Sara's glare on Leon was far from loving. He cut her off again, before the inception of a rant guaranteed to bring down the walls of the alcove.

Leon walked to her, cupped her chin and lifted it up, sure to make eye contact with her. "I will not jeopardize our operation for the sake of sentimental details. We are *Marranos*, my love. You must never forget it."

One of the three men who stood witness the evening before at the wedding, walked into the alcove. "Forgive me, Rabbi. A messenger from the house of Montes just rode in.

A hunting accident of some sort. The young son of Fernando Montes is seriously injured. They fear the worst."

Leon brushed a swift kiss on Sara's nose and left the room.

"Take Cid," Sara yelled after Leon.

The meeting was adjourned. Jaime took his leave promising to join them later that evening for dinner. Maria and Sara set out to explore the underground palace, granted that they could find it since no one at the House of Gardens seemed to know of its existence.

The search for the palace's hideout gave Sara the opportunity to see the sights of her new home. Although built close to the heart of the city, and not far from the Jewish Quarters, the House of Gardens stood cocooned in the curve of an *S* at the bend of a road, which reached a dead end beyond the palace's grounds.

Tired of walking under the sun and itching to gather the palace's formal staff—if there was one—Maria abandoned the hopeless search. Sara was left free to rummage around until some secret gate leading to the pleasure palace would open magically at the touch of a stone.

Sara became frustrated by her fruitless search and reclined against the wall of a large fountain on which was erected a gigantic statue of an angel. Six large colorful fishes, with wings like butterflies, swam in its crystalline water. From here she had a perfect view of an orange rose garden, one she had never seen before and adopted instantly as her own. The beauty of her newly discovered garden did not diminish the fact that she was hot, as a result of the searing sun, and tired and sore, as a result of their passionate wedding night.

She admired the dance of the fishes against the calm tide of the water, and considering the heat striking at midday, she felt a tinge of jealousy at how cool they seemed to be. She was tempted to dip her fingers in the water, but the strangeness of the fish kept her from sinking any parts of her body in the fountain's pool. Instead, she stood on the edge and, dangling from the statue's wing, she reached for a spray of cold water coming out from the angel's mouth. Sara almost lost her footing when as if by magic, a portal opened beneath the body of the angel. Sara held on strongly to the wing of the statue and peeked down the open gap. She smiled triumphantly and stepped down to a long marble stairway that led directly into the underground palace.

After surveying the numerous chambers of the underground palace, Sara was convinced she had found the answer to her prayers. The accommodations in this newly found treasure were as habitable as the ones above ground, except for some explicit graphics on the walls, and some disturbing apparatus targeted to pleasure the sexual fantasies of the most perverted of beings, which would have to be immediately removed for the sake of morality.

***

The young Montes died moments after Leon entered the Montes' manor. He found the boy lying in a pool of blood atop a large desk in Señor Montes' study. The lad's mother was slumped over her son, sobbing and pressing down on his wounds with the weight of her own body. Wounds that would undoubtedly take away the life of her only child.

The young boy, barely fourteen, had gone out hunting with his father on what was meant to be a test of his manhood. The boy was of delicate nature and did not possess the aggressiveness to kill. Fernando Montes doubted his only son's virility and had bullied him into going after a red boar they sighted in the woods. The boy, goaded by his father for his weakness, charged forth determined to kill the boar with his arrow. But the arrow fell short, creasing the boar's thick head, maddening it. The beast charged young Montes, startling his horse, and thrust his tusks under its belly, overturning him. The horse rolled over trapping the boy underneath. Unable to escape, the young Montes was savaged by the angry boar. By the time Fernando Montes arrived at the scene, the boar had done its damage. The horse was bleeding out and so was his son. The boar was intent on ripping the young boy's body with its thorny teeth. Fernando Montes stabbed the savage beast until it's jaw slacked, finally releasing his dying son.

There was nothing Leon could have done to save the young boy's life. The boar chewed through his internal organs, granting the boy a slow and painful death.

A step behind Leon, a monk came to deliver the boy's last rites. Señora Montes, angered by the unjust fate of her dear boy, screamed profanities at the priest and to the heavenly Lord he represented, demanding a logical explanation for her son's death. The young priest's job turned out to be impossible, since he could not approach the body of the young man, or his crazed mother, without being spat at or hit with angry fists. At the end, the last rites were administered swiftly from a safe distance, and the priest darted out of the house afraid of being possessed by the hysteria of the mother.

Leon stood silently beside the woman. There were no words of consolation he could bring himself to express. Her son was dead.

The brave Fernando Montes had not been courageous enough to accompany his son during his last excruciating moments.

In a strangled croak, Señor Montes confessed to Leon his boy's last moments. His mangled son had looked at him straight in the eye when he pulled him from under the boar and horse. "Do not be angry with me, please father," he had mumbled before succumbing. For Fernando Montes the last words of his son were a death sentence by burning. He was consumed by the flames of hell, forever in pain, forever guilty.

Although they were a Catholic family, as a rabbi, Leon had the moral duty to see the Montes couple united and supporting each other in this moment of grief. The body of the boy had to be removed from the study, washed, and prepared for burial. The mother would not hear of any clerics attending to her son. She would wash him, and care for him, because it was to be her last time. Leon convinced her to detach herself from her son, and with his aid they cleaned the maimed boy. Leon took special care to stitch the hollow wound in the center of the boy's stomach, preventing bodily fluids from seeping through the clothes the mother so lovingly dressed her son in.

After a draining process of exculpating Fernando Montes for the accidental death of his son, Leon was able to gather the couple around the boy's corpse, and finally help them come to terms with his death.

***

Leon arrived back at the House of Gardens past dinnertime. All he wanted was to feel the warmth of Sara's body next to his. He was sick with death and grief. He questioned God's decision on that fatal incident. "Why teach the arrogant Montes a lesson with the death of his child? Why not take away Fernando Montes from the boy's life instead?" Leon yelled at God the way he had done many times when enraged with his creator's judgment.

He called out Sara's name with the authority of a master and found no response.

Maria heard his anxious shouting and rushed to him while wrapping herself in a throw. "She's gone. I tried to stop her, but she rushed out to the city. She said she will explain everything when she is back."

He stared at her blankly.

"She hinged Señorita to a ratty cart she found abandoned in the stables and left."

Leon closed his eyes trying to control the surge of fury rising in his chest. He turned on his heels and headed to the door.

"She is yours in heart and soul, Leon." Maria's words echoed through the grand entrance. "But her spirit belongs to no one."

Maria sat with Leon under the dim glow of a solitary lamp in his study. Eventually, Jaime, a steady guest at the House of Gardens, came to join them as they sat watching the night grow into dawn.

***

Faint footsteps echoed beyond the doors of the study. Maria nudged Jaime, who had fallen fast asleep, and they both left the room.

Sara entered the study, dressed in her riding attire. Leon's temper had been under control while Maria and Jaime kept him company. He had sat silently thinking about all the horrible things that could have happened to his wife, while he was patiently waiting for her. Then, his mind shifted to all the horrible things he would do to her upon her safe return. He even contemplated beating her until she would promise never to leave the palace unaccompanied or without his consent. He knew he was only fantasizing. He could not hurt Sara physically, yet her thoughtlessness hurt him.

Sara stood by the door waiting to be scolded. Leon glanced at her while closing his fists tight until his nails dug into the skin of his palms. He kept silent and so did she.

After a few moments of tense quietness, Sara yawned and said sleepily, "I need rest," and without a backward glance she walked out of the study leaving the door open.

Leon sat on his chair feeling like a fool. This woman, his wife, kept him up the whole night dreading for her safety, and when she returned she went about her business as if nothing out of the ordinary had happened. The constraint he had exercised up until that moment boiled into an uncontrollable rage that sent him running after her.

Leon broke down the bedroom door with a solid kick. Sara was slipping into her shift and started at Leon's explosive entrance. He was almost out of breath and his eyes shone dark with a mixture of emotions. He walked to Sara and grabbed her arms with an iron grip.

She did not say a word. She looked up coldly into his eyes declaring a duel.

"Where the hell were you?" Leon roared. She kicked his shin but only succeeded in hurting her bare toes since Leon's fury had taken him past physical awareness. He repeated his question, this time shaking her.

Sara kept her defying eyes on him.

Leon lowered his face to hers and sniffed her like a dog. "You've been drinking!" He frowned in disgust. "Where, Sarah? Where were you?" After a few failed attempts to extract a word out of her by force, he stepped away from her and slumped on the bed. His shoulders dropped and his head fell to his chest like a heavy boulder.

Sara was almost to the door when she heard his quiet sob. She climbed on the bed behind him and wrapped her arms across his chest. "There are things I must do as a *Marrano*, Lev. It is my duty."

Leon threw his head back and leaned on Sara's chest. "I needed you." His voice was raspy and low. He turned to her and grabbed her arms again. "I am sick with death, Sarah. I smell it, I touch it. I, Rabbi Lev, speak for a God that rewarded a man's arrogance with the gruesome death of his only son, and then I think, how is he going to repay my constant insolence towards him, my endless doubts? And I run to you, because I fear he will take you from me—because you—you breathe life into me." With each word his grip on Sara tightened.

"You are hurting me," she said in a firm voice, but he was not done with her.

"I come home to you, to make me forget, to make me feel that not everything I touch is death." He pulled her up within a hairbreadth of his face. "And death plays with me, Sarah. And I feared he finally did it, he stole you from me." He shook with grief.

Sara could not look at him in the eye any longer and turned her face from his. "I'm here now," she whispered. "Let go of my arms and let me hold you." Her voice grew louder and commanding, yet tender.

Leon's big frame collapsed on her like a falling tree. Sara undressed him and took him to bed. He buried his face in between her breasts and inhaled her scent, erasing the stench of loss that followed him all the way from the Montes' manor till the moment he watched Sara saunter into the house alive. He spent his anguish by losing himself in her. And she let him have her in the way he needed to. Later, when Sara felt Leon's breathing easing up, she got out of bed and slipped into the music room and into the usual dreamlike state that connected her with Angelina.

When Leon woke, Sara was not in the bed. The memory of his earlier actions shamed him. He was not a man to lose his temper so easily, but then again, he had never feared for anybody's safety before as he feared for Sara's. It had been his choice to marry her, even though he knew she would not be an obedient wife.

Leon made to leave the bed when Sara suddenly walked into the room with a tray of food and juice. She settled the tray on the desk opposite their bed, poured juice in a mug, and offered it to Leon who took it eagerly. Sara walked back to the desk and waited for Leon's interrogation, one she knew she could not escape.

"Come closer. I won't bite, I promise." He summoned her while he took another swig of his juice.

"I spent the night at a brothel," Sara spurted out bluntly. Leon burst into a coughing fit as he choked with the half-drained mug of juice. Sara rushed to him and thumped his back until he was able to gasp some air. She quickly stepped away from him and lifted her hands defensively. "Let me explain…"

The notion of children being sold as sex slaves because their families abroad did not want them, had haunted Sara since that morning's meeting. She had the resources to help and the desire to foster those children until other arrangements could be made. She had to find a solution.

The Jewish crisis was escalating and spreading across Western Europe. Who knew how long it would take for the rest of Europe to adopt the anti-Jewish policy, and have the mass of newly arrived immigrants from the west expelled once more?

"The solution has to be found outside the European limits," she put simply to Leon, as she sat on the bed next to him.

An idea formed in Sara's mind. "I envision organized groups, not just single families, settling in lands where Jews are not treated as pariahs, demons, or second-class citizens."

From the little she knew about Jewish history, the people had always survived as a community and not as individuals. In the current political and religious environment the Jewish crisis in Spain was dire. There were many parents who had lost children, and many children left as orphans. If the community as a whole was to join in raising children while supporting each other, new families would be born out of tragedy, and the continued existence of the Jewish people would not be threatened as long as a strong community existed. But, where?

Constantinople was still safe. The Holy Land was a constant target of Muslims and stray Crusaders. Who knew? Maybe India, even China.

The amber in her eyes glimmered with passion as she poured out her ideas to Leon. He could not help but love her more than he already did for her idealism. If it only were so simple, he pondered. "The brothel," he demanded, feigning severity.

"Yes, yes… of course… the brothel."

Leon got out of bed and poured a second mug of juice and gave it to her. He raised his eyebrows, an order to proceed. "Lev, I cannot leave those children in the hands of—I simply cannot." She swallowed hard, unable to control her emotions. "I rode Señorita to the brothel, the one by the tavern outside the Jewish Quarters. I walked in and asked to see the Madame. I gave her two bags of silver coins. I bought them, Lev. All six of them."

Leon closed his eyes to organize his thoughts without losing his common sense to Sara's glistening stare.

"There's more…" Leon opened his eyes resigned to digest the information as it came. "After two jugs of wine, and some very interesting suggestions, the Madame gave me valuable information to enhance my wifely duties." Sara tilted her head and threw Leon a suggestive gaze. "It was a wondrous meeting, I must say. At the end of the night we became comfortable with each other, like good acquaintances."

Leon fixed Sara with a sardonic glare. "Will we be expecting Madame for dinner this coming Friday for *Shabbat*?"

Sara shrugged. "Well, not exactly, but she is my new partner."

"Partner? Sarah, have you gone insane? A brothel?" Leon's voice escalated until it became a booming threat.

Sara burst out with laughter. "Oh, my dear Lev, you give me less credit than I deserve. No, I will not go into the brothel business." Sara wiped her face and cleared her voice. "As I was saying before, after two pitchers of wine, the Madame disclosed a secret, a dangerous secret. The children are the property of the Church. She gets a *lot*, as they call them, twice a month. The kids are brought to Cordoba from all over Spain. The soldiers, who raid Jewish homes and arrest the adults in the house, make sure to deliver the children safely to the Church in exchange for a reward. Then, a small group of monks pick the most desirable ones and distribute the *lots* amongst brothel houses in Cordoba. I doubt the Church is directly involved with it. This only happens in one diocese, as far as the Madame knows. There's a particular friar who runs the ring and protects the brothel houses, in exchange for the payment the children get for their services." Sara shook her head obviously affected. "Sadly, children are highly sought after."

Leon felt sick to his stomach. "How will Madame justify the six missing children from her house?"

"Lev, most of them die within one or two months after arriving at the brothels. She will house them in the brothel's storage room for a week. Then, I will pick them up and pay her for all of them. In the meantime, the friar will only get payment for the services of two, maybe three at most. Eventually, she will tell him the children died or ran away."

"I gather we have six children in the house now," Leon concluded.

Sara nodded slowly. The fire in her eyes was replaced by a veil of sadness. "Some of them need doctoring, Lev. They are… damaged."

"Where are they, Sarah?"

"The underground palace," she said matter of factly.

By the time Leon went down to the secret rooms, the children were bathed, fed, and clothed with clean garments. Even after the gentle loving treatment they received from Sara and Maria, they were all huddled together against a wall, protecting each other.

The children were specters of their former selves. Cracked lips, battered faces, and bruised wrists. It took Leon several hours before the children would allow him near them. That night, Sara, Maria, Jaime, and Leon slept in the underground palace in close proximity to the children.

Before falling asleep Sara whispered into Leon's ear, "Can you imagine if a new world were to be discovered, where we would not have to hide, where we could live in peace?"

Chapter Twenty-Nine
The Tribe

The events of the following day reflected the true life of a *Marrano*. In the morning, Sara and Leon were wed under Catholic law at the Alazars' chapel, with the marquis standing as witness, followed by a small feast at the marquis's castle.

Later that day, a meeting of paramount significance—far from a celebration—was held at the House of Gardens. In a small room in the underground palace Sara, Leon, Jaime, Maria, the rabbi from Bilbao, and the three men gathered to discuss Sara's proposal of going back to Jewish tribal life.

The idea, although appealing, needed to be carefully planned. It was necessary to spread out the operation between several residences in Cordoba in order to diffuse the traffic of people from the Fernandez's Palace.

Jaime suggested Casa Di Laurenti as one of the locations. The Di Laurenti manor had been used successfully as a hideout for refugees over the years. The staff was blind to the newcomers and its remote location made it easy to smuggle people in and out of a region surrounded, as it was, by dense woods. His familiarity with the area and its scarce neighbors made Jaime comfortable to run the operation from there.

Maria was to stay in Cordoba with Sara and do the runs to the brothel. The three men, a teacher, a silversmith, and a baker, were to manage a training program for the exiled. The main idea of the program was to teach the refugees of the *Tribe* basic skills from the many talents brought in by the newcomers. The future of the members of the Tribe in foreign lands was uncertain. Knowledge was not a bulky load, but an invaluable asset that the Tribe would need to carry when transitioning into a new life.

Another important aspect of the Tribe's rescue mission was finances. Most of the Jewish families across Spain were in possession of great wealth. Fleeing and leaving their fortune behind simplified the major objective of the Inquisition, which was recruiting souls to Christ while fattening up Fernando and Isabel's coffers. The core of the Inquisition consisted in amassing the riches of the subdued in the name of the Lord, to empower the dominion of the Catholic Church across the world as a political force.

Leon was as certain of this fact as he was of his need of air to breathe. His undesirable connection with the two-faced marquis provided him with access to earnest confessions. Confessions made by nobles as well as high-ranking monks, during functions at the Alazars' castle, when their tongues were sodden with the best of wines. Clouded with alcohol, the truth of the Inquisition was spelled out in blurry messages, yet clear to the ears of a *Marrano*.

Massimo Di Laurenti and his ring of agents across the Orient, Africa, and Constantinople were the answer to the immediate transfer of funds needed to empty the vaults of the wealthiest *Marranos* in Spain. The money would have to be invested in foreign trade ventures, shipments of spices from India, or African ivory transported across the Sahara Desert into Northern Africa by camel caravans. Once delivered, the profits of the transaction would go to moneychangers abroad who would allocate the earnings to a bogus mercantile account. To justify the loss, fake documentation of failed businesses and lost shipments to pirates would be produced in order to deceive the tax collectors in Spain. The main objective of Leon's plan was to show the financial ruin of the most solid *Marrano* fortunes in Spain. In reality, the biggest downfall the supposedly bankrupt families would suffer would be the loss of their main residences.

Leon was conscious that his financial plan would not be widely accepted by the wealthy Jews of Spain, people accustomed to living better than monarchs themselves. However, he was certain that there were others willing to take a loss if they could leave Spain with their lives and a healthy portion of their wealth safely invested in foreign lands. When signing on to the Tribe's financial scheme, each bearer would be assessed a percentage on their investment to be distributed as payment between the agents responsible for keeping the operation rolling. Also, a fund would be created to aid victims of the Inquisition left unable to fend for themselves.

The founding members of the Tribe voted unanimously on all aspects of their new venture. A sense of pride rose throughout the small room of the underground palace, a place which gradually became the axis of a clandestine community where dismembered families came together as one.

***

As she had been doing for many months, Sara drew the rattling cart to a stop upon the stone paved alleyway at the back entrance of the brothel. It had become her custom to drive Señorita and the beat-up cart for *The Lot Runs*, a new phrase coined by members of the Tribe. It was the best cover up she could come up with given the unfortunate looks of the sweet mare. Señorita, pulling the decrepit cart almost in shambles, was sure to escape the attention of anybody, as they went about their business under the cover of the Cordoban nights. Sara also declined to wear her usual riding habit. Instead, she wore a hooded monk's robe which concealed her shapely body as well as her face. The lot of this night was to be the largest so far since her partnership with the Madame began four months before. Thanks to the work of María and the Madame, they were able to spare over twenty children, ranging from ages five to fourteen, from the terrible fate of child prostitution.

***

The Madame looked at the wooden clock in her chamber, she expected Sara Fernandez to come in at any time to take the lot from her hands. In the meantime, she lounged in her chaise chair and counted her blessings. Sara Fernandez was one of them.

She considered her trade an art. She welcomed her courtesans only if they knew the risks of the profession and its repercussions. It was their choice to sell their bodies for money, and it was their own consciences that they had to live with.

A big bulk of the whorehouse's business came from the local clergy. The advantage of servicing the men of the cloth was the ritual of soul salvation they performed for the prostitutes after the deed was done. Regardless of their profession, the prostitutes were all devoted Catholics and their yearning for eternal salvation was paid with the agony of their flesh. At least that was the indisputable explanation a number of priests gave the well-used harlots after leaving their chambers.

The day the Madame received an official visit from a friar of the Inquisition, a large man who enjoyed being flayed by Hugo the gatekeeper, while mounting the ample assed Juana from behind, she became worried. She did not wish for any connections with the Church beyond the unlimited access the monks had to her working girls.

The large friar reclined petulantly on a red upholstered French chaise, across from the Madame in her office. He declined the glass of cognac that she saved for her most valued customers and jumped directly to the purpose of his impromptu visit.

"My jurisdiction has encountered a problem with the young heretics," he explained in a leveled tone. "While I wish wholeheartedly to convert the children to Christ, the cost of supporting them is beyond what the Inquisition allocates for the seed of nonbelievers."

His plan was to make the youngsters work their way to the Lord with the sacrifice of their own bodies, binding into Christ, in body and soul. The Madame was to be allotted a small portion of the earnings, enough to feed the lot, as the friar referred to the children, while a delegate of his priory would collect the rest of the proceeds every fortnight.

The proposal was a dirty one and the friar knew it. He was a perverse man when it came to satisfying his lust, and took advantage of his powerful status to impose his will. Before the Madame could utter a word of contradiction, he ratified his continuous protection over her business as long as she complied with his orders. He also mentioned the fact that her name had been brought up for investigation by the Holy Tribunal and it had suddenly vanished from their minds as if by a miracle.

"Miracles are hard to come by these days, Madame, unless we are willing to make sacrifices," the sweating friar said casually while eyeing his dirty nails.

The Madame was cornered with no other choice other than to take the children in, along with a whole new clientele of perverted men from all corners of society.

The Madame was sick with fear and grief for consenting to the rape of those little souls. Fortunately, the youngsters did not last long. The Lord was kind to them and welcomed them to heaven before the children reached the second month of torturous abuse under her roof.

When Sara Fernandez walked into the brothel for the first time, dressed as a Turkish warrior, the Madame thought her to be another deviant character and wondered what sexual fantasies a woman dressed in men's clothes had in mind. To her relief, Sara did not seek pleasure—she came to her for help.

After hours of conversing and two pitchers of her best wine, the Madame gave silent thanks to God for sending a woman to teach her a lesson on courage. Sara helped the Madame, more than the Madame helped Sara, because on her own she would have not had the guts to defy the friar in order to save her own life, never mind the lives of others.

***

Señorita was always cooperative when pulling the cart to the brothel and back to the House of Gardens. Yet on this night the mare was unusually restless. Something had shifted in the air and the unnerving silence and stillness of the night, accompanied by Señorita's impatient hoof beats pounding on the paved road, crept darkly over Sara.

The children were late and there was no indication of any activity inside the brothel. Sara started to step down from the cart, when a man, hose around his ankles, ran out of the building screaming. Before she could recover from the shock of the man's strange exit, pandemonium broke loose from every narrow door leading to the innards of the brothel. A half-dressed mob of panicked men and women fled into the streets pushing and trampling each other in their haste to run away. Concerned for the children's safety, Sara jumped off the cart, and pushed her way through the crowd and into the building.

There was an unnatural quietness in the cleared-out brothel house. The hairs on the back of her neck prickled with the anticipation of an imminent attack from any of the silent corners of the main room where she was standing. Sara surveyed the first floor and found it to be deserted. The brothel's working chambers were housed on the second floor. The children's hideout was on the same floor at the end of the hallway in a storeroom.

Sara crept up the stairs careful not to make a sound on the creaking wood. A ghostly presence, that felt as if it watched her every move, lay heavy in the air around her. She touched the handle of the knife she always carried belted to her hip bone, and pulled it free in one swift motion. The doors to the rooms stood ajar. Sara pushed the first door to her right open, one of many doors lining the hallway.

She drowned a cry of panic when the body of a courtesan lay sprawled on the floor, her severed head inches away from her bloody torso. Sara ran from room to room, and found the same grisly scene in each one of them.

A killer was in the building and she was right there with him. The way to the storeroom at the end of the hallway, where the children were supposed to be hiding safely, seemed miles away. Sara felt numb. She forced her body, heavy with fear, to reach the door. It was the only closed door in the whole house. She opened it. The room was dark but the stench of terror told her it was not empty. Sara shakily held onto her knife with both hands, uncertain of what her next move should be. She could not see him, but she sensed the killer's menacing presence.

A warning cry broke the silence. Out of the darkness, a devil embodied in the form of a priest slashed out of the darkness and sliced the space between him and Sara with an executioner's sword. Sara fell backwards and dodged his murderous blade only by a hairbreadth. She recovered and ran out of the storeroom and down the stairs to the main floor.

The crazed priest did not look pleased with his failed attack and charged after her with his sword held high, pronouncing the sinner's prayer fervently, "Heavenly Father, I confess to you that I'm a sinner, that I can't change on my own, that I'm in need of salvation. I believe you sent your son Jesus to be my savior, my redeemer, my Lord. Through his death, his resurrection, and his ascension, my sins can be forgiven and I can be assured an eternal place in heaven with you."

Sara refused to leave without the children. Out of breath, she reached the first floor, and hid behind a massive couch set against a corner.

The priest was not to be fooled. Kicking and pushing every obstacle in his way, he made it to Sara's hideout. She jumped out from behind the couch and stunned him, taking the opportunity to plunge her knife into his left shoulder. The priest looked at Sara wide eyed, but regained his murderous composure before she had the chance to free herself from the confinement between the couch and wall. The priest raised his sword to deliver a fatal blow when something sharp struck him from behind. A child, smeared in blood, gaunt and with the biggest brown eyes, jabbed a poker through the priest's back. The priest looked back at the child, surprised, but still holding onto the sword.

He smiled sweetly at the scared boy, and then he ran his sharp blade through the child's middle. Only then did the priest let go off the sword and fall on his knees in prayer, "Heavenly Father, I confess to you that I'm a sinner, that I'm in need of salvation..." The rest of the words were lost as he collapsed on the bloodied carpet.

Sara jumped out from behind the couch, knelt beside the child and lifted his head on her lap. Her hands trembled. "Please, God. Please, God."

The child smiled faintly at her. "Is it over?" he asked. "Is the bad man gone?"

Sara held the boy tight to her chest and carried him up the stairs. Blood drained from his body rapidly. *He will be all right*, she told herself. Leon had taught her how to control the bleeding. She knew how to do it. She knew she could do it. She would mend the little boy's wound and they would soon leave this horrible place and be safe at the House of Gardens.

Sara walked into the first room she found and stepped over the dismembered body lying on the floor. She placed the child on the bed, ripped strips of bed sheet, and secured a tight dressing around the boy's sliced abdomen. The boy was slipping into unconsciousness. She caressed his hair and his face. "Wait for me, my dear child. Don't sleep yet. I'll be only a moment." The boy nodded faintly and Sara rushed out of the room.

She reached the door to the storeroom, where the Madame sat on the floor, soaked with blood, surrounded by the lifeless bodies of seven young children. She looked up at Sara with hollow eyes. "He said they were saved. He killed them all."

The gruesome scene was more than Sara could bear. Those children were gone, but she could still save one, the one who saved her life. The two women looked into each other's eyes and with a faint nod Sara left to tend to the only surviving child.

When she ran back into the room the young boy was barely breathing. His eyes remained open, alert. He had waited for her. She picked him up, cradled him close to her bosom and carried him down the stairs. "What is your name, my beautiful boy? Your Jewish name."

The boy moved his head close to Sara's ear and breathed his last word, "Yehuda."

Sara walked out into the desolate street holding the dead child in her arms. A full moon illuminated his young face. He looked peaceful, drowned in deep sleep. She rode slowly back to the House of Gardens, careful not to disturb his eternal dream.

***

Leon was ready to leave the stables with Cid when he saw Sara approaching. He rushed to her and stood silent at the sight of the little boy's body hanging limp from Sara's arm. There was no need for an explanation for the unusual delay.

They had argued heatedly when she set her mind on riding on her own to the brothel every time there was a lot to pick up. In the beginning, he had forbidden her from doing it. His attempt to impose his will on her was short lived as she argued her right to action as a member of the Tribe. It had been difficult for him to consent to it, but he knew that her heroic initiative to save the children was part of being Sarah.

It always amazed him to see how she managed to appease the children she rescued from the brothel. As soon as they arrived at the House of Gardens, they would follow her like a row of ducklings into the harpsichord room. Maria would be waiting there with bowls of warm milk, and fresh sweet rolls. Comfort food, she called it. Then they would all gather around the harpsichord, and Sara would not stop playing uplifting tunes until the last of the children had given in to some sort of a smile.

This night they would not gather for milk, music, or laughter.

Tonight there was to be a funeral.

Sara stepped down from the cart, still holding the child, and walked straight into her harpsichord room. She placed the boy in the crook of her left elbow and freed her right hand to play. She needed to escape from the cruelty of that night and she wanted to take the boy into the light of her melodies. She could not. She was numb with pain.

Leon came into the room with his *tallit* rolled under his arm, a bowl with warm water, and a sponge. Sara laid the boy on the floor and in silence they washed him and wrapped him in Leon's *tallit*. The child was now ready for a proper Jewish burial.

Sara sat on the floor beside the boy and kissed his forehead a few times. Leon stood back silently. Hours passed until Sara was ready to release the boy to Maria.

She never left the harpsichord room that day. She sat on the bench and stared at the keys as though they were foreign to her.

Leon stood behind her. He was also struck with grief. "He could have been ours, Lev. Our son."

She turned to him, her face masked with pain. Her lips were set firmly because she would not allow herself to cry. She swallowed hard and put both her hands on her lower abdomen. "I'm with child, Lev. His name shall be Yehuda."

Leon reached for her hands, but she moved them swiftly to the keys of the harpsichord before she would succumb to the shelter of his warm touch. She closed her eyes to the material existence of the space around her. She was not in the harpsichord room any longer. She flowed into a weightless space where nothing mattered. She was back with Angelina.

Part III

Chapter Thirty
Turmoil

Argentina - 1978

Angelina no longer needed music to communicate with Sarah. The bond established between them was the closest thing to what Angelina had once read in a medical journal about the intricate connection of twins. She loved to fantasize about the idea of having a twin with whom words were not necessary to communicate.

Throughout her years with Sarah, she questioned her sanity. In the beginning, she attributed her journeys to an alternate space and time, to the shock she experienced when she was so violently removed from her family and placed under the care of the Church. But that would have been extremely unfair to Mamá Lucia.

Lucia was the most wonderful mother a child could have yearned for. She was different from Marta, her birth mother, because Lucia had adopted her with her heart.

The memory of her birth parents faded slowly throughout the twelve years in which she had been at the *Trapa*. She could not remember her mother's face or her father's smile without the help of the only photograph she had left of them. She did remember the events they shared as a family, especially the last one. The memories of the day after her sixth birthday were seared with a pain that never left her.

There was nothing she could do to bring her parents back, but at least she could find answers to what she had become. She was torn in two. She was woman and child. Past and present.

Books. She needed to find answers in books. Angelina was barely thirteen when she started reading through the few medical and psychological tomes the convent held in its library.

It was then that Lucia's suspicions were confirmed. Although obedient and a faithful Catholic, Angelina's spirit was not made for a convent life. Perhaps her future would lay in the medical field, added to the fact that she was a gifted pianist. The sisters usually stood in awe when watching Angelina play the piano. She did not play publicly. It happened in the wee hours of the morning when most of the convent was asleep. The beautiful melodies she played danced around the convent grounds, luring a peregrination of sleepy nuns into the chapel.

Angelina's gift for music could no longer be overlooked and, Lucia did what any mother would have done. She searched high and low until she found a music teacher who could teach Angelina how to write the melodies she so passionately played on the chapel's old piano. She learned quickly and within a couple of months Angelina had several spiral notebooks filled with musical notes. When played together, they sounded like heaven to Lucia's ears.

Leaving the convent grounds for music lessons opened Angelina's eyes to her new favorite place, the public library across from her teacher's home. Angelina noticed the excitement in Mamá Lucia when she watched her sit for endless hours researching medical books. There was something about medicine that attracted her. She was not disturbed by the sight of blood or open wounds. She often thought about Leon Fernandez and his journey as a physician in the late fifteenth century. However, her main interest did not lie in traditional medicine. She concentrated her reading in matters of the psyche.

Long ago, she had dismissed the presence of the other woman who inhabited the core of her being as an imaginary friend. The other woman, Sarah, although from another time and place, felt as real as Mamá Lucia to her.

To her dismay, after some thorough research she feared she was a victim of what mental health professionals called Multiple Personality Disorder. Her case fell under the traditional description of the mental illness. She had experienced a traumatic event during her childhood, which had led her to forgo her desire to communicate. Instead, she had created an alternate dimension, where somebody she had never met before filled up the void with stories of a life far removed from the one at the *Trapa. There,* she concluded, *I'm crazy.* If she could only push herself to communicate with the outside world and not only with the fantasy in her head, she might break the spell and attain something close to normalcy.

Through Angelina's frequent visits to the public library, Lucia noticed her eagerness to part from the routine imposed by a life surrounded with old, boring nuns, and scored a second victory in favor of her child. After heated arguments with the other sisters about the pros and cons of secular education, Mamá Lucia happily enrolled Angelina in a public high school.

Lucia, a true Italian with a straightforward manner, brought up the issue of Angelina's speech with the school's headmaster. "There is nothing wrong with her speech—she just chooses not to use it. The day she'll find something worth saying, she will do it."

With the finality of that statement, the headmaster's questions about Angelina's mental competence were quickly dismissed and the subject was avoided throughout the three years Angelina attended the school.

During her last year of schooling, Angelina deepened her research into the Jungian theory of racial memory and collective unconscious. In lieu of her mental sanity, she favored that theory better than the one of Multiple Personality Disorder.

Jung's theory of genetic memory explained that people have certain memories encrypted in their psyche which may have belonged to their ancestors, such as feelings or ideas. Other venues to explore Angelina's phenomenon were through hypnosis, to regress the subject into a probable past life or consult with a psychic. But Angelina did not need to be regressed in time. Being Sarah in the fifteenth century felt as real to her as being the introverted orphan walled up in a convent. She was both past and present.

Aside from her personality phenomenon and all the plausible methods to explore it, she chose psychology as the one most fitting to quench her thirst for knowledge. To her advantage, she had all those years of silence and deep observation in the field of human behavior. She had turned into an expert on the ways of people's interaction, body language, and manipulative roles. For Angelina, the study of psychology was merely an academic passion, not a path to unravel the mysterious origins of her alternate life. In a way, she wanted to keep Sarah separate from her books and rather as a part of her persona waiting to unfold.

Throughout the years filled with Sarah's melodies and stories, Angelina came to know a passionate woman willing to risk her life for what she believed to be just. Angelina yearned to become that person in her own time. She was ready to reclaim her old self, the person she was before being brutally torn from that tiny stucco house in Pueblo Brugo.

Angelina's interest in the study of the psyche made her consider it as a career path. When graduating from high school, Mamá Lucia asked her about her plans for the future. "You could take the oath at any time, my child. But I know that's not what you really want."

Angelina, who by then had grown into an attractive young woman with deep glowing brown eyes atop high cheekbones, rich dark curls, and a svelte figure, looked into Lucia's eyes and shook her head side to side.

"So, tell me. What do you want?"

Angelina set her lips firmly suppressing the urge to speak up, but nonetheless words flowed out of her. "I want to study psychology at the University in Buenos Aires."

Both women sat stunned at the sound of a voice that seemed like it did not belong to anybody in the room. It took Lucia a few moments to come to terms with what had happened. Her little girl had finally spoken. She had a voice and as Lucia had predicted years before, she would use it only when she felt it necessary to do so.

Lucia had foreseen this day. She knew her daughter would eventually wake up from the lethargy imposed by sadness and become the beautiful, intelligent woman she was destined to be.

The good nun had kept a savings account with what her family had given her when leaving Europe, and ever since Angelina arrived she had added the small monthly allowance she received from the Order. With a child's future to think of, she could not rely on the Church to provide it all. She did what her mother did for her and her siblings. She saved.

Even though neither Lucia nor Angelina knew life outside of the convent walls, the move to Buenos Aires was easier than they had envisioned. The prospect of settling into an apartment in the city, one the Order kept when higher-ranking monks came to pay their visits to the neighboring convents, was scary, nonetheless exciting for them both. It only took the vivid sparkle in Angelina's eyes for Lucia to set aside any reservations about life outside of the *Trapa* and face the situation with the same courage she did when leaving Italy.

Through Church referrals, Lucia was guaranteed work in an all-girls Catholic high school. It was only a few blocks away from the University of Philosophy and Arts Angelina was to attend.

Within a few weeks in the city they had developed a routine. They took the bus together early in the morning, Lucia walked Angelina to the front steps of the university, and then she made her way to her own workplace. At the end of the day, the two of them met up at a bakery a block away from the bus stop. They would buy their bread for the evening meal, and ride back to the apartment while Angelina filled Lucia's ears with an array of French and German names that had been the founding fathers of psychoanalysis.

Lucia did not dare interrupt the never-ending chatter coming from her daughter. In every way imaginable, this child turned out to be the miracle that saved Lucia from succumbing into dry, old age. Before Angelina, she was certain she had lost her ability to love. Loving God was easy, it didn't take the daily effort to feed Him, bathe Him, or even worry about His future. Angelina, on the other hand, was a constant worry. But, she did not see Angelina as a weight on her shoulders. In fact, she looked forward to worrying about this girl who had gotten under her skin so deeply that she had become blood of her blood. Every concern, every pain Lucia felt, was the amazing result of loving and being loved. But not all was a fairytale. With Angelina attending university amid the tumultuous political atmosphere in the country at this time, Lucia could barely breathe until she saw her daughter safely back at the bakery every afternoon.

Two years before their move to Buenos Aires, on March 24, 1976, Argentina was blasted by yet another military coup that rattled the stability of a country that was far from stable to begin with. The notorious *Junta* was established, snatching the country from the inept hands of Isabel de Peron.

Isabelita, as she was commonly known by all Argentineans, was the widow of the famous populist Juan Domingo Peron, Argentina's late president, a close acquaintance of Italy's Mussolini and an enthusiast of Hitler's ideology.

The focus of the *Junta* was to eliminate anybody whose beliefs did not match theirs. Throughout the previous couple of decades, a significant portion of Argentina's youth developed a sense of national identity aimed to reclaim the country's Latin American roots. Argentina, a country built mostly by Europeans, lacked a sense of national pride. These political movements, which tended to veer more to the left than to the middle, were felt as an imminent threat by the long-established Argentinean hierarchy and the ever controlling *Yanquis*. Even though the effects of the coup barely permeated through the walls of the *Trapa*, Lucia was well aware that the *Montoneros*, a guerilla group responsible for terrorizing anything resembling capitalism, was active and murderous. Many innocent people were blown up only because they were wealthy or because they were American-born— imperialists by *Montoneros* standards. But the word on the street was that most detainees of the military regime were not associated with deadly bombings, kidnappings of foreign dignitaries, or factory owners.

Most of the missing persons were ordinary men and women, young and idealistic people who would chat at a *café* about the social revolution. But fears ran high among the oppressive government. The military kidnapped people from their homes or schools, to later disappear into clandestine centers of detention. Throughout this indiscriminate massacre, the ones sitting at the top of the social pyramid looked away while chewing on their Sunday *asados*.

Considering the troublesome state of affairs, Lucia feared for Angelina's safety at the university. The talk of the *missing*, which was not linked with any social movements or political parties, was whispered amongst frightened citizens at bus stops and supermarkets.

***

It was a Wednesday in the middle of May and the weather felt unseasonably warm considering that autumn was already upon them. Lucia had left her job early that afternoon, and with some time to spare before meeting Angelina at their usual spot, she ventured to the central market in search of some cheaper produce than that sold at her neighborhood stall. That Wednesday, the image of a woman in her mid-forties, pacing around the central market, clutching the picture of her missing son to her chest, haunted Lucia.

The desperate mother asked every stranger in the streets if they had seen her son. At the sight of Lucia dressed in her religious habit the woman ran to her and grabbed onto her wide flapping sleeve. "I swear, Sister. I swear for all that is holy that my son is not part of the revolution. He's just a boy, Sister. He is my son."

Rumor had it, that all it took for a person to be hunted by the military police, arrested, and gone forever, was for their name to be found in the phone book of one of the many detainees.

The encounter with the mother of the missing boy was enough to rattle Lucia's nerves. She could kick herself for having acceded to move to the big city, allowing Angelina to study at the university. But, how could she deny her? Lucia was about to become the proud mother of a professional. Her daughter a psychologist, who would have thought?

Lucia came back to her senses when she realized that in Angelina's exciting accounts of her daily activities at school, there were no signs of anything political or ideological. Yet, when she arrived at the bakery shop, she couldn't wait for the clock to strike the fourth hour to see her Angelina stride through the door.

When Lucia walked into the bakery that Wednesday afternoon, the baker, a good-humored man, greeted her with the same amicable manner he did every day. He handed Lucia her bread, already packed in a brown paper bag and along with her purchase he gave her a message. "Angelina came by about an hour ago. She said she was meeting some friends and she would be home in time for dinner…"

Before the man finished his sentence, Lucia felt the blood from her face drain. The baker noticed and placed a comforting hand on Lucia's. "Sister, she is a good girl. Don't worry, she'll be fine."

Anxious for Angelina's return, Lucia paced the small apartment intermittently, when not kneeling in prayer at the foot of the small shrine dedicated to the Virgin. The apartment walls seemed to close on Lucia with every passing hour Angelina was not home. She surveyed the layout of the place memorizing every detail. A living room with a small piano against a wall, a simple white Formica coated table surrounded by four wicker and wood chairs, and a white tiled kitchenette connected to the family room by a narrow door. Two bedrooms and a bathroom were to the sides of the short hallway at the opposite end of the kitchen.

Lucia could still remember the astonishment Angelina experienced, when walking into the apartment for the first time, to find the old piano set against the family room's wall. The girl did not care if she had to sleep in the street as long as there was a piano she could lay her fingers on.

Lucia had kept it a secret from Angelina. Before leaving the *Trapa*, she had phoned all the parishes in Buenos Aires until one of them, compelled by Lucia's pleas, let go of an old off-tune piano they had in storage.

Lucia sat at the piano and pressed one of the keys receiving a soundly vibration in return. *She will be back by dinnertime. She will be back,* the tone assured her. As the clock struck seven thirty, their usual dinnertime, Lucia heard the jiggling of keys at the door. She did not give Angelina the chance to unlock the door from the outside. Her hands moved with urgent speed to the latch and unbolted the heavy door before Angelina had the opportunity to insert the key in it.

Lucia was not conscious of having slapped Angelina across the face, not until she felt the stinging on her own palm. Angelina stared at her with the surprise of being stricken without notice.

Lucia looked into Angelina's eyes. "I don't even have a picture of you," she said in between choking sobs. Lucia raised her trembling hands to Angelina's shoulders, and drew her into her arms with a distressed embrace. "I don't even have a picture…"

Angelina returned Lucia's squeeze with reassuring strength. Her mother was obviously shaken and Angelina felt horribly responsible for it. But how could she tell Mamá Lucia about the events of the past couple of months?

***

Before enrolling at the university, Angelina promised Mamá Lucia that she would never look away from her studies to become involved in politics. But, ignoring the current state of affairs went against her nature. Her interest had started as mere observation, and soon Angelina found that she could gather more meaningful information along the university's hallways than in the classrooms. The asphyxiating state of turmoil was evident in the increasing emptiness in the school's corridors. Students who had shared classes with her and others who were a fixture at the corner coffeehouse, suddenly vanished from the university's daily scene.

She was not naive to the underlying revolutionary activities of the student body at her school. The activists were mostly those who championed the works of Karl Marx or the ideologies of their own Argentinean revolutionary Che Guevara. In the beginning, she kept to herself and her books, making clear to all who considered inviting her to any questionable meetings that she would refrain. However, her involvement was not inspired by student activism, but rather by a couple of French nuns she met at the bottom of the stairs when leaving school due to a cancelled class.

She approached them with close familiarity. Although she was becoming more sociable every day, the sight of two nuns, not very different from Mamá Lucia, gave her a sense of security similar to the one she had felt at the *Trapa*. On the spot, she decided they had to come to the apartment and taste Mamá Lucia's Wednesday homemade ravioli, which she usually made in quantities enough to feed a small army.

The French nuns did not dine with her that day, or the following day, or any day, even after meeting her regularly at the bottom of the stairs. In fact, the French nuns were polar opposites from the nuns Angelina had grown up with at the convent. These women were missionaries and had a purpose beyond a religious life. They fought for humans and their rights. Angelina joined their cause fully aware of the risks and consequences. In working with the French nuns she could finally relate to the sense of purpose Sarah felt when taking charge of her life.

The clandestine meetings took place in the cloister of an almost desolate monastery, a forty-five-minute drive from the university. Besides the two French nuns, there was a steady group of women, all mothers of missing students, who gathered religiously every Tuesday and Wednesday afternoon. The purpose of the meetings was to orchestrate ways to keep the population informed and warned about the ongoing massacre taking place at the School of Mechanics of the Navy.

Through the grapevine, the nuns had information about a torture center set up in the heart of the dreaded building, where most of the missing persons were taken before meeting their deadly fate. The nuns assured the Mothers of Plaza de Mayo, the name they used to refer to themselves, that the chances of finding their children alive were almost impossible.

The cause was in a way close to Angelina's spirit and to the experiences she had had as Sarah. In her mind, there was no difference between persecution for a religious belief and persecution because of a certain political ideology. Nobody she knew had been captured and evaporated like the sons and daughters of the Mothers of Plaza de Mayo. But she didn't have to have a missing loved one to step into action.

She had unjustly experienced uprooting when torn away from her family. She had experienced in her own skin the courageous actions of a woman, distant from her time and space—a woman that became a part of her, who chose to fight because of her convictions.

During the first meetings, Angelina just sat and listened, while brewing up ideas for the group. Having been through Sarah's time, she stirred together the plans of the Tribe and the suggestions of the church group, gradually developing a course of action to defy the Dirty War.

After days of contemplating the critical situation of hiding dissidents, she suggested their transport to Europe by cargo ships. "It worked effectively throughout the Spanish Inquisition," she explained.

The mechanics behind scattering fugitives in secret places across the city, the communication with the fishermen at the docks, and the smuggling of human cargo into the ships came explicitly out of her mouth as though she had been in charge of the operation for centuries.

A mutual agreement amongst the church group was reached and the Tribe's strategic plan was given life once again almost five centuries later.

The French nuns had a network of informants that had led them to reach those on the government's black list before the military police could. The Mothers of Plaza de Mayo spread the word amongst their supporters, obtaining a number of safe houses for the fugitives waiting to be exiled.

By the time the group was in full motion and embedded in the underground exodus of political dissidents, two men had joined in. The first one to join was Lito, a young man in his mid-twenties.

He had soft, fair skin and thick blond hair. His eyes were a pale light blue, eyes that never left Angelina's face while she reported the latest events at the university to the group. Lito was obviously head over heels for Angelina, and the *Mothers* who had taken a protective role over her did not miss the chance to banter about it when Lito was absent.

Lito joined the church group because of his missing younger brother. Through his church, he had heard of the French nuns and the Mothers of Plaza de Mayo. He underwent a painstaking interview conducted by the fearless nuns before being allowed into the meetings. Soon after Lito, another young man, close to his age, joined the group.

El Gallego, the name given to David Moreno by the group, was a true Spaniard from the south. He towered over six feet two and his features were the perfect fusion of dark intense eyes, sharp nose, and strong jaw, reminiscent of the blending of cultures in that part of the world. David, a man of apparent wealth, had direct contact with lower ranked military. His connections were key to freeing political prisoners or smuggling the ones with any affiliation to the arrested out of the country.

David kept mostly to himself, although it seemed to some of the women that he had a perceptible dislike for Lito, especially when Lito sat or stood too close to Angelina.

It was in the midst of that silent confrontation when Angelina decided to invite everybody to her apartment for dinner. If they were to work together, it wouldn't hurt to do it in a friendly environment. She couldn't think of anything better to break the ice than Mamá Lucia's cooking. Also, she worried about Mamá's reaction to the message she had left with the baker. Since joining the nun's group she had been careful not to give Mamá Lucia any reason to worry, making sure to stick to their schedule. But today's meeting got pushed back and her deep involvement in the group did not allow her to miss it. Yes, inviting her friends over for dinner could distract Mamá Lucia. And maybe, if surrounded by others, she would not reprimand her for arriving home late.

***

She was wrong. A deathly silence followed the whip of Mamá Lucia's outburst. As Angelina waited at the door for Mamá Lucia to let her in, she stepped aside to reveal four persons standing behind her. The two nuns, Lito, and David.

Angelina's friends did a double take at the sight of Mamá Lucia's religious habit. To her, having a nun as a mother was as natural as brushing her teeth. But her dinner guests looked shocked.

Everybody except David.

Chapter Thirty-One
The Spanish Connection

Fortuna Fernandez learned her lessons early in life. Favored by her father and resented by her mother, she developed an unwavering strength of character that would lead her to achieve most of the things she wanted in life. In a way she was thankful for her mother's bitterness. It taught her that there was nothing more uncompromising than the grudge held by the female sex, a fact she acknowledged when faced with Marta Fernandez's cold-hearted stare.

That June afternoon in 1966, when she was turned away by Ramiro and Marta in Pueblo Brugo, Fortuna was quick to lick her wounds. She planned to return to them with a proposition they could not refuse. It was one of the few times in her life that she had let her guard down and allowed her feelings to act on her behalf. Fortuna was at her best when approaching situations as though they were business transactions. Her vast experience in dealing with people from all walks of life, including Spain's president and monarchy, taught her that nobody can pass up a good opportunity, regardless of their rank or upbringing.

As far as she could tell, despite the stormy welcome Ramiro rolled out for her, the Fernandez family of Pueblo Brugo was no different from anybody she had met along her sixty-odd years. Fortuna was bent on taking Angelina under her wing, even if that meant doing it from afar until the girl reached an age where she would hopefully decide for herself to meet with Fortuna. Ramiro was a smart man, and even through his scared eyes, she could tell he was a dreamer. She hoped she was right and that Ramiro secretly wished for his daughter to leave Pueblo Brugo in search of a better future. After all he was a sailor, and his breed possessed an urgency to sail away at any given moment.

Fortuna knew his kind. She was like him. There was something in their blood that made them wander in search of an unfinished quest. They were all the same, even Angelina. But Marta did not run on Fernandez blood. Unlike the rest of her family, she could not bear the notion of uncertainty.

Fortuna had done her homework on Marta and found out about her prized herb business. When driving into Pueblo Brugo, Fortuna noticed the expanse of open land which served as an invitation for bums and drunks to make it their own. The price of land in the *pueblo* was cheap, and money was not an issue for Fortuna. She was ready to approach Marta with a business proposal she could not refuse. But, as with any business offer, there was a catch. The catch was to accept Fortuna into the family, and in doing so, Marta would become the owner of the largest greenhouses that the Entre Rios Province had ever seen.

With Marta busy building a new business and Ramiro agreeing to a better future for Angelina, the girl was going to be protected from the limited instruction the only school in town imparted. When older, she would hopefully be open to learn about her ancestors. It was a sound plan, but Fortuna doubted that she would live to see that day.

Two days after being thrown out of the Fernandez home in Pueblo Brugo, Fortuna visited a real estate agent and bought land for the immediate building of the greenhouses. Then, she made her way back to the small stucco house where a six-year-old girl stood as her only hope.

Her carefully developed plan shattered when her car approached the charred remains of the stucco shack. A low cloud of smoke loomed over the rubble, as though a ghost was the keeper of the ashes left behind by the devastating fire.

A crowd of women stood a few feet from the house, Rosaries in hand, mumbling prayers. Fortuna grabbed one by the arm and woke her from her trance, demanding details of the fire.

"The Devil. It was the Devil, Señora. He took them... like a wolf... only the Devil cries like a wolf." With a visible shiver, the woman closed her eyes and intensified her prayers.

Fortuna stepped into the remains of the structure. Scraps of furniture and broken china hid amongst scorched mattresses and drapes. Instinctively, her legs moved her forward to the room where the fire had started. The springs of the big mattress, the one shared by Ramiro and Marta, stood upright like naked winter branches, spiky and dark. The glass windows had exploded, rendering the room the appearance of a skull, full of hollow cavities and death.

Her body trembling, Fortuna knelt by the remains of the bed unaware of the sharp rubble cutting through her skin. Her eyes glanced over the debris and she cursed the moment she pushed her arrogance on the Fernandez family of Pueblo Brugo two days before.

Her fantasy of reuniting with her only remaining relatives in a lost little village in South America had sentenced them to death. In reality, she had no factual proof of them being related to her other than the sight of Sara's pendant in Ramiro's hands years before. The existence of that pendant had given her a glimmer of hope for the survival of the Jewish Fernandez lineage. But now everything was lost.

The memory of Marta's hateful eyes flashed through her memory. And Fortuna wondered if she had driven a family, as foreign to her as any other family in Pueblo Brugo, to burn to death because of their Jewish roots in a modern day *Auto de Fe*.

***

Fortuna's quest to find a trace of her family started after the death of her husband. She found herself childless, older and with no one to inherit her estate. She was the last Fernandez of her lineage that she knew of in Spain, yet there was a possibility that lost relatives existed in other parts of the world. She launched a worldwide search for any familial links to the Fernandez's of the fifteenth century.

During her investigation, she met Jose Moreno, a beautiful man of olive skin and eyes as rich and dark as Turkish coffee grounds. Jose's ancestors had wandered the globe like so many other *Marrano* families after being expelled from Spain by the Inquisition. The traces of his family went as far as Jaime Moreno, a jack-of-all-trades, deeply involved in foreign investments and shipping. Jose held several documents which originated back in the fifteenth century, where the names of Leon David Fernandez and Jaime Moreno were clearly associated as partners. They had been involved in countless shipping transactions of goods from Spain to the Far East.

Historians had concluded after the analysis of those documents, that they were obviously connected with the smuggling of live cargo, human cargo to be more exact. Jaime was known to have fled Spain in 1492 with his wife and newborn baby to Constantinople. After digging through more documents, Jose found that two whole generations of Morenos had later settled in Israel, and then a small branch had returned to Spain in the late eighteenth century. Jose's passion for his ancestry and his documents were proof that Leon and Sara Fernandez—Lev and Sarah—had weakened the devastating effects of the Spanish Inquisition by perpetuating the lives of others.

Fortuna's branch of the family came from a distant cousin of Leon Fernandez. Her family, *Marranos* to the core, had been successful in avoiding the exposure of their true identity. Originally from Aragon, they moved around Spain until finally settling in Cordoba at the turn of the nineteenth century. Always in possession of a solid fortune, her predecessors acquired every piece of property ever related to the Fernandez name in Cordoba, and that was how she came to inherit the House of Gardens.

With Jose's help, she came across an almost insignificant mention of Salomon Fernandez's offspring in South America. The hope of meeting the descendants of the only surviving child of Sara and Leon sent Fortuna across the ocean. Her first attempt had been a failure. Ramiro had refused to learn of their common roots. But, when she found out about Angelina a surge of hope rose within her. New blood. A gate to the future. While crossing the ocean to Argentina, she felt like a crusader in search of somebody to carry forth the Fernandez name. Her crusade had ended with the same impact as those of the eleventh century, death.

***

She was ready to leave the burned house behind and admit her defeat as well as her guilt, when a sparkle amongst the charred ruins drew her in. Fortuna stepped into the empty space left by the scorched mattress and dug out the shining object. For a moment her breath came short at the sight of what she held in her hands. It had the size of a gold coin with rubies and diamonds surrounding the Hebrew letter *Fey* engraved in the center of the pendant, enclosed by a golden Star of David.

She had seen that pendant every day for the past sixty some years. The image of the family heirloom was painted around the neck of the portrait of Sara Fernandez, which hung right above the harpsichord rescued from an old parish in Madrid. Her heart skipped a beat as she realized that the original pendant, the one Sara Fernandez once wore, was in her hands.

Fortuna went to the police station to inquire about the remains of the Fernandez family. She had considered transporting the remains to Cordoba and having them buried in their family graveyard. But she could not bring herself to do so. The Fernandez's from Argentina had lived as Catholics, and she would make sure they received proper burials.

Pueblo Brugo's own sheriff, a comely young man, welcomed Fortuna in his office. "The fire started in their bedroom." He shook his head slowly. "They could have escaped..." His voice trailed off and he met Fortuna's eyes. "Ramiro and Marta, what was left of them..." he said with a frown, "we buried them early this morning, next to Marta's grandmother. A good woman, the old lady was. And Ramiro..." the sheriff dropped his head and choked back tears, "you should have seen the line of men that came to pay their respects. He was a true captain that Ramiro. We loved him here in the *pueblo*, you know?"

Fortuna was reduced to tears as the young sheriff recounted the details of the burial service.

"It was a miracle little Angelina was sent away the morning of the fire. Thank God she is safe with the sisters in Hinojo."

Without solid proof of being her relative, other than a pendant that dated back to the fifteenth century, Fortuna was not allowed to see Angelina when she went knocking on the *Trapa's* door. After weeks of waiting and pleading for a private meeting with a nun, Fortuna was finally granted one with the gruff character of one Sister Lucia.

Fortuna poured her heart out to the sister with the hopes of being eligible to adopt the little girl and take her away from the convent. The sister sympathized with her story, but honored the strict orders of the deceased mother. Marta's wishes were to keep her daughter away from one specific woman, Fortuna Fernandez.

No amount of pleading made Lucia falter from her determination. Angelina was there to stay, at least until her eighteenth birthday. Before leaving, Fortuna trusted Lucia with the pendant and the promise that when the girl turned eighteen, she would give it to her along with the account of their meeting. The nun agreed reluctantly and the two women parted, never to see each other again.

Fortuna did not trust the nun's promise and hired a private eye—a Vietnam veteran who had become a Nazi hunter in South America—to follow Angelina closely. Through his reports, Fortuna had a glimpse of Angelina's every day and she hurt with the knowledge of the girl's gloomy life.

Since the tragic visit to Argentina, Fortuna was never the same. A woman full of arrogance and thirst for life was reduced to a shadow of her former self. She stopped attending social events and ceased to host any more fundraisers or cultural events at her palace. Her only consolation was her close relationship with Jose Moreno and his precocious son David.

David was her godson and she had taken the responsibility to heart by becoming completely involved in the child's life. She was aware of the child's eating habits, his grades in school, and his visits to the pediatrician. David's parents had busy lives—his mother was an acclaimed painter and his father a high-powered attorney.

The little boy had put up with their starchy events for the most part of his first ten years of life until one day he faced both parents and stood his ground. "No more! You can go and have fun without me. I'm off to *Tía* Fortuna's."

His parents sat dumbstruck for a few minutes. They could hardly believe that their ten-year-old had claimed his independence so early in life. "Another attorney in the family," Jose concluded cheerfully as they accepted the new arrangements. From that day on, David spent most weekends at the House of Gardens with Fortuna.

David loved Fortuna and admired her greatly, respecting her word as if she was a third parent. When he asked about Fortuna's change in spirits, Jose told him bits and pieces of the tragic story of the long-lost relatives in Argentina. David made it his job to replace Angelina in Fortuna's life, and little by little through his teenage years, he moved in with his godmother. His presence brought life back to Fortuna and once more she ventured into the social sphere on the arm of her handsome godson.

The day Fortuna was diagnosed with pancreatic cancer was the day David graduated from law school. The House of Gardens radiated with the biggest celebration it had seen since the fifteenth century. Fortuna knew it was going to be the last time she would enjoy a feast and she had meant to make it memorable. After her physician broke the news of her deadly disease, Fortuna smiled with resignation. She could not complain about the life she had. She had been a powerful woman, had her share of lovers after her husband's early death, and later in life, although not from her loins, she was granted a son—David. Fortuna was a woman of eighty plus years of age and through sickness or old bones her time was drawing near.

Throughout the years, she tried not to think about the deaths of Ramiro and Marta Fernandez. That part of her life was a dark chapter she avoided, yet the memory of the lonely girl in the convent disturbed her. In her heart she knew she had tried remedying her tragic mistake, but she was denied the opportunity to make it up to the girl.

Three months after David's graduation, Fortuna slipped into a pleasant nap and did not wake up to play rummy with him as she had promised she would. He cried his loss for hours before he informed the rest of the household of her death. During those hours together, while her soul was still in the room, he promised Fortuna to keep her mission alive. He swore to bring Angelina to Cordoba, to the House of Gardens, to Sara Fernandez, to her.

David shuffled through the stack of pictures the informant in Argentina had sent regularly for the past twelve years. It felt as if he had grown up together with Angelina. Those photographs had become as familiar to him as his own picture album. The first one was of Angelina at age seven in a nun's habit. The second one he held in his hands was of the girl at age eight in the same habit looking out a window. He went through several others and paused at one of Angelina playing the piano with her eyes closed. Many times he had sat at the harpsichord and had stared at the picture of Sara Fernandez. She too had been a piano player in her day. The two looked so much alike and the unusual connection they had with the instrument was close to metaphysical. David laughed at the idiocy of his nonsensical presumption and kept looking through the pictures. Angelina, at thirteen, finally out of nun's clothes and off to a regular school. The next one was one of his favorite snapshots of the young Argentinean, a beautiful Angelina at fifteen with dark curls framing her almond shaped eyes. And finally the one picture which he could not tear his eyes away from, Angelina at eighteen on her graduation day, a stunning young woman. A woman he had never met, and would likely never meet. A woman he felt he had known his whole life.

***

When David arrived in Buenos Aires, the private eye who had kept Fortuna informed of Angelina's whereabouts met him at the airport and fed him the latest news on Angelina.

She and the nun were in the city. The girl was enrolled in the school of psychology and had been attending some meetings of dubious nature at an old church. Fully aware of the charged political climate in Argentina, and an activist himself, David's heart jumped to his throat at the thought of Angelina becoming another unexplained missing person.

In Cordoba, he had held a fundraiser to help Jews flee Argentina by buying their way out through the Uruguayan border. The Jews were not particularly interested in the country's politics, but the youth was deeply involved in Zionist groups, tightly linked in spirit to the socialist party. But in the eyes of the military they represented a growing danger for a dictatorship bent on submission by force, a situation they easily controlled with a significant portion of these young men and women gone missing. Unlike North American, Central American, or European Jews, the Argentinian Jews were mostly middle class and their pockets were not full enough to bribe the military for the lives of their children. The international Jewish community was aware of that and joined forces to help their Argentinean counterparts.

As soon as the private eye related all the information about Angelina to David, he contacted the French nuns. He had to become a member of their group to keep a close eye on her. The nuns kept changing their minds about meeting with him. The two women ran a risky operation and conducted their own inquiries before disclosing their activities to anybody.

After three weeks of cancelled meetings and unanswered calls, the French nuns finally met with David. The women were sharp and straight to the point. David did not play games with them, and told them exactly who he was and about his intentions of helping those wanted by the government. However, honest as he was, he did omit one small detail—Angelina. Beyond his active role in the human rights movement, his reasons for joining the group went beyond altruism. He had promised Fortuna that he would bring Angelina to her and he was determined to do it with Angelina in one piece and breathing.

The day he walked into the secret meeting held at the abandoned cloisters of the church, the Mothers of Plaza de Mayo were already there. He was introduced to some of the women who were enchanted by his Spanish lilt. David realized, after being asked to repeat over and over again words containing *Ss* and *Zs*, that women in Argentina found his accent somewhat sensual. The nuns, with an accent of their own, were proud of the new addition to the group and explained David's role in saving dozens of people from death by torture.

David was engrossed, explaining the details of the operation to the hopeful mothers until Angelina arrived hand in hand with a man.

He felt as if somebody had punched him full in the stomach. Of course he did not expect her to be with a man, the girl grew up in a convent for crying out loud! A few months out of it and she was already in someone's arms. So much for being raised in a church and by nuns. Once the unexplained anger faded and he was back to his senses, he understood where the shock had come from. Besides seeing her in person for the first time, it was as though Sara Fernandez had walked out of her portrait and into the meeting. Yes, he could see a difference in the coloring of the eyes, and Angelina's hair was wilder than Sara's, but the similarity was disturbing.

They were formally introduced. Angelina's face lit with a gracious smile when she greeted him with a soft nod. But when David shook Lito's hand, he detested the feel of it. It was not a firm grasp. Lito was hiding something.

It was Lito's idea to name David *El Gallego*. Argentinians had a fascination with calling any Spaniard *Gallego*, regardless of whether they were from Galicia or not. In detail, David explained his Andalusian birth, a fact the whole group chose to ignore, christening him with the common name of *Gallego*. Throughout the meeting, information was exchanged, and David, keeping a critical eye on each one of the members in the circle of trust, decided to sit and watch the interaction within the group.

The nuns led the meeting by announcing the completion of the most updated list of missing people, set to be published in two days' time, the day of the highly anticipated inauguration of the *Futbol* World Cup in Buenos Aires. The list would appear on the front page of *La Nación*, the country's leading newspaper. It was the best chance for those opposed to the government to unveil the massacre happening, all while the world cheered for its favorite soccer teams. The Mothers of Plaza de Mayo welcomed the news as a major step forward in their efforts to oust the government.

The Mothers spoke next, providing details of their daily routines. It always started with a quick early meeting with *mate* and sweet rolls, and then off to the police stations to inquire about their missing children. As always, they broke down while recounting the ways their hopes were shattered time and time again. The sardonic officers they met did not care to register their children's names or even look at the photographs the women carried religiously.

Angelina gave the mothers time to recover from their discouraging update, and then addressed the group with some unsettling events that had just happened that afternoon. She had visited a number of residences where fugitives were hidden. On her way to one of her assigned hideouts, she noticed a military green Ford Falcon parked at the corner. The two officers sitting in the car followed every pedestrian roaming the area with hungry, hound eyes.

Angelina smiled calmly at the alarmed reaction of the group. "There weren't any fugitives in that location. All of ours are safe. I received information last night about suspicious traffic around the building, so I relocated all of them. We can never be too careful. People talk. Information leaks."

Lito eyed Angelina with a mixture of bewilderment and pride. "Who would have thought," he said in between smiles, "our puppy here, a strategist. Well done, doll."

Angelina accepted his praise with a timid smile.

Regardless of her composed demeanor, the group fell victim to a deathly silence after Angelina's report. Two harsh realities hovered over the room. Not only were they being watched, but there was a mole in the group.

David surveyed the people in the room and focused on Lito. He did not like him. He did not believe in the story of his missing brother. Furthermore, Lito's reaction to the obvious treachery within the clandestine group seemed forced, if not fake. So far, David could not let Angelina out of his sight. Not until he had more information on Lito.

To lighten up the dreadful mood of the group, Angelina offered a ravioli night at her house as they were breaking up for the evening. The Mothers of Plaza de Mayo passed on the invitation, while the rest accepted eagerly.

David opened the door to his car and drove the French nuns, Lito, and Angelina to dine with Lucia, the cruel nun his godmother had told him about.

Chapter Thirty-Two
The Mole

Dinner turned out to be more unpleasant than David had expected. The sour faced nun, Lucia, did not take her eyes off him for most of the night. Each one of the guests played a role. Lito played the sweet, tender, obedient young man, obviously seeking approval from Angelina's guardian. The French nuns played the *remember when* game with Lucia, reminiscing about events that they had experienced during World War II.

David did not enjoy his evening in that stuffy apartment. The conversations held during the meal were shallow, always revolving around the food and the cook. Not once were the matters of Angelina being slapped at the door, Lucia's meltdown at the sight of her daughter, or the unexpected company for dinner mentioned. As David chewed the last of his dinner, he confirmed that the raviolis lived up to their fame—the nun could definitely cook.

During the car ride to the apartment, the French nuns had decided it was best to leave Lucia out of their secret. They would all pretend to be schoolmates, even the nuns. When disclosed to Lucia, it was evident that she did not believe a word of it, but it was also evident she had decided beforehand not to ask any questions.

From the corner he was sitting in, David perceived the small family room as a chessboard, a game he had enjoyed playing with Fortuna when she initiated him into the world of politics. The French nuns were perfect knights, standing on their own with a specific goal to attain. Lucia was a mere pawn. Although she thought herself powerful, her control over Angelina's life would disappear as soon as Angelina would claim her independence. By the looks of it, it was happening sooner than expected. Even without proof, David saw Lito as the bishop, the two faced, double dealing bishop. David was the tower, his mission was to protect the king, who was no other than Angelina. Without the king the game was lost, and unbeknownst to her, he carried the responsibility of seeing Angelina to the end of the game.

After dinner, when cups of coffee were passed around, Lucia asked Angelina to play one of her melodies for the guests. The obedient daughter she was, Angelina put her coffee cup down on the table and sat at the piano.

Angelina summoned a moment of concentration. Her eyes closed in the same way David had seen so many times in that picture he left back in Spain. Her hands rested on her lap, waiting for her mind to command them to play. The room stood silent for what seemed like an eternity. The poise in which Angelina dwelled over her choice of melody was unsettling for him. If he had not have been the arrogant intellectual that he was, he would have believed that at that moment Angelina was possessed by the ghost of Sara Fernandez.

The next event was the most unnerving. While David struggled for the second time that night with the metaphysical notion of ghosts and possession, Angelina turned to him, chin upturned, eyes deep and glinting. She fixed him with a gaze that hinted the affirmation of his mystical thoughts.

He must have looked panicked, because Angelina disrupted the strangeness of the brief moment with her voice. "You might be familiar with this melody. You heard it some time ago…"

Her words did nothing to appease him. If anything, he felt the hairs on the back of his neck rise with the same uneasiness he experienced as a little boy when his nanny forgot to leave the nightlight on.

David chose to close his eyes, in the same way Angelina did, and allowed the music to play it's magic. He had heard that melody before, he just couldn't recall where. His mind hummed to the music. The tune took him back to Fortuna's house, to Sara's portrait, to the harpsichord, and finally it laid him gently on the plush lawns of the gardens. The music stopped, but his eyes remained closed. He was afraid to wake from a dream in which he lay on the green of the House of Gardens next to a woman. Next to Sara.

A wave of applause broke the enchantment followed by Lucia's flat voice. "*Mi niña* writes all her music. She is a gifted pianist."

Angelina turned on her bench and waved her hand shyly. "Mamá Lucia, I told you, these are melodies I heard somewhere. I cannot take credit for any of it."

Lito, *the sucker*, as David had secretly named him, was at Angelina's feet taking her hand. "If I may, my dear, you were fantastic."

The French nuns assented with enthusiastic nods before getting up on their feet. It was time to leave. Curfew was soon to start and none of them wanted to risk the chance of being detained and interrogated in the streets.

Before leaving the apartment, David thanked Lucia for her hospitality and bent his head to kiss Angelina on the cheek, the customary greeting in Argentina. Something stirred in him at the touch of her skin against his and he whispered in her ear, "I do remember that afternoon by the fountain."

She suddenly backed away and her gaze locked in his. He felt his face flushed and hot. He opened his mouth but nothing came out. Her eyes followed him as he hastily turned on his heels and left.

She too remembered. She remembered the warm afternoon. She remembered his gift. She remembered everything.

***

Sara was lying on the tender green grass surrounding the angel fountain admiring her prized rose garden. She was tired and felt cold down to her bones. She did not want to alarm Leon with the symptoms of what seemed like a common chill, especially after the tragedy which had struck the family the year before. A bit of warmth under the sun would do. She closed her eyes. Her mind unwillingly wandered to a fresh memory still too raw to heal…

After ten years of continuous absence from Spain, Massimo and Camila returned to claim their eccentric life back at Casa Di Laurenti. Since their arrival, it had been a non-stop celebration. Paola and her seven children traveled from Portugal to Onuba where they spent a few months visiting, and Sara and Leon joined the feasts as often as they could.

Camila came back from the Orient filled with the most unconventional ideas for fabric patterns and embroideries. Soon after, she was back at the top of the fashion industry in Spain. Massimo relented most of his business to his agents across Europe and the East, and divided his time between his Andalusians, his grandchildren, and his beloved wife.

Having her parents back in her life had given Sara the sense of completion she lacked during their time in the East. She was the happiest she had ever been. She had a man in her life that she adored, three beautiful boys who breathed life into her with their daily mischief, and now she had her parents with whom to share all that happiness.

But her joy was short lived the afternoon Jaime walked into the House of Gardens, panic in his face, filthy and weary from his ride. Massimo had fallen seriously ill and required urgent attention.

It had started with a chill of the bones and some minor bloating. On the second day of his confinement, Massimo assured Camila he felt stronger. He left his bedroom, eager to break in a new mare which was busy snorting murder to anybody who dared to walk by the stables. The afternoon died into dusk and there were no signs of Massimo. A party of grooms went about the Di Laurenti lands and found Massimo unconscious by the jealous mare which refused to leave his side. Massimo's condition looked alarming and Jaime did not spare a moment before he was on his way to get Leon.

Massimo's intestines exploded before Leon and Sara made it to Casa Di Laurenti. The smell of bloody stools indicated the advanced stage of the disease. It was a matter of hours before Massimo would die. As predicted, he died early the next morning in his wife's arms, deliriously mouthing his undying love for her.

Camila did not know how to live without Massimo. She stopped eating and spent every waking hour sitting in her balcony, overlooking the valley as if Massimo would ride out from the forest to take her with him. After a week of being gone, Massimo finally came for her. She was found dead hours later, beautiful as ever, a smile on her lips. She had reclaimed the only life she wanted when she died. She was reunited with Massimo who was not willing to face death without her.

The unexpected death of her parents left Sara aching for their lively presence. It had been a gift to witness the way they had thrived off each other. It would have been impossible for either of them to inhabit the land of the living without the intense passion they ignited when together.

In a way she consoled herself when thinking of them together in death. With a hint of a smile, she looked around knowing they were there. Loving and protecting her as if they had never left.

The temporary comfort she had found in the memory of her parents' love was suddenly broken by Leon's latest concern. By nature, he was a worrier. He worried about her safety and that of their three boys, Yehuda, Salomon, and baby Yoshua. He worried about the secrecy of the Tribe, and lately he was deeply worried about his strained relationship with the despot Alazar.

Their safe time in Cordoba was coming to an end. Yehuda's *bar mitzvah* was to be soon celebrated and they were set to leave Spain for the East right after. Between the marquis's demands and their fictitious financial collapse, people raised eyebrows questioning the legitimacy of their situation. Their plans to leave Spain had been postponed repeatedly due to lack of leadership within the Tribe. Jaime and Leon, deeply embedded in the whole operation, failed to relay responsibilities on the younger and most capable members of the Tribe. Sara and Maria were guilty of the same doings. The children's rescue mission they ran was basically theirs, and in recent years, Elmede's. Moved by the stories of the rescued children, the tough loving woman left Casa Di Laurenti for the House of Gardens.

***

It was on the fourth day of the month of April of the year fourteen hundred and ninety-two, that the Fernandez's of Cordoba fell out of favor with the Marquis of Alazar.

Leon, like all the other members of the Tribe, was cleaning out his coffers and investing in foreign ventures. In Spain, just as planned, he showed his share of losses to the point that his readily available cash diminished significantly from the years before. The marquis, a festering wound for Leon, had grown greedier than ever and was determined to kiss the king's feet by providing him with a fully equipped army, sure to take over Granada and the Moors. Leon did not have the gold necessary to finance the marquis's latest delirious campaign, and was faced by an outraged Alazar, ready to denounce him to the Inquisition.

"Take my father's gold, his coffers are still in the vaults at Casa Di Laurenti. We will repay Paola her share of the estate once we meet her in India," Sara suggested at the terrifying notion of being questioned by the Church.

Leon finally consented to Sara's suggestion and complied with the marquis's ambition once again, leaving Leon with a bad taste in his mouth. He felt imprisoned around the marquis and he cursed the time his great-grandfather had dealt the most unfair hand of his life.

When Leon requested an audience with Alazar to relinquish the gold at once, the audience was denied. He was informed, at the foot of the front steps of the castle, that he should surrender the coffers to the marquis's secretary and leave. With his stomach in a knot, Leon did as he was told. The gold was unloaded from his coach and taken into the castle while he waited at the door like a serf. The heavy gates to the Alazar castle closed on his face when his carriage was finally emptied.

***

Sara dozed off under the blanketing warmth of the autumn sun. She was awoken by a soft brush on her lips, one she returned with the same tenderness given to her. Leon lay next to her, his blue eyes studying the face of the woman he never tried to love. "Feeling better, love?" His fingers played with the silky curls forming at the ends of her long hair.

Sara started at the question and made to sit up, but Leon pushed her back gently, nesting her head in the crook of his arm. "There's nothing wrong with me, Lev. Sometimes I feel tired, that's all."

He kissed her forehead. "I'm sorry, my love."

She reached for his face and her fingers traced the arches of his brows, his strong nose, his sweet mouth. "I would do everything we did a thousand times over. I am not sorry, Lev. I am pleased."

His face turned grave. "I do not want you to wait for me. You shall leave for the Di Laurenti Palace in India with the children in two weeks' time. I will join you in a month."

Sara sat up and faced him, determined. "The children will depart with Maria and Jaime at the appointed time as agreed. I will stay until we can both leave, together."

He knew there was no point in discussing it any further. His wife was as stubborn as a deaf mule. He also recognized the benefits of sending the children out first, making it look like the three Fernandez boys were joining their older cousins and aunt currently vacationing at the Di Laurenti palace in India.

They sat staring at each other for a long time. Both their thoughts were on the dangers lying ahead of them. With a nod, Leon finally consented to Sara's final verdict. She clung to Leon's neck and he pulled her to him with urgency. Every moment they spent together was precious. The words Leon spoke to her the day after their wedding suddenly echoed in her mind. *Any moment could be our last.*

They came together with the hunger of two lovers who happened to discover their bodies for the first time. Leon's fingers revisited the scar his wife sheltered underneath her shoulder blade. The memory of their first encounter, of death looming over Sara when he found her in the forest, drove him to take her stronger, deeper.

They lay in each other's arms until the afternoon turned cold and gray clouds obstructed the rays of sun that had served as their shelter. Sara snuggled closer to Leon and he covered her body with his. He looked down at her and smiled. "I have something for you."

Her eyes shone bright and she sat up clapping with excitement. "What is it?"

Leon touched the soft spot between her breasts. "Close your eyes."

Her eyes closed on command, and then she felt the coldness of a metal necklace around her neck. A round pendant fell right where Leon had touched her only seconds before. She kept her eyes closed but her fingers traced the shapes of the jewel her husband had designed with her in mind.

"I have been wanting to give it to you for many days now," he said apologetically.

She opened her eyes and without looking at the pendant, which she had already memorized in detail, reached for Leon's hand and placed it on the spot the pendant rested. "I love you, my Love, my heart. I love you for making me yours. I love you for loving me in the way that I am. I love you because without you, I would have never been me."

Leon drew her to him and they remained linked together by the touch of the pendant until night fell over the House of Gardens.

***

David woke up the next morning with the worst hangover he had experienced since the night he graduated from high school. And that dream! His head felt like a boulder.

Dinner at Angelina's the night before had been a bizarre experience, if he had to give it a name. The tense environment during the meal, the phony Lito, with his round cherubic face, and Angelina's music… What the hell had happened to him? He was not conscious of the words forming in his mouth, not until the full sentence was out in the open. Yet, she did not look surprised. Damn, his head hurt! He couldn't think straight. He looked around the room and found a bottle of Irish whisky, drained to the last drop.

When back at his apartment the night before, the vision by the angel fountain was still playing over and over in his head. The music, Sara, the mind-blowing sex, the pendant. He had to erase that strange memory out of his mind and he had found nothing better to do it with than whisky. He remembered opening the bottle, as for the rest… a pounding headache told him the end of the story.

After a cold shower and four cups of dark coffee he felt ready to face the traffic of the city. He had seen crazy drivers before in Madrid and Rome, but the drivers in Buenos Aires had nothing to envy them. Once behind the wheel, the chance to make it out of the car alive was a lottery draw.

David phoned the private eye before leaving the apartment. They met at a coffeehouse on *Avenida Nueve de Julio* across from the Obelisco. After some more coffee and a butter croissant that stirred up the nausea from the hangover, the private eye left with the promise of calling him before day's end with information on Lito.

In the meantime, he could not sit still and wait. His next visit was long overdue. It was about settling old scores. For the loving memory of Fortuna, David was determined to finally put them to rest.

Lucia was cleaning up the chalkboard in the classroom where she taught religion, when David knocked softly on the open door. "Sister, can we talk?"

Lucia turned around with a certain look of panic in her face. She suddenly snatched her purse from the desk behind her, and hastily moved to the door. "I have a previous appointment, young man." Without further word Lucia fled down the corridor with quick steps.

"The name is David Moreno, and I'm here to make you honor a promise you made twelve years ago, Sister. I'm here in the name of Fortuna Fernandez, Angelina's true blood relative."

Lucia's mouth felt dry and her heart pounded with fear, her feet became unresponsive. She later realized that it was David's stronghold on her elbow that had prevented her from falling flat on her face.

David walked her back to the classroom and gently set her down on the chair by the desk. He was truly concerned. There was no love lost between the nun and himself, but he did not intend to kill her with a sudden heart attack. "Can I get you a glass of water, Sister?"

She waved her hands in the air. "No, no. I'm all right. Slightly faint, but fine."

The two remained silent. David had already informed the nun of who he was. Now it was her turn to speak. "I take it you don't go with *mi niña* to school." Lucia looked up and met David's eyes. He replied with a slight shake of the head.

"Or the other three that ate with us last night..." David did not respond this time. He didn't have to, Lucia already guessed. "Is Angelina in trouble?" she asked with the genuine concern any mother would have in such turbulent times.

David felt embarrassed for his resentment towards the nun. If anything, she had kept Angelina safe and it was obvious she loved her. "She could be, yes." David folded his arms over his chest, ready for the next question.

"I never promised anything to Señora Fernandez. Angelina is not hers. She is mine. She is my daughter. God gave her to me." Lucia's eyes were misty as she struggled to her feet, making her words more eloquent.

"Nobody is blaming you for any wrongdoing, Sister. But, she has the right to know. You owe that to her. She has to know she belongs somewhere."

Lucia stood taller, her face upturned. "She belongs to me, young man."

David kept his composure. "Give her the pendant, Sister. Talk to her or I will."

Lucia felt suddenly exhausted. She sat and looked down at a crack on the desk and traced it with her fingers. "Will you take her away from me?"

David hated to hurt this woman. He moved next to her and knelt, meeting her eyes.

"I am not an ogre, Sister. All I want is for her to know. The choice is hers. I would never take her from you or anybody she loves. If she decides to travel to Spain to learn about her family, I expect you to go along with her."

Lucia searched under her robes and produced the pendant. It was hanging at the end of a chain, the same thick gold chain depicted in the portrait at the House of Gardens. David ached to touch it. He was so familiar with that piece of jewelry, but only from an image that stared at him from the past.

Since his meeting with Angelina, he felt trapped in a time machine. Her face, the music, the scene by the fountain, and now the pendant. It was as if Lucia read his thoughts, and handed the pendant to him. He held it in his hands with the same care one holds a newborn baby. For no reason known to him, his eyes filled with tears.

"*Mi niña* talks in her sleep." Lucia smiled. "She knows where she belongs, David. The pendant is but a detail. I have slept in the same room with her for the past twelve years and I've watched her dream dreams of the past. She knows about the House of Gardens." David's eyes opened wide in shock.

The nun continued, "Sometimes I believe that the one person who had lived next to me all these years was Sara Fernandez—Sarah." Lucia lifted her eyes from the crack on the table. "I fear for her safety, David."

He laid a reassuring hand on hers. "Me too, Sister. Me too."

Lucia left the school with David on the way to his apartment.

During the drive, he told Lucia the extent of the danger Angelina was involved in. "These are not the times to defy the government, Sister. We are in the middle of a manhunt, a lawless war, and Angelina could be the next victim."

The moment David stepped into his apartment, his butler greeted him with urgency. "There's a message for you, *Licenciado* Moreno." The butler handed him a note. "The man said to call him back urgently."

Without wasting a second, David dialed the private eye's number. It rang once. The words that traveled through the phone line froze David's blood. "Lito is no other than Brigadier Marcelo Ortiz from the Armed Forces. He gave the names out, David. They were all arrested this morning at the church. Angelina was amongst them."

Chapter Thirty-Three
Inquisition

"Come on Lito, we are running late. You know how the nuns hate it when we walk in late for the meetings." They were sitting in Lito's mousy grey Citroen. He had been toying with the keys, taking his time, thinking. Angelina looked at him and folded her arms in frustration.

She was flustered and for a good reason. Lito had tried to kiss her a few moments after they had gotten into the car. She liked him, but not to the point of kissing him. He was a sweet, noble guy, everything a girl like Angelina would want, but she was not attracted to him. She had been unsure of her feelings towards Lito, but they were made clear when David Moreno joined the group.

El Gallego was far from humble, if anything pretty arrogant, and radiated a worldly air about him, unlike the boy next-door simplicity that defined Lito.

She had zero experience when it came to men. Yet, there was a universal inherent sensation that an individual felt when attracted physically and emotionally towards another. In the case of Lito, she liked him, she liked him a lot. But the touch of his skin on hers felt uncomfortable. They had held hands before and he had expressed on more than one occasion, amid his shyness, his interest in her beyond friendship. Angelina did all that she could to discourage him from thinking they could be anything other than friends. And she had considered him a friend. She had opened up to him. She told him about her upbringing in the convent, her years of silence, and her lack of friends. Especially male friends.

Lito had apologized for imposing his *male selfishness*, as he called it, on her. He was happy to remain friends with her, but something inside her told her his insistence was far from over.

She had shared her story with Lito, but not in its entirety. Although raised within the confinement of her silence and the walls of the *Trapa*, Angelina was not foreign to passion. Her travels outside her bodily form through the melodies Sarah provided her had stripped her from the naivety and purity of a convent education. She had experienced love for a man and she had felt his love for her. She knew about the anticipation of lovers and about games of seduction. She had lived through the fear of losing the man she loved and through the assurance of being nestled in his strong arms. Lito was none of that. He inspired in her feelings of camaraderie, a feeling where physical attraction was not a possibility.

On the other hand, David Moreno stirred something in her ironclad vault of secrets. When she sat the night before at her piano, she had been transported to an alternate reality away from the crowded little room. Through the years, Sarah had only come to her when she was alone. However, last night, Angelina felt the barriers of time coming down. For a moment, while playing the melody, she was Sarah, and David was Lev, the love of her life. She had seen Lev in David's eyes and had felt him when his skin touched hers.

Angelina had attributed the episode to an electric energy that surrounded David, begging her to bring forth the cherished moment by the fountain. When looking at David before playing the melody, she knew that Leon— Lev—had walked in the room, longing to hold Sarah in his arms the way he had done that afternoon in the garden.

She obeyed David's silent request. Subconsciously, she knew she could not deny that man. She felt David being sucked into the music and taken to a place where the language of the body was stronger than the words of the mouth. She shared the vision of the scenes in his head, played out like a love story, which although latent, found an outlet in that tiny room.

She read the story in his eyes. Her senses did not betray her. He had been there too.

***

She glanced sideways and saw Lito under a new light. He was far from the tender, shy young man she came to love as a friend. His face was set and his hands were angry, clamping his car keys and making his knuckles stand out like a row of bullets. "We're good friends, Lito, that's all. Please, understand the way I feel about you."

He turned to her with cold eyes and suddenly she felt scared. "So the chaste virgin from the convent knows how to heat up water for *mate,* but she won't drink it."

Angelina shrunk in the corner of her seat and stared at Lito with apprehension. She slowly moved her hand to the door handle. He sneered at her in a way that made her skin prickle with fear.

"Where are you are going, doll?"

Angelina pulled the handle and pushed the door open, but her escape was halted when Lito clamped his fist in her hair and pulled her back into the car. She struggled to free from his painful grasp on her hair. It was in vain. The man was angry. He reached over her and slammed the door shut securing the lock.

Tears streamed down her face. "Lito, please, let me go."

His grip on her hair tightened, and he pushed her down on the seat and forced a kiss on her. He thrust his tongue in her mouth.

Revolted, angry and scared, Angelina bit his lower lip and tasted his blood. The pain caught him off guard, and for a second, he loosened his hold on her. She struggled to unlock the door, but her sweaty fingers slipped off the short, black lock over and over again.

"Damn bitch!" He yanked her backwards and banged her head on the dashboard. Angelina went into a momentary daze. The hard blow opened a gash on her forehead and blood flowed freely down the corner of her left eye. Nevertheless, she fought against Lito's forceful hold and kicked the door until it blasted open. Lito climbed on top of her, and struck her. Darkness descended on Angelina. She was not afraid. A melody embraced her.

***

Sara was sitting at her harpsichord with one-year-old Yoshua on her lap. The baby, the next promising musician of the family, was the spitting image of Leon, with dark, thick hair and the deepest blue eyes.

All her children had a look of their own and a personality that defined them as unique individuals. Yehuda, their first-born, had her light brown wavy hair and Camila's emerald green eyes. At thirteen he was tall for his age and promised to be as broad and strong as his father. He loved spending time in Leon's surgery and had already declared his ambition of becoming the next Doctor Fernandez.

Salomon, barely ten years of age, was of a lighter build and had the dark handsome looks of Massimo. He was quieter than Yehuda, a trait that allowed him to become more observant. Salomon inherited the gift of his great-grandmother Sarah Espinoza. The child possessed the mastery of art and was able to depict his surroundings in beautiful strokes of color. Sara and Leon marveled at Salomon's ability and displayed his paintings with unmitigated pride all over the House of Gardens.

Sara looked down at the baby on her lap and smiled. Years had passed since Leon and Sara had given up hope on having more children. Yoshua had taken them by surprise when he came to complete their circle. The two older boys were protective of their little brother and had loved him from the moment they noticed the little bump in their mother's belly.

To Yoshua, everybody in the house was Mama. Sara was Mama. Leon was Mama. Maria was Mama, and the boys were Mama and Mama. Jaime, Yoshua's godfather, loved that baby with utter tenderness. Since Yoshua's birth, Jaime had pressured Maria into marriage, yearning for a stable life and a baby of his own. Although of advanced age to bear children, Maria married Jaime all the same. It had been a day of joy for the Tribe, when under the *chuppa*, Leon proclaimed Maria as Miriam Moreno, a Jewess by choice.

Sara looked around the room and for a moment she closed her eyes. This palace, her home, held a fortune of memories she would carry in her heart wherever fate would take her.

She allowed Baby Yoshua to slam happily on the keys of the harpsichord while he chanted a composition of his own with unending *mamama* lyrics. She held him tightly, and took in his sweet scent, long enough to last her until they could be reunited in India in two or three months' time.

The trunks with the children's belongings were packed and Maria and Jaime were ready to depart with the three Fernandez boys. It had been Sara's choice to send them ahead. She had dwelled on that decision for weeks and changed her mind several times, but she always went back to her initial gut feeling. It was safer to send them without her. The air surrounding the Fernandez name had grown thicker since the incident with Alazar. Although still living off the Fernandez allowance, Alazar was said to have found another *Marrano* willing to indulge in his abuse in exchange for protection from the Inquisition and possible advancement as a court Jew, a position Leon had refused flatly when Alazar offered.

Another worry also lay heavily on the Tribe. The rabbi from Bilbao had left for Toledo over two months before to secure the finances of other *Marranos* interested in diverting their fortunes out of Spain, and they had had no word of him since. Of all the members of the Tribe that had passed through the House of Gardens, the rabbi from Bilbao was the only one who had consistently refused to leave Leon's side. Leon was pleased to have him in Spain, even though he insisted on the rabbi's departure for a safer land. Leon regarded him with high esteem, and second to Jaime, the rabbi from Bilbao was his other right hand.

Samuel Ben Rey was his name and he was not much older than Leon, although he looked much older. His hair had gone white for the sorrow he felt when he fled Bilbao. His wife and children had chosen the Church over him, and had abandoned him to his own fate. Yet, in the life of the Tribe, he had found a purpose and a woman to love. Weeks after Yehuda's birth, the rabbi from Bilbao married a young woman, the daughter of a prominent lawyer, a *Marrano* with close ties to Court.

"Mama." Yoshua's call pulled Sara out of her thoughts. She followed his stubby, little index finger pointing at the freshly painted portrait of Sara hanging on the wall behind the harpsichord. "Mama," he exclaimed again with the biggest smile. She grabbed his chubby index finger and kissed it. "Mama," he called out once more.

"Yes, that is me, your mama, my sweet boy." She pointed at the portrait. "That is your mama."

Yoshua turned to Sara and planted a slobbering kiss on her chin, struggled out of her arms, and climbed down her lap, when he spotted a shiny black beetle languidly inching towards the legs of the harpsichord.

Sara rolled her eyes and smiled. "Leave that poor creature alone, Yoshi."

The baby followed the beetle and stood his ground at the threshold dividing Sara's chamber and the harpsichord room. He exclaimed with seriousness, "Mama!" The tone in the baby's voice was different from his usual cheerfulness when encountering an insect. Sara found his sudden graveness unsettling. She stood up from the bench and walked towards her bedroom door…

***

A door suddenly opened and Angelina felt a splash of cold water over her naked body. She shielded her bruised skin. The cell she was in was dark. She squinted several times until her sight adjusted to her dim surroundings. The room was bare, and smelled of feces and blood. She looked up and saw a single light bulb dangling at the end of a wire. She heard others moaning or crying, but they seemed to be distant. Maybe in adjacent rooms, maybe in another time…

***

A gown of deep green silk lay across her bed. Sara turned to Yoshua who still stood at the threshold, and smiled at him. "That's Mama's dress, baby." It was the one she was to wear for Yehuda's first reading of the Torah.

Her big boy was becoming a *bar mitzvah* in a private ceremony held in the underground palace. It was to be short, but Leon as well as Sara saw the ceremony as a necessary ritual in order to bless the departure of their children. Besides, Yehuda, proud to have come of age within his religion, was excited to gloat with his newly acquired status to Salomon, and could not wait to assume a man's role before his two younger siblings.

A knock on the door set the moment of departure closer. Elmede, her face puffy from crying, walked into the room and helped Sara into her gown. Although unconventional for a married woman and the wife of a rabbi, but not for a Di Laurenti, Sara still wore her hair loose like a maiden. Her amber eyes shone like jewels against the color of her gown, and the pendant Leon gave her by the fountain completed her striking beauty. In the meantime the baby trudged back into the music room and came back with a triumphant smile as he held the hopeless beetle in his little fist. After some explaining about the beetle missing his mama, Yoshi surrendered the insect to Elmede asking her, "Mama? Mama?"

Elmede couldn't help but laugh through the flow of tears. She bent to wipe the baby's hands on her apron and was rewarded with a hug about her neck and a slobbery kiss. "Mama," he said to her.

Elmede broke out crying harder than before and lifted Yoshua in her arms. "How I vill miss the children, Lady Sara!"

Sara handed Elmede a handkerchief to wipe her tears. "It does not have to be forever, Elmede. In a few months' time we will leave to join them. Come with us."

Elmede's sadness was lifted with a wave of gratitude. "I vill, Lady Sara. I vill." Elmede settled the baby in the arms of his mother and left to attend to the last details of the small meal the guests would share after the ceremony. With the baby in her arms, Sara left for the last celebration they would hold as a family in the underground palace.

Leon stood by the wooden paneled Torah's ark, beaming with pride as he watched Yehuda wrap himself in a prayer shawl. Salomon, although still a boy in the eyes of the religion, was awarded a prayer shawl of his own, a parting gift from his father. As little Yoshua almost dived head first to the ground, excited to join his elder brothers and father by the ark, Sara gazed at them with tenderness. They were all hers. They were her men.

The *bar mitzvah* party consisted of eight other families, a little over thirty people. A last-minute detail in closing Casa Di Laurenti had held Jaime and Maria back in Onuba longer than expected, and Leon started the ceremony without them. Time was of the essence. The more he delayed the departure of his boys, the more heart wrenching it became for him.

As Yehuda intoned the first chant of the Torah portion, Leon smiled at the irony of the scene. The portion was *Shelach Lecha*, Send To You. In it, God instructed Moses, as he led his people into the desert, to send spies to the Land of Canaan to survey the grounds of the territory which was to become their home. Upon the spies' return, they said to have found figs and pomegranates and a land of milk and honey.

Leon, like Moses, had led his people into an exodus out of a land that had held them slaves of a faith they did not believe in. A land that forced them out of their identity under threat of death. Unlike Moses, Leon did not see fit to overextend the suffering of his community by sending them into the Holy Land, where they would have to defend their freedom against the same dark forces they fought against in Spain. Perhaps God did not approve of his actions. As he stood by the open ark, with his older son submerged in the reading of the Torah, and his two younger ones standing solemnly by his side, he felt at peace and he did not care about God's approval. He felt at peace with what he had done for his community. Leon looked up and found the eyes of his wife resting on him, deep with love. In his heart that was all the approval he needed.

***

The underground palace vanished from Angelina's mind as a thread of light filtered through the room she was held in. The last thing she remembered was being hammered by Lito's angry fist. At one point everything turned dark, still her mind and senses registered all that had happened to her since the beating in the car.

She could trace the length of the hallway she was dragged through. She still felt the dampness of the cement floors, where her face had rested until Lito walked into the room. She would have fought him fiercely if her body would have responded to the commands of her brain, but the obvious disconnect gave him free rein to strip her naked and rape her.

The splash of cold water helped her regain some of her consciousness back. She was not afraid of Lito or the men walking in and out of the room yelling dreadful threats. He could make free use of her body and beat her until she bled, but he did not have the power to crush her. She had no fear of death because of a pact she had struck with fate long ago. Her link to life ran deeper than her flesh. Her existence transcended the walls of the room where she was being held. It even transcended the body she inhabited, because she was made of the past, and a legacy of courage. She was the product of men and women with a will to survive.

Somebody walked into the room. By the sound of the footsteps it was more than one person. Some furniture was moved about and the yellow dangling light bulb revealed the shadowed profiles of two men sitting comfortably. A third man with calloused fingers bound her hands with a rope and hung her like a cattle carcass from a hook in the ceiling. Angelina felt every joint pop with the weight of her limp body dangling down. She lifted her face and focused on the two men sitting in front of her with notepads on their laps, as if they were attending a conference. One of them had a thick mustache, and the other one was Lito.

Lito got up from his chair and walked to her. He lifted her chin to face him. She looked at him with indifference. If hatred was what he wanted, he would not get it from her. She had to save her energies to outlast the torturous questioning to come. During her time in the cloisters with the French nuns and the Mothers of Plaza de Mayo, she had heard gruesome accounts of the way the military extracted information from the detainees.

"Let's show the new guy here how we deal with *putas* and traitors," Lito said as he turned to look at the other man.

For a moment she felt a pang of fear for the physical pain to come, but it was instantly replaced by an urgent melody that swept her far away from the torture room and into the underground palace…

***

Baby Yoshua became restless before Yehuda reached the end of the first paragraph. Luckily, Elmede was there to entertain the baby until the ceremony was over. Sara looked around the makeshift temple held in the former ballroom of the underground palace. The people attending the *bar mitzvah* had consented to be blindfolded when transported in and out of the residence. Nobody knew exactly where they were, and there was a reason for it.

These were desperate times and it was common to witness neighbors turn against neighbors, denouncing one another to the Tribunal of the Inquisition in order to obtain a portion of the prisoner's estate. The *Marrano* community was not foreign to such practices. Unfortunately, a vast majority of *Marranos* facing Judaizing charges were brought forth to stand trial by their counterparts, desperate to save their own skins from burning at the stake. The knowledge of the passageway to the underground palace was exclusive to four persons besides Leon and Sara. It was their trusted circle formed by Maria, Jaime, Elmede, and the rabbi from Bilbao. To ensure the safety of each member of the Tribe, secrecy within the community was key.

Thus when footsteps echoed through the marble-floored hallway leading to the small temple, a tense silence froze the air. Yehuda looked up and Leon stood in front of his son, shielding him from palpable danger. There was nowhere to run except to the one and only exit. Elmede hid behind a curtain with the baby, and Salomon crawled under the chairs. He tiptoed his way out of the temple and into the corridors that streamed to the wings of the underground palace.

To the relief of the congregants, it was Samuel Ben Rey, the rabbi from Bilbao. Leon smiled at his friend. "I am pleased to see you, Samuel! I feared something of ill nature might have happened to you. Thank God you are safe and back with us."

The rabbi from Bilbao smiled uncomfortably at the attention he was getting from the small congregation.

Leon waved him in. "Come, my friend. Do us the honor to read on my son's *bar mitzvah*."

Sara watched the rabbi from Bilbao with a wary eye. He looked uncomfortable, not like his usual self. She stepped in front of him and stared straight into his eyes. "Is there anything amiss, Rabbi?"

Samuel Ben Rey shook his head slightly and avoided Sara, but couldn't escape Leon's accusing gaze. Yehuda walked from behind the shelter of his father's body and stood next to him. Leon kissed his son's forehead. "Go to your mother." Yehuda did as told. When he reached Sara's side, he stood tall next to her and took her hand.

"How is your business in court, Samuel?" Leon said casually while he rolled the Torah parchment. "Come and help me with…" Leon gazed up sarcastically. "Or perhaps not. Perhaps you have already traded your sacred *tallit* for a *Sanbenito*."

The rabbi from Bilbao had stood petrified on the same spot ever since Leon guessed his treachery.

"Do I have time to send my family away, my friend?" The rabbi from Bilbao looked down ashamed.

"I guess not," Leon retorted.

Leon stepped down from the pulpit and walked to his son and wife. The baby crawled out from behind the curtain and tugged on Leon's leg. Leon picked him up, hugged him tightly and kissed his soft hair.

Baby Yoshua reached for his father's nose and looked at him with curiosity. "Papa?"

Sara smiled at him with teary eyes. "Yes, my baby, that's Papa."

Yehuda whispered softly in his mother's ear, "Where is Salomon?" Sara eyed him briefly and he understood not to ask any more questions.

"They are in the main house," Samuel Ben Rey finally said. "You could still escape."

Leon stood by his wife and children, fixing the rabbi from Bilbao with curiosity. "How much did you sell us for, Samuel? How much did you promise Alazar?"

As though summoned by Leon's words, Alazar marched into the room leading an army of over forty armed men. Alazar, sweaty and trapped in layers of fat, smacked his lips against his rotten front teeth. "Doctor Leon Fernandez, by orders of the Holy Tribunal of the Inquisition, you are arrested under suspicion of heresy, Judaizing, and evasion of taxes."

Leon ignored the marquis, looked down at Sara with the tenderest of smiles, and kissed her thoroughly as if they were the only two persons in the room. Then he addressed Alazar scornfully. "My dear Marquis, you of all people should know my real name, Rabbi Lev David Fernandez. After all, thanks to the wealth of the Fernandez family you have secured yourself the role of inquisitor… although not a man of the cloth, I gather." Leon sneered. "Or perhaps your appointment came from a powerful Dominican monk who likes to share your bed."

Drops of sweat poured down Alazar's face. The hatred he had accumulated for Leon throughout the years spurted out with a spitting order. "Arrest them! Arrest them all. Arrest the Jewish witch and her offspring. Send them all to the dungeons. Let the Jew beg on his knees for the life of his family."

Pandemonium broke at the orders of the marquis as a clash of slaying swords slashed through the desperate crowd.

A soldier pulled Yoshua from Leon. Leon retrieved the *navaja* he always carried with him and jabbed a number of soldiers in his attempt to reach Yoshua. Held back by the chaos, Leon watched as the soldier lost hold of the baby. As he desperately fought his way to his youngest son, he helplessly witnessed the moment when baby Yoshua was trampled underneath heavy boots, bodies, and swords. Leon's heart stopped at the sight of his dead baby boy on the bloodied floor.

"Fernandez!" the marquis called out.

Out of breath, Leon turned to Alazar to find Sara and Yehuda held at sword point.

Sara's eyes were fixed intently on the floor where the baby lay unmoving. "Let me get to my baby. Let me get to my baby," she pleaded.

Yehuda shook with fear and kept looking from his mother to his father. Two soldiers restrained Leon while a third one punched him in the face and stomach until his legs buckled beneath him.

The marquis walked to Leon savoring the fall of the Jew. Grabbing a fistful of Leon's hair he yanked his head, and bored his hateful eyes on Leon's. "See what happens to heretics, Jew? Look at your whore and look at your satanic seed, Jew. Look at him for the last time."

The marquis smiled at the soldier holding Yehuda, and before the boy could call out for his father, a sword slashed Yehuda's throat sending him into a slow, choking death.

Leon fought to free himself from the soldiers' grasp and was beaten until left unconscious.

The rabbi from Bilbao, who until then had hidden behind the ark, stepped forward and pleaded with Alazar to let Sara tend to her children. The marquis looked at her with disgust, but ordered the soldier to release her.

Sara was suddenly fueled by a strength she knew did not come from her, but from Angelina. She gathered her thoughts and refused to go into shock. She still had one child left, and there was nothing in her power to bring her other two boys back. But there was one thing she could do. She would make the man responsible for the massacre of her family pay with his life.

Sara knelt by the baby first. She cradled him in her arms and arranged his dark hair which was matted with blood. There was a line of blood marring the corner of his mouth, but otherwise he looked at peace. She kissed him. "Mama loves you so much, my sweet baby." Sara ripped the skirt of her gown and wrapped the baby in the green silk. She walked to the pulpit and left the baby at the foot the ark. She kissed him one last time.

She walked back to Yehuda. His green eyes were still open, in shock. She closed them and laid his head on her lap. She ripped another piece of silk from her gown and dressed the bloody wound across Yehuda's throat. "Take care of your little brother. You are a man, my boy. The way you wanted to be. A man to take care of your baby brother."

The rabbi from Bilbao lifted Yehuda in his arms and placed him next to Yoshua. Sara knelt in between her two sons. The marquis was losing his patience, but the rabbi pleaded with him once more. Sara seemed unaware of what was happening in the room or of Samuel Ben Rey standing guard behind her.

She placed a hand on each one of her sons and sang the lullaby that had lulled her three babies into sweet dreams since their birth, "*Durme, durme mi itzico de madre sin ansia y dolor. Durme Durme con hermosura de Shmah Israel.*"

With a lingering look over both her dead sons, Sara mouthed a last goodbye and stood up ready to face her enemy. Her gaze fell on the rabbi from Bilbao who looked back at her with guilt. The waistline on her gown was torn and a hole on the slip beneath it showed her bare skin. She placed her hand over the rip and inhaled deeply when her fingers traced the knife still strapped over her hip bone.

Sara walked to the rabbi and stopped only an inch from him. He did not yell, or gasp. The magnitude of his crimes weighed heavily on his conscience and he welcomed the judgment of Sara's merciless knife in the softness of his lower abdomen.

Behind thick scarlet velvet drapes, Salomon witnessed it all.

Chapter Thirty-Four
For the Love of a Child

David silently thanked his luck, his enormous fortune, and the many crooked military men he had met along his frantic two-day search for Angelina. As feared, she was a prisoner at the notorious School of Mechanics of the Navy. Angelina was held in a remote wing of the building in a secluded room, separate from the rest of the other church members. Rumor had it Brigadier Marcelo Ortiz, also known as Lito, had a special interest in the dissident and was handling the interrogation personally. David tried to keep the horrific images of Angelina's torture from assailing his sanity. He had to stay focused and free her from the hands of that fucking sadist.

From the moment Lucia learned about Angelina's ill fate, she surrendered to David. The fear of losing her daughter to death was greater than losing her to the story of her past. As much as she wanted to cry, her eyes were dry and her heart hardened. She could not bring herself to pray for her daughter and refused to think of Jesus, the Holy Virgin, or God as help. If any of them would have watched over her child, then she would have been safe at home and not in a torture chamber. She doubted that the Lord had valued her unwavering years of devotion and servitude. Her child had not been spared from the ordeal she was subjected to, and that had been His choice. Her daughter might die under His watch.

God had slapped Lucia with yet another trial when she needed him the most. Was it because she came to love her daughter more than she loved him? If that was the case, there was no sense in trying her now. She had made up her mind years before. Never ask a mother to choose between a man and her child. God or not, Angelina would always come before Him.

David had forbidden Lucia to go back to her apartment. Lito would surely have the premises destroyed, searching for evidence he knew did not exist.

During the past few months, Lito spent most of his waking moments with Angelina and the church group, and all the details of their activities were fully disclosed to everybody involved. Lito's undercover operation failed miserably when his aching balls had distracted him from his appointed mission. His obsession with Angelina had partially blinded him from the nuns' activities, and he was too late to stop the list of missing people from being published on the *Futbol* World Cup's opening day.

With the world's eyes on Argentina, the government could not afford to close down the most prominent newspaper in the country, but they could censor it. Yet, the list was already out in the streets by word of mouth, and the public would have access to it regardless. Lito had to make amends for his mistake, and by handing over Junta dissidents with international connections, such as the French nuns, or communists like the Mothers of Plaza de Mayo, his hiccup would surely be overlooked.

In exchange for a small fortune, Oscar, one of the military crooks David met during his search for Angelina, contacted him with information. Oscar, a middle-aged colonel, a transplant from a sleepy southern province, viewed the big city as his opportunity to be noticed by the Junta, and milk money out of desperate parents in exchange for their missing children.

David met with him once. He developed an instant disgust for the heavily mustached colonel, but he couldn't afford to snub him, the colonel was his only hope. David gave Oscar a hefty advance of the ransom money he demanded for slipping Angelina out of the Armada building. The remaining balance was going to be paid off upon her release, but there was a gray area in their deal. The colonel was careful not to guarantee his delivery of Angelina alive.

"The Brigadier has his reputation, you know? He is an animal." Oscar laughed at his own remark while David fought the urge to take him down with his fists.

Instead, he patted Oscar amiably. "I forgot to mention it, but there is a bonus for getting her out in one piece, Colonel."

For the past two days, since the raid at the church, Lito had become the closest thing to the Pope in the eyes of the School of Mechanics of the Navy. With his newly acquired status as the terrorist hunter, he easily upgraded the peaceful church group to that of vicious guerillas for his own personal gain. He was said to be conducting the interrogation of the youngest member of the group. According to him the girl had close ties with the Tupamaros, the guerilla movement in Uruguay. His methods of extracting information were known to be cruel but effective.

David was not the only one who had to pay his way to Angelina. The colonel had to do it, too. Oscar gathered as much information as he could about Lito's schedule and proceeded to sweeten up Lito's secretary's pocket. As a result, Oscar was appointed as a transcriptionist during Angelina's interrogation. It was as such that he finally met David Moreno's prize face to face in that very room where Angelina was being tortured.

The girl looked awfully battered, and by the blood and bruises on her upper thighs, it was obvious she had not only been beaten but also raped.

As soon as Lito began interrogating Angelina, it was clear to Oscar that his interest in her had nothing to do with Montoneros, Tupamaros, or Communists. Lito was merely enjoying inflicting pain on the girl. His favorite method of torture was the *picana*, an electrical prod. He did not ask questions after shocking her with the prod, he mouthed resentful statements like, *I would have been good to you*, or, *You should have not denied me*.

Just as Oscar had planned, a knock on the door interrupted the session. An emergency required Lito's immediate attention. The list of missing persons appeared on the front page of *La Nación* in black bold letters, and President General Jorge Rafael Videla had ordered Lito to appear in front of the Junta at once. Even considering the danger his career was under, Lito hesitated before leaving Angelina behind.

"Orders to proceed with the prisoner, Brigadier?" Oscar was on his feet, arms firmly to his sides.

Lito looked at Angelina and bit his lower lip while thinking. "Cut her down. I'll be back for her later tonight."

With the help of the other soldier in the interrogatory room, a frightened kid no older than Angelina, they wrapped her in a white bed sheet. After signing her out of the building as deceased, they stuffed her in the trunk of a dark green Ford Falcon, the Argentinean military's signature car, and Oscar drove out of the naval building. No one asked questions. It was customary to dispose of the bodies in landfills or the river.

Oscar met David at the intersection of Highway 9, on the route to Uruguay. When David lifted Angelina out of the trunk, he feared her dead. She bore a lifeless weight, and the hand that had slipped out of the shroud was bloodied. The son of a bitch had yanked all her nails out. His fear increased when he placed her on Lucia's lap in the backseat of his car. The nun lifted the bedsheet from Angelina. Her whole body was burnt, bruised, and slashed.

Lucia did not waste her energies grieving over the poor state of the girl, and while David finished off the transaction with the colonel, she checked Angelina's pupils and pulse. The signs of life, although weak, were still there.

"She is alive," Lucia yelled out of the window to David, "but we must hurry."

David retrieved an extra wad of bills out of his pocket and handed it to Oscar. Without missing a beat, he jumped in the car and sped to an empty house en route to Zarate where a doctor was waiting for them.

Angelina's eyes fluttered under her closed eyelids. Their time was drawing near...

***

When Maria and Jaime finally arrived at the House of Gardens, the place felt disconcertingly empty. Ordinarily, the grounds resembled an ant farm, busy with working gardeners, grooms walking or training horses, and kitchen maids harvesting fruit and vegetables for the daily meals. None of these activities were visible and Maria looked at Jaime knowing his thoughts trailed along hers. They did not bother to take the horses to the stables. They dismounted by the main house and dashed in. "Sara! Leon! We are back!" Jaime ran in and out of several rooms on the main floor only to find them all empty.

Without further delay, they made their way to the underground palace. Maria's heart plunged when she found the secret passage gate wide open. Jaime went down before Maria and ordered her to stay by the fountain. Her initial intentions of obeying her husband died away when she spotted Sara's pendant lying at the bottom of the stairwell leading to the heart of the underground palace.

She hurried down the steps past Jaime and bent down to pick up the pendant. When she stood up, Maria stifled a cry at the sight of the slain bodies lining the hallway to the makeshift temple. Jaime stood frozen behind her, taking in the horror before them. Even though he was a strong man, hardly foreign to death and violence, he felt courage betray him, leaving him vulnerable. Elmede lay sprawled at the threshold of the temple. Her face, contorted in panic. Her eyes, wide open. Maria knelt and averted her gaze from the fatal wound inflicted on Elmede. She desperately wanted to say a prayer of farewell for the departing soul of the woman who had become a trusted friend and dear member of their family. Yet, she could not find the right words. The sight of Elmede dead brought a surge of anger inside of Maria which she could barely contain.

Maria closed Elmede's eyes and moved forward, stepping over bodies until she stumbled upon the rabbi from Bilbao. Sara's knife stood plunged deep into the rabbi's lower abdomen. Maria looked over her shoulder. "Jaime!"

Jaime stood a few feet away from the temple, taking in the mayhem around him. Another trail of innocent blood left behind by the Spanish Inquisition.

He had spotted Samuel Ben Rey's body before Maria called out his name. He had had his doubts about Ben Rey's loyalty, but he set them aside until he could corroborate his suspicions with substantial proof.

***

Jaime was a well-liked man across Cordoba. He had an innate charm that made people volunteer information to him without having to ask for it. He took advantage of this particular trait of his and always kept his ears open. A few months back, a groom from Castle Alazar had traveled down to Casa Di Laurenti to acquire a handsome Andalusian for the marquis. It came as a surprise to Jaime that Leon was not informed of the marquis's need for a new horse, and he pressed into the matter after the groom was two cups of wine too drunk. The groom's tongue loosened up and disclosed all the knowledge he had at hand. The marquis had been appointed to a high office and had a new guarantor on site, the son-in-law of a powerful lawyer. There were not many powerful lawyers in Cordoba with sons-in-law. To Jaime's knowledge, Samuel Ben Rey was one of three.

He esteemed Ben Rey and decided to give him the benefit of the doubt. In truth, the rabbi from Bilbao had not shown any signs of being involved in anything other than his own business dealings and the Tribe. But before leaving Spain with the three Fernandez boys, Jaime was distracted by the final arrangements and had failed to follow up on the vital information Alazar's groom had handed down to him in Onuba.

It was entirely his fault. The carnage, the loss of his dear family, the treachery of the rabbi from Bilbao. All of it, his fault. A slight movement behind the heavy scarlet velvet drapes at the far end of the former ballroom caught his attention. With sword in hand he slowly slid the drapes open. He found Salomon, bathed in blood, leaning against the wall, holding each one of his brothers in his thin arms. He looked up at Jaime. "They are safe with me. The soldiers cannot take them."

The burial of Yehuda and Yoshua took place at twilight. Jaime dug the two graves by Sara's favorite Valencia rose garden. Through a fog of tears, Maria could still envision the happy moments the Fernandez family had enjoyed around the rose garden.

On the hottest Cordoban nights, the boys and Leon used to sneak out of the house with Sara's best bed sheets and set up a tent to spend a night of laughter outdoors. A pang of grief hit Maria hard at the realization that those moments would never happen again. From that day on, they would become a chapter stored in her heart as memories.

"*Earth you are, and to earth you will return. And the earth returns to the land as it was, and the spirit returns to God, who gave it.*" The finality of Jaime's words pulled her out of the lapse of choking pain. They had to flee Cordoba without delay. The soldiers would surely come back to loot the place, and the marquis would not be satisfied until he saw the full dismantling of the Tribe.

Before parting from his brothers, Salomon insisted on marking the graves. "So that we can always find them," he said to Maria as he pulled out long stem orange roses from the ground. With the artistry he had inherited from a great-grandmother he had never met, Salomon arranged petals and stems over the graves, and with them he wrote the names of his beloved brothers.

At dusk, they left the palace with Jaime's horse hitched to the flat cart that was once used for the lot runs. Maria and Salomon lay hidden under a heap of hay, and endured the rough terrain of the forest until they reached the only place where they could find safety—Florica's tavern.

Florica had never met Samuel Ben Rey and that made her the only person they could turn to. Her association with Leon was exclusively known by Sara, Maria, and Jaime. Several of the fugitives the Tribe harbored were Gypsies persecuted by the Inquisition. Most of those Gypsies were women who found refuge at the convent in Toledo, where the sisters kept Mother Ignacia's good work alive long after the nun had passed.

In the dead of the night, Jaime, Maria, and Salomon arrived at Florica's inn. She, like most of the residents of Cordoba, had heard of the arrest of one of the city's most prominent families. It was Alazar's first arrest as Inquisitor and he meant to impress the population with his abhorrence to heresy.

Florica broke down when Jaime recounted the details of what they had found at the House of Gardens, and the little information they were able to extract from Salomon. The boy looked hollow eyed and refused to eat. He curled up in a corner of Florica's room and fell asleep. Brokenhearted, Jaime cuddled Salomon in his arms with the intention of guarding him from nightmares that would certainly haunt him throughout the night.

By dawn the next morning, Florica was at the gate of the Alcazar promising free drinks to a few guards on duty in exchange for information about Sara and Leon Fernandez. The negotiations with the guards took over a week to finalize, and in the end, Florica was forced to throw two prostitutes into the deal. She waited three long hours outside of the Alcazar's walls until she got word on the status of the prisoners.

***

Leon was held at the dungeons of the Alcazar in a damp, rotten cell. His hands, feet, and neck were shackled to the wall as though he were a wild beast.

Escorted by two guards, Alazar went to him on the third day of his imprisonment. The marquis, who resembled a pig more than a man, held a handkerchief to his nose and jumped back in fear when Leon stood tall and daring. "Well, well, well, Doctor Fernandez, how are you faring, my friend?"

Leon tensed up, the clank of his chains making his approach to the marquis threatening. Yet, his intentions to crush the marquis's fat neck with his bare hands were cut short by the length of the chains.

Alazar exploded in a mocking laughter. "You can have it all again, Fernandez. A simple confession on the whereabouts of your entire fortune and you could be back in the comfort of your bed tonight."

Leon masked his grief behind the revulsion he felt for Alazar. He could never have his life back. Two of his sons were dead. Salomon was missing. And what about Sara? "Where is my wife?"

"Let's not get greedy, Doctor. Why would I give you information for nothing in return? The location of the gold first, Fernandez."

Leon kept his eyes on the marquis. He did not care about the money. All he wanted was Sara and his little boy. Their life was ruined, but they could start anew, the three of them together. Perhaps they could sail to the New World, with the expeditionary caravels set to leave soon, and fulfill Sara's dream of building their lives in a land where they would not be persecuted because of their faith.

"The money is invested in foreign ventures," he said level toned, "it will only be released to my wife or myself. If we fail to claim it personally, it will then be distributed amongst families who adopted orphans of the Inquisition."

Alazar lost hold of his handkerchief and his face turned beet red with rage. "Are you mocking me, Fernandez?"

Leon did not waver at the inherent menace in the marquis's voice. Even if the money could be released to Alazar, the fate of hundreds of families would be in danger upon his disclosure of the Tribe's transactions to Alazar. No, Alazar would kill them all. He was a dead man already, he had nothing more to lose. "I am telling the truth. Now, where is my wife?"

At the nod of the marquis, Leon was unchained and dragged out of his cell into an interrogation dungeon. A few torches illuminated the dark, cold room. Still he could make out the contours of a table with several greased instruments of torture on top. The wooden frame of a rack, with two ropes hooked to the bottom, and another two tied to a handle on the top, stood above ground in the middle of the room.

Leon was familiar with the devastating effects of *the rack* as method of torture. Many of the prisoners the Tribe was able to free from jail were victims of this device. Usually the torturer turned the handle until the limbs of the victim dislocated from their joints.

Leon heard a faint moan. He could recognize that voice anywhere. His eyes struggled to find the location of the sound, and they finally rested on a foot roasting bench that held Sara captive. The remnants of hot coals were aglow below the soles of her scalded, raw feet. She lay on the floor almost unconscious.

"Sara!" Leon elbowed the guard next to him on the face, and in spite of the restraint of his chains, he fought to get to her. She turned her head in the direction of his voice and met his eyes before the brutal thrash of an iron rod to his back took him down.

Leon lost his balance and fell. The guards pulled him up and forced him down on the rack. The blow of the rod did nothing to diminish Leon's beastly resistance against the guards. He used his elbows, head, and knees to fight them, but their incessant thrashing finally won.

Alazar, with a look of sincere concern, loomed over him. "It is most unfortunate that we have come to this rather awful situation, Leon. But, you leave me with no choice."

A guard freed Sara from the hooks and dragged her to Leon as if she were a hunted animal. Leon noticed her skin bore burn marks and the distinctive spider tracks of the tails of a whip. Her eyes, although open, looked distant. Leon fought the ropes that tied him to the rack. He wished to touch Sara's face, to reach for her hand, to hold her, to save her from the slow death the marquis had planned for them. "Forgive me, my love, for I could not save them. Please forgive me."

Sara closed her eyes and gave him a feeble smile.

Alazar turned to Sara and grinned at her, displaying all of his rotten teeth. "What say you, Lady Fernandez? Your husband for your wealth?"

Sara blinked slowly. Her eyes surveyed the room, the marquis, and finally Leon. "I love you," she mouthed.

The room was soon filled with Leon's grunts of pain.

The interrogation on the exact details of the foreign investments, the whereabouts of their remaining son, and their accomplices, Jaime and Maria Moreno, lasted four more days. Leon had most of the bones in his body broken, his joints dislocated, and several fingers and toes crushed. The marquis had forced Sara to watch Leon while he was being tortured.

On the seventh day after the raid at the House of Gardens, the Marquis of Alazar officially proclaimed Doctor Leon Fernandez an unrepentant Judaizer, and sentenced him to be publicly burnt at the stake. Subsequently, his wife Sara Fernandez was sentenced to life in prison.

Outside the city walls, a crowd gathered to witness the burning of another Jew. Leon, tied to a mule and paraded along the streets of Cordoba, was spat at, stoned, and insulted by a mob that only two weeks before had considered him the best physician in the city and the most compassionate of men. Leon was unable to stand or walk since his limbs no longer supported him. Two soldiers dragged him off the mule and tied him to the stake in the center of the square. Sara, sick and fragile, was taken to the burning site and was ordered to witness the murder of her husband.

Leon's deep blue eyes found the face of his wife in the crowd, and with her image embedded in his eyes, the world ceased to exist. She smiled at him, beautiful as always, and placed her hands softly over her middle.

Leon smiled back at her thankful for the love they had shared and for they life they had created.

The next morning, a jail warden stood at the doorstep of Alazar's office in the heart of the Alcazar. Deep in reading, the marquis kept his attention on the documents about his desk. "State your affairs, warden."

The man looked down to his feet and balanced his weight swaying left to right.

Alazar lifted his fleshy eyelids and glowered at the warden with disdain. "I do not have time for idiots. Speak or take your filthy carcass out of my office!"

Fearful the man looked at the marquis and cleared his throat, "Your Excellency…"

The marquis drummed his finger on his desk and looked sideways. "Yes?"

The warden cleared his throat once more. "The woman—the prisoner—Sara Fernandez…"

The name caught the marquis's full attention. He was on his feet, holding onto the edge of his desk with his thick short fingers. "Is she ready to confess?"

The warden shook his head and pressed his lips firmly. "We found her dead this morning, Your Excellency. The prisoner Sara Fortuna Fernandez is dead."

The marquis grabbed a marble statuette from his desk and hurled it angrily at the warden. The warden sidestepped in time to avoid the flying object, which hit the doorframe leaving it significantly splintered.

"What do you want us to do with her body, Your Excellency? Do you wish to see her?"

Alazar turned to contemplate the imposing crucifix nailed high behind his desk. "Burn the damn bitch."

***

The doctor David had arranged to meet had conducted a thorough check up. The torture Angelina had been subjected to had injured her terribly, but she would heal.

"It'll take time," he said to David and Lucia, "especially the psychological damage. That, *mi amigo*, that might never heal."

Angelina stirred, involuntarily shaking and gasping for air. David, who sat by her side for most of the night, placed a hand on her forehead and eased her down gently on the thin mattress he had laid her on when they arrived at the house.

Lucia heard the gasping and ran into the room. Angelina's eyes were open but glassy. She did not know where to touch her daughter or how to hold her. Her hands were bandaged, so were her shoulders, and rib cage. She chose to lie beside her.

Feeling her mother next to her, Angelina turned her head towards Lucia's shoulder. "Mamá Lucia?" Angelina muttered.

"Yes, my child, it is me. I'm here. Right here by your side."

Angelina relaxed at the voice of Lucia. "I'm so sorry, Mamá Lucia."

Lucia felt hot tears rolling down her face. "It's all right, my angel. You have the strength of God about you. You'll get through this." Lucia placed her hand softly on Angelina's forehead. "You must leave soon. David is a good friend and he will take care of you until we can be together again."

Angelina's face was damp with tears. "No, Mamá, don't leave me."

Fighting the will to scream and cry, Lucia gathered all the strength remaining in her and sat up. She searched under her robes, produced Sara Fernandez's pendant and hung it around Angelina's neck.

Angelina did not need to look at it to know what it was. She recognized the weight and the shape of the object resting on her chest. She could describe every stone, every detail.

"I'm not leaving you, my child. We will always be together because you are my daughter. You will always feel my presence the way you feel your parents watching over you, the way you feel Sarah."

Angelina closed her eyes and allowed for the medicated induced stupor to claim her, for she could not say goodbye to Mamá Lucia.

The first rays of light filtered through the half-opened window and kissed Angelina's face with a golden, warm glow. Lucia stroked Angelina gently on the bridge of her nose, the way she used to when she was a little girl. She glanced at her one last time, stood up and headed for the door.

David stood in her way, "Where... why... Sister Lucia, you must not be on your own. You must come with us. She needs you. I... I need you."

Lucia placed a gentle hand on his cheek. "You will do fine, David. I can see it in your eyes. You are a decent young man and you will take care of my Angelina."

David felt winded and shook his head trying to clear his mind.

Lucia smiled a sad smile. "For the love of my child, I must go into seclusion and sort out my affairs with God." She stood on tiptoes, kissed him on the cheek, and left the house.

Chapter Thirty-Five
With the Touch of a Key

Leaving Argentina through Uruguay was easier than arriving at the airport with proper documentation. A wad of bills and a couple bottles of wine did it for the *gendarme*, the lazy border patrol agent in charge who sat around a game of *Truco* with his three subordinates.

Once in Uruguay, a counterfeit Spanish passport with Angelina's picture in it was handed to David by an immigration officer, before they boarded a hired private plane to Cordoba, Spain.

David worried about Angelina's emotional state once completely conscious, uprooted from Lucia, the only family she had left. He had shared his concern with the doctor at the house in Zarate, and in return, he was strongly advised to keep her under the effects of sedatives until her physical injuries improved. She was in no condition to suffer a setback, and the realization of loss could send her spiraling into depression. David played with the pack of pills the doctor gave him. He had seen her at her worst and he could not bear to watch her suffer any more. He hated the idea of drugging her, but he felt powerless when she moaned in pain. The sedatives would help them both. She would rest and he would have time to think things through.

On the day of Fortuna's death, David made her a promise. Ever since, he had fantasized about bringing Angelina to the House of Gardens. He had a speech prepared for her, in which he would recount the story of the Fernandez family up to and including the tragic death of

Leon and Sara, and Salomon's narrow escape to America. Furthermore, he was prepared to show her the records Fortuna had managed to find in South America to validate his claim.

Amongst the documents, there was a written entry with Salomon's name listed as a settler of Hispaniola, later called the Dominican Republic, where he had resided with other Jewish families who had also fled Spain. There were other records which showed solid evidence of Salomon marrying a Jewish woman. The trace of his family tree, which throughout the years had moved southward to Argentina, looked thoroughly Jewish up until the turn of the twentieth century. Somewhere around that time, the Fernandez family had suffered an unknown event, leaving its identity hidden under secrets and silence.

As a trial attorney, David had the whole process of discovery staged in his mind. In it he would expose Angelina to the truth of her past, confronted by the imposing portrait of Sara Fernandez. He envisioned his closing argument as if he were before a jury at a courthouse. He would plead the case of Sara, Leon, and Fortuna Fernandez in front of Angelina and he would expect her verdict to be one of acceptance.

But he never expected to bring Angelina to Spain under her current condition. The vibrant, beautiful woman he had met in the cloisters of the church in Buenos Aires was reduced to a traumatized young girl who did not need to be confronted with anything other than time and peace.

When they finally arrived at the House of Gardens, David had a team of nurses and a doctor ready to see Angelina through her recovery. She was dazed, but smiled faintly at her surroundings, especially when David carried her into the room that had once been Sara and Leon's.

After surveying the room with groggy eyes and finding the door which centuries before led to Sara's music room, Angelina fell into a peaceful sleep for the first time since being rescued from Lito.

David had urgent business to attend to after his long absence from Cordoba and made arrangements to leave Angelina under the care of the medical team. Before leaving, he sat by her side and watched her sleep. There was something unsettling about her that made his insides stir. Her nearness brought back memories he did not recall living. He could swear he had sat on that same spot countless times before, staring at her in sleep. Déjà vu, they called it. He shook his head, and left the room.

His day did not go as expected. From the House of Gardens he drove straight to his office where a mountain of messages and neglected deadlines waited for him. His brain was fried and he felt emotionally drained. For the past five days he had functioned on adrenaline alone. The prospect of having to concentrate on business was enough to make him walk away from his office and order his secretary to put everything on hold for another week.

With his last drop of energy, he drove to his flat, located in the center of the *Judería*. He filled the bathtub with warm water, got out of the clothes he had been wearing for the past forty-eight hours, and sank in the water with a cathartic sigh. He closed his eyes as the afternoon sun seeping through the window embraced him like a golden blanket.

He realized that he had fallen asleep when a ripple of gooseflesh woke him. It was dark and for a moment he did not know where he was. One thing was for sure, the nightmare he had lived through for the past few days was as vivid as if it had not ended. He jumped out of the bath and phoned the House of Gardens.

"The doctor is gone for the night," the nurse informed him. Angelina was hooked to an I.V. and medicated. She would sleep for many hours. David put the phone down with certain relief, walked to his wet bar, poured a glass of whisky and slumped onto the nearest couch.

He helped himself to a second glass of whisky and walked to his room with the intention of not leaving until the next day. Five minutes later, he found himself dressed and rushing out of his flat.

The House of Gardens was dead asleep by the time he arrived. As a teenager, he had his suspicions about the house and shared them with Fortuna. "This is not just a house, *Tía* Fortuna," he remembered saying, "it's an entity with a life of its own. Sometimes I can hear music when I walk in. And other times, I swear *Tía*, I can hear voices."

Fortuna often laughed at his boyish fears and warned him not to watch horror movies anymore.

The music he heard when he approached the room where Angelina was resting was not a product of his imagination. The nurse on duty was asleep on a chair outside the room, and he slipped in silently.

Angelina's bed was empty, bloody bandages were strewn over the covers, and the line to the I.V. hung unhooked. He heart lurched with a short-lived panic until his eyes found the door to the attached chamber ajar.

Angelina sat at the harpsichord. Her eyes closed. Her damaged fingers, flowing through the keys. From the portrait, Sara's amber gaze fell over her protégé. Finally together in one place. The music spoke words David could not understand. All the same he stood by the door and listened.

Angelina paused and turned to look at David. He felt like an intruder. "I'm sorry... the music..." he muttered. He should have reprimanded her for ripping off her bandages and breaking free from the I.V., but her presence was almost hypnotic, and for the first time he was at a loss of words when with a woman.

He noticed she had the pendant on. It fell on the right place, right beneath her breasts. On that spot where her skin was soft and smelled like the rose petals of her garden. David closed his eyes. What was happening to him? He had never been with Angelina in an intimate way, and had no idea how her skin felt or smelled. Yet, the raw memory of the evening by the fountain and her silky skin fresh on his fingers filled his senses.

She patted the bench. He walked to her and silently sat next to her. Her hands went back to the keys and played a tender melody which wrapped around his heart and made him look up at Sara.

"She is not dead." Angelina's voice broke the spell the music held over the room.

He turned to her and noticed how frail she looked under her nightgown. "Angelina, let's get you back in bed. You need to rest. And your hands…"

Angelina looked down at her fingers. Her hands were trembling. "Can you hear her, David? She is not dead." Angelina's battered hands rested on the keys and she closed her eyes, allowing Sara's melody to fill the room. Allowing Sara to tell the rest of her story.

***

The guards from the Alcazar helped Florica for a significantly higher price than they originally agreed to. They fully disclosed Alazar's intentions of hunting the remaining members of the Fernandez family, even Jaime and Maria. For an extra bag of gold, they agreed to dump Sara's body into Florica's flat cart and burn another woman who died on that same day instead.

Florica hurried back to her tavern where Jaime, Maria, and Salomon waited to be transported to their new hideout. The ride to the convent in Toledo took them ten days. Florica made sure to avoid the main roads where soldiers of the Inquisition could stop to check the cargo in the back of her flat cart where she hid Alazar's prey under a heap of hay, oranges, and a few clucking chickens. Upon her arrival, the nuns in charge of receiving provision deliveries unloaded the cargo through the backdoor and hurried the fugitives up the stairs to the tower room.

Jaime walked into the chamber that once belonged to Sarah Espinoza, carrying Sara in his arms. The nun, who accompanied them to the tower, opened the drapes to the alcove at the end of the room. The cot, where Sara spent the last few days of her grandmother's life, remained intact. With utmost care, Jaime laid her over the soft covers and stepped back, powerlessly bunching his fists to his sides. Maria came forward and unbundled Sara from the rough linen sheet, stifling a sob at the sight of her poor body. Jaime stood behind her and placed a hand on her shoulder. "At least she still lives."

Salomon had stayed behind in the antechamber of the tower room, fearing to learn about his mother's fate. He overheard Jaime's words and gained the courage to step into the main tower room. The murals of Sarah Espinoza shone bright on the walls of the grand chamber. Salomon was drawn to them as if by magic. His fingers gently traced the lines of the figures in the paintings.

His mother had told him and Yehuda about Sarah Espinoza, how she had lived hidden in a tower for most of her life. Salomon thought it a mere tale. He sometimes wondered if his mother, the wonderful storyteller that she was, had fed them with stories of heroic imaginary family members with the sole purpose of strengthening their identity. Yet, the evidence on the walls was not a product of his mother's imagination. Sarah Espinoza had lived and it was now his turn to paint the saga of his family on those same walls.

The remnants of Sara's green silk dress lay crumpled at the foot of the cot. Maria washed Sara with the warm water and soap the nuns provided. She then dressed her with a dark tunic, which hid most of the dreadful wounds Alazar's weeklong interrogation had left on her skin.

"Salomon." The weak voice of his mother pulled him out of the tragic story of his ancestors, placing him back into their precarious reality. He walked to her counting the number of footsteps that it took him to reach the cot.

Salomon felt relieved when he saw his mother, although sickly, propped up. Her hands trembled when she reached for him—he clasped his hands firmly around hers in reassurance. The fate of his father had not been discussed between them. There was no need to. He knew his father was dead.

Mother and son stared at each other for what seemed like an eternity. She studied his features carefully, and he hers. Words were not spoken. There was no need to. They both knew their time together would be short. That they would soon part, never to see each other again.

"I asked the sisters to bring you Sarah Espinoza's brushes and paints. They stored them after she died. Would you like them?"

A ghost of a smile lit Salomon's face. He nodded.

"Would you do something for me, my beautiful boy?"

Salomon gulped his tears. He had to be brave. He should not cry. "Whatever you want, Mama."

Sara smiled at her boy. "Paint the rose garden for me. I want all of us to be there, with Yehuda, and Yoshua, and Papa..." she paused and placed her hands on her stomach, "and a baby. I know he will be a boy, I can feel him. Your new baby brother. We shall call him Lev."

Jaime and Maria, a few steps behind Salomon, stood stunned at the news. Sara looked up and acknowledged them with smiling eyes.

For the next few weeks, Florica kept them informed of Alazar's frantic search in the attempts to find them.

Every home in the *Juderia* was ransacked, all the roads leading to Cordoba were blocked. Through his torturous methods of interrogation, he extracted information from other members of the Tribe, and soon learned that Salomon, the last Fernandez, became the sole recipient of the family fortune. He swore to claim the Fernandez's fortune as his. He swore to kill the boy.

When Sara heard of Alazar's ruthless determination, she sent Salomon out of the room and expressed her wishes to Jaime and Maria. They both knew better than argue with her. Sara's wishes were commands.

However weak her body was, her mind was as sharp as ever. She knew exactly what she wanted for her son. "He must leave Spain. He cannot stay here with me, or with you. I want him gone to the New World. I want my son on one of those ships. He must start a new life, free of hatred and death."

Maria pleaded with Sara to let Salomon stay with them. She spoke about leaving together after the baby's birth.

"That will never happen, my dear Maria. I will never see the face of my newborn baby. That is why Salomon is painting him for me, so I can store him in my memory along with that of Yehuda, Yoshua, Salomon, and Lev. When he finishes, he must leave."

It was evident that the pregnancy was draining her of the little energy she had left. The distinct olive tone of her skin had faded into a jaundiced color. She was no longer able to stand on her own, and the trembling of her hands worsened to the point that Maria had to feed her.

A week after Sara made her decision clear to Jaime and Maria about Salomon's fate, Florica sent word of a ship leaving from the Port of Cadiz in ten days' time. A number of Jewish families, victims of the devastating expulsion of Jews conducted by the Catholic king and queen across Spain, were to board that ship. One family, former members of the disbanded Tribe, had agreed to care for Salomon as if he were their own.

The time for Salomon's departure grew near, but the face of the baby in the painting was not finished. Sara followed the progress of her family's mural. She marveled at the ability her son had. Through his boyish strokes, he had captured the essence of each member of his family— Leon, sitting next to Sara, looking at her with his blue eyes filled with love. Baby Yoshua, on Yehuda's shoulders, and Salomon on one side, watching them, smiling at them.

"How do you want baby Lev to look, Mama?"

Sara closed her eyes and searched in her heart for the face of the baby who grew stronger every day in a body that could not harbor him for much longer. "He will have Papa's eyes, Yehuda's hair, Yoshua's smile, and your beautiful skin color. He will be a part of all of us. Just like you are."

Salomon looked at his mother, and for the first time since the death of his brothers, he could no longer hide his grief. He buried his face in his mother's lap and cried. "I don't want to leave you, Mama. Don't make me go. I will never get to know my baby brother. I will be alone forever."

Sara closed her arms around him. "You will get to know your brother, my beautiful boy. You'll see. Maybe not in this life, maybe not in this time. But I promise you, I will bring our family back together."

He slept in his mother's arms until wakened. Soon after, he left the convent with her scent forever embedded in him. Risking her life, Maria hid Salomon in the back of the cart that very same night, after the face of the baby was completed.

Sara spent the next five months staring at the mural Salomon painted. She barely spoke anymore and slept for most of the time. Before the pregnancy reached its seventh month, Sara woke up in a pool of blood. The labor pains ripped through her fragile body, nevertheless, she felt stronger than ever.

She could feel Sarah Espinoza's strong presence in the room. She, just like her grandmother, was about to perpetuate the line of her blood while hidden in the tower room of a convent. As Sara pushed the small scrap of life out of her, she felt at peace with the promise she had made to her grandmother more than fourteen years before.

The last thing she saw before her world went blank was the picture of her whole family enjoying life in the rose garden.

Sara was laid to rest next to her grandmother's grave later that evening. In her arms, Maria held a tiny baby boy with the strongest will to live. A wet nurse was called in to feed the baby. Although small and premature, little Lev suckled on her breast hungrily.

Maria and Jaime Moreno hid in the tower room for three more months after Sara's death. Everyday, Maria would sit in front of Salomon's mural with the baby in her arms, to tell him the story of his three brothers, his mother, and his father. Just like Sara imagined him to be, little Lev had Leon's eyes, Salomon's dark skin, Yoshua's smile, and Yehuda's hair. And from his mother, he had life.

Jaime, Maria, and little Lev left for the Holy Land via Constantinople. To the eyes of the world, little Lev grew as Leon David Moreno, the only child of Maria and Jaime Moreno. But in his heart, he always knew he was Lev Fernandez.

***

David looked up at Sara's portrait and then at Angelina. His eyes, swimming in a sea of tears that did not seem to ebb, saw blurred images of the past and the present. He saw the Fernandez family of the past, and he saw the Fernandez of today. It was him and Angelina. They had been together before, and they were together now. Angelina nodded as though she could read his thoughts, but David was not surprised for they had lived within each other for centuries.

Angelina placed her fingers on the keys of the harpsichord and felt the vibration of each generation pass. The promise Sara made to her grandmother was meant to last an eternity. It had transcended her life and the life of her children, and now it was theirs to fulfill.

She glanced at her past, staring back at her from above. Angelina felt whole. The emptiness she experienced from the moment she was taken from Pueblo Brugo was suddenly gone. She had Sara and Leon. She belonged to Salomon and now her lonely days were over because she was home, with David.

Angelina turned to him. "She did it. She brought us together. Just like she promised Salomon, she brought us back home."

Angelina traced the thick links of the chain that held the pendant nestled between her breasts and took it off. She reached for David's hands and placed it in his palm closing his fingers around it. He held it tightly and then looked into her eyes.

She cuddled closer to him and he gathered her in his arms. Angelina wondered if in another time and place someone was listening to the melody of their story.

About Sandra Perez Gluschankoff

Sandra was born and raised in Argentina, and immigrated to the United States a little over two decades ago. While her academic background in her birth country is in psychoanalysis, anthropology, Judaic studies, and Hebrew language, she is best known for her accomplishments in Spanglish as a best-selling, award winning historical novelist and award winning screenwriter.

Social Media Links

Website: www.palabrasandstories.com

Facebook page:
https://www.facebook.com/palabrasandstories/
@palabrasandstories

Twitter:
https://twitter.com/SandraGluschank @SandraGluschank

Amazon Author page: https://www.amazon.com/Sandra-Perez-Gluschankoff/e/B009TDKBNU

If you enjoyed this story, check out these other Solstice Publishing books by Sandra Perez Gluschankoff:

International Best Selling/ Award Winning novel Franzisca's Box:

Mystery, betrayal, murder, and passionate love were things Sofia Lazar only experienced as a movie producer. All of that changed after her grandmother's sudden death when she comes face to face with an unwanted revelation contained in a tattered box. The meager contents of the box take her back to her childhood and the fantastic bedtime stories that Abuela, her grandmother, used to tell her of a heroic warrior girl named Franzisca. Now, two decades later, fragments of Franzisca's stories creep back into Sofia's life, tying Franzisca and her grandmother to an unknown past. With the memories of her childhood bedtime stories to guide her, Sofia sets out to piece together her grandmother's mysterious history, leading her to discover the truth behind her life.

Set against the backdrop of World War II Romania, the immigration of Nazi criminals into South America, the later years of the Military Regime in Argentina during the 1980s, and present-day California, Franzisca's Box is a story of war that ultimately affects three generations of women who will never find peace until they call for a ceasefire in their own wars and surrender to forgiveness and love.

http://bookgoodies.com/a/B01BX2M7A4

Best Selling short story Wednesdays With Maria

Wednesdays are the days for mates, gossip, and the reading of cards to foretell the future....

Caught in a web of deathly secrets in a country where corruption rules over truth, Andrea, a young investigate reporter, lurks between life and death. She ultimately leaves behind an unsolved mystery as legacy for her newborn daughter.

http://bookgoodies.com/a/B01JJ7IB3C